IN A DARK GARDEN

BOOKS BY
FRANK G. SLAUGHTER

In a Dark Garden
A Touch of Glory
Battle Surgeon
Air Surgeon
Spencer Brade, M.D.
That None Should Die

FRANK G. SLAUGHTER

IN A DARK GARDEN

GARDEN CITY, NEW YORK, 1946
DOUBLEDAY & COMPANY, INC.

COPYRIGHT, 1946, BY FRANK G. SLAUGHTER
ALL RIGHTS RESERVED

PRINTED IN THE UNITED STATES
AT
THE COUNTRY LIFE PRESS, GARDEN CITY, N. Y.

CONTENTS

1. Glasgow 1
2. Nassau 73
3. St. Augustine 114
4. St. Marys 170
5. Vicksburg 202
6. Atlanta 237
7. New York 353
8. Richmond 385

IN A DARK GARDEN

1

GLASGOW

HALFWAY down the ugly cobbled street, he paused to look back. The hackney still waited at the door of his inn, grotesque as an overgrown pumpkin in the fog. Below, where the pavement slanted to the water's edge, the river was drowned in that same gray cotton wool. He walked slowly downhill, welcoming the cold sting in his lungs.

This afternoon the weather had slicked the cobbles from brown to greasy black; the dampness highlighted the flanks of the dray horses and spangled the whiskers of the porters sweating at warehouse doors. The quays themselves were blurred ghosts of commerce; but the loadings went on regardless, despite the weather. They would continue until the last ship had cleared. Too many others were waiting in the murk down-river, eager to nose in for their share. It was the autumn of 1862, and Glasgow bustled with the freight of Mars from Clydebank to the firth. It hardly mattered to these ironmasters that the American war they served was a whole ocean away.

Julian Chisholm damned the ironmasters adequately as he waded deeper in their Scotch mist. It occurred to him to damn his own strange errand too, but he resisted that healthy impulse. It had been some time now since he had noticed his eyes in a mirror and ordered the brain behind to cease its brooding. Today the fog fitted his mood like a thick wet glove.

At times like these it helped to focus on externals. He had learned that simple trick long ago. For example, the Baltimore clipper that would be taking him to the Bahamas tomorrow—assuming that he could make up his mind to go aboard. He picked out her topsail spars above the sheds along the river. The *New*

Providence lay snug in her moorings, but even a landsman could tell she was ready for sea. . . .

He paused under the trussed-up martingale and admired the lines of this aged lady from the China trade. She carried her years beautifully, though every bulkhead would surely creak once she was under way: it was the fate of ships that came back from the graveyard to help their owners turn an honest penny. He patted her figurehead (a surprisingly respectable elder, complete with stovepipe hat and biblical beard) and walked down the dock until he stood beneath the stern. Above him the spar deck was half lost in fog. It made an adequate screen for a man who had no idea what his next move might be. Now that he stood in the clipper's shadow, it seemed incredible that he would sail for Nassau tomorrow. It was much more logical to wait here patiently, to keep a rendezvous with a woman he did not even know.

Of course rendezvous was not quite the word for his impending encounter with Mrs. Kirby Anderson. She would have no inkling of his presence here—when, and if, she drove down to the water front. But she had smiled at him three days ago, when they had met on the inn staircase; she would remember him now, if he stepped forward and spoke.

He had followed that smile into Argyll Street, in time to see her enter the waiting hackney. Thanks to the crowded road, it had been easy to trail her progress to the quay—where he had lingered to watch her board the clipper. Yesterday he had repeated the tactics of a hunter who could be patient for a while. Today he had promised himself to force the issue, on the conviction that her desire to go beyond smiles would match his own.

Mrs. Kirby Anderson. The widow of a late major of the C.S.A. Booked to sail home via Nassau, to put her husband's affairs in order. That much he knew from taproom gossip. As the clipper's richest passenger, she had rented Captain Shea's own quarters for the voyage: it was only natural that she should go aboard these last afternoons, to make her cabin comfortable. . . . Natural, too, that she should have a cottage piano in her suite at the inn and play brilliantly in the hour before dinner; that Swanson (her estate manager) should pout with pride as he brought her down.

It was, in short, a virtuous façade as well as an attractive one. But Julian Chisholm—wise beyond his years in such matters—had dismissed it long ago. The invitation in her eyes, he repeated, was as genuine as the copper gleam of her hair, the frank enticement of warm white shoulders, smooth thighs, a waist that owed little to whalebone. If he could judge by externals (and who could judge better than a doctor with a Vienna degree in his pocket?), Mrs. Kirby Anderson's body was made for the act of love. . . . With the proper approach, would she be an antidote for Lucy Sprague?

Lucy—and her husband—had taken a westbound packet some weeks ago; thanks to Victor Sprague's somewhat peculiar mission in the Bahamas, they would be well settled in Nassau when the *New Providence* docked. It was no new thing that his heart should pound at the thought; in planning the seduction of Mrs. Anderson, he was only following the theory that one nail will drive out another. After all, he would have to face Lucy eventually. It was ridiculous that he had not yet brought himself to pay Shea more than a deposit on his cabin.

Byron, he told himself firmly, was well buried now; Byron's *homme fatal* was a sadly outdated role. Especially for a young man with frayed cuffs and a purpose in life peculiarly his own. Yet he had played the role for years. He had played it to the hilt when he came up to Glasgow for Lister's lectures—and lingered because Whit Cameron's company had made Glasgow bearable. When he had fought the urge to take the first ship—any ship—to Nassau, and Lucy. . . .

Three years ago he had put an ocean between them for the second time. He had gone back to his courses in medicine, insisting that American men did not ruin themselves for a woman's sake. Not even in the supposedly romantic South. Now, at last, he could say that those years of dedication had not been wasted: he had been born with a surgeon's hands, even if he had also been born unlucky in love.

For three years, while the money came from Chisholm Hundred, he had burnished his skill with the masters. From the Rotunda in Dublin to Semmelweis's great clinic in Budapest. From the Hôtel Dieu on the Seine to the stench of the Allebemeines Krakenhaus in Vienna, where he had taken his final degree. Glasgow was merely the end of all that, as it had been the beginning. He had turned back to the dank, outmoded old buildings of the university as a man might turn home again, knowing that this was his final stop before he went home in earnest.

Tonight he would attend his last lecture. It was high time he took his hands to war.

Would he have the courage to face Lucy, in her fine house in Nassau, and tell her that? Hearing the squeak of carriage wheels in the fog, he turned to face Mrs. Kirby Anderson instead—just as she opened the hackney-coach door and put one small sandaled foot on the step.

She was wearing a hooded pelisse that muffled her to the chin; in the murk she seemed almost nunlike and smaller than he had remembered. When she stepped out to the quay, the hood fell back, revealing the dim copper aureole of her hair, already curled in tight ringlets by the fog. For a moment she stared at him with no sign of recognition, a strategy he applauded as he lifted his not-too-shiny beaver and offered her his hand.

He found that they were of a height after all—that her eyes, deep brown in the pale blur of her face, were weighing him with interest. Her mouth (was it too large for beauty, and were the full lips carmined?) just escaped smiling. He handed her up the gangway to the clipper, realizing that she was managing the meeting more neatly than he.

"Dr. Chisholm?"

"Your servant——"

"Are you surprised I know your name?"

"A little."

"After all, we're to be fellow passengers."

There was no doubt of her smile as she leaned down from the gangway and met his eyes. "I'm putting the final touches on my cabin. Won't you come aboard—and tell me I've done well?"

He had been taught to bow acceptably almost before he could walk; it helped to cover his blind panic now, when he took a long stride up the gangway and breathed the scent she was wearing. When she vanished abruptly into the clinging fog and Lucy Sprague stood laughing in her place.

Lucy had worn heliotrope their last night in London. (Sometimes he needed even less to bring her back.) She had stood laughing at him, on the frayed carpet of his room at the Temple; in a black-and-gold evening dress, she had gleamed against the dingy background like an orchid in a swamp. Beyond the windows the same fog boiled in the ancient courtyard. He had shut it out with one sweeping gesture before he turned and held out his arms...

The mist cleared, and he saw that Mrs. Kirby Anderson was standing on the deck of the *New Providence*. He was quite certain now that she was laughing at him.

"So you refuse to come aboard until we sail, Doctor?"

"You must forgive me. I'm late for a lecture now."

She murmured something in the fog. Julian turned away without hearing. It was a long walk to Lister's clinic, but Lucy would whisper beside him all the way. It was really incredible how often that light, teasing whisper had shut out the world and its invitations.

ii

The gloom of the amphitheater funneled downward, melting in the cone of light above the operating table. Julian pushed his way through the packed benches and, with a little forcing, found a place at the rail. The reek of chloroform hung about the frock-coated surgeon who stood ready under the battery of oil lamps; heads craned in unison as he bent above the patient who was still writhing feebly on the table. Joseph Lister was a teacher who sought always for the new and untried—some even said the impossible. Judging by the great, gaping wound below the merciless bite of the tourniquet, Julian concluded that today's problem was a hip-joint amputation—a formidable procedure for any surgeon.

The instruments beside the patient were shining clean. Julian checked the familiar alignment of razored scalpels, forceps, bone saws. Most of them had been devised for use before the present vogue of anesthesia. He remembered his own first clinic (in this same amphitheater, not too long ago), when the presiding surgeon had scoffed at chloroform as an impious attempt to circumvent the laws of God. Watching the well-scrubbed fingers of Lister's dressers darting at their work, Julian wondered when the theory of cleanliness would also be accepted as something less than mumbo-jumbo. It was practiced now only at the University of Budapest: he had seen the great Semmelweis operate there and had come away all but convinced. . . .

Strange how simple it was to banish Lucy at the clinic door. He leaned forward now, as eager as the others to hear what Lister was saying.

"The severity of the injury here makes it almost certain that infection will ensue if the limb is not amputated. What is the continental view, Dr. Chisholm?"

Julian answered with no sense of shock; it was not the first time that Lister had asked his opinion.

"In Vienna some surgeons favor excision of the bone fragments, especially in compound fractures and traction."

There was an audible murmur in the front row of benches; this was a radical departure from accepted practice in amputations.

"What are the results?"

"Gangrene, in many cases. A large percentage of mortality."

Lister nodded. "I, too, would save the limb—if I could prevent gangrene."

In Budapest, Julian had watched Semmelweis operate without gangrene. Semmelweis argued that particulate matter was the cause of that dread "hospital disease." But in Vienna, Virchow had insisted that the connection was absurd. There had been little hesitation among the students, when it came to choosing between the Hungarian and the Viennese. Yet Semmelweis continued to deliver clean-healed wounds from his clinic, and cadavers with "hospital gangrene" continued to appear on the dissecting tables of the Vienna deadhouses, the medical center of Europe.

A student spoke from the dim cave above them. "What is the cause of gangrene, Doctor?"

Julian shrugged off the challenge and sat down.

"Guerin claims that air gets into wounds," said Lister. "I have noticed that gangrene seldom occurs in medical wards where there are no open wounds." He turned to wash his hands at a basin proffered by one of his dressers. The nails of those pudgy fingers, Julian noted, were both clipped and clean.

"The patient is ready, Doctor."

Lister held out his hand for the scalpel. The mound of inert flesh on the table did not flinch as the steel bit through mangled tissue: it was evident that the assistant pouring the chloroform knew his job thoroughly. Once more Julian marveled at the dexterity of those spatulate digits as they tied in ligatures and reduced the rasp of the bone saw to a mere whisper. Already Lister's fame in these emergencies had penetrated through Scotland and England. Who else could claim eighteen thigh amputations without a death?

The clamps came off at last, and the surgeon stepped back from the table. His frock coat was still immaculate: this, too, was a far cry from the practice of Lister's colleagues, to whom a bloodstained lapel was a badge of prowess. Lister, however, was not only deft but clean. Lister scrubbed his hands after each operation as well as before—a practice unheard of save in Semmelweis's Budapest clinic. And, like Semmelweis, Lister got results— when others lost patients from the very gangrene the operation was supposed to prevent.

The stump was neatly sutured now and covered with linen compresses; the dressers wheeled the patient away, and Lister rolled down his sleeves and bowed to the applause from the crowded benches. Julian allowed himself to be carried out with the jostling crowd of young men, most of whom were several years younger than he. In the doorway, he resisted the impulse to bid the surgeon good-by. It was enough that Lister had rescued him from himself for an hour; enough that he could now follow silently down the trail he had blazed.

iii

He stood for a moment on the steps of the surgery. A raw wind had begun to sigh up the Clyde valley from the sea; Julian turned up his frayed collar against its bite as it whistled mournfully along the eaves. Glasgow seemed no less grim by dark, but he was sorry to turn his back on this dingy hall of mercy.

Walking slowly toward the Paisley Inn, he dared Lucy to ambush him in the night. Usually this first hour of darkness was the worst, unless he had begun drinking before sundown. Tonight he found that he could rehearse Lister's fluent technique—for whole minutes at a time—without thinking of Lucy at all. Was it the fact that his postgraduate work, as such, had ended with today's lecture? Or could he thank Mrs. Kirby Anderson for a temporary deliverance, after all?

He weighed that last question carefully, and let his steps quicken on the cobbles. At least he knew now that he would pay Shea his passage money. He had crossed that Rubicon when Mrs. Anderson laughed at him from the deck of the clipper.

So far, so good. It would be easy enough to knock at her sitting-room door tonight and apologize for his strange behavior on the quay. Easy to breathe her fragrance again and assure himself that she would not always be replaced by Lucy's mocking phantom. Of course he had tried this route to forgetfulness before and found it a blind alley. For all those memories, he could not slow his steps as he turned into a narrow lane that seemed to twist upon itself in its steep descent to Argyll Street. Already the aroma of Clydebank assailed his nostrils, a mud-and-fish-head aroma older than legend. It was still a short cut to a rendezvous (he could use the word now). A hope, however tenuous, that another woman could offer the release he had wandered over Europe to find.

How much of his life had he wasted in mean streets like these? In short cuts from dissecting table to half-empty bottle? In grimy doorways, where he waited patiently for the turn of a key, the gleam of eyes at a stairhead? He totaled the score without self-pity. If Mrs. Kirby Anderson would add her name to the list— if she would help him over that last waiting hurdle in Nassau—he would thank her from the bottom of his heart.

One more turn of this crooked lane and he would enter the side door of his inn. He lifted his eyes to the strip of night sky above the housetops, seeking an omen:

Thence issuing, we again beheld the stars.

Mr. Cary's translation of Dante, he reflected, was appropriate to the moment—even if Dante did sound a bit odd in Glasgow. He had every right to speak the last line of the *Inferno* aloud, since he was still playing *l'homme fatal* and enjoying the role. It would sound more dramatic tomorrow—in Mrs. Anderson's cabin on the *New Providence*.

Something moved in the dense shadows ahead. Julian pulled up warily and saw that it was two drunken navvies, clawing for each other's throats at the entrance to an alley. He had witnessed many such brawls in his wanderings. Freezing to his own patch of shadow, he watched the smaller combatant wrench free and cock his fist for an overhead smash. The other man, apparently a trifle less fuddled, had already anticipated the move. Julian started forward just as the *coup de grâce* crashed home—in this case a cloth-wrapped blackjack that swept downward in a short, vicious arc. The victim spread-eagled in the gutter with an almost contented sigh; the winner vanished down the alley like a homing bat.

The instinct of a physician had overridden Julian's wary pause.

Now it forced him to kneel above the prostrate figure, to feel along his hairline for a possible fracture. He found no wound, no blood —and no reek of alcohol; there was a suspicious tension in the man's muscles as he tested the arms for possible injury.

The warning came almost too late. Still he managed to twist aside and avoid the punishment of the savage knee thrust up at his midriff. Again the realization that this was expected of him jolted his senses wide awake. But there was no time to avoid the sudden shadow that blotted out the stars. A shadow with a flail that lashed expertly downward. The cloth-wrapped persuader connected neatly with his skull, just behind the ear, blotting the stars in earnest.

His back somersault into darkness lasted only a few seconds, though he was too stunned to rise at once from the gutter. His assailants had propped him against the curb before they vanished: he slapped just once at his pocket to be certain of their motive. His wallet was gone—and, with it, his passage money to Nassau.

He let the thought sink deep as his fingers touched the laceration just behind his temple. They came away wet with blood, but he knew that the injury was not serious. An experienced fist had swung that cloth-wrapped bludgeon, placing the blow directly over the motor area of the brain. The preliminary lure had been well planned too—even if it was an old item in the footpad's repertoire. He might almost assume that he had been followed from the university, that the thugs had known a doctor would hasten to the aid of a supposedly injured man. . . .

Julian was on his feet now, swaying a little as he waited for the last wave of dizziness to pass. His money was gone—that was the important fact. Unless he kept his head, the *New Providence* would sail without him—to say nothing of the invitation Mrs. Kirby Anderson had offered with such refreshing boldness.

He laughed aloud as he groped his way down the last damp pitch to Argyll Street; still laughing, he lifted a fist to the stars. It was a gesture worthy of *l'homme fatal*, but he felt that he had earned it. No one but a fool would pause to admire the stars from the depths of an alley. Only a brassbound idiot would count his blessings before he held them in his hand.

There was one blessing he could still enjoy, if he reached his room in time: the half bottle of whisky he had hidden carefully that morning. Without even pausing to brush the mud from his coat, he broke into a shambling run.

There was no time to pause for details: a man as shabby as Julian Chisholm (of Chisholm Hundred) could hardly gibe at a little dirt on a broadcloth sleeve. That coat (like Chisholm Hundred) had seen better days. Like those once-bountiful acres on the Cape Fear, it would see worse before its owner struck his truce with life.

iv

The throb of his headache was gone when he entered the inn. He plunged straight for the stair well, turning from the inviting bustle of the taproom. MacGregor, the manager, was helping at the bar tonight—and MacGregor lived up to his name. This was not a moment to remind him that a certain account was a week in arrears.

On the first landing he was held for an instant by the door number across the way. Tonight those brass numerals stared back at him like dim yellow eyes in the frugally lighted corridor. Number 33 had been Mrs. Kirby Anderson's quarters since her arrival; more than once he had paused before that oaken panel and raised a hand to knock. Tonight he continued up the stair as his vision cleared. He was panting in earnest when he reached the top landing and unlocked the room he shared with Whit. The eyrie sprang into its dour, familiar outline in the lamplight. A smallish nook under the pitch of the mansard roof, it had been used originally as a servant's bedroom: the gray walls matched the gray fog seeping in at the oriole window. Julian sat down on his own doddering bed and reached into the clothespress for the bottle. For a long moment he sat staring at the label without seeing it at all.

A drink, at least, would start his brain ticking. He shook off his apathy and poured himself a quarter tumbler, feeling his head clear in that all-too-familiar alchemy almost before he could gulp the whisky down. He poured again, and put the glass on the floor beside the bottle. After all, it was time for the inventory.

Finances would do for a start. His friends in the alley had overlooked the few coins in his side pocket. He dropped these to the floor between the cracked toes of his boots and smiled as the last worn halfpenny rang true. Nine and six, exactly—not counting the pfennig he always carried for luck. . . . He took his watch from its fob, wondering again why it had not been filched along with his wallet. Placing it carefully on the floor beside the little heap of coins, he opened the worn hunting case. The faces of his parents stared up at him, two faded daguerreotypes under glass. The small, demure mother he had never known. The father like a medallion from a more dashing century. Tonight Harrison Chisholm's eyes seemed even more reproachful than usual.

The watch would bring a few pounds more if he could make himself part with it. His clothes hardly counted, after their months of neglect. He turned briefly to the sagging door of the press and let Whit's wardrobe mock him with its splendor. Sleek broadcloth claw hammers, with magnificent satin lapels; waistcoats that only a born dandy would dare; doeskins that remembered their owner's trim shanks. . . . He stroked the hearty fabric of Whit's boat cloak, the Scotch cap done in the Cameron tartan. Whit had bought them on Bond Street for the voyage they had planned to make together. . . . On the shoe trees a pair of dancing pumps glowed like dark mirrors. Julian's own walking boots were an affront in such company; his hatbox (slapped with the second-class labels of Europe) elbowed Whit's topper like an importunate poor relation. He knew its contents all too well: an odd stock or two, a change of tattered linen, and dueling pistols that had stayed with him (like an outgrown habit) since college days.

Of course there were the tools of his trade. He lifted the small mahogany chest from beneath the bed and took out a plush-lined scalpel case. He opened it carefully: the slightest pressure against a blade could dull the edge, requiring a half hour's honing to bring the steel to concert pitch. With the knife nestled in his palm, he remembered Lister under the operating lights. Semmelweis in Budapest. Himself, performing his first major in Vienna, with the glare of the great Virchow burning his shoulder blades like a second knife.

Still nursing that tingling memory, he replaced the scalpel and took up a flexible probe, tipped with porcelain to seek out deep-lodged bullets. For a moment he saw himself operating behind a battlefield, under a strip of canvas broiling with summer. A working surgeon, stripped to the waist, dedicated, secure at last from the private wars in his heart. But the image faded fast; he made no effort to call it back. That deadly quarrel a whole ocean away was no subject for melodrama.

He had bought the chest of instruments months ago, when his decision to join the Confederate forces had first taken form. Each item had been chosen carefully, from the slender forceps (only the artisans of Berne could fashion steel so delicately) to the button trephines. Surely he could be forgiven for clinging to them now. Besides, they would not fetch a tenth of their value in a forced sale.

Was there no other way to obtain the balance of his passage money before Captain Shea resold his cabin? On his feet again, Julian paced to the cheval glass, pausing to snatch the whisky from the floor in one practiced swoop. Staring hard at his mirrored image, he found no real weakness there. Only an anger that went well enough with a lean profile and straight-knit brows. A promise to himself—to break free of an impasse that, at the moment, seemed unbreakable. Never in his life had he felt so futile, or so trapped.

The Chisholms, as a clan, had seldom questioned their destiny. Yet other Chisholms (not too long ago) had fought their way from traps no less desperate. The only surviving Chisholm continued to stare bleakly at his image. This next inventory would be more damning, and much more detailed.

To begin with, he discarded the carapace of *l'homme fatal*, once and for all. In its stead he welcomed Julian Chisholm, M.D.—a surgeon with the skills of a continent presumably lodged in his finger tips. As a friend of humanity, he was determined to offer those hands to the Confederate States Army, for what they were worth. As a born romantic (who could quote Dante thirty seconds before a footpad's bludgeon connected with his skull) he had fumbled his chance to make that offer. It was as simple as that, so far.

The blunder could be repaired, in time—even if he did not sail with Mrs. Kirby Anderson tomorrow. There were other ships— and there was more than one Mrs. Anderson. The Confederate agents in London would pay his passage, once he had produced his family tree and his diploma. The Confederacy was already desperately in need of doctors. Of course the red tape would be endless, the delays maddening . . .

His father's face still stared up at him from the open watch-case. He restored the case to his fob and took out Harrison Chisholm's last letter. Though he knew it almost by heart, he scanned the bold flourish of the script one more time:

MY DEAR SON [the elder Chisholm wrote]:
As I set down these lines, I cannot help asking myself if you will ever receive them. I am positive that we can never meet again on this earth. Though I have been treated well enough, my health is not good. Arrangements go forward for my exchange, but I feel that I shall be gone before they are consummated—even as I feel certain that the Cause, for which so many have offered their lives, is doomed—unless Europe or England intervene.

Perhaps you can answer that last hope better than I. Your letters speak of an early return: I trust that you have completed your arrangements for running the blockade.

We have never been close, I know. Yet I am sure that our sense of responsibility to our State has always been identical. Believe me when I say that I understand (though I can never quite forgive) your decision to be a doctor—and your determination to persist in that career after your brother died.

I can even understand that Chisholm Hundred could mean but little to you, by comparison with the lifework of your choice. So be it. You are still my heir—a part of this world of ours, as well as the new. Perhaps you can serve it more fully as a surgeon than you ever could as master of a plantation on the Cape Fear.

Here in the North the Yankees are glum enough as news comes of our victories (though there is some doubt of the outcome at Sharpsburg, or, as they call it here, Antietam). As a Southern commander in the field, I can guess how dearly those victories were bought.

Come back to your own people, Julian—and come quickly! As I say, I have left everything to you. It is not much any more, now that the war moves into another winter. Good-by, my son. And God bless you.

YOUR FATHER

Julian folded the letter between his fingers. Like all his father's missives, it had come from Fort McHenry, the Union prison in Baltimore. The letters had reached him regularly since his father's capture at the First Manassas. Delayed as usual by the censor, this one had followed official word of the elder Chisholm's death.

Try as he might, he could not blame the Yankees too much or feel a burning desire to avenge his loss. Over the years other and more telling blows had lessened Harrison Chisholm's will to live. Mark's passing had been the first, his own desertion the second. The crash of civil war, capture in the first pitched battle, months of prison life—all these had been only the final links in the chain. Colonel Chisholm had been lucky in his captors, lucky in his one brief taste of war. A hell-for-leather cavalry charge (ridiculous as grand opera) had carried him with his men across the flank of a routed Massachusetts brigade at the first battle of Manassas. In the end it had been pinched off neatly—between two companies of Yankee marines guarding the main army's retreat to Washington.

Julian could never picture his father as a cavalry colonel. Save for the flattering reproductions in London magazines, he had yet to glimpse the Confederate gray. The South's hard-working diplomats in England did not appear in uniform; perhaps they never would, despite their string of victories at home. . . . It would have been easier, in a way, to imagine Harrison Chisholm riding off to the Crusades—a jingo that had more than surface kinship with the field of Bull Run.

Crusader, champion of North Carolina's sovereign rights, master of ten square miles of prime valley land—— He tried hard to warm to each of those images. To Julian his father was more credo than man; he had died as he had lived, with the essence of his integrity intact. Harrison Chisholm had been a good man, in his way a useful man. He had not been a father who aroused affection in his young.

His one surviving son bowed his head to the memory. His father bowed back from the past—a symbol of his time. For all its feudal basis, it had been a debonair, well-planned world. But from his beginnings Julian Chisholm had moved through it like a stranger.

v

He made that world come back again, forcing the images a little and adding a spot of whisky to the tumbler to keep them sharp. Harrison Chisholm, who had had the finest cellar in his county, had once called whisky a drink for overseers. His younger son was a more democratic alchemist: Johnnie Walker had served him well before, when he tried to pin down his past.

Chisholm Hundred had faced the Cape Fear River for more than two centuries now, across the great flat checkerboards of its fields. High on the slope of the hill, its south portico seemed remote as a cloud when viewed from water level—as unreal as another Parthenon created (for no visible reason) in this green corner of Carolina. Actually those Corinthian columns were only a façade of the older Georgian mansion that Timothy Chisholm had raised here in the beginning, when he had surveyed and claimed his ten square miles under a royal patent. The wine-red brick spread in warm wings along the hillside: Chisholm Hundred combined the dignity of the past with its even prouder present, and the blend was sound. Here was an aristocrat among houses. As such, it took a half acre of gleaming parquet for granted in the foyer. It would have felt naked without an ancestor on every wall, a houseboy for every guest.

Like all real aristocrats, the house was at home with its background, enhancing it even as it dominated. Julian remembered the soaring beauty of the portico against dove-gray winter skies —the snowless Southern winter, when the fields were umbered with dead cottonstalks and the wind that keened upriver from Wilmington just escaped a freezing bite. And then—overnight, it seemed—gray changed to tender green as spring marched up the valley, painting the hills with bursts of dogwood, coloring the formal gardens with well-planned magic, burying the breezeways in a mantle of cape jasmine.

Summer was the easiest season to bring back: the lazy shimmer of heat mirage between fields and river; the shouts of the overseers as they marshaled the hands after their nooning; the rhythm of those myriad, sweat-slicked backs, dipping down the straight-ruled furrows—where bursting white bolls presaged another annex to the warehouse, another hunter in the stables. . . . The too-warm nights that always felt a little lonely, even when they throbbed with music. The fine September rain, like a suspended mist, when the gins closed down at last. When you could ride with Mark again, beside the river, as far as the tidal marshes. Or take the wood road across the river to the north, and give the roan her head in a vain scramble to match Mark's breakneck pace.

Turning home in the smoky dusk after one of those long gallops, Julian would sometimes rein in at the gatehouse of a neighbor's estate and watch the lights wink on across the lawns. It was a luxury then—to yield to this dawning wonder. To ask yourself why your suave, hand-tailored world seemed unreal as a stage setting. Or why you could pose so naturally in its midst, like an extra actor who had no wish to assume a stellar role.

Thanks to Mark, Julian knew that he could go on being an extra indefinitely. Mark would always be an ideal heir apparent, whether he was leading a cotillion at a levee or chatting (like a good seigneur) on a doorstep in the quarters. True, some of his elder brother's private musings might have shocked their father greatly; but the master of Chisholm Hundred was far too occupied to eavesdrop on the thoughts of youth.

Mark said, "You're a fool to be a doctor, Ju. Isn't being a gentleman enough?"

"I don't know what you mean."

"You will, in time," said Mark. "As you see, I'm making it my lifework. So will you, if I have my way."

"You'll be just as busy as Father when you take over here."

"Not if I can help it. Not if King Cotton lasts out our time. Our esteemed parent goes through the paces because he enjoys it. I have other pleasures I enjoy more."

"But, Mark——"

"Wait till you come up to the university," said Mark. "You'll give up this dream of being useful."

Julian remembered that conversation on the Sunday the new headman assumed his office. Zeno had led the pickers for a long time now; but Zeno had been bought by a visiting trader for two thousand dollars, for resale to a rich redneck in Texas. Most of the estate's four hundred field hands had turned out for the ceremony in their gaudy best; Harrison Chisholm had stood on the top step of his portico to hand the traditional glass of whisky to Lolly, who was to be Zeno's successor.

When the black tide had broken into segments again and ebbed from the formal gardens, Julian sought out Mark. Seeing the Chisholm slaves en masse had depressed him, for no reason he could name. Lolly, of course, would drive his fellow hands no less grimly than Macalastair, his father's head overseer—and Julian could only wonder why. Another question (and this was both novel and unsettling) concerned both his father and Mark. Why, when the estate ran so effortlessly, was either of them needed at all? His mind refused to put that last thought into words when he found Mark on the upstairs breezeway, enjoying a cold toddy. He was fond of his brother, and the question smacked of disloyalty, to say the least.

Today the heir apparent of Chisholm Hundred lolled like a contented god in his basket chair; his personal houseboy knelt before him to massage his master's bare feet and calves. The master's riding boots, an apple-green hunting coat, and sweat-stained smallclothes were tossed in a heap beside the chair. Even in Irish-linen drawers, Mark Chisholm kept his authority intact.

"Before you say a word, Ju, I'm sorry I missed the ceremony. Did Father notice?"

"I'm afraid he did, Mark."

"The fact is, I was detained. At the quarters."

"I thought Macalastair turned everyone out."

"I had business with Queen's Tandy," said Mark. "Macalastair let her stay while we—transacted it. Don't blush, Ju; you're old enough to know what I'm talking about."

Understanding instantly, Julian held his tongue; at their feet the kinky head of the houseboy had stopped bobbing for a moment, showing that he had grasped Mark's meaning too. Mark himself merely yawned and pushed the small Negro aside with a bare foot—a gesture of dismissal that was both curt and kind.

The black boy scurried down the breezeway with his master's soiled clothes piled high in his arms. Mark walked to the rail and parted the vines to let the hot blond light drench him for a moment. Pallor was an asset then, even in athletes—so the heir apparent did not stand too long in the full sunlight. Julian knew that he would always remember the perfection of his brother's body: shoulders just broad enough, corded back muscles that rippled like silk to blend with narrow flanks. Why was Mark's skin almost *too* white at that moment? Like a snake's skin in the dark, when he returned to the green shadow of the vines.

Laughter rumbled in the barrel chest, and Julian felt his question vanish with his doubts.

"After I've bathed," said Mark, "I'll offer the pater my regrets. Ceremony is important, Ju—and don't you forget it. I might even say that our lives are based on it. Most lives are—when society insists on doing things the wrong way."

So the question was answered, even as Julian had put it aside. It was wrong to live by slave labor (even as the Yankee abolitionists were screaming). It was doubly wrong to use a slave as Mark had used Queen's Tandy. Yet those same slaves had seemed as contented as sheep during the ritual on his father's lawn. It was a slippery thought for the mind of a fourteen-year-old to pin down. Mark did not help as he stood there in the lazy river breeze, flexing his leg muscles and smiling at thoughts of his own.

"Ceremony is a fine thing, Ju," he said at last. "But it must be handled properly—with enough good whip hands at the bottom, enough real brains at the top. We've plenty of both, here in the South. If the Yankees will let us be, we might make things last forever—just as they are."

Like many of his brother's offhand remarks, the words came back to Julian later, freighted with new meaning. For the present it was enough to take one of Mark's cuffs behind the ear—and go down to the kitchen gardens to blaze away his doubts in pistol practice.

At fourteen Julian could already shoot feathers from the old cocked hat they used as a target. A year later—when he was all but ready for the university—he could drill the spots from a playing card at ten paces, a feat not even Mark could duplicate. And Mark had already come through a half-dozen meetings with only a splintered collarbone. . . . Prowess with the smooth-bore dueling pistol, said Mark, was essential to every young man's education—along with the ability to walk a chalk line with two bottles of claret under one's belt. Julian, who followed most of his brother's dicta, had never thought of arguing. He even repaid Mark by coaching him in algebra and the mysteries of Tacitus. This, too, was a necessary chore, since the elder Chisholm had insisted that Mark complete his degree—and Mark persisted in thrashing every tutor that Harrison Chisholm summoned to the estate.

Latin, Greek, and a little logic. French and mathematics. Enough history to season the young Southern mind without unsettling it with the ferment of change. Julian had absorbed it all, even as he soothed their tutors' feelings. He had known that he would be a surgeon—ever since he had helped old man Cagle set a broken hip. Hilary Cagle, who doubled as stock expert and plantation doctor (and actually boasted a degree from Glasgow), was a cynic who did not offer compliments lightly, even to the son of an employer. When he had told Julian that his hands were born for just such work, Julian had accepted the statement as a fact. Later—when he had probed unaided for a bullet in a poacher's thigh, tied off a bleeder under Cagle's exacting eyes, and delivered a half dozen babies at the quarters—he knew that he had found himself, and his dedication.

It was a solemn discovery to make at sixteen, and he clung to it gratefully. Here, at least, was a refuge from his mounting doubts.

. . . Slapping breath into the latest of Tandy's progeny, knowing (even before he carried the child to the sunlight at the cabin door) that the infant's skin was the color of coffee with cream, he let the most pressing of those doubts find words at last. Old Cagle had merely snorted derision.

"What of it? It's *droit du seigneur*. An ancient and honorable privilege of every laird. Trust an American nabob to turn it to his account. A high brown like this will fetch top money as a houseboy."

At sixteen a few young men have already dreamed of changing their cosmos for the better. But Julian merely shook his head, without shaking off the puzzle. It was enough, for now, to have his own *raison d'être*. And yet, while the newborn child squalled under Cagle's ministrations, he stared at Tandy's dwelling place as though he were seeing it for the first time.

Harrison Chisholm had always been generous. Though the bed on which Tandy lay was a mere wooden trestle with a moss mattress, the blankets were new. So were the cooking things beside the wide clay fireplace, the Sunday clothes that peeped out of a box in the corner. Like every cabin, this one had a fieldstone base and a well-shored floor. It was whitewashed, inside and out; Macalastair often boasted that his sick list was the shortest on the river. Of course Tandy would be back in the fields again in a few days, and the whole family would share this small room tonight. The aftermath of that sharing hung in the sunlit midday—though Cagle had aired the cabin thoroughly before the accouchement. A dark animal aura, primitive and sad. . . . Julian, breathing it cautiously, knew that it was part and parcel of Chisholm Hundred. Would Queen's Tandy—or Lolly, or Zeno—be happy in any other air?

But that same spring—when his young blood stirred in earnest, and Mark suggested a way to quench its ardor—he had held back. He had been neither chivalrous nor afraid—nor, for that matter, in the least repelled by the slant-eyed grins that Queen's Tandy, and a few other wenches in the quarters, had begun to throw his way. Certainly he had had no hesitation (beyond his first moment of panic) when Mark had taken him instead to Madame Denise's maroon-and-gold parlors in Wilmington—where the young ladies were companionable, expensive, and imported.

From that moment the question sank to limbo. He was certain

now that something separated him from the destinies of Chisholm Hundred. The fact that he could not force himself to go to the quarters on such a common errand was his most vivid proof. At least he was grateful to know that there were other, more natural escapes. For the rest, his work was waiting around the corner of tomorrow. It helped him to forget, sometimes, that a way of life (whose destiny he could not share) was lonely at times.

vi

Julian had expected a battle royal when he asked permission to pursue his studies in medicine. The Chisholm studbook had yielded its quota of officers for the Mexican war, and an oversupply of senators, governors, and lesser luminaries. But Chisholm men had yet to venture into trade—or even the sciences. True, a collateral branch (on the Randolph side) had turned up at least one doctor of repute—and doctoring in general was beginning to be recognized, however cautiously, as a profession. . . . Julian never knew just what prompted the elder Chisholm's consent. Perhaps, with the succession assured, his father had merely resigned himself to what seemed a whim—a stubborn whim which his second son might yet outgrow.

It was agreed that Julian would begin his studies at the University of Virginia—for the sake of polish only, with no reference to the medical course offered there. Later, if he persisted in his resolve, he would follow old Cagle's suggestion, take a degree at Glasgow—and follow it with postgraduate study on the continent. It was an ambitious program for the time, but Harrison Chisholm could be openhanded when he made up his mind.

If he was disappointed in Julian, he gave no sign when they shook hands at the river landing that fall. Standing at the rail of the side-wheeler that would take his trunks down to Wilmington and the railroad, Julian was sure that his father had sighed over that handclasp. He would never know if that sigh had been born of relief: the elder Chisholm was too poised to admit (even by his demeanor) that his second son was an enigma he could not solve.

Julian lived with his brother during his first term. Mark had come back for a fifth year, to clear up some credits for his degree, and permitted Julian to parse his Sallust with perfect good humor.

In return, he had introduced his brother to every young nabob in their dormitory. Jack Stuart, who loaned Julian his hunter and applauded his skill at the bars. Harry Lucas (of the Maryland branch), who permitted him to lose handsomely at his poker parties—and came off a poor second when he tried to match the Chisholms drink for drink.

Both young men considered it odd that Julian should come to their campus without a valet, or a tutor to write his papers. They found it even odder when Julian insisted on attending an occasional class, with no prompting from the dean. But they accepted him as Mark's brother—as well as a man who could bet a hundred dollars on a four-card flush without turning a hair.

If this acceptance had come naturally, Julian's first duel was plotted, by himself, to the last detail. Duels at the university were fought for a hundred reasons, though political quarrels ranked high on the list. As an eccentric who had decided to study medicine abroad, Julian was excused from most of the debates that went on past midnight and ended, all too often, with a double report of pistols in the dawn. Still, he was expected to fight at least once before the first recess, if only to round out his pattern. . . . When young George Raleigh, flushed with one drink too many, had blocked his path on their stair, he could have given way with honor. It had suited his purpose to send George sprawling, for George was both a fire-eater and a nuisance.

They had met at the far end of the Long Meadow, in a misty dawn. Shooting at the barked command (from the hip, as Mark had taught him years ago), Julian had simply blasted George's pistol from his hand before his opponent could fire. A broken finger (which he had set on the spot) was enough to satisfy George Raleigh's *amour-propre*. If that young gentleman's fire-eating was checked for a time, Julian's initiation into campus life was complete.

Just before the Christmas recess the dean had reluctantly handed Mark his overdue diploma. According to the elder Chisholm's wishes, his heir apparent would now perform the customary grand tour abroad—and return to Carolina in time for the next ginning. The brothers had parted tranquilly enough.

"Give it another year," said Mark. "It'll make you one of us."

"Just what does *it* mean?"

"The mold," said Mark. "The ancient Southern matrix no man

can escape, if he's well born. God knows I've done my best to fasten it on your fledgling soul."

"How well do I fit?"

"I'll answer that on my return," said Mark.

"And if I still want to be a doctor?"

Mark's darkly handsome profile had knotted in the briefest of frowns. "I'm relying on Harry and the others, Ju. I think they'll help you to outgrow that notion in my absence. You see, my lad, I'll want you around when I take over."

"Why?"

"Someone must listen to my philosophy," said Mark. "You won't have time if you insist on being useful."

"I could be useful at Chisholm Hundred."

"Chisholm Hundred is a place for gentlemen," said Mark. "Must I define that word once again?"

Julian had expected to hear no more of Mark until summer. His brother was no letter writer and his father's own duty letters contained little but reports on the heir's progress from London to Paris to Rome—with *de rigueur* weeks in Cairo, Constantinople, and the Holy Land. But Mark had been gone less than five months when the elder Chisholm wrote that he was returning home at once— with a prospective bride.

. . . Your sister-in-law-to-be is Lucy Taylor, of the Port Royal Taylors [Harrison Chisholm wrote]. She has been an orphan for some years now, and was living quietly with an aunt in London when Mark was presented. Judging by his letters, I gather that it is a Love Match: since the young lady's connections are beyond reproach, I was only too happy to give my consent at once.

Naturally I deem it essential that you return home for the announcement of your brother's marriage—an event which neither party wishes to delay.

Julian had arrived by steamer the night of the engagement ball. Walking up the hill in the close spring twilight, he thought that the house had never looked more remote—or more a picture of its time; and he had stood on the driveway for a while, watching the lamplight pattern the lawns, hearing the scrape of fiddles as the orchestra (brought across a state line for the occasion) prepared to welcome the guests. For all its elegance, this had been a man's world since he could remember; it seemed strange that it would soon boast a chatelaine again. He walked under the white beauty of the portico without asking himself why the prospect should be so disquieting.

Miss Taylor, said his father's butler, was still at Oak Point, her cousin's estate. Julian climbed the great soaring curve of the stair well—striving, as always, not to glare too hard at his forebears on the facing walls. His forebears (having no such reticence) stared back at him without pity from their tall gilt frames. Mark was waiting on the first landing with both hands held out. In evening black, he could have stepped into a picture frame of his own: the future master of Chisholm Hundred looked the part tonight, down to the last jeweled button of his London waistcoat.

In his own quarters, Julian found that Mark had brought him presents from abroad. A set of pearl studs from Rome. A topaz-and-emerald boutonniere from the Grands Boulevards, shaped into a perfect cornflower. Mark straddled a chair and watched while a houseboy fastened the straps under Julian's dancing pumps.

"Won't you congratulate me, Ju?"

"But I have——"

"You aren't happy to see me settling down. Youngsters never are. But you needn't pull a long face. We plan to be gayer than ever here. Wait till you meet Lucy—you'll see why."

Julian was sure that he didn't resent Lucy's coming, despite that strange moment of doubt on the driveway. He could even rejoice that Mark had found something of real interest outside himself. But the sense of strangeness, of threat, persisted. He searched for words that would bring his malaise in the open without hurting Mark.

"I suppose I'm confused—now it's happened so suddenly."

"Love can strike without warning," said Mark. "I thought that was poetry once. Now I know better."

He did not say it happily. Julian saw, for the first time, that his brother's face was drawn. He studied Mark carefully in the glass as he gave his cravat its final inspection and accepted evening gloves from black Roy's hands. There was a hot, inverted gleam in Mark's eyes tonight. Like hunger turned inward, thought Julian —though he guessed, even now, that the strange light burned even deeper.

"Just how did it happen?"

"We met at Aunt Sukie's," said Mark. "I proposed the same evening. Lucy thought me slightly mad. I told her I *was* mad—

for her. . . . I've said that before, of course. This time, worse luck, I meant every word. I knew I couldn't rest until I'd brought her home with me." He smiled briefly, and that smile, too, was quite unlike Mark. "So I showed Aunt Sukie our account books—and brought her."

"You make me eager to meet this paragon."

"I was afraid of that," said Mark. "Dance the first waltz with her, Ju. A younger brother can't do less, I suppose. But remember she's mine. You've grown much too handsome for a freshman, and Lucy's much too fond of flirting."

Julian knew that his brother's laughter was forced, but he echoed it dutifully. They went down the staircase, pulled into the great, shining foyer by the whisper of the violins.

Lucy had not yet appeared, and for the next hour he danced dutifully with girls he had always known. He flirted with them, just as dutifully, as an unattached male has been expected to flirt since formal dancing was invented. As luck would have it, he was in the library with Cagle when Lucy entered on Mark's arm. So he was entirely unprepared when he crossed the floor, as a new waltz was beginning, and found her standing on the last step of the stair.

vii

The picture would be with him always, down to the last item. The rattle of watch seals in his father's white-gloved fingers, as he bowed to friends among the dancers. His own black Roy, agile as a wasp in a white jacket, offering a tray of tall glasses. Lucy declining the offer absently (already her eyes were fastened on him, drawing him). The Paris couturière who had designed it could not have described her ball gown more accurately than he. How the panels of draped tulle (caught up in a hundred acanthus leaves) swept over the classic bell of her hoops and met at the slender waist. How the gleaming bodice swelled upward, into prodigal ruching that covered the tiny sleeves—and let the girl's arms and shoulders gleam forth like warm ivory in the lamplight.

A single jewel winked in the hollow between her breasts as she lifted her head proudly and waited. Already he knew why Mark's voice had gone taut that evening when he spoke of her. Already he was glad that his brother was elsewhere when his father spoke the formal presentation.

"Of course it's your waltz, Julian," said Lucy. "Why else would I wait?"

As a younger man he had cursed the dancing master who had come out from Wilmington to teach him to bow properly. Tonight he blessed the man's capers, for Monsieur Albert had known his business. So had certain young women at Madame Denise's, where he and Mark had learned to waltz to perfection long before that dance was admitted to the drawing room. Whirling Lucy now, watching the light shine on her coronet of ash-blonde braids, he hoped that his skill would atone for his silence.

"It's always a shock," said Lucy, "when things turn out as you expect. I sometimes wonder why."

"I beg your pardon?"

"You and I, for example. Surely I'm what you expected, if you've talked to Mark. Don't be gallant. Just be truthful."

"You are all I hoped you'd be and more."

"I'll be truthful too," said Lucy. "I hoped you'd be like this. Shy on top. Knowing just what you want——"

He took the plunge—and risked the easy patter of the ballroom. "And what do I want now, Miss Taylor?"

"Call me Lucy, brother-in-law. You want *me*."

He whirled her without trusting his voice. This was beyond all bounds. Even at Madame Denise's (where the surface deportment was flawless) such conversation would not be tolerated for a moment.

"I'm only clearing the air," said Lucy. "I'm only sorry you didn't see me first. Can't you be resigned, if I am?"

"Since I've no choice——"

"Not that I regret my bargain. Dance me into the fresh air, and I'll try to tell you why."

But he continued to spin like a grim top, pretending that he had not heard. No woman on earth had the right to peer into a man's heart and read what she had burned there. He dared to glance down at her quickly: Lucy lifted her wide blue eyes to his —candid eyes, for all their mischief—and he saw for the first time that she was beautiful. When they had met at the stair, he had known only that he must take her in his arms and keep her there, as long as he dared. . . . The soft, full mouth could pout charmingly, without losing its strength. Despite the whalebone armor between them, he could feel her sweet warmth like a visible current between her body and his own. Instinct (maddening in its insistence) told him that he could bend to kiss her now—that she would only purr like a sleek blonde cat and ask for more.

"I said I'd tell you why," she murmured. "Aren't you even curious?"

He whirled her through an open french window at last and across the flagged sweep of the portico. They walked in silence toward the formal garden, through a night heavy with unfallen rain. The throb of the waltz followed them; in the deep dark Lucy dropped his arm and whirled down the path ahead, still in waltz time.

He took the dare, forcing her solo waltz into an ever-narrowing compass, until she had whirled back into a cul-de-sac of boxwood, her arms spread against the hedge, her small, firm chin tilted in laughter. He stood above her then, still gripped by brooding silence—and prayed that she could not hear the thud of his heart. To his mind it seemed to shake the sixteen inches of lawn that lay between them. . . .

"Why are you staring?" said Lucy. "Can't you imagine me as a bride?"

"Until tonight, I couldn't have imagined you at all."

"I'm not really wicked," said Lucy. "I'm just honest. And, like most honest people, cruelly misunderstood."

"You were about to tell me why you accepted Mark," he said stiffly.

"I'll be honest about that too, Julian. I can give Chisholm Hundred all that it needs. I can't offer your brother genuine affection —but he's much too conceited to miss that. As for me—well, I still owe three thousand pounds in London—and I haven't a friend in the world. Only relatives who take it for granted I'll marry well." She was still laughing up at him, with those wide-open, candid eyes. "I've told Mark this, in the same words."

From the portico they were only one of a half dozen dimly defined couples, lingering for the correct quarter hour of badinage as a dance ended. He had stood on this same path a hundred times —a tall, correct figure, playing an impromptu of compliments against his partner's reproving sighs. Perhaps even bending to kiss a lace-embroidered wrist, with lips that combined reverence and ardor. Tonight he ached to fasten both hands at the spot where Lucy's décolletage just masked the swelling points of her breasts.

To rip downward, as a man husks corn, until she stood naked before him.

Lucy said, "Will you take me as I am, Julian? Or is that too much to hope for?"

He might have borne it had her eyes held less of wisdom; had he been less than certain that she understood his desire, and accepted it, as a matter of course. Instead, when her hand touched his (light as a moth in the dark) he crushed it between his own before he lifted it to cover it with kisses. Oddly enough, the arrested romance—so rigidly in pattern—saved him for the moment.

Lucy said, "You're unhappy because you want me. And even more unhappy because I know. It's nothing to be ashamed of, really I only brought you here to tell you that I keep my bargains."

He knew that she was flaying him deliberately, daring him to smash her easy defenses, simply by crossing the sixteen inches of lawn that still separated them. He pictured that meeting: white moth shadow, fusing with his own dark silhouette, swaying in a kiss without ending. The music had begun again, and the other couples had answered its call. There would be no eyes to see when he carried her into the darkness of the boxwood maze and possessed her completely.

But she was still laughing up at him as the mist cleared; the sixteen inches of lawn still lay between them like an unfought battle ground.

Lucy said, "I could have pretended, I suppose. Young ladies usually do, when they know they've made a conquest." She used the phrase deliberately, almost solemnly. "Would that have eased your mind and your conscience?"

"I'm glad you didn't," he said.

She swayed toward him, still laughing a little. For one blind moment he thought she would offer him her lips. Instead she slipped a cool arm through his and lowered her lashes modestly.

"Take me back, Julian. I'm quite refreshed now."

Ten seconds later they walked into the ball, and a dozen would-be partners swooped on her in unison.

Julian did not linger to watch her whirl away in Jack Stuart's arms. Nor did he venture into the ballroom again to meet Mark's eyes. In the stables he flung himself on the back of the first horse a sleepy groom could saddle. At the crossroad he had considered riding in to Wilmington—and the safety that lay in flight. Or, perhaps, the doubtful nepenthe of Madame Denise. . . . Instead he reined in at the river's edge and sat for hours in the cleft of a water oak, watching the broad, serene flood widen into the tidal reach downstream. Only when the last light had winked out on the hill did he dare whistle to the roan and ride back to the stables again.

Next morning, when he wakened in a cotton-wool dawn, he could almost hope that he had dreamed that black moment of desire in the garden. He had dressed without ringing for his houseboy; seeing that the sun was already above the misty river, he tucked his dueling pistols under his arm and started for the kitchen garden. The old target was still in its place. He had blazed other moods away against its splintered profile.

Lucy's laughter drifted up to him as he crossed the breezeway, and he drew back into the leafy shelter of the vines. She was crossing the lawn, swinging the skirt of a velvet riding habit, her eyes lifted to the tall house that loomed above her in the morning mist. For a moment he was sure that those appraising eyes had found him out. Then he realized that Lucy was only admiring the house that would soon be hers. Storing each feature in memory with that quiet, possessive glance.

He stood in his ambush, staring down at her as though he could never get enough of staring, the pistol lax in his hand. Mark called from the paddock and joined her on the lawn; for a moment they stood close together in the hush of early morning, then Lucy gave a little chuckle and drew Mark's mouth down on hers. It was the kiss he had dreamed of last night, beside the boxwood hedge; it was no less shameless—though he could not have said why—now that she offered it to his brother.

Madness could not drive him all the way; his hand faltered in time, before his rigid right arm could flail the dueling pistol down on the base of Mark's skull as Mark swayed on the lawn below him, with Lucy deep in his embrace. He even remembered to catch the pistol in his free hand before it clattered to the slatted floor of the breezeway.

He must have stumbled, without sound, into the house again, though he had no memory of reaching his room. The mist cleared while he clawed at the bellpull, and he poured himself a brandy with steady hands while he waited for his houseboy to answer.

Now, at least, he knew what he must do; he thanked a remote Heaven that he had found wisdom in time. When Roy hurried into the room, Julian had already opened the first of his bags and begun his packing.

viii

Knowing that Roy would never survive the Glasgow climate, he left the houseboy behind when he sailed for London. His decision to begin his medical studies abroad without a manservant had shocked Harrison Chisholm even more than his original resolve; his insistence that he must sail before Mark's wedding was received with the same disapproval. But Julian's father had promised him an education abroad, on his own terms; at Chisholm Hundred a promise once made was absolute.

Once he was established in Scotland, he found that he could drink away the memory of Lucy by noon; sometimes she was only a phantom by midmorning, if the first glass steadied his mind. In time (but this was a slower process) he found that work was a better antidote: that anatomy could be an absorbing subject, and the foul cave of the dissecting room a sanctuary where he could shut out the world, along with the memory of unkissed lips in a dark garden. Looking back on that first dour year, he felt that he might have lived her down completely if his luck had held. He could have continued to write pious lies to his father —of the progress he was making, of the practice he could buy in London. Yes, he could have persisted in his resolve and held his ground if Lucy had stopped writing those light, teasing notes. If Mark had lived . . .

On the surface, her letters were as innocent as any sister-in-law's. Sometimes they were mere lists of changes she had made at the estate. Silk drapes from China via Boston, *capitonnage* from Paris via Charleston. The new chef (also from Paris) had taken over the kitchens, to the vast annoyance of the black major-domo. Monsieur Felix Laurentier (another French item), the fashionable portrait painter, was adding the new chatelaine to the gallery. Then there was the bijou summerhouse that Mark had built for her on their first anniversary. It stood on the hilltop, with a magnificent view of the river. Gulls from the tidal estuary quarreled for the bread crusts that Lucy tossed them as she sat there alone, sketching the afternoon away.

He had no right to read meanings into such lines. When Lucy spoke of the ball that her father-in-law had given to celebrate the Dred Scott Decision, he tried hard to weigh the overtones of that celebrated political blunder—and the fact that the South could find it a reason for festivity. Instead he cursed Jack Stuart for stealing three waltzes with Lucy, and wondered if Jack had spirited her out among the boxwoods.

In the end he burned all her letters (none of which he had dared to answer) and returned triumphant to his work. But he knew even then that his triumph would be short-lived; that his hope for the future was a bravura gesture, nothing more. His father's next missive drove the point home like a thunderclap.

. . . Your brother is dead [the elder Chisholm wrote]. Though I set the words on paper, I cannot quite believe that they are true. Still, I must write them down, if only to call you home at once.

He was riding with a groom across the pine barrens. Lara, who has never stumbled since she was broken, pitched forward as she cleared the wood-lot fence. Mark was thrown from his stirrups—and, by all accounts, died instantly.

I need hardly add that this fearful news greatly alters your future, if you will it so. For your shattered father's sake, Julian, keep an open mind on the questions I cannot help but ask you.

Lucy has borne up well under the blow. Though you cannot be here for your brother's funeral, she joins me in the hope that you will hasten your return.

Three weeks later he walked up the hill to Chisholm Hundred, through another rain-haunted afternoon; once again he paused under the last oak on the driveway and let the strangeness settle about him like a protective cloak. His father's tall house looked confident of its immortality. What right had he to say (even in his heart) that its days were numbered?

A few moments more and he would be putting that thought into words. He need only tell his father that his determination to continue in medicine was unchanged—that he would never accept the inheritance or its ties. It was enough, for now, to walk quietly among the boxwood hedges, to stand (silent as a thief) in their shadow before he slipped into the house by the first door.

The formal living room was already drowned in twilight, but he saw that Lucy had made good her changes. Her drapes were frivolous at each of the high windows; the overstuffed armchairs she had ordered from Paris (done in golden yellow and sapphire blue) had the air of reformed rakes beside the grave marble of the fireplace. Lucy's portrait, framed in the overmantel, looked down at him in the half-light; he lighted a candle at the hearth and went up to stare at her remembered smile. The French artist had painted her in a gown gleaming with sequins; her ash-blonde hair was molded in a silver band. Despite her classic pose—and the pillar on which her hand was resting—she was more *gamine* than *grande dame*. At any moment, thought Julian, she might have changed that smile to a full-throated laugh.

He turned his back on that possibility and walked out of the house, postponing his moment of decision and damning himself for the weakness. Beyond his mother's old rose garden late sunlight cut through the water oaks to mark the stone on his brother's grave. He had never felt depressed in the family burial ground: today it was almost soothing to pause, of old habit, at his mother's headstone.

Mary Randolph Chisholm
April 2nd, 1816—September 3rd, 1837
"Too Soon with the Angels"

He had always blamed his father for that pious footnote, even though he admitted that the sentiment was genuine. Today he hated himself still more for his empty heart as he stood beside that neatly tended grave and wondered what his mother had sought from life. Wed at sixteen, she had given her husband three sons before she died. Two of the sons were buried near her now: Matthew, the eldest, had gone in infancy, Mark at full flower. And now her youngest could bring her no assurance that her marriage would have lasting fruit.

The grass was already lush on the sharply defined rectangle of Mark's grave. Julian read the inscription dutifully and murmured a prayer before he turned back to the house. This time he marched straight through the front entrance and knocked on the study door. He could guess, without asking, that Harrison Chisholm would await his arrival there.

He found his father seated at his mahogany writing table, staring down at Macalastair's account books and spinning the great terra-cotta globe that always stood at his elbow. But the elder Chisholm had surrendered none of his poise. When he lifted his hand from the globe and offered it to Julian, the pressure of the fingers was firm with purpose.

"Sit down, my son. I trust you had a good crossing?"

"I came by the first packet, sir. There wasn't time to write."

"There was no need. I am sure that your sentiments, at this moment, are only an echo of my own."

You know my answer now, thought Julian. That standard burst of rhetoric is only a refuge. I'll miss Mark as much as you ever could, though my reasons are different. What's more important, neither of us can put his reasons into words. We can only face each other, with his memory between us, and admit (once and for all) that we are strangers.

"I'm sorry, Father." He forced the words. "I haven't come back to stay."

"You'll return when your studies are completed?"

"I've made up my mind to be a surgeon. It's my one aptitude, and I must perfect it."

Harrison Chisholm considered. "I hardly suppose you could be a doctor and manage this estate as well?"

"Is that what you had in mind?"

"Frankly, no. It's too much to ask of anyone."

You believe that too, thought Julian. Each day you sit here and review your head overseer's accounts; each day you ride to the four corners of your empire, like a good seigneur, and watch it function. What you don't see is the fact that a canny Scotch manager and four hundred black serfs earn every dollar of your wealth. *Your* only importance in the scheme is to keep the pattern intact. To stand foursquare against change in a world that must change or die. But that I can never put in words. You've never hurt me consciously; I'll get out of your way without hurting you, if I can.

His father broke the silence. "May I hope that you'll reconsider —and give the estate all your energy?"

"It will be some time before I can complete my studies. Perhaps I'll return to America eventually. But even if I settle here, I must come as a doctor."

"The land and slaves will go to you someday, in any event. I might say that they are your responsibility."

Suppose I said that I'd accept neither? thought Julian. Or suggested you free the slaves over your lifetime and let them work the land themselves? It's what I'll do, if history gives me the chance. Again he was silent, and guessed that silence was wounding his father more than violent argument.

"I wish you'd talk to Lucy before you decide."

His heart leaped, but he met Harrison Chisholm's eyes steadily enough. "How could Lucy influence me?"

"I have not yet questioned her as to the future. But it has occurred to me that you might pay her your court, after a decent interval."

Julian tried to speak, but the elder Chisholm held up a soothing palm. "Don't think I'm callous when I make the suggestion. Mark would be the first to approve. It's common practice when a family line is threatened with extinction."

He paused at last. Julian opened his mouth to speak but found he did not dare, after all. He knew now that he had expected this from the moment he left Glasgow. By the same token, he knew what his response should be. . . . As his father had just remarked, it was quite usual for a younger brother to wed his sister-in-law when that sister-in-law was left an early widow. Lucy, by her own admission, had married the Chisholm money, rather than Mark: why should she balk at the idea?

"Do you think she'd have me, sir?"

"She has taken her bereavement well. Lucy is young, Julian, but she has a strong, alert mind. She'll make a perfect mistress here someday; I hope she'll look forward to that position, as your wife."

"Would you understand if I insisted on continuing with my medicine? If I turned the management over to Macalastair?"

Harrison Chisholm just escaped smiling. "Certainly, my boy. To be frank, I'd trust your wife to—make you see the light in time."

She's charmed him completely, thought Julian. He remembered her words, in the shadow of the boxwood hedge: *I always keep bargains.* She had brightened life at Chisholm Hundred, just as the fabrics of her choice had brightened the classic repose of the drawing room. What could he lose by asking her to stay?

"You'll find her in the new summerhouse," said his father. "She goes there often to watch the sunset." Again he hesitated. "Don't think I'm forcing you to a decision, Julian, but—this morning she said she'd be waiting there for you."

"Are you suggesting I broach the subject now?"

"By no means. But there's surely no harm in testing her mood."

"No harm at all, sir." Julian got quickly to his feet. The movement broke his indecision. Before he turned to the study door he realized that his father had won, after all. At this moment Lucy held his future in the hollow of her hand. If she would make herself part of his inheritance, Chisholm Hundred might still claim him forever.

Harrison Chisholm pressed his advantage quietly, as befits a gentleman. "May I take it that the future is still open?"

"As you like, sir."

Julian closed the study door without avoiding the unspoken bargain. For once his father's eyes did not quite meet his. Instead he heard the well-oiled whisper of the steel axis as the globe turned under the elder Chisholm's fingers. He guessed that those fingers were much less restless now. His father could afford to twirl his private world—quite as though the serrated mountains and terra-cotta seas were part of his own acres.

Outside, in the golden evening, he took the path to the summerhouse by instinct. Lucy's letters had told him that it stood alone, on the last steep slope of their hill. A thicket of cedars made a windbreak to the north; to the east and south the land opened to the tidal estuary, pale blue in the lingering day. Already the tiny building was part of its decorous background—a warm-white jewel of a house, snug in its setting of green. The jalousies were drawn against the angry red glow in the west; even the door was barely ajar, so that he could not see within as he came up the path.

When Lucy spoke his name, he had an insane conviction that she had been waiting here from the beginning—that this last, steep climb from the lawns of Chisholm Hundred was only the culmination of their destinies.

"I saw you leave the steamer an hour ago," said Lucy. "What kept you?"

"I was remaking my future," he said, with one foot still on the threshold. "That takes time, you know."

"Tell me about it," said Lucy.

He made no effort to answer the challenge, since this was destiny at work. In spite of the mad pulse in his throat, he felt strangely at ease when he closed the door behind him and stood facing her in the latticed light. She had been seated on a low couch that stood beneath the west window of the summerhouse: as she rose, her hand brushed the blind, letting in a few chinks of the dying light. Before her hand could quite fall at her side, he took her in his arms—and the last shreds of his self-control snapped before his mouth could close on hers.

His senses reeled as he felt her lips part under his own. Then the iron compulsion of desire steadied him, making his hands swift and sure as they fastened on the throat of her low-cut gown. Only then did he realize that this whisper of silk between them was her only garment.

"Why are you staring?" said Lucy. "Are you the only one who's waited?"

ix

When she left him at last, he did not speak. He knew that she had created this moment deliberately; he could trust her to break the spell—probably in a way he least expected. Now that he had possessed her fully—now that the wild need to destroy and be destroyed had won its own surcease—he could afford to wait a little for the words that would seal his future.

The lash of self-reproach would come later, of course. For the present it was enough to watch her open the door of the summerhouse a little, to let in the last gleam of day. For an instant she stood there, bathed in gray light. She had only begun to dress: in low-heeled slippers and pantalettes, she could have passed for a demure child, until he let his eyes move up her body. In the thin cambric sheath of her undervest, her breasts were saucy as silver apples and still proud with the passion they had shared.

But she did not speak until she had stepped into her hoops, and he had gone to her at last, to hold her laces. It seemed quite natural now, to help her thus.

"I've all but lived here, since Mark died," said Lucy. "Didn't your father tell you?"

"My father sent me here to sue for your hand. He didn't mention details."

Lucy nodded—and took up her mirror. "It's been in the back of his mind for some time now. Harrison Chisholm is a gentleman, Julian—but he's practical too."

"He mentioned a decent interval, of course——"

"And it was decent of you to wait."

"But I didn't—*we* didn't. That is——"

"Don't feel ashamed," said Lucy. "I made a contract and kept it. I can assure you that Mark had no regrets." She paused on that, dwelling on a memory all her own. "He died happy, Julian—without even guessing the sort of wife he'd married. Remember that, when you begin listening to your conscience. Remember, too, that we're out of bounds here. . . . The summerhouse is all mine: we had that understanding when he built it for me. I told him that I came here to be myself——"

Julian watched her smooth the last of her petticoats over her hoops, watched her inspect the severe part in her pale hair. Contentment settled upon him again, a barrier to the questions clamoring just outside the threshold of his mind. This was their moment, whatever its outcome: this was their sanctuary, no matter how wantonly they used it.

"Be honest," said Lucy. "Do you really want to marry me—now?"

"I'll do anything to keep you. How often must I tell you that?"

"So far you've told me nothing," said Lucy. "In fact, Julian, you're a remarkably silent lover. . . . Suppose I agreed with your father and insisted you take Mark's place here?"

"I could let Macalastair manage the plantation and go into practice in Wilmington." Julian was on his feet now, pacing out his thoughts. "Give me six months, Lucy; then marry me in London. I'll be ready for Paris then—and my gynecology. We could rent a house in the Quartier while I was working at the Hôtel Dieu——" He paused abruptly when he saw that she was laughing.

"Don't mortgage your future for my sake," said Lucy. "I'm quite through with Chisholm Hundred."

But his voice went on against that easy laughter. "We could have a wedding trip in Italy. Or Spain, if you prefer."

"On Saturday," said Lucy, "I go to my aunt in Charleston. In August I shall probably marry Victor Sprague."

He stared at her, without quite taking it in. "You mean—the Yankee senator?"

"We met last year at a ball in Wilmington," said Lucy. "We planned to meet again at Saratoga this summer. Why shouldn't I go, in widow's weeds?"

"You made these plans when Mark was still living?"

"He promised to take me North in August."

"You'd have given him up for Sprague?"

"Probably," said Lucy.

Hate rose in his throat like a giant's pulse. Just in time he remembered how that same red rage had almost put a bullet through his brother's head. At the moment he could hardly shoot a man he had never met. . . . He turned away from Lucy, controlling himself with a great effort. At this moment he was in no position to condemn her.

"Let's go on being honest," said Lucy. "We both know that Mark died happy. The way our world is going, he's better dead. So would we both be, if we stayed on here. I'm leaving in time, and I'm marrying the richest Yankee I can find, if he'll have me. Can you blame me too much?"

He forced himself to face her, and found those wide blue eyes as candid as ever. He could hardly quarrel with her wisdom. Or blame her, if she chose to marry Victor Sprague—or the devil.

"Don't pretend you were too young to see Mark clearly," said Lucy. "You know as well as I that he was a handsome, charming animal—and quite useless. He belonged to this land, just as your father belongs; he couldn't have survived the crash that's coming. . . . It's surely coming, Julian. When the North elects its first President. Sooner, if the scalawags have their way."

"Is that why you're marrying in the North?"

"I prefer the winning side," said Lucy. "What woman doesn't?"

"Why did you accept Mark in the first place?"

"I was younger then," said Lucy. "I really believed this world would last awhile. This past year I've grown up fast. It's another trick women have, when they're treated as jewels—and given too much time to think."

She hesitated, and her lips curved in a faint smile, as though she wondered if she could trust him with another confession. "Let's say that your father and Mark were born a century too late —you and I, a century too soon. I still know what I want. And it's a great deal more than a French chef and my own summerhouse——"

He stood above her then, with his hands twitching, as though he would strike her at last; and her blue eyes blazed up at him, daring him to complete the gesture. "Don't be a hypocrite, Julian," she said at last. "You know I'm right. So far I've broken no hearts here: I'd like to keep the record clean."

"What about me?"

"Your course is simple. You'll return to your medicine and pray that you're qualified before the storm breaks. When it does, my guess is you'll go with the South. You've a quixotic side, even if you are a born doctor. There's one thing Don Quixote can't resist —a war that's lost before it's begun."

He faced away from her on that, letting her last bit of insight build its wall between them. Behind him he heard the rasp of a lucifer as she turned up the lamp that hung above her mirror. The brisk sound of a comb told him that she was putting the final touches to her hair, but he did not dare to look. Instead he stared down at the couch beneath the west window. A few stray splinters of afterglow spread a patina across the cushions. It seemed incredible that their bodies had been locked in love on that same couch a scant half hour ago.

"Why did you give yourself to me?"

"I felt you deserved it," said Lucy. "I hoped you'd enjoy it. Be gallant and admit you'll never forget me. A Chisholm can do no less."

He heard the lamp chain rattle as she blew out the wick— and the quick whisper of her hoops. When he turned, she was standing on the lawn outside, bathed in the last pale light from the west. For a moment she seemed to float between lawn and sky—a sprite whose slenderness was accented only by the great bell of her gown. He could have touched her merely by taking two long strides through the open door, yet she had never seemed more remote. At that moment, she could have stepped into her gilt frame in the drawing room, with that parody of a classic pose intact.

Lucy spoke over her shoulder. "We've two whole days before I go. Shall we meet here again tomorrow?"

"After what you've told me?"

"Everyone respects my widowhood and leaves me alone," said Lucy, as though she had not heard. "Your father thinks you've begun to court me—so what could be safer?"

He whipped through the door and offered her his arm without another word. A year ago—the night of their first meeting—they had walked through the gardens thus. Tonight it was only seemly that they should return to the house arm in arm. . . . On the slope below, Chisholm Hundred—a proud phantom in the dusk—

winked at them from a score of windows as the house slaves lighted the downstairs rooms. He could not escape the conviction that the house was laughing at a joke all its own.

x

The next afternoon he had ridden Lara for hours through the pine barrens, knowing, long before he put foot to stirrup, that he would ride back in time to take the path to the summerhouse again. The following evening (while Lucy sat in the drawing room in symbolic loneliness) his father had questioned him discreetly over the claret. Julian had been shocked at his ease in turning the elder Chisholm's questions aside.

"You mentioned a decent interval, sir. I could hardly presume——"

Quite beyond shame, he would have lied by the clock to cover his tracks. Fortunately his father was called to Richmond on business the day of Lucy's departure, so there had been no need of lies. It had been easy to give her an hour's start before he left an ambiguous note, packed his portmanteau, and followed her.

But in Wilmington he found that Lucy had taken a coastal steamer to Baltimore—that her aunt in Charleston had been dead for years. In Baltimore he found no trace of her whatever, though her tactics were now plain enough for any thwarted lover to grasp. He had gone down to Washington on the first train and walked through the mud of Pennsylvania Avenue, in a pelting April rain, to sit in the Senate gallery and plan his next move. It would be absurdly easy to kill—or be killed by—Victor Sprague. He had only to ask himself if it was worth while.

Luck was with him that afternoon, for the senator from Pennsylvania was speaking in defense of the Free-Soilers. Sprague had changed his front before, as business warranted. Now, as a Solon of the new, and disturbingly vigorous, Republican party, he shouted for the extension of freedom at the expense of slavery. Julian sat on for a long time, watching the man's head bob down the dark aisle below him. Tall without too much majesty, both leonine and well-groomed, Sprague was the epitome of the new crusader, the heir of Webster. It seemed quite logical that this ironmaster (who had made one fortune in Pittsburgh and another in shipping) should invade Congress without slowing the hard, sure beat of his success.

Today Sprague brought his own party to its feet with cheers: the Democratic phalanx could only stare in silence when he returned to his desk. Here, thought Julian, was the titan of tomorrow, even if his origins were common as brass. Perhaps he could give Lucy what she demanded of life.

Had his brother's widow come to Washington to meet this suave mouther of phrases? It would be simple enough to follow Sprague to his bachelor quarters at the Willard and surprise a rendezvous. Easier still to challenge him—for a reason that had nothing to do with Lucy. Sprague (as the world knew) was not averse to dueling, if a duel could serve his ends: his last fist fight on the Senate floor was already part of Washington legend. . . . But reason crept in as the day waned, and the Senate abandoned its oratory at last. Julian sat on in the visitors' gallery, watching Sprague march out with his colleagues, letting him escape to whatever future he willed.

When the lamps were turned out and a page tapped his shoulder, he quitted the nation's unfinished Capitol and turned his face toward the railroad depot. Glasgow (and his courses in surgery) was waiting over the edge of tomorrow. At least he had grasped the fact that passion is no substitute for honor. Lucy had merely played with him while she waited for bigger game. It was a bitter admission for a young man to make. The fact that he could make it at all was a long step toward maturity.

xi

That fall he began his gynecology at the Hôtel Dieu. Paris welcomed him with her gray, remembered smile; he found an entresol not too far from the Ile de la Cité and plunged into his new work with an all but normal zest. There were days when he told himself that he had outgrown Lucy at last; there were fragrant midnights when Bette (the girl who had come so casually to share his life) promised to help him forget that madness in the summerhouse.

It was Bette who brought his father's letter up from the concierge. It contained the news he had both expected and feared. Lucy, he read, had married her senator in Washington—a month before the fateful national elections. Though it had been preceded by a discreetly intense courtship at Saratoga, the ceremony had been private, in deference to the bride's widowhood. . . .

By all accounts, the man is a thorough scoundrel [wrote the elder Chisholm]. Though I must add that his Manner was above reproach when he visited Wilmington. There are stories that he is spending thousands to insure the election of Mr. Lincoln—a political calamity that can only mean war.
I still cannot believe that Lucy would wed another man, less than six months after Mark went to his grave. Still, I cannot blame her too much: she is alone in the world, with her own future to consider, and has every right to divorce her Destiny from ours.
As for you, my boy, I can only repeat the hope that you will recall your own True Interests when our moment of crisis arrives. It cannot be long in coming now.

Watching him read, Bette had tucked herself into the curve of his arm like a friendly kitten.
"*T'as cafard, Julien. Pourquoi?*"
"*Moi triste? Jamais de la vie!*"
He had taken her to a students' ball that evening and tried hard to drown this new, sullen heartache. Knowing that it must come sometime, he had not believed that the news could hurt so much. Bette (he recalled this later, with gratitude) had sensed his despair and done her best to console him, as only a Frenchwoman can. But both of them had fought a losing battle from that moment.

Lucy's own letter came a few months later, when his courses at the Paris hospitals were completed, and he lingered on with an inertia born of too much philosophy—and too much brandy with his breakfast coffee. More note than letter, the missive went to the heart of his problem—and offered an inevitable solution.

MY DEAR JULIAN [Lucy wrote]:
Why have you not yet congratulated me on my new marriage? I refuse to believe you have forgotten me so soon.
Will you prove me right, and steal time from your studies for the All-Nations Ball in London? I will be in the American booth: Victor is now in England on diplomatic business, as you may have read. I will save a waltz for you, and give you my news as we dance.

The letter had been forwarded by the university secretary in Glasgow; the ball of which Lucy spoke (a polyglot charity affair, for which tickets could be bought at any London embassy) would be held in two days' time.

Julian had burned the letter and gone to make notes on an operation at the Hôtel Dieu. An hour later he found that his notes were gibberish. An hour more and he was standing in the shed of the Gare du Nord, pressing a thick fold of bank notes on a not-too-tearful Bette, feeling his heart pump like a schoolboy's as the guards called, "*En voiture!*" down the grimy length of the Calais train.

Another twenty hours (he had spaced them with half tumblers of scotch whisky) and Lucy was in his arms again, whirling to the "Blue Danube."

She was wearing the same white ball gown she had worn that first night at Chisholm Hundred. The only added feature was a great rivière of diamonds. He resented the jewels particularly. After all, she could have made her point without them.

"I'm glad you're still curious," said Lucy.

"Where is he?"

"Victor is in Birmingham. Next week we sail for the Bahamas. He's much too busy for parties these days. . . . Was it so wrong of me to make sure of a partner?"

He laughed aloud at that, remembering the cloud of young officers that had clustered around her. "I've kept rather busy too, Lucy."

"But you came to this ball for my sake?"

He held her decorously as they reversed on the crowded floor. She was Lucy Sprague, the wife of a diplomat: there would be prying eyes, even at a London charity ball.

"You know why I came, Lucy."

"For *both* our sakes, then," said Lucy. "Shall we go to my hotel or your rooms? Your rooms, I think, would be safer."

She was past shocking him now, but he felt his breathing quicken. "What about your present bargain?"

"Victor again? Can't we wait to talk of Victor?"

"But I came all the way to London to congratulate you."

"You came to London to make love to me," said Lucy. "Why not begin?"

That night he took her to his chambers in the Middle Temple; it gave him a certain savage pleasure to spirit her there, to remind her how dingy a student's life could be. But he had forgotten such petty revenge long before he could hand her down from their cab to the fog-wet stones of the courtyard. Nothing (to put the matter bluntly) seemed too important beside the promise in her humid eyes, the whiplash of the perfume she was wearing. . . .

That night—and the next—she had stayed until the black fog outside his window had begun to gray with dawn. For the first time she had talked outside the facile ambush of her wit: Lucy Sprague was real in those London nights of love, a woman as well as a flame. He could even understand why she had married a scoundrel, though he could not forgive her.

For all that, he could not quite resist putting the question into words.

"Mrs. Victor Sprague," he murmured. "It still doesn't sound real."

"Victor is real enough," she said. "Would you care to meet him?"

"Heaven forbid!"

"For better or worse, he's the future. I want to move with the future, Julian—not trail behind."

"You seem to be managing admirably."

"I'm happy enough. Victor's a pirate, and he fights without rules. So am I. He doesn't happen to love me—or anyone. But he finds me decorative when he wants decoration. I'm as free as a woman can be in this year of grace. What adventuress could ask for more?"

"Don't dismiss yourself so lightly."

"And don't misunderstand me," said Lucy. "To you, an adventuress is a harlot with drawing-room manners. To me, she's simply a woman—who knows what she wants and wins it—with all the weapons she has. All my life I've wanted power—and the chance to do as I like. Victor Sprague is power—and he gives me my head. So, as I say, I'm content."

"Life isn't that simple, and you know it."

"Of course it isn't, Julian. If it were, would I risk it all to be with you?"

Life, Julian added privately, might turn out to be far too simple for them all if Sprague should return unexpectedly to London. For his part, he was prepared to meet the ex-senator—and kill, if he was lucky, with the firm conviction that Victor Sprague's death would benefit the human race. It was obvious (even here in London) that the ironmaster from Pennsylvania was gambling heavily on civil war at home. With that outcome in view, Sprague had transferred most of his shipping interests to British hands; and arrangements had been made (with certain mills in Sheffield and Birmingham) to divide the arms market sensibly. As a political power, he had a roving commission—an ambassador without portfolio. It would take him to Nassau now, to iron out details. . . . Already—they said it freely in London—goods must continue to flow to both sides, in event of a brothers' war.

He wondered how much Lucy knew of her husband's affairs. She had mentioned her love of power: the wife of Victor Sprague could not help but feel that history, and its molding, lay just within her grasp. Yet how much of his power would Sprague really share with a wife—or with anyone?

He explored that imponderable the night Lucy came to his rooms in traveling clothes, with the news that she must join her husband in Liverpool.

"Aren't you going to ask me why, Julian?"

"I'll tell you why. British factors are building extra piers on the Nassau water front today, to handle our wartime shipping. Your husband is going to check cargo—to make sure his hulls carry their share."

Lucy smiled. "According to our State Department, he's to sound out British sentiment in the Bahamas. The hope being that the governor will observe a Union blockade——"

"When blockade-running promises to be a major industry? Both sides are already in agreement on profits."

"Is this a criticism of Victor?"

"It's a statement of fact. Are you willing to face it?"

"I've already said he was a pirate. But don't think I've a part in his piracy."

She had gone on that defiant note—after an hour of love that still burned his dreams. Her last words came back to him often: in a way, they summed up Lucy perfectly.

"Don't ask too many questions of life. Remember it's always a jungle—and try to enjoy it."

This time it was easier to go back to Glasgow. Easier still to cross the Irish Sea for his courses at the Rotunda. Lucy did not write from Nassau: he knew only that she had settled there, in a mansion not too far from Government House. Sprague, he read, was shuttling busily from that port to England, as the first secession was proclaimed in the Alabama statehouse—as Mr. Lincoln delivered his inaugural at the still-unfinished Capitol in Washington. . . . In those wild months of rumors his infatuation with Lucy seemed a small thing. So small, indeed, that he had yielded to it almost mechanically when she appeared in London that spring and summoned him.

"Victor says it'll be a long war. So I'm to go to Paris next time, to renew my wardrobe. We might meet there, for variety——"

We might, thought Julian, but we won't. Not if I can put a few countries between us. Not if I go to Budapest for a year with Semmelweis and neglect to leave my address.

The name of Fort Sumter was inked on British newsstands now. With the smell of gunpowder on Carolina's doorstep, a second secession was inevitable: war, in the worst sense of that short, foul word, was only a matter of weeks now. He had faced the fact for some time—and faced it calmly. As a doctor, he would complete his studies and offer his services. It was the one sure way to banish Lucy from his mind.

He had seen her just twice in the year that followed this resolve. Once when he had picked up a French newspaper in a Vienna coffeehouse, read that Lucy was in Paris, and missed a fortnight of lectures to join her. Again in London—when his Vienna diploma still crackled cleanly in his portfolio.

By that time he had already joined forces with Whit Cameron. But Whit was the sort of friend who never asked questions at inopportune times.

xii

Julian came back to the inescapable present. The room under the eaves of the Paisley Inn was gray with the fog that still boiled through the oriole window. He crossed to slam it shut, blowing on his hands as he walked. There was still a little coal in the grate and an inch of whisky in the bottle at his bedside. Watching the flames lick the black heart of the stove, and pouring himself a last half tumbler, he wondered if he could ask Whit to help him now.

At college in Virginia—thanks to the ingrained snobbery of the castes—Julian had found it all but impossible to move from group to group. Only Whitford Cameron had dared to flaunt that taboo during his short stay. Whit belonged, by rights, to the mannerless gentry, the sons of small planters and tradesmen who had inched their way to the campus and were expected to stay where they belonged. Whit had merely moved into the nabobs' dormitory—and paid his way. Since no one was sure of his background, no one complained. Whit's spreads were much too prized, his whisky much too mellow for doubting.

Julian remembered that the Cameron waistcoats had been the envy of the spendthrifts, his pallor the despair of the dandies. It was soon remarked that the interloper was never seen by daylight, save on the rare occasions when he could not bribe a sheepskin man to serve as his proxy in the classroom. It was also remarked that Whit's guests were heavy losers at his poker parties. The gentlemen involved could afford their losses, but the mutterings grew. They reached a climax when it was learned that this same Whitford Cameron had attended the V.M.I. the previous semester —where his winnings had been no less phenomenal.

For all that, Whit had departed from the campus as elegantly as he had come—if a trifle more abruptly: old Ted, his dormitory servant, had always been tipped handsomely, which explained the gambler's head start on a posse clamoring for his blood. Julian had not joined the hue and cry. His losses had been heavy enough, but he had sighed at the loss of a friend. Expensive as they were, he had enjoyed his visits to the gambler's rooms.

A month ago Whit had emerged from a crowded Paris sidewalk and sat down at his café table without being asked. It had seemed only natural to shout for the waiter, and offer his hand. Whit had returned the greeting cordially.

"You want your money back, of course. Shall we match for it?"

"To prove you're honest?"

"To prove I'm in funds," said Whit. "Or you could merely buy me a brandy—to show you've no hard feelings."

But after they had driven to a restaurant in the Bois and dined royally at Julian's expense, Whit had admitted, quite candidly, that he was down to his last sou.

"I remembered your face. It still looked kind, so I sat down."

"I'm glad you did."

"Does that mean you'll stake me?"

"Within reason. We can't ship much cotton these days, you know."

Whit had named a figure, and Julian had blinked, then passed the bank notes over. Expecting to see the last of the gambler, he was pleasantly startled when Whit appeared at his hotel a few days later, with the money—and a dinner invitation of his own.

"You won't believe this, but I've never run out on an I.O.U. or marked a card. Say I live by my wits, if you like—and I'll agree. Or say I'm a student of character, who knows when to bet and when to stay out."

It pleased Julian to accept this statement at its face value. Whit was one of those rare beings who enjoy each day for its own sake, without quibbling over cost. If Julian never learned his creed or parentage, it hardly mattered: it was part of Whit's pose to be always a bit larger than life. An air of mystery suited him, along with his astounding cravats and the nugget of raw gold that hung at his watch chain.

"Never mind your conscience," said Whit. "You're the sort of man who would bring a conscience to Paris—because your state is at war with Old Abe and you aren't. Tell me why you're still out of it. You'll feel much better."

"I've told you. I'm waiting for my diploma."

"Never mind your diploma. What's her name?"

Julian frowned at his drink. It was a relief to unburden himself—to a point. "She happens to be married."

"Where is she now?"

"In London—waiting for me to join her."

"Why don't you?"

"I'd hoped to sail for Bermuda from Cherbourg."

"Glasgow's cheaper," said Whit, "I'll go with you via London, if you say the word. If you pause en route, what's the harm?"

Julian looked narrowly at the gambler across their café table. He was sure that this was an impromptu decision on Whit's part. Now that it was made, his new friend would find a dozen ways to vindicate it.

"Don't tell me you plan to volunteer?"

"There are many ways to enjoy a war," said Whit. "Let's say I'll look the ground over—and choose one that suits my talents."

Julian laughed aloud. "Perhaps you're a Yankee spy. I'd never know by your accent."

"Don't cramp me with a local label. And don't call me a bad patriot because you found me in Paris—instead of in Richmond with the bombproofs. I've been raising passage money for six months now—or trying to."

"Any luck?"

"I've had nothing else since you made me that loan. That's why I suggest we join forces, pro tem. On the surface we're an ill-matched team, but I feel we get along."

"Why do you say that?"

"You're in a mold. Call it what you like. Southern gentleman will do, I suppose. Unfortunately, you've never quite cracked the plaster. It still hurts when you violate a commandment, even if it's only the seventh."

"If you don't mind——"

"Very well, let's talk about me. In a way I'm luckier than you, Julian. When I was born, the mold was broken. Since then I've taken whatever color suits my fancy. Right now it pleases me to put you on your feet—and on the way to what you consider your duty."

"What of this detour in London?"

"Detours are good for duty, if they don't take too long," said Whit.

On that note they had crossed to England. Whit had taken rooms on Park Lane, while Julian met Lucy for the last time. When Lucy had boarded the Bahama packet at Liverpool, the gambler and the surgeon had taken second-class tickets to Glasgow.

Whit smiled comfortably at his friend as they settled into their shabby carriage on the railroad; Whit's silences could be soothing, too. But he had permitted himself the luxury of just one remark.

"It must be love. What else but the tender passion could keep a Carolina boy away from the wars?"

"It's love, right enough. And whoever called it the tender passion was lying in his teeth."

"Which means you'd prefer to outgrow it?" said Whit.

"More than anything."

"Give me a few days to study the problem. I'll deliver you."

After that promise, Whit had seemed to doze in his corner of the carriage, with the short, curled brim of his beaver tilted debonairly over one eyebrow. Sitting bolt upright with his memories, Julian was sure that the gambler was studying him carefully under that hatbrim. Asleep or waking, his lips were still curved in their habitual lazy smile.

Whit was smiling now as he burst into their bedroom at the inn, twirled his cape across a bed, and reached for the whisky.

"Out with it, Julian Chisholm of Chisholm Hundred," he said. "What private hell are you toasting in tonight?"

xiii

Julian looked up from the tumbler that held only the reek of whisky now and found that he was smiling too. As always, he felt both shabby and reassured at the sight of Whit Cameron. His own attire could never match the gambler's fawn-gray pantaloons and violent plaids; his stubborn conscience could never agree that life was a joke to be savored endlessly. Whit happened to be a born actor: in his presence, one could never be quite sure where reality left off and illusion began. One's own reason for being took on an added sturdiness, if only in self-defense.

"Tell it from the beginning," said Whit. "You've been rolled in some gutter and robbed. Instead of coming to me at once, you sit and wonder how you'll settle with Shea——"

"How did you know that?" Julian got to his feet none too steadily. "How could you know?"

"Point one: the turned-out pockets in what was once a coat," said Whit. "Point two: the mud you've yet to wipe from your cheek. Point three: the neat swelling behind your left ear." The gaunt fingers flicked Julian's temple. "The skin is hardly broken. Your assailant must have used a cloth-wrapped bludgeon, rather neatly."

Julian reached for the bottle. "You're right on three counts. So right that I've nothing to add. All I want is advice."

He paced over to the window and stared out at the fog, hearing the creak of springs behind him as his friend stretched out on the bed. Clearly, Whit was in an expansive mood. If he had won tonight, he might advance the balance of the passage money without being asked.

"This is the first time you've solicited my advice," said Whit. "The answer requires thought."

"I need a hundred pounds tonight, if I'm to sail tomorrow. Where can I get it?"

"Not from me," said Whit. "At the moment I've not one sovereign to rub against another. Fortunately I settled my own account with Captain Shea before I sat down to play this afternoon. I even promised to remind you that your own payment is overdue."

"That wasn't too kind."

"I've never felt kinder," said Whit. "Nor have I felt more like a god."

Julian looked hard at the gambler. "It isn't like you to bait me."

"But I'm not. Curiously enough, I'm already prepared to—how shall I put it?—make you a financial proposition in another's behalf? I came up that stair just now with an overflowing heart. Which means that I think you'll accept."

Julian sat down on his bed again and glared briefly at the empty bottle. "*You'd* best begin at the beginning."

"How much did you have when we arrived in Glasgow?"

"Under a hundred pounds."

"You'll remember I said that would hardly pay your bills and get you aboard the *New Providence*."

"There are secesh agents in Nassau. I'd hoped to arrange my passage through the blockade."

"Cash is better than hope," said Whit. "Hope can be a cold bedfellow—especially in the Bahamas."

"What are you talking around?"

"I'm preparing you for good fortune, my friend. Can't you be patient?"

Once again Julian looked sharply at Whit. The gambler's manner fitted the moment much too neatly. Had those two footpads really followed him from the University, as he had at first suspected? He started to blurt out the question—and held his tongue. Whit Cameron would offer his surprise in his own way or not at all.

"Answer this once more," said Whit. "You're both penniless and desperate?"

"Penniless yes—desperate, never."

"The reply is worthy of a Chisholm. Still, you've made no other plans to raise your passage money?"

"I've no friends in Glasgow, if that's what you mean."

"There I disagree. Your passage to Nassau can still be paid tonight. With enough over to buy you a berth from Nassau to Georgia."

"What must I return for this service?"

50

"Nothing that any gentleman wouldn't do for a lady."

"Then be specific."

"That would hardly be fair to Mrs. Kirby Anderson," said Whit. "Swanson, her agent, is waiting downstairs now to introduce you. She insists on making her offer in person."

"Mrs. Kirby Anderson?"

"Don't pose," said Whit. "I'm the poseur of this team, not you. *You*, my friend, have had your eye on the lady for three days now. Aren't you pleased to learn that the regard was mutual?"

The memory swam back into Julian's brain as he continued to stare at Whit. How that same Mrs. Anderson had smiled at him on the stairway of the inn; how she had laughed outright from the deck of the clipper. Strange how completely that tap behind the ear had driven her from his mind. It was stranger still that she could come back like this—with plans of her own.

Or perhaps it was entirely natural, once he had the missing bits of the puzzle.

Whit said, "Why shouldn't you do business with a woman, if her offer is honest?"

"When was it first made?"

"Three days ago, via Swanson. I might add that he's a clever agent. At least he knows all about your past—and a great deal about your future."

"Does that enter into the bargain?"

"References are always important."

"Do I understand you've—come to terms?"

"Pending your consent. Passage to Nassau, paid in advance, aboard the *New Providence*. Five hundred dollars to take you from there to Georgia. Money to be paid in hand, if you'll answer just one question correctly. Mrs. Anderson will put it to you, alone."

Julian nodded. The puzzle was complete now—only one missing piece was needed to define the pattern. He held it at arm's length, to admire the workmanship. Someone had most certainly planned this moment; even Whit's arrival had been carefully timed.

"Shall we go to the lady now?"

"Not until you're presentable. Just to prove *I'm* a good manager, I'll lend you a coat—and that gilet you admired in Paris."

"Thank you, no. She'll take me as I am."

"At least you can wash the mud from your cheek. Will you need more than a moment for that?"

"Wait for me. We'll go down together."

But the gambler was already at the door. "I'll tell Swanson you're coming; we can meet in the taproom——".

Julian stopped Whit with his voice. "It didn't happen this simply. Admit it."

"Life is always simple if you've something somebody wants," said Whit, and closed the door precisely.

xiv

Julian got up from the horsehair sofa one more time and roamed the parlor where Swanson had left him. The door in the far wall must certainly open to Mrs. Kirby Anderson's bedroom. Just as certainly, Mrs. Anderson was within, and fully aware of his presence.

He pulled up abruptly, before he could hammer that door with his fist. Instead he sat at the cottage piano and let his hands roam the keyboard in a dry run. He had played well as a boy at Chisholm Hundred; only common sense kept him from striking a few wild chords now.

For almost ten minutes he had fidgeted here, while preserving an outward calm. Swanson had left him at the hall door; Swanson had said his client would be out directly. The man had been smooth as cream: a perfect City type, he had made this moment respectable, even when he lifted an eyebrow with his good-by smile.

Two things, Julian pursued, were evident at this moment: Mrs. Anderson had planned the meeting well in advance—and planned it her way; Mrs. Anderson, armed with knowledge of his needs, held the whip hand. If these were unhappy facts for any man to face, they were better faced at the beginning. What—without descending to an obvious conclusion—did he have that she wanted? He cursed Whit for playing the game according to Swanson's rules, and let his hands dance down the keyboard after all. The first notes of Donizetti's mad aria from *Lucia di Lammermoor* . . .

Mrs. Kirby Anderson walked into the room as though she were answering a cue. Like an actress fresh from the wings, she paused for a moment in the sudden bath of light and smiled at her leading man. She was in pale green evening dress. Diamonds gleamed on wrists and fingers, and there were other jewels in her copper hair. At her throat, where the décolletage of her gown began, a jeweled cameo hung by a narrow black riband, echoing the promise of half-revealed breasts. Julian, playing Donizetti to the hilt, kept his eyes on the keyboard. Perhaps he had misjudged her approach after all. Perhaps he had known just what she wanted, from the beginning.

"Did you guess that was my favorite, Doctor?"

She walked easily to the horsehair sofa and sat down just outside the circle of lamplight. Even in the penumbra there was a glow about her that went deeper than the jewels at wrists and throat.

"Perhaps you should understand one thing first," she said. "This is not an assignation."

"Do I seem to labor under that fallacy?"

"A little. I can scarcely blame you."

Julian smiled and rose from the piano for a tardy bow. The faint tremor in her voice told him that she was not too sure of her ground after all.

"Forgive my misapprehension, Mrs. Anderson. It *is* Mrs. Anderson?"

"You knew that much on the quay."

"But my knowledge ends there. Yours, I gather, goes deeper."

"I accept the rebuke. Or was it a compliment?"

"At the moment I'm not quite sure."

"Correct me if I stumble." There was no tremor in her voice now. "You are one of the Cape Fear Chisholms. Your father was captured at Bull Run; he died some weeks ago, in a Baltimore prison. If you'll permit me this much poetry, you're about to take his place in the ranks——"

"As a surgeon."

"Precisely. From what I've heard, you are much too levelheaded to think that fratricide can produce anything but—more fratricide. At this moment you are without funds—and might accept my help, if the service I ask in return is within reason." Mrs. Anderson spread her fingers and smiled down at the cold white fire of her rings. "Is your silence an endorsement, Dr. Chisholm?"

Julian kept his voice level. "You're much too thorough for comfort."

"But those are only essentials. Mr. Swanson is well connected in London; he has many Southern friends who know your family. As for my help"—once again the rings made their dance of fire—"I assume you would not be here if you had no intention of accepting it."

"May I ask the conditions?"

"Assure me of one point first. You plan to take a commission in the Confederate Army?"

"I've gone beyond plans. My application is on file in Richmond. With an uncle on headquarters staff, it won't be overlooked."

"That would be General Clayton Randolph. Your friends in London weren't sure you had written." Mrs. Anderson nodded thoughtfully; he felt that she was endorsing something in her own mind rather than his own remark. "Would you care to question me, for a change, or shall I make my point at once?"

"I think you've made it now," said Julian. "You're anxious to reach a Confederate port. Anxious enough to help me financially, if I'll return the compliment."

"Will you, Doctor?"

"Gladly—but how?"

"Surely it's simple enough," said Mrs. Anderson. "Will you marry me before we sail?"

He stared at her in silence. The question had not been unexpected; it left him just as breathless, now it had come. As for Mrs. Kirby Anderson, her poise was perfect. Looking back on it later, he knew that he resented her calm most of all.

"Perhaps I'd better ask those questions now," he said at last.

"Do. I'll answer them truthfully."

"You are the widow of a Confederate officer?"

"My husband was killed this summer, on the Peninsula."

"You are also a Southerner?"

"I was born in the South. Later I moved North. I returned to marry Major Anderson shortly before the war."

"Must you omit geography?"

"I'm afraid I must." Her composure was still flawless. "If we do marry, we must do without aftermaths."

"I'm afraid that is beyond me."

"I'm anxious to enter the Confederacy with the least delay. My husband was wealthy. Unlike most of you, his wealth is still intact—and he left me everything. Already his relatives are trying to break the will. They'll succeed if I don't defend my rights."

"That's clear enough."

"Hear me out, please. Among my—my husband's people, I'm called a Yankee. They could keep me from returning if I took passage at Nassau under my present name."

"How could they manage that?"

"They've managed pretty well now, Dr. Chisholm. Perhaps you didn't know that blockade-runners carry black lists. My name has been down for some time."

"So you've planned to return as Mrs. Julian Chisholm?"

"Of the Cape Fear Chisholms," she said, and he was sure that her voice had taken on a thin edge now. "Of course we'd separate the moment we reached a Confederate port. Permanently. Therefore I omit geography from my life story."

"What makes you think I'd disturb you later?"

"The way you're staring at me now," said Mrs. Anderson. "Surely you're human enough to be curious."

"I'm more than curious."

"The fact remains that we can use each other. Will you accept my offer?"

"What have I to gain?"

"A boat ticket, which you need badly. The knowledge that you've helped a Confederate widow in distress."

He walked to the window and stared down at the wet pavement of Argyll Street. Her armor, it seemed, was quite without chinks; whatever her secret, she meant to keep it. The coolness of her proposal—and the certainty that he could not but accept it—still tingled in the back of his brain. But he could afford to smile, now his back was turned. For all his thoroughness, Swanson had apparently learned nothing of Lucy Sprague, and Lucy Sprague made his acceptance all but inevitable.

His smile broadened into an abashed grin as he remembered how he had planned to use this same Mrs. Anderson. Only a few hours ago he had hoped to flaunt her before Lucy, if occasion offered. Why should he complain if she used *him*, for reasons of her own? She might serve him better as a temporary bride.

Once in the Confederacy, he could take up his trade and forget her—as he hoped to forget Lucy. She could make no claims on his future: the legal tie could be annulled with ease. If she were a demimondaine fleeing from old troubles, or seeking new fields, she might plague him later. But that, too, was a chance he could ignore. Already he guessed that she was out for other game.

He turned to her on that note, with his mind made up; if he seemed to hesitate, it was only to make the bargain definite. "I gather you'd agree to an annulment later."

"I'd insist on it. I'll be rich when I've secured my husband's estates. Don't think I'd make the least claim on yours."

"I've only your word for that, of course."

"Swanson will put it in writing, if you like."

"Your word will do nicely," said Julian. "To be frank, my own estates will hardly be worth claiming, until the war ends. Besides, I'm a doctor, not a planter—and I'm eager to prove it. Much too eager to balk at details."

"I counted on that too," she said.

"Perhaps I should add that I've turned into something of a vagabond these past years. Or did your Mr. Swanson uncover that fact as well?"

"I guessed that much on my own."

"And did you guess that I might have a hidden motive for accepting you?"

"Don't tell me her name. We must keep a few illusions."

Julian forced a smile. "How can you be sure it's a woman? Suppose I'm a jewel thief who always strangles his brides?"

Mrs. Anderson returned the smile, much more serenely. "One always takes chances in marriage."

He stood above her and found once again that they were almost of a height. Since he couldn't precisely tower, he did his best to stare down her composure. Only a tiny pulse at the base of her throat betrayed the fact that she was tense with waiting. He remembered how casually he had planned to kiss that same throat as another prelude to forgetfulness.

"The advantage is yours, Mrs. Anderson. I trust you won't abuse it."

He did not attempt to outface her on that; instead he turned again to the window and the drear vista of Argyll Street. He heard the rustle of her hoops as she went to the piano—and, when no music came, guessed that she, too, was giving her fingers the discipline of a dry run.

"Play for me," he said, still without turning. "When a man offers marriage, he needs background."

"What is your favorite, Doctor?"

"Do you know 'Lorena'?"

He had no idea why he had suggested that sugary ballad. Even if Lee's men had wept over it in bivouac, it was hardly her style. Mrs. Anderson struck one hard, bright chord and spun away from the keyboard.

"Let's dispense with background, Doctor. You have your incentive—is it yes or no?"

"Yes, of course," said Julian, and lifted her hand to his lips. "To the success of your ventures," he added, turning her fingers in his and pressing a second kiss against the palm.

"Success to yours," she said, and took her hand away.

"That, too, was a venture," he reminded her. "Why did you discourage it?"

"To save you time, and effort. I've already said that this is not an assignation."

"Thank you for reminding me."

"Our marriage will be a matter of convenience, nothing more. Surely you've grasped that by now."

"Most marriages are."

She rose from the piano. "Would you prefer to call off the bargain?"

"By no means. Nor would you. I'm sure your business is too urgent."

It was a blind shot, and he smiled as he saw it sink home. This time it was her turn to go to the window, his to sit at the piano and ripple through the chorus of the ballad he had requested. When she spoke, he saw with approval that she had regained her poise.

"So you insist on 'Lorena'?"

"The song of Lee's Invincibles," he said. "At times, I hear, they can be sentimental too. So can I—now I'm betrothed."

Her eyes were still on the fog-streaked pane. "I think we've hurt each other enough."

"It's a temptation few men can resist, when they're crowded in a corner."

"Would it help, if I said that I—that I feel no contempt at your acceptance?"

"That I can scarcely believe."

"If I promise to respect your reasons and ask that you respect mine?"

He offered Monsieur Albert's best Sunday bow. "*Affaire entendue, madame.*"

"There are a few details," she said. "As you know, I've taken the after house aboard the clipper. To be exact, the captain's stateroom—and the mate's. You will occupy the latter cabin. There is a connecting door, which I shall keep locked. Is that both clear and agreeable?"

"It is clear, at least."

"The ceremony will be performed aboard, the moment we have cleared Port Glasgow. I have already made arrangements with Captain Shea."

"How could you be so sure of a bridegroom?"

"It was the one chance I took, Doctor. Thank you for vindicating my trust."

She held out her hand to him. This time he shook it firmly. Once again, he admitted freely, she had won her point.

"We leave Clydebank in midafternoon," she said. "We should be in the firth by sunset. Don't be late for our wedding; it would create a bad impression aboard."

"I'll remember. We must be careful of impressions from now on, Mrs. Anderson."

"My name is Jane," she said. "You might remember that too."

"And mine is Julian. Good night until tomorrow, Jane."

For a moment more he held her eyes, waiting for that steady glance to drop. Then, since there was no more to say, he bowed again and walked out of the little parlor, closing the door carefully behind him.

On the landing he paused to listen to her playing. Her hands were wildly confident on the keyboard of the cottage piano: for a moment she only improvised. Then her fingers glided into a familiar melody—folded at first into the bass, then picked up in sweet treble octaves. Finally her voice, light and clear, blended with the tremolo accompaniment:

> "A hundred months have passed, Lorena,
>   Since last I held thy hand in mine,
> And felt the pulse beat fast, Lorena,
>   Though mine beat faster far than thine . . ."

He found that he was humming the tune as he walked into the taproom. Poor Jane, he thought, you're fooling no one with that bravado. For all your firmness, for all your jewels, you were just as afraid as I.

xv

MacGregor himself brought the bottle when Julian found a seat in the inglenook. He returned the innkeeper's booming salute with a brief nod. Apparently the news of his change in fortune had traveled fast: it would be quite like Whit to drop a hint that Dr. Chisholm's score could now be paid.

"Bring me pen and paper too. Can I still post a letter tonight?"
"Where to, Doctor?"
"To the Bahamas, via Liverpool."
"If it's ready within the hour, sir."

When the writing materials came to his table, he found that he did not need a drink after all. He drove the pen swiftly, without pausing to think:

My dear Lucy:
On the eve of my departure for Nassau, I want you to be the first to know that I am returning to the Confederacy with a bride. . . .

If he could cleave to facts—and leave out the emotion—he could make the letter real. It would go by the next mail packet; Lucy would have it long before the *New Providence* could dock in Nassau. He could hardly hope that the news would hurt her; it might purchase him a measure of immunity while he waited in Nassau for a place aboard a runner. Lucy was not proud, but she was practical. Surely she would leave an ex-lover in peace if that ex-lover appeared with a bride.

His bride. Mrs. Kirby Anderson, whom he was now permitted to call Jane. But Lucy need have no inkling of that bargain.

Jane is a Southerner like myself. I won't say like *us*, Lucy—for you are one of us no longer. . . .

He stared at the sentence for a moment, wondering if that much of the letter were true. Jane Anderson's accent, so far as he could place it, suggested the mountain rather than the seaboard South. It was too trained a voice to be classified readily. Clearly, her residence in the North had refined away most of the telltale slurring.

We are returning to take up our common cause. Perhaps that quixotic streak you discovered in me is broader than you think. I can say this honestly: I feel that I have been away too long—and so does she.

Why was he returning, after all? Jane Anderson's words came back to him, and he let his pen pause while he weighed them. *You are much too levelheaded,* she'd said, *to think that fratricide can produce anything but—more fratricide.* Certainly he could find no sympathy for either side in this war. He would offer his services to the Confederacy, simply because the Cape Fear country was his home. That much he could admit privately, now that his father was gone.

So much for his own motives. What of Jane's? Her defense had been perfect just now. Could she still hold him at arm's length in the after house of the *New Providence?* He thought of the nights to come, when only a locked cabin door would separate him from a legal bride. Already this was far more than the familiar adventure he had planned. Jane Anderson's mystery was a major challenge. Solving it might be quite as important as the minor triumph of possessing her.

A waiter stood beside his table when he looked up again. He stuck down the flap of the letter and tossed it on the man's tray, along with the last silver in his pocket.

"It's an express letter—see that it's posted at once."

"Very good, sir. This just came for you."

The envelope the waiter handed him was heavy in his hand. He knew the sender even before he broke the seal and peered inside at the neat row of gold pieces. Twenty-five American eagles—and twelve words, in a square, bold hand:

I appreciate your gallantry—but don't you want your money in advance?

He tried to curse her, but no words came. Instead he chuckled and dropped the envelope in his coat pocket before he walked over to the cashier's desk with the still-unopened bottle cradled in one arm.

"Take my reckoning out of this. I'm keeping the bottle."

MacGregor stared at the gold piece doubtfully. "American specie, Doctor? I don't know that I can——"

"Don't be stupid, man. You're getting rich on it."

He walked out of the taproom without waiting for the innkeeper's reply. The fog outside had changed to rain. At the first crossing he paused to bite the cork from his bottle and raised it to his lips. Then, with a shout of laughter, he flung Scotland's finest whisky into the gutter, untasted. The private war with Lucy

Sprague was not the only victory he had begun to win this past hour. Besides, a Chisholm should be sober on his wedding morning.

xvi

The *New Providence* had danced out of Port Glasgow under topsails. Now (with darkness clamped on the firth like an iron curtain) she fought to hold her course. The autumn gale had howled down from the north, with spindrift boiling at its edges; in the space of minutes it had boxed the clipper in its gray menace, forcing her to fight for seaway.

Dr. Julian Chisholm, a bridegroom of two hours' standing, braced himself in his small cabin and decided he was too sober to be seasick after all.

With that point settled, he felt it was safe to ignore the storm: the crash of the boarding seas, the thud of feet on the spar deck overhead, the nightmare twang as a guy rope parted to let another square of canvas wing into oblivion. Captain Shea was a rascal, but he was a seaman. His ship would ride out the storm. Dr. Julian Chisholm (a married man, now, thanks to that same captain's benediction) would ride out his own storm in time.

Before this voyage was over he might even learn to face the door across the cabin—and smile at the impulse that urged him to smash the lock tonight.

Shea's own cabin (it was Mrs. Julian Chisholm's bedroom now) was much roomier than the cubicle in which the doctor himself was boxed—like a wolf who did not dare to match howls with the wind. Jane had done herself well for the voyage. There was a carpet on her floor, and a real bed was nailed to the bulkhead. An easy chair and a combination desk and table made her cabin a self-sufficient world. Julian had not needed to count the trunks that had come aboard that afternoon to guess that his bride's trousseau was *dernier cri*. He did not need to listen at the locked door to decide that she was snug in that soft bed now, preparing to sleep out the storm and the cursing of a brand-new husband with equal calm.

Had it been less than an hour since he had carried her over the threshold of that same cabin? Even then the wind was freshening; he had staggered just a little in the spume-wet companionway, though his bride was light enough. Behind them the half dozen

61

women passengers had cooed like idiot doves. Whit, an adroit best man, had handed their champagne glasses through the door. Shea's monkey grin had been framed in the cabin window before a shouted question had sent him scurrying to the deck above.

When the door slammed behind them, Julian thought that the draft had snuffed out the overhead lamp. Then the ship righted; the lamp, still burning, eased back on its gimbal—and he smiled at his bride, with one arm still around her. She stepped out of the embrace coolly and tossed her plaid cloak across the bed. He remembered how her skirts had flared in the gesture, for all the world like a toreador's cape after he has fixed his bull and knows he can turn his back in safety.

"Can you believe we're at sea?"

"Can you believe we're married?" he had countered.

She pivoted toward him then, rising easily on her toes, the panels of her gown expanding with the movement. The cameo she had worn last night (pinned, like a brooch, to the wine-red pelisse she was wearing now) took the lamplight in its jeweled circle. Settling on her low heels again, the new Mrs. Chisholm seemed to settle into her dress and into her cabin.

"It was a convincing wedding, Doctor. Thank you for a good performance."

"You didn't mind the kiss?"

There had been no avoiding that kiss, he thought. Not with the whole passenger list watching the ceremony in the forward deckhouse. He could still rebel at the pretended response of her lips as they had met and held his own. Her body had been a hard mockery against him then. Yet he knew that from the others' viewpoint (Whit, a wise djinn, had already poured out the champagne) she had seemed all sweet yielding. . . .

"Without that kiss," said Jane, "our nuptials would hardly be legal."

"If you were half as tense as I——"

"Women are seldom tense at their weddings," said Jane. "Remember, it's their one moment of triumph in a man's world." The ship leaned with the wind, shivering as she righted. He put out a hand to steady her and saw her face go white.

"Should we be more formal when we're alone?"

"It might be wiser."

"As you wish, Mrs. Chisholm. And good night."

He'd gone into his own cabin on that, without even slamming the door. She had bolted it on her side, without attempting to ease the cheerful scrape of brass. . . .

There he had his wedding, blow by blow. The pacing had come later—the cursing later still, after he'd barked his shin a second time in the freshening storm.

Reality, he reflected (fumbling at the magnificent cravat Whit had knotted for him in Glasgow) can be confusing when it measures precisely with expectation. But he had no right to curse her for that—simply because she had carried off a well-planned moment so coolly. No right at all to crouch against a bolted door and imagine how casually she had slipped into the peach-bloom *robe-de-nuit* that had waited (like a bad joke in its satin setting) at the foot of her bed. . . . He settled on his own bunk and found it narrow but adequate. He had bought it for a price, and the price was paid. He would learn to sleep there, in time.

But he was still braced against the headboard—with the white silk mass of his cravat crumpled in one fist—when he heard the bolt whisper in its socket and Jane's knock on the panel that separated them.

The ship complained through all her length, as another sea crashed aboard. Holding his breath in the comparative stillness that followed, he heard the wave pour down the coaming before the knock was repeated. The door swung open almost before he could bark an answer. She stood on the threshold, still fully dressed—though her hair was tumbled about her shoulders in a bright flood. Her face was set; he had to look twice at her staring eyes before he realized she was trembling with fear.

"It's the storm, Doctor—"

"Why didn't you tell me?"

"I didn't dare, then. Will you—sit with me awhile?"

He offered her his hand as they moved from mate's to captain's cabin—and she took the offer, with only the smallest pause. Overhead the lighted lamp still danced gaily on its gimbal: the furniture, creaking with each heave of the ship's bows, looked as smugly self-assured as ever. The nightgown case, he noted with a smile, had vanished from the bed. For all her slow yielding to terror, Mrs. Julian Chisholm had been woman enough to hide that satin lure.

63

Her voice was almost steady now. "Will you forgive me—for being a fool?"

"You might have knocked sooner. You knew I wasn't sleeping."

"Of course, the moment you're really tired——" He dropped her hand and stepped back as she crimsoned to the roots of her hair. "I suppose anything we say tonight will have two meanings."

But the fist on the outer door had already broken the confusion neatly. An insistent hammer that was no respecter of wedding nights.

"Dr. Chisholm!"

Julian looked quickly about the cabin before he whipped off his coat and tossed it across the bed. The ports were snug: no one outside could have heard their words against the keen of the wind.

"*Dr. Chisholm!*"

"Your invitation came just in time," he whispered, and opened the outer door. Rain lashed at his face: in the utter blackness outside, the dripping figure was part of the night, a wet shadow rather than a man. Then a voice came out of the dark, and Julian saw that this was Bosley, the second mate.

Bosley said only, "It's the captain, Doc. Captain Shea. He's bleeding like a shoat. Could you come at once?"

xvii

He remembered how he had groped for his surgeon's kit, how he had paused to tuck the mahogany case under his shirt before he joined Bosley in the open companionway. He remembered thinking of Whit Cameron, and canceling the thought in advance. The gambler had earned his sleep tonight: this was a doctor's job, and he would go to it alone. Without sense of transition, he was following the mate along the safety rope that led up to the spar deck. Ducking, just in time, as the mizzen boom swooped above them with inches to spare. Running, with shoulders thrust against the aching cold of the wind, to gain the oasis of the wheelhouse.

Shea was lard pale in the binnacle light, but his grin was intact in its frosty frame of whiskers. Above him two quartermasters clung to the bucking wheel, with the first mate beside them. The captain was watching the little group rather than the hideous, red-welling tide that bubbled from his left sleeve. An order croaked in his throat, emerging in a whisper. But the helmsmen

64

heard and eased off a point on the wheel, bringing the deck up from its crazy angle. White water roared down the scuppers and spilled like a waterfall from forecastle hatch to martingale.

"Easy does it, lads," said Shea. "The old lady can ride it out. . . . What about me, Doc?"

Julian was already on his knees, his toes fighting for purchase on the slippery deck. His mind had not quite kept pace with his body, but there was no lost motion in his hands as he ripped the sleeve aside to expose the wound. Not even a layman could mistake the rhythmic pump of the spurting red column. A rough tourniquet, he saw, had already split under the captain's writhing. He twisted his own handkerchief under Shea's arm and knotted the ends. Bosley passed him an open clasp knife. The handkerchief sling tightened under his hand, biting deep into the flesh of the captain's upper arm. Shea's cursing was already competing with the scream of the wind.

"How did this happen?"

"Mizzen spar," said the second mate under his breath. "He would help lash it down, before the wind took it. Caught him, just inside the elbow. Neat as a cutlass."

Shea fumbled at the side of the wheelhouse and all but made his feet before he crumpled in the arms of two seamen. Watching the tourniquet, Julian saw that it was holding firm this time. He clutched his instrument case and started for the forward deckhouse. Bosley caught his eye and signaled to the seamen to follow.

His instruments were ready on the table when Shea rolled in, his cursing feeble now but no less picturesque. Julian did not look up as they stretched him on the settee that ran along one wall. He was in his chosen world now. Knowing just what he must do, he could keep his hands from trembling as he faced his first real test—and faced it alone, away from the purring of his teachers, the hush of the amphitheater.

When Bosley folded the slit sleeve back from the wound, the younger of the two seamen lurched toward the door. Julian understood the man's reaction: the edge of the spar, as the mate had said, had slashed the flesh from elbow to shoulder, as cleanly as steel. In the depths of the wound the muscles bulged through lacerated fascia; blood was already clotting here. Julian knew he must work fast if he meant to locate the severed artery, before the natural elasticity of its wall retracted beneath the surface of those punished muscles.

"Can you handle it, Doc?" asked Shea.

"Of course I can."

"I don't see a bone saw in that box. Aren't you going to take all of it?"

Julian considered the captain with new respect as his fingers flew among his tools. Shea was a sharp customer, but he was no coward: he had seen too many accidents like these to forget the usual procedure of the surgeon.

"I can repair the wound. If there is no inflammation, the arm can be saved."

"If you say so, Doc."

For once the captain's whisky-pale eyes were full of trust: glad of a chance to avoid them, Julian sat on the worn leather couch and bent close above the wound. In his postgraduate clinic at Vienna, such an injury would almost certainly have become gangrenous; gangrene meant inevitable amputation later, and, almost as inevitably, the loss of a patient. What right had he to risk Shea's life now, when to amputate might prevent gangrene? Yet Lister would not have hesitated to save the arm if he could.

He drew a deep breath and made himself face the captain once again. "Have you any chloroform or ether?"

"Never ship the stuff. If you ask me, we're lucky to have you and those knives." Shea's bravery was a trifle forced, but his voice was steady. "I can make it on whisky, if you can."

Julian nodded. "Someone must help with that tourniquet."

"May I assist, Julian?"

He looked at Jane for a moment as though she were a stranger. It seemed a long time since he had left her in their honeymoon cabin. Apparently she had paused only to toss a boat cloak over her dress; her hair, still streaming about her shoulders and drenched with spray, looked almost black in the unsteady lamplight.

"I've done some nursing," she said. "I promise you I won't faint."

Julian nodded to Bosley, who turned in to the galley and came back with a bottle. Shea downed the whisky as though it were tea; while he drank, Julian led the mate and the remaining seaman aside.

"One of you must anchor his legs. The other will stay at his head and shoulders. No matter what happens, that arm must be kept steady. I may have to go deep for the bleeder."

"We can strap him down if you say so."

"We should manage without straps." He had watched enough patients scream out their hearts under the harness of the old-line surgeon—the gentry who still looked on anesthesia as an invention of the devil and considered pain the patient's normal lot. They could spare Shea that if they moved fast.

In the galley he scrubbed his hands as best he could. Lister always washed his hands before an operation: in Vienna they would have laughed at such frippery. Semmelweis would have scoured everything in a solution of lime chloride, but he had no such chemicals handy; besides, it was well known that Semmelweis was mad. . . . Back in the saloon, he noted with approval that Jane had drawn up a small table for his tools and arranged them on a clean towel: delicately serrated artery clamps were laid neatly beside his scalpels, and several sharp-bladed needles had already been threaded with whipcord and arranged ready to his hand. He smiled at his bride before he glanced down at Shea. The captain, still working hard at his bottle, refused to meet his eyes.

"This won't be easy," said Julian. "As you see, I've controlled the bleeding; but you must release the tourniquet so I can find the injured vessel." He hoped his voice was not too academic and smiled again at Jane. "When I say, 'Tighten,' you must twist it again quickly."

Jane's cheeks were pale against the dark mass of her hair, but her voice was quite natural. "I understand, my dear."

The fact that she could play her bride's role, even now, was all the assurance he needed. "Let's begin, then. Ready, Captain?"

A final gurgle was his answer. Shea tossed the empty bottle across the saloon and braced himself against Bosley's hands. The seaman had already straddled his skipper's legs, with a fist clamped hard on each thigh.

"Steady we are," said Shea. "As steady as we'll ever be."

"Release, please."

Julian waited, with a patch of soft linen in his hand, as Jane slowly eased the tourniquet. When the wound bubbled red again, he swabbed quickly and found he was quite unable to locate the source.

"Tighten, please." He watched her hands, rejoicing in their unexpected strength as they obeyed him instantly. "I must enlarge the wound."

Her face changed as she grasped his meaning. Shea did not budge, but the tobacco-stained tooth that held his lower lip seemed to dig deeper. Julian had already located the region of the large artery with an exploring finger, just at the crevice that lay between the two great muscle groups of the upper arm. With a quick motion he drew the scalpel along the skin, laying it open for a distance of several inches. Shea's head jerked up, but no sound came through the blue line of his lips.

For a few moments Julian worked in the bloodless field, separating the muscles until he was in the region of the artery itself. So far—thanks to the infiltration of blood between the muscle layers—he could not distinguish the vessel from the surrounding tissue.

"Release again—slowly."

Again he sponged the steady flow of blood, and this time he could see the pulsing mouth of the vessel lying in the wound, far deeper than he had hoped. He went in with the forceps, filching the artery from its bed, letting the delicate blades pinch off the mouth. His tension lessened as the notch of the handle ratchet clicked and he saw that the cloture was complete. Another pair of forceps, placed below the first, closed the opposite end of the damaged vessel. The bleeding had already lessened noticeably. He worked quickly, anchoring other forceps along the line of puncture. When he sponged the blood away and raised his head, the wound was dry. At his nod Jane loosened the tourniquet completely.

"We must tie off now. Can you remove the clamps for me?"

It was the most difficult part of the operation, and he knew that she had sensed the fact instantly. It meant that her unskilled fingers must follow his, into the depths of that gaping wound—releasing the forceps as he put in his needles and knotted the whipcord streamers. But he gave her no time to hesitate as he stabbed the first steel point home, slipped the needle free, and pulled the knot taut.

"Take off the forceps, please."

Her fingers, cold but steady, were close to his now. The bloodstained instrument flicked out of the wound; he finished his first knot, watching from the corner of his eye to be sure she did not flinch when she dropped the forceps on the table and slipped her hand beneath his own again. Then he tightened the next knot, letting the whipcord ends stream free.

"Only a few more——"

She nodded mutely; her hands did not falter as she removed the remaining forceps in rhythm with the loops he was making on the barrel of the throbbing artery. With the last tie made, he placed his stitches and began to close the wound. Only when he had covered it with a compress of clean linen did he dare glance down at Shea. The captain's forehead was dark with sweat; the tooth that clamped his lower lip had made a neat puncture, and a trickle of blood oozed into the jungle of beard below. But he had not even stirred in Bosley's iron grasp.

"Steady did it, Doc."

Julian met his bride's eyes across the table and saw that she was trying hard not to stare at his blood-smeared hands. Her own hands, red from finger tips to wrist, lay limp on the table. He nodded toward the galley and stood aside as she groped for the door; she had promised not to faint, and he trusted that promise now.

"Do I keep the flipper?"

Julian came back to his patient. "You'll be as good as new, barring inflammation."

"How d'you bar it?"

"I don't know." The surgeon could afford to be frank now. "No one really knows. There's this in your favor—some doctors believe that wounds on shipboard never show inflammation. This is my first experience."

He found that he could make the admission quite calmly. Looking down at the neatly compressed wound, it was good to remember that his own hands had put the dressing there. That his own skill had given Shea a fighting chance to save his arm. Despite himself, he turned sharply—as though he half expected to find a hard-eyed professor seated on the observer's stool. But there was only the second mate, staring at him in openmouthed respect. . . .

Jane came out of the galley with color in her cheeks again. Just in time, Julian remembered to step forward and slip an arm about her waist. For a moment they stood thus, smiling down at Shea.

The captain, biting a cork from a second bottle, grinned back cheerfully.

"I'll say it to your face, ma'am—if I got him out of bed for this, I'll never forgive myself."

Jane's blush, at that moment, was all that any bridegroom could ask for; Julian knew that he was red-faced, too, when he bent down to take the whisky from Shea's paw.

"I'd go light on that, now it's over. Bed down here till morning, and don't move that arm for anyone."

"Give me another four fingers, and I won't wake up till we lift Nassau," said Shea. "Did I say I'm proud to be your first patient?"

"Even if you had," said Julian, "it would bear repeating."

xviii

He kept his arm at Jane's waist until they stepped through the deckhouse door and into the banshee dark. Then, taking her hand instead, he groped for the safety line that led to the comparative shelter of their own companionway. He heard her gasp behind him as the air seared her lungs; a wave splintered on the starboard quarter, sending them reeling against the after house before they could wrench open the door of her cabin and tumble in.

For a moment he leaned back against the closed door, feeling the sudden quiet lull his senses. Jane spread the wet boat cloak across a chair. Her eyes were withdrawn, but there was no barrier between them now. He made the discovery, even as his mind grasped the reason. They had come back (for all the world like husband and wife) from work well done—from a victory they had shared. For the moment, at least, the fact had established an intimacy of its own. He breathed softly and did not speak: one wrong word might destroy a spell he had no wish to break.

Jane knelt beside a trunk, turned a key in the ornate brass lock, and swung back the lid. She spoke as her hands delved in the top drawer.

"It seems a long time since I knocked."

"You aren't afraid now?"

"Not in the least. That's the strangest part."

He smiled and kept his place. "Not even to be alone with me?"

"Not even to give you this." She rose with her words and offered him a wallet in the cup of her palms.

For a moment Julian stared down blankly at the square of worn leather. "It's yours," she said. "You'll find your money inside."

Still he made no move to touch the wallet. She came forward and forced it into his hands. "I meant to give it back in Nassau."

"So you did hire those thugs to follow me?"

"Your friend handled that part," said Jane. "Are you beginning to see how badly I needed you?"

He opened the wallet mechanically, glanced at the folded pound notes within, and dropped it into his pocket. "Isn't this rather unwise?"

"Perhaps. I couldn't keep silent after what—well, after what you've just done."

"You knew I was a surgeon."

"I've treated you shamefully," she said. "Don't hate me for it, please. At least I had my reasons."

"Suppose I told you that I guessed?"

"About the footpads?"

"And Whit." He found that he could smile quite without bitterness. "You worked hard to be sure of me, didn't you?"

"You won't let me apologize?"

"Why? I'm still enjoying our wedding."

When she spoke again, he knew she was following a tangent of her own. "I thought you were just another spoiled nabob," she said. "I assumed you had more good looks than brains. . . . So I didn't mind using you in the least. Tonight I've begun to see you as you really are. Nabob or not, I think you're just unhappy—and lonely."

He kept his smile inviolate. "Shall I plead guilty and fling myself on your mercy?"

"I respect you," she said, still on a tangent. "I want to say I'm sorry. Please let me."

"You've nothing to be sorry for. All you've done is rescue me from myself."

"Were things so bad, then?"

"Perhaps I'll answer that before we dock."

"It's a long voyage," said Jane. "I'll live in hopes."

"So shall I."

"You still won't accept my story? Believe me, I *am* a widow who needs a husband——"

"You aren't a widow now," he said.

She colored on that but made no effort to avoid him. "And you assume I never was?"

"I'm asking you nothing. I'm just human enough to hope for an answer."

"You've every right to revenge," she said, and turned to face him at last, with cheeks flaming.

"Be careful of words," he said. "They're easy to misunderstand."

"Revenge is a simple word," said Jane. "So is *wife*."

"Are you testing me, by any chance?"

"Perhaps."

"Reminding me I'm a Southern gentleman—and assuming that I won't abuse the privilege?"

"I'm trying hard to be honest," she said. "It isn't always easy for a woman."

"It isn't always easy to be a gentleman."

"I said woman—not lady. I'd never be called a lady in your world. . . . Perhaps that's why I can speak my mind tonight. I can even say I admire you, Julian. Enough to forget that locked door—if you insist."

He smiled before he lifted her hand and pressed a kiss into the palm. "That's for being a good nurse tonight. . . . If Whit were here, he'd say that the mold is stronger than I thought."

"What does he have to do with us now?"

"Like you, he understood me too well for comfort. Will you accept my compliments—and bolt that door, regardless of the progress we've made in matrimony?"

For all his pretended poise, he didn't quite dare look back at her as he stepped again from captain's cabin to mate's. When the door had closed behind him he sat for a long time, straining his ears to catch the whisper of the bolt. There was no sound beyond the partition. He needed no sound to tell him that she had gone to that wide, snug bed at last, that there was no obstacle between them now but his own will.

Stretched on his narrow bunk, he expected to lie awake for hours, tortured by his barren triumph. But he was asleep a moment after his head touched the pillow. For all the pitching of the *New Providence*, his sleep was deeper than any he had known for years.

NASSAU

"*WATLING'S* Island," said Whitford Cameron. "Columbus named it San Salvador. Now it's *our* first landfall too. Would you call that an omen?"

Julian made room as his friend the gambler joined him behind the bowsprit shrouds. Like everyone on deck at that moment, his eyes stayed on the bluish shadow that had just swum above the eastern horizon. A few moments before it had all but merged with the milky morning. Now it was an unmistakable island, real as a ghost come alive in the sunlight.

"Who said it was Watling's?"

"Our friend Bosley. They've just made the entry on the log; with luck, we dock in Nassau tomorrow."

Nassau—and Lucy Sprague. Julian asked himself why he could face the prospect so calmly.

Five weeks at sea, he reflected, should be long enough for any man—especially a bridegroom in name only. Yet he had enjoyed these sun-steeped days for their own sake; he would be sorry to leave the cramped cabin where he had begun to find himself again. He had even enjoyed his bride, in a way Whit Cameron (to take the first convenient example) would never understand.

He let his eyes dwell on Whit. In a smart box coat and trousers patterned in the Cameron tartan, Whit suggested Pall Mall rather than the foredeck of a clipper. Yet Julian was glad that they were standing side by side to watch this outpost of America take shape in the growing day. He bore the gambler no malice for the part he had played in his marriage: regardless of methods, he felt that Whit was his ally. Yet he knew that Whit would only chortle at the truth, and refuse to believe it. Unkissed brides did not exist in the gambler's cosmos, to say nothing of unkissed grooms.

The *New Providence,* heeling sweetly under a full suit of canvas, dropped San Salvador down her starboard quarter—and the coral outcrop that spouted white water, even in this lazy breeze. The beaches of the island gleamed with morning as they slipped by; Julian could see the shoulder of a low hill or two, beyond the seaward-facing savannahs. San Salvador looked lonely as the day Columbus had marked it on his chart, but it was still a part of Nassau's doorstep.

"We might call Jane," said Whit. "This is a solemn moment. Or should we be sensible, and ask ourselves a few final questions? We may not have another chance."

Julian smiled. Clearly this was not a belated attempt at honesty on Whit's part. He had already suspected that the gambler was as ignorant as he of Jane's past.

"What would you like to know?"

"Where she's really bound—and why. Can you answer that much?"

"By the book. Her agents in Nassau are working now, to get the three of us aboard a runner. We're to try for St. Marys, just above the Florida line."

"Does it trouble you to know she has people working for her everywhere?"

"Not at all. After all, you were working for her in Glasgow."

Whit took the reference with aplomb. "Thank you for including me in the lady's entourage—when my contribution was so slight."

"So, I fear, is mine."

"Yet you take pleasure in your—may I say your *work,* without offense?"

"You may call it what you like. I'm keeping a bargain: if Jane has no complaints, I'm satisfied too. It doesn't mean I must go into her life history, or her motives. In another month I'll be in uniform—and she'll be settling her husband's estates."

"If that's what she is really after."

"Would you have introduced us otherwise?"

"Probably," said Whit. "Would you have married her?"

Julian faced the question. He had been desperate that night in Glasgow, desperate enough to accept Jane's offer blindly, even though he had doubted her story from the first. As Whit had hinted, it was quite possible that she was both adventuress and Union agent. He could not have given her his name had he been positive. Still, it was comforting to cling to the hope that his bride was as virtuous as her manner.

"I'm a doctor," he said. "I want to practice. That was my first thought, and my last."

"The scalpel before the sword," said Whit. "Well, that's as it should be. I still insist you must know something. Surely she's let a few facts drop——"

"Only that she comes from a mountain state and has lived in the North. Only that she considers the war senseless—which is a sentiment I can share."

Whit shrugged and turned to blink at the golden motes that spangled the sea ahead. The sun, just clear of the horizon now, promised to bring in a flawless day: even the plume of smoke that had lifted like a dirty pennon behind Watling's Island could not spoil the perfection of the morning. Julian had noticed it some time ago and supposed the island was inhabited after all. Now he saw that the smoke was pouring from the funnel of a vessel bearing down on them at top speed.

Already the other ship was near enough for him to observe that she was making seaway on the strength of her boilers, though a pair of masts were stepped into the sharply raked deck. Low to the water, and businesslike as a beetle, she moved with astonishing speed. Her single stack (shiny as a congressman's hat) belched vapor in short, hard gasps. Under her starboard gunwale, the row of gun ports was no less grim because they were closed. . . . The flag at her mizzen was all too familiar. Staring hard at the peppermint stripes and the thirty-odd stars of union in the blue field, Julian told himself that here, at last, was the enemy.

Neither of them spoke as the Yankee ghosted up, cut a white arc in their wash, and slipped toward its hide-out again. It was a sight they had expected for some time. For a moment the watchdog seemed to hang on their wake: they could see her young, bearded skipper clearly as he stumped the cleated walk above a paddle box, with his glass trained on the red duster at their mizzen. Julian found his own eye straying to that magic talisman that protected a future surgeon of the Confederate Army as well as a thousand Enfield rifles in the hold. There was something in the slant of the Yankee's telescope that expressed both rage and derision.

Whit said, "It won't be so simple in the Bahama Passage."

"These are British waters. How do they dare?"

"They wouldn't open fire here, even if we flew the Stars and Bars: they'd simply stalk us into open water. Once they've run down a prize on the high seas, it's a short haul to Key West. The Yankees have stayed there from the beginning."

"They're in St. Augustine, and Jacksonville, too."

"Don't call me out for this, Julian—but have you thought of signing with *them?*"

"I may have my faults, but I'm not a turncoat."

"Spoken like a Chisholm," said Whit. "Are you sure you aren't talking nonsense?"

"Quite sure, though I couldn't tell you why."

"Being a knight-errant has its drawbacks," said Whit. "Don't let it fog your common sense."

"Why don't *you* go North, instead of South?"

"My reasons are simple. I'm a fisher in troubled waters, and I enjoy gambling for its own sake. Fortunes are being made on both sides in this war. I'm merely trying my luck at one end of the table."

Julian chuckled: it was hard to resist Whit for long. "Has anyone ever told you that you're a complete scoundrel?"

"Has anyone told you that the Southern gentleman is the world's queerest anachronism?"

"Men have been shot for saying that."

"Hear me out, Julian Chisholm of Chisholm Hundred. Open your eyes to that Yankee gunboat and read your doom. Already they've a strangle hold on your ports; the rat pack will make a few fortunes slipping through, but the rats' days are numbered. How long will Europe supply you, when it's plain you're dying by inches?"

"Don't say *you* so bitterly. Remember, you were born one of us."

"My brains were my own from the start," said Whit. "I've lived by them well enough. I'm lucky on two counts: I was born free, and I was never a nabob. You call me a scoundrel: I agree—and say it helps me to grasp facts."

"What would you do in my place?"

"Take the first packet out of Nassau and offer myself to the Surgeon General of the United States. You could save as many lives in the end—and you'd come out of the war a general. But no: you'll go to your uncle in Richmond, insist on being a field surgeon, and save lives for the losing side. Afterward you'll go back to Chisholm Hundred and end your days regretting what might have been. Unless you're already dead, which is quite likely too."

"In my place, you'd do the same."

"No doubt. It's hard to outgrow one's mold—or did I say that once?"

"You've said it frequently," laughed Julian. "Let's have a look at the captain's arm. At least I'll have the right answers there."

ii

Shea was working at his logbook in the chartroom, with Jane beside him. Today her hair was hidden in a gypsy bandanna; her eyes, sparkling in a face she had dared to tan lightly (despite the clucking of the lady passengers), sought Julian warmly.

Once again he found that he could sit beside her with no leftover tension. The feeling that had built up between them this past month was too tentative to call itself friendship. But it was no less definite a bond. *Perhaps it's only an armed truce after all,* he thought. *Perhaps all marriages would run like clockwork if they were uncomplicated by passion, and assured of a definite time limit.*

"I've brought up your instruments, dear," said Jane. "Shall I remove the captain's bandage?"

Sitting across from Shea, Julian remembered how deftly her fingers had managed the first change of dressing, three days after the accident. He had dared to examine the wound then, only because Shea had insisted on returning to his duties; and he had held his breath, expecting to be greeted by the rank, familiar stench that was a herald of death in every hospital. But the wound had healed well from the start. Today the scar had knit from shoulder to elbow, a long, healthy welt that had already begun to change from red to white. Julian tossed the bandages aside and got up from the table.

"I hope I'm as lucky with all my patients, Captain. You're as well as you'll ever be."

Shea accepted the verdict with a wide grin. "I always figured you're safe from gangrene at sea. Happens you're the first sawbones who got the point."

"I don't accept the theory. We took a chance that turned out well: it's as simple as that."

"Have it your way, Doc. What's the damage?"

"I'll take no money from my first patient. Just promise to stay out of trouble, if you can."

"I'll do better," said Shea. "Let me talk to your agent when he comes aboard tomorrow. You'll get a rock-bottom price for that trip to Georgia."

Julian stepped through the deckhouse door and stood for a moment in the full blaze of morning. He knew without turning that Jane would rise to follow him. Whit was already laying out a game of patience beside the captain's log. It was the sort of patience that would turn into five-handed poker when enough passengers had rolled out of their bunks. If Whit seemed to shun the light of day at times, he had his reasons.

Jane slipped an arm through his. "Shall we walk our mile now?"

"This morning I'll say a mile is ten times around the capstan."

They fell into step together on the straightaway between the forecastle head and the after house. Julian bowed to the wife of the Jamaica planter who was reading *Pendennis* in the shade of the deckhouse awning; the lady stared coldly at Jane's bandanna and bowed back. The Yorkshire governess at her side was too queasy to risk a smile today.

He compared his bride to these hulks and found that she gleamed like an alert bird in the sunshine. Tomorrow, perhaps (he made the admission grimly), he would compare her to Lucy Sprague.

"I should have called you when we made our landfall," he said.

"You mean *I* should have wakened you. I've been on deck since dawn, with the captain's telescope."

"Are you so anxious to be ashore?"

"Speak for yourself, Julian."

He avoided the challenge. "Shea said your agent is coming aboard before we dock. Is that usual?"

"I gather it's quite usual when an important passenger is involved. Remember, he isn't my agent—he's yours. At least he was put to work in your name."

"Does that mean I must haggle with him too?"

"I'm willing to pay up to three hundred dollars for our passage if the runner is steam-driven. So is Whit."

"Apparently you studied that Yankee watchdog rather carefully."

"The moon is dark this week," said Jane. "Perhaps we can go on at once. Is that agreeable?"

Would he be delivered from Lucy this easily? He felt his heart leap at the prospect, and did not know if he was glad or sorry.

Aloud he said, "Why do you ask? We must arrive in Georgia together: it's the vital part of our bargain. Unless it's the impression we leave in Nassau."

"Other things are important," said Jane. "Don't pretend there isn't a woman in Nassau."

They swung around the capstan and faced down the straightaway again. He did not speak until they were under the white shadow of the mainsail.

"How long have you known that?"

"Long enough," said Jane tranquilly. "I even know her name is Lucy Sprague. I'm not sure if she's your past, present—or future."

"Nor am I," he said, a bit surprised at his own frankness.

"Tell me this, at least. Would you avoid her, if you could?"

"Not unless I could be sure of forgetting her too." He felt a strange lightness of spirit, now he had admitted so much. "You see, I was in love with her—long before she married Sprague. It isn't her fault that I've done a poor job of living her down."

"Isn't it?"

He plunged on, if only to enjoy his mounting sense of release. "I mean to face her in Nassau and have things out."

"You mean you'll insist you're happily married—and hope she'll believe you?"

He kept his eyes on the shining towers of canvas above them. "With your permission, of course."

"I begin to see why you married me," she said.

"Are you angry?"

"Who am I to complain, Julian? In fact, it will give me pleasure to help you deceive your Lucy."

"I've said too much," he murmured, instantly contrite. "Please forgive me."

"You've told me nothing, really. Only that you were in love once—which, I'll admit, is quite a revelation." She smiled up at his scowl. "But I shan't plague you further. Just don't be startled if I invite the Spragues to dine with us. Or vice versa."

"I've never met her husband. I don't care to meet him."

"In Nassau," said Jane, "you can hardly avoid meeting Victor Sprague. Now smile at me, for heaven's sake—or our fellow voyagers will say we've quarreled."

He managed to obey the warning, after a fashion—and, for good measure, lifted the hand on his arm and pressed it warmly. Then he swung his bride toward the rail just as the clipper came about. The plume of Yankee smoke was gone from the horizon now. In its place the palms of yet another cay stood like feather dusters against the copper edge of morning.

iii

Nassau, he observed, was precisely what he had expected. Standing at the forecastle head to watch the snug harbor open out before their bows, he felt no elation at his voyage's end. . . . The town climbed its hills in sun-faded contentment; the ensigns of Empire hung limp on the flagstaffs of two lichened forts; Government House straddled the spine of Fitzwilliam Hill like a bilious beachcomber who has signed the pledge. Even in the hard white glare of noon the pattern was muted. He was too far away, as yet, to hear the clang of commerce on Bay Street, though he could already see the masts along the water front, thick as a forest wall.

The clipper coasted in the harbor mouth as the crew scrambled to furl topsails. There was the pilot boat, scurrying to round the Hog Island beacon. There, beyond a doubt, was his shipping agent, a man in bleached linens, who seemed to be rubbing his hands in anticipation long before he could toss a leg over the clipper's gunwale.

Julian faced away from the smaller vessel as she came alongside. This was not an interview he relished. It would be better if the fellow sought him out after he had talked to Shea. And yet, despite his reticence, it seemed only a matter of minutes before the factor had charged toward him, like a dog hard on the scent.

There was something doglike in his handshake, too—the trick of a canine who has learned to despise his master long ago.

"Dr. Chisholm? A pleasure, sir. Jarvis is the name. Shall we talk here, or would you prefer your cabin?"

"Here will do. Mrs. Chisholm is still packing."

The man's appearance puzzled Julian almost as much as his manner. Blockade-running, as such, was surely a Confederate perquisite. Yet this Jarvis smacked of a New England counting-house, from purse-string mouth to nasal twang. So, for that matter, did the brisk thumb that turned the pages of a notebook under his arm.

"What would you say to the *Sewanee*, Doctor—sailing at sunset tomorrow?"

"Steam or sail?"

"Steam, sir." Jarvis looked hurt. "Steam—*and* screw-driven. Shoe leather and Irish potatoes under hatches. Captain Nichols. He's booked for Savannah, but he'll unload at St. Marys, too." The factor spoke casually, a booking agent familiar with his details. "The fact she's not in munitions is to your advantage. The Yanks have their nose in Nassau; generally know when we sail, what we carry——"

"Speaking of Yankees, aren't you one yourself?"

"Boston born, thank you, sir. But I'm a British subject now. Shall I book two places—and another for your friend Mr. Cameron?"

"What sort of places?"

"Bunks only, sir. The lady in her own quarters amidships; the gentlemen in the fo'c'sle. Crew sleeps on deck, when they can. Which isn't often once you're in blue water. Speed and more speed: that's Captain Nichols' motto."

"I gather this is the best you have?"

"The very best, Doctor—and the best price. Two hundred Union dollars, if you please. Or forty pounds sterling." Jarvis closed one eye in an alert wink. "And that's only because Shea caught me first."

"Suppose I see Mrs. Chisholm and let you know?"

The factor shook his head. "Won't do at all, Doctor. Since I had your letter I could have sold those berths ten times over."

In the end Julian paid with only a routine protest and went to question Shea. Jarvis had already bustled down the deck on further business: the Chisholms, Julian gathered, were not the only passengers aboard who also planned to run the blockade.

Shea stood beside the pilot as the latter conned the *New Providence* into easy water; he stepped down into the companionway at Julian's nod.

"Two hundred for the pair of you is dirt cheap," he said. "Sprague can name his own price for the Georgia run."

"Did you say *Sprague?*"

"The one and only, Doc. Came to Nassau last year, with Washington backing. It's a strange world, till you get the hang of it."

"The man I refer to is a former senator. He's in the Bahamas on diplomatic business. Are you telling me he'd fight blockade-running at Government House and finance it on the side?" Julian was forcing anger for the captain's benefit; actually he was rather grateful to Victor Sprague for stepping so boldly into the role he had provided.

"The *Sewanee* was one of his ships before the war," said Shea. "Six months ago he sells her in Liverpool, to a Savannah firm. Then he takes shares in her under another name. Jarvis works for that secesh outfit—and takes pay from Sprague to keep 'em honest."

"Say that again."

"The Confeds have what it takes to fight a war, but they've no hard money. Someone's got to fill the gap—and that someone gets paid more than he's worth. If I told you what Sprague's cleared on cotton, right in this corner of nowhere, you wouldn't believe me."

"I believed that much in Glasgow," said Julian. "It's rather hard to face the reality."

He made himself face it when he returned to the rail and watched Nassau take definite shape in the blaze of noon. He could see the town clearly now, above the bustle of the harbor. The buildings were tall and many-windowed; most of them were surrounded by latticed porches. He wondered if Lucy was watching the clipper come into her berth and dismissed the notion. Lucy was not a woman to look through her lattice at the world.

At the taffrail above him a seaman swung a cable overside; it smacked wetly on the pierhead, where a black stevedore snubbed it home. The *New Providence* swung into her berth, between an asthmatic side-wheeler and a schooner-rigged yawl whose deck was still white with the remnants of a burst cotton bale. On the pier, Julian noted, the goods of war were mountain-high. He had heard that both England and France had shipped food as well as cannon to the Confederacy, almost from the beginning. Judging by this bursting pierhead, the trade was still at its peak.

While he watched, the side-wheeler lumbered into open water, loaded deep and creaking mightily. A trim screw-driven vessel slipped into the empty berth: the stevedores were aboard her instantly to pass down her cargo—the inevitable cotton bales again, packed into the last square inch of her narrow hold, lashed down under canvas on her decks. As the first gang unloaded, a second moved in on their heels, to hurry a procession of packing cases into the hold. Long, straw-filled cases that could contain nothing but rifle parts. . . .

"Dr. Chisholm, I presume?"

The claret-faced Englishman who stood beside him at the rail might have stepped from the pages of *Punch* without altering a line of his friendly scowl. The white drill coat and broad-brimmed hat were only a minor masquerade: under them the starched manner was intact. The accent of the right public school echoed in the clipped greeting; the strength of the Empire was in the handclasp.

"Dr. Steed, sir. Surgeon of the Port. Just hopped aboard to give your Mr. Shea a clean bill of health. My compliments on the old rascal's arm. However did you save it?"

The man's bounce was infectious; Julian forced himself to respond. "Blame Shea for that, Doctor—and salt air. All I did was tie off——"

"Youth," said Steed, "is seldom so modest. Is my friend Jarvis lying—when he says you take your bride to Georgia tomorrow?"

"That is our plan. I've a commission waiting——"

"I know about that commission, Doctor—asking your pardon. Here in Nassau we have a way of keeping tabs on our visitors. I do wish we could persuade you to stay and get rich here. His Excellency is crying for doctors. I could use a colleague myself."

Julian glanced out over the confusion of the quay to the jammed walks of Bay Street. No matter how adequate the facilities, this island capital would be hard hit by an epidemic—and epidemics, he knew, were persistent camp followers of war. The Bahamas (sick child of the crown colonies since a British admiral had wrested Nassau from the buccaneers) could hardly escape forever.

"I'd be honored by a visit, regardless," said the port surgeon.

"Hospital's on Windward Point. The West End, you know. Good mile from Government House, but any driver can take you there. *Had* to locate in the environs, because of the stink: the founding fathers insisted." He was on his way with an offhand wave as someone shouted his name from the pier.

Brief as the encounter was, it restored Julian's sense of balance. This time he turned back to the quay with only a faint disgust that such hurly-burly could exist in the service of Mars. It even seemed natural now, when a leonine head thrust up between two overloaded drays and he found himself looking down into a familiar face.

He knew his man instantly; he hoped that Victor Sprague knew him too. Certainly the ex-senator's stare was malevolent enough for any enemy's taste. His man was a trifle grayer, but no less vital. *He only looks heavy,* thought Julian. *Actually he's as light on his feet as a bobcat, and just as deadly.* He glared back from his greater height and choked down a shout as Sprague turned aside —contemptuously, as a man might ignore an antagonist he had measured and found wanting. In another moment the gray-tufted head was lost in the crowd; only the memory of the cold eyes remained.

Julian stayed rooted to the clipper's rail, trembling with the aftermath of unreasoning rage. He could not believe that the encounter—if it could be called that—was accidental. Thanks to Jarvis, Sprague had certainly heard of his impending arrival in Nassau.

He was almost calm when he felt a hand touch his arm. Jane smiled under the pert halo of her bonnet.

"We can go ashore when we like, my dear. Our carriage is waiting."

Their journey from gangplank to dock was almost an anticlimax. Bay Street, he found, was wide as an esplanade and packed with a sluggish stream of vehicles from curb to dockside. He settled beside Jane under the prodigal white fringe of their surrey and tried to stare back at its raw, bright colors as a tourist should. Not that he felt like a tourist at the moment: merely by closing his eyes, he could whisk himself to any Southern port when the cotton buying was at its height.

But it was profoundly strange after all, when he looked again— though his compatriots still thronged the tin-roofed arcades. Nassau might grow fat on American wars, but Nassau retained an out-at-elbow charm of its own. A sea-haunted, faintly evil charm that was part of the cloying heat, the stench of the fish market, the slap of black feet in sandy roadbeds. For all that, he bristled properly when two blades in the coats of Her Majesty's Army ogled the surrey at a crossing.

Jane said, "I hope you admired the *Sewanee*. She looks fast enough."

He remembered the runner that had berthed so debonairly beside the *New Providence*. "That can't be the *Sewanee*. She was loading rifles——"

"Did the factor pretend she wasn't in munitions? I hear that's a trick to fool the Yankees."

"To say nothing of passengers." He wasn't too surprised at Jarvis's lie. The *Sewanee* did look fast: the deception fitted the whole soulless scramble of the Nassau water front.

"I prefer to reach home in time, and take the risk," said Jane. "We're lucky he saved us the best. Of course your name helped us there——"

"Let's hope it won't also mark us for a Union gunboat."

Jane dismissed the threat. "They'd never get word offshore in time. Can you bear to leave so soon? We've almost no time for the Spragues——"

"I'm afraid we must postpone that reunion," he said, pleased that he could make it sound so natural. "I've an appointment that'll take most of my time."

"How could you?"

"The port surgeon has asked me to look in at his hospital. I can hardly refuse."

Jane glanced up at their driver's back and dropped her voice. "Are you that afraid of your Lucy?" Her lips brushed his ear as she spoke. From the sidewalk, she was a model bride, teasing her new husband with a butterfly kiss. "Don't you see, Julian? You *must* face her sometime—and tell her you're in love with your wife."

"But I'm not," he floundered. "That is, I haven't——"

"Still, you agreed to pretend."

He kept his eyes ahead. "Surely I can leave my bride for an afternoon."

"Perhaps I misunderstood. Are you meeting Mrs. Sprague alone?"

Let's hope I've put that part of it behind me, he thought. What would you say if I admitted I need all my will power to keep free of her? That I can't even enter our hotel with you now—for fear a note will be waiting? That I'd go to her at once if she sent for me, Sprague or no Sprague?

If he could read men's eyes at all, there had been death in Sprague's glare. A man who could shoot a fellow senator for political gain would hardly hesitate where his honor was concerned. But even now Julian knew that it was not fear of Sprague that held him back.

"I'll be at Steed's hospital until nightfall," he said. "We can meet again at dusk. I suggest we dine early—and alone. Tomorrow promises to be a long day."

Jane bowed her head, but he knew that she was studying him narrowly, for all her gesture of wifely submission. "As you wish, my dear. Forgive me if I misjudged you."

The carriage swung into their hotel grounds. The Royal Victoria stood on the slope to Government House, with the town below its gardens. Brand-new, and arrogantly handsome as a white sultan on his throne, the hotel seemed to burst with prosperity. In the curve of the porte-cochere he sprang out under a great spray of bougainvillaea. Jane took his hand demurely and stepped to the carriage block.

"I'll keep the surrey," he said.

"As you wish, my dear."

"Windward Point, please."

The driver stared down at him briefly, then cracked his whip again. Jane had already walked through the hotel entrance with her head high. But when he risked looking back, he saw that she had paused to watch him drive down the hill, after all.

He smiled wanly as he recalled the implication. On their first meeting, in Glasgow, he had fled to Lister, rather than accept her challenge. His flight was no less abject today.

iv

"Typical tertian fever," said Steed.

"You are exhibiting quinia?"

"In small amounts. They'll pay any price for quinine in your

Confederacy, Doctor. We can scarely keep a supply on the island."

Julian nodded and looked down again at the black man thrashing on the pallet. The malarial crisis was both acute and unmistakable: the man's eyes rolled, his teeth rattled; limbs and muscles quivered, in a paroxym of cold which seemed oblivious of the cloying heat.

"Really, Doctor," said Steed, "I'd hoped to spare you the wards."

"I was trained on wards," said Julian. "May we make the rounds?"

Despite himself, he glanced up at the high, boarded windows that lined the room on the seaward side. Steed's hospital was well placed on its promontory just beyond the harbor's mouth—but, from what he had seen so far, the planning had stopped there. Here in the men's ward the stale air seemed to press down on the long row of pallets like a visible miasma. Most of the patients were naked under the coarse sheets. At one end of each pallet stood a table for their belongings; between each pair of beds was an iron bucket, the only apparent sanitary provision. One whiff of the complex stench would have driven most laymen into the fresh air, but Julian had trained himself to ignore it long ago. As he said, his training had inured him to the dark brown reek of poverty; the poverty here was only a trifle more pathetic than its counterpart abroad.

"Must these windows be boarded?"

"Night air's damp as pea soup sometimes. Besides, most of these beggars believe in vampires."

Julian had worked hard to choke down his anger ever since he had walked into this pesthole. He moved on to the next cot.

"An interesting case," said Steed. "I've called it typhomalaria."

Judging by the tattoo marks, this patient had been a sailor once. Not even a shadow of his brawn remained; his skin was saffron yellow, with dark, bruised areas on face and body. The breathing, Julian saw, was rapid. The pulse was small and thready.

"He's almost *in extremis*."

"It's a severe disease. Especially when it comes in epidemics."

"You're having an epidemic now?"

"Perhaps a dozen cases. Nothing unusual in this foul climate."

Julian glanced at Steed; the port surgeon of Nassau was dropping in his estimation with each crisp phrase. He considered the other cases the English doctor had classed as epidemic. All were desperately ill: the last man in the line was deep saffron from chest to hairline. He lifted a lid to check the yellow, clouded eyeball. The thin black trickle at the patient's lips canceled out his last doubt. Even when he had worked with Cagle he had known the dread import of the black vomit. He forced the words down, remembering that there was one more test that could convince even Steed.

"What do you think of this case?"

"Typhomalaria," said the Britisher. "Undoubtedly fatal."

"May we return to it later?"

"The hospital is yours this afternoon: I'm only the cicerone."

In an open gallery outside the wards they paused to breathe deep of the sparkling sea air. Then Steed led the way through a whitewashed door beyond. Julian saw at once that this was a private ward, complete with beds and head-high partitions. A nurse came up for a consultation, and the Englishman turned to his visitor with his best smile.

"Will you confirm another of my diagnoses?"

They followed a long corridor to an isolated room that seemed, at first glance, to be part of a storehouse. The patient, a giant Negro, lay on a high bed with no covering but a fouled sheet; a glance told Julian that the man was moribund. He had seen many such cases abroad; hospital gangrene, or peritonitis, was generally the controlling factor. Always there was the picture of complete mental and physical collapse, as if the patient were stunned by some poison too strong for the body to bear.

Steed took the man's pulse and frowned. "I'm afraid it's too late for an examination after all. He's almost gone."

"When did it begin?"

"A week ago. It's cholera morbus—complicated by a tumor. I prescribed calomel and bleeding, and he improved somewhat. But he's lost ground ever since I brought him here."

"Why is he in this room alone? Do you fear contagion?"

Steed looked down briefly at the patient. "The fellow happens to be my gardener. All yesterday he howled like a lost dog. Had to strap him down. Seemed much simpler, keeping him away from the others."

Julian kept his voice steady. "You spoke of a tumor, I believe?"

The Englishman flicked the sheet aside and pointed to a monstrous dilation of the abdomen. "It appeared the first day after I brought him here. Naturally I diagnosed dropsy also." He thrust a finger deep into the man's right side. "He's too far gone to react, I suppose. Yesterday he screamed whenever I touched that spot. The tumor is obviously malignant."

Julian was already at the bedside, running his fingers over the area Steed had indicated. Skoda, the great specialist in percussion, had taught him that technique years ago in Vienna. Testing the "tumor" which Steed had diagnosed so blithely, he outlined a hard, ill-defined swelling that had stretched the flesh almost to the bursting point.

Peritonitis was surely indicated—but was a tumor really the cause? He remembered his own clinic on typhlitis—and the laughter that had greeted his theory of its genesis. He had been new to the Krakenhaus then, with only a few autopsies behind him. Yet he had dared to suggest that typhlitis—that new concept of inflammation of the bowel—was often caused by disorders originating in the *processus veriformis,* that deformed appendix which hung from the caecum like an unwanted worm.

"What do you call it, Dr. Chisholm?"

"It could be typhlitis."

The British doctor shrugged: clearly the word was unfamiliar. "How do you base your diagnosis?"

"On two years' work in Vienna. I handled many such cases there."

"I still feel it is a case of cholera morbus, complicated by a malignant tumor."

"Only an operation would answer that."

"Would you advise one now?"

"It's rather late for surgery," said Julian. "Your patient is dead."

He stepped back from the cot while Steed verified the statement. In Vienna he had urged operations for more than one such case. He had even suggested that it would be possible to remove the appendix itself with a minimum of risk. If this dunderhead had permitted it, he might have taken that risk now. He wondered if Steed would consent to an exploration.

"Could we perform an autopsy?"

"In heaven's name, why?"

"In Vienna every case came to post-mortem," said Julian patiently. "Surely it's the best way to study disease."

"I know it's the continental custom." Julian saw that Steed was impressed, under his polite truculence. Vienna was a name to conjure with in surgery.

"If you'd give me permission to explore, you could send the findings to London. It might well be reported in the journals."

Steed yielded the point with his starch intact. "I'll send for a set of instruments, Doctor. The cadaver is yours."

"Shouldn't he be removed to your morgue?"

"*This* is my morgue, sir."

Julian went out to the seaward-facing gallery while he waited for the instruments. A breeze had set in with the declining day, and he felt his spirits rise a little in that whiff of ozone. It would be simple to forget Steed's glaring incompetence.

Already it was evident that the man would not budge from his prejudices. It was equally evident that his visit had plunged him into a cesspool that would go on stinking to heaven, regardless of his efforts.

He was a surgeon, after all; he had come to Windward Point to forget his personal problems, not to wrestle with the problems of the world. Why not ignore Steed completely—and walk down the point for a swim before he returned to Nassau? Why not save his breath, and escape a futile argument? He stripped to the waist as he stood there in the brazen sunlight, tossed his coat across a palmetto clump, and walked slowly back to the storeroom that doubled as morgue.

Steed hovered in the background as he began the autopsy. A few strokes of the knife opened the abdominal wall above the region of the tumor. Evidence of widespread inflammation was instantly apparent—a massive swelling, reeking with the smell of death. Julian frowned as he reached for a retractor and spread the incision yet wider. At this moment it seemed possible that the port surgeon had blundered on a correct diagnosis after all.

"We can write down peritonitis," he said.

"It is noted," said Steed.

"Now for the cause."

The knife explored deeper, to open a cavity black with a purulent oozing. Steed bent above Julian's shoulder and nodded sagely.

"A malignant tumor, ending in abscess and death."

"Let us be sure."

The knife moved on, following the distended barrel of the caecum: Julian saw that the tissue here was iridescent with decay. A true case of typhlitis had involved this dangerous segment of the bowel; so far he could not even locate the appendix normally attached to its lower curve. When the knife exposed the wormlike organ at last, he found it all but destroyed—almost as though it had exploded near its middle. He lifted the livid remnant and stepped back from the table with a round, stonelike object in his palm.

"Shall we say this stone lodged in the appendix, causing a severe inflammation which spread to the bowel—before and after the smaller organ ruptured?"

"How can you prove that inflammation didn't begin in the caecum itself?"

"I can't, of course. Nor can I see evidence of a tumor, malignant or benign."

Julian knew he was wasting his breath before he laid down the knife: in this instance Steed could rely on the skepticism of the scientist, as well as old-fashioned dogma. But he could not surrender his clinical pattern without a final word. He took up the scalpel again and tapped the steel against the hard little stone that had expelled itself from the abscess.

"The vermiform appendix is a vestigial organ, useless to man. Why shouldn't it be a troublemaker, too? Suppose the surgeon excised it at the first sign of pain? After all, this is like any other abscess."

"It's still peritonitis," said Steed. "Can you name a patient who's recovered?"

A nurse had already appeared in the gallery with soap and hot water; Julian gave up the argument and stepped outside to scrub. Only as he dried his hands after a second cleansing did he remember the fever patients.

"That typhomalaria diagnosis. Could I have another look on the way out?"

Steed turned to the nurse for a whispered question: Julian could read the doctor's answer from his sudden frown. "I'm afraid we've lost him too."

"Have I brought you bad luck, by any chance?"

"Of course not." Steed rumbled with laughter. "We knew he had only hours to live: the same is true of the others."

"I'd like a look, just the same."

The body was already covered with sacking in a corner of the ward—ticketed, evidently, for a pauper's grave without further attention. Julian stood aside while Steed lifted the coverings; the nurse had already brought a screen to shut off the examination from the other patients. The port surgeon turned back the dead man's eyelid, but Julian only glanced at the evidence revealed. The examination was for Steed's instruction, not his own.

"Deep-saffron eyeballs," he said. "Lids black with hemorrhage. Will you expose the chest?"

Steed drew the sacking down still further. Behind them the nurse gasped and bolted from the room. The port surgeon jerked to his feet, wiping his palms as he rose.

"What do those dark blotches mean?"

"Your nurse knows," said Julian. He could almost enjoy Steed's discomfort now. "She was raised in the tropics."

"My diagnosis is still typhomalaria."

"Your diagnosis is incorrect, Doctor. This is the *coup de barre* —known in America as yellow fever."

"That I refuse to admit." Steed's voice was hoarse; he turned abruptly from the body, flicking the sacking over the jaundiced face with one angry toe. Julian dogged his heels as the Britisher stalked into the fresh air.

"Yellow jack is not a phrase to play with, Doctor."

"I agree," snapped Julian. It was a relief to let his temper rise at last. "I've seen many cases in the Carolina lowlands. It has wiped out whole towns. Would Nassau be luckier if it got a real start here?"

"I resent your tone and your implication." The port surgeon had recovered his aplomb. "I must also remind you that my diagnosis is final."

He knows I'm right, thought Julian. He knows that there could be no greater threat to Nassau's wartime prosperity. Therefore he'll stop any rumors of an epidemic on the threshold of this pesthouse. It was incredible that a licensed physician could stoop so low—yet the man's attitude was unmistakable.

"Perhaps you were unwise to invite me here," he said at last.

Steed was polite but frigid. "I need only remind you of the ethics of our profession. These suspicions must go no further."

"You mean facts, don't you? Jaundice, terminal fever, gastric hemorrhage. In short, the *coup de barre*."

He watched Steed redden at last. "I have shown you every courtesy here, Doctor. You must admit that."

"I admit it freely."

"I must insist you keep your theories to yourself. There is no yellow fever in Nassau."

"And I insist there is."

"Your stubbornness is most unwise. You are a foreigner in a British colony. Must I remind you that it is an offense against the Crown to spread false rumors?"

"Is that a threat?"

"Let's remain friends, and call it a warning."

"I accept the warning—and refuse the friendship." Julian also ignored the proffered hand as he turned on his heel. But he could not resist a parting shot from the doorway. "I wonder where you took your medical oath, Steed. Or did you ever take one?"

Outside at last, he snatched his coat from the palmetto bush. His driver still snored in the front seat of the surrey. He yielded to the impulse he had stifled before and turned his back on the hospital. Walking down the point, he turned into the shelter of a dune, stepped out of his other clothes, and plunged for the open sea.

A strong swimmer since boyhood, he had wrestled with problems before in Atlantic surf. Today the one lazy wave that creamed the sands of New Providence was a poor substitute for the pounding seas of Hatteras. But he swam far out, as he had always done, and floated with his eyes on the pale tropic sky. Merely by turning his head he could have looked back at the port of Nassau. But he knew what was waiting for him in Nassau, without a backward glance. As Jane had reminded him, his problem was still there: he had not solved it by running away.

The sun was on the horizon when he dressed, but his mind was hard with purpose now. His driver sat up promptly as he stepped into the surrey and cracked his whip without waiting for orders. Hospitals, like graveyards, should be avoided at all times, the gesture said. Especially now, when the dusk was creeping over the mud flats of shanty town. Dr. Julian Chisholm settled back and rehearsed the words he must speak.

"Take me to the residence of Victor Sprague."

v

Pacing Sprague's study a half hour later, he paused again at the tall, latticed window to stare out across the garden. The house stood on the slope of George Street, beside the stair to Government House; its occupant, reflected Julian, had only a short walk to his political duties—and the harbor was almost as close. The quiet elegance of the room annoyed him almost as much as the long wait. The rosewood highboy and matching desk, the morocco-bound volumes under leaded glass, had no relation to their owner as he remembered him. Without quite knowing why, he had expected something gaudier. Or, at the very least, a touch to remind him of Lucy.

He forced himself to pause and settled in the chair facing the desk. The murmur from the drawing room upstairs reminded him that the Spragues had guests; the host could hardly rush down at a moment's notice to receive a visitor who refused to state his business. When he had given his name to Sprague's black majordomo he had listened for a moment in the stair well, but he could not pick out Lucy's voice from the babble upstairs. He was listening now, tense with the fear that she might answer his summons, in lieu of her husband.

"Dr. Chisholm? It's high time we met, isn't it?"

Ex-Senator Victor Sprague was bowing in the polished frame of the doorway. Julian apologized silently for an error in judgment. Sprague fitted his background perfectly: in austere evening dress, he could have posed for a statesman in any century. Only the tired, hooded stare betrayed him—and a clever artist would have painted that out for posterity's sake. . . . But when the ex-senator stepped into the full circle of lamplight, Julian saw that his show of vitality was only a part of his pose. Under it he seemed tired as most moneygrabbers at the day's end, and ill to boot.

"You should have come straight up, Doctor."

"This is not a social call."

"Forgive me for misunderstanding, but——"

"I've come to warn you of a grave danger to yourself and your wife."

Sprague continued to stare with that same grave unfriendliness: an attitude that contrasted pointedly with his surface politeness.

He's weighing me now, thought Julian—just as he weighed me when our eyes crossed on the pierhead.

Aloud he said only, "I assure you that I'm thinking of Lucy's welfare—and your own. Will you hear me out?"

"You have my attention, Doctor."

Sprague gestured wearily toward the armchair and settled at the rosewood desk, but Julian ignored the parody of manners. "You seem to doubt my motives, sir."

"You have yet to state them."

"I've just come from the hospital on Windward Point. An epidemic of yellow fever is imminent in Nassau. Steed is doing what he can to cover up, but——" He had kept his voice steady. It wavered now, against Sprague's indifference.

"Is that all, Doctor?"

"Have you ever seen yellow jack sweep a town?"

"I know little of the disease. So, I imagine, do most doctors. But speak for yourself."

Julian hesitated. Instinct told him that the present threat was terribly real, but he had no yardstick for his belief. It was true that this strange scourge had decimated many towns. But the death rate was sometimes light; patients even recovered, and were immune thereafter. Yellow jack seemed to strike, for the most part, from swamps and rivers—never from the sea. A miasma borne on the wings of death, it could miss one town entirely, even as it ravaged another. Respecting no social barrier, it had invaded both manor house and slave cabin in the Carolinas. Were it to stalk through Nassau, this house would be no more immune than the hovels of shanty town.

"Would you listen if I suggested that *you* might be suffering from fever now?"

Sprague's head came up, giving Julian another chance to note the unnatural brightness of his eyes once they were opened wide. In the full light the spots of dull color above the jowls were even more apparent.

"Isn't that a rather hasty judgment?"

"I'm trying to make a point. When a fever epidemic is in the making, there might be a hundred walking cases in a town the size of Nassau. Will you let me examine you?"

Sprague shook his head; his eyes had narrowed to sleepy slits again. "Our mutual friend Steed looked me over only this morning—he said I'm fit enough for my age. I'll grant you this climate is hard on white men: I still hope to survive it."

"May I ask how long you plan to stay in Nassau?"

"Until this business of the blockade is settled."

Until blockade-running ceases to turn a profit, thought Julian. "I'm taking my own wife to the mainland tomorrow," he said. "I advise you strongly to send Lucy away too."

"With you, Doctor?"

The question threw him off balance; he knew that he was flushing like a schoolboy. "I'm suggesting that you send her North—or back to England. At least until this threat is ended. Naturally I wouldn't ask Mrs. Victor Sprague to run the blockade."

"I'm trying hard to value you, Doctor," said Sprague. "And I'm still puzzled. You should be fighting me and all I stand for——"

"Granted, sir."

"Yet you offer to save my life. I can't see why."

"It's my business to save lives."

"Even the enemy's?"

"Why not?"

Sprague got to his feet. "Shall we join my guests—since I refuse to be saved?"

"You simply won't see the danger?"

"I can deal with men who fit their patterns," said Sprague. "Why don't you fit yours?"

"I am only speaking as a doctor."

"Be a man of the world, and yield to Steed."

"Steed happens to be a stiff-necked fool. You may take my word for that much."

"Do you class me with him, because I refuse to listen?"

"Suit yourself, sir."

Julian held his breath and waited. It was provocation enough for a challenge. Would Sprague fight him after all—for an insult that had no direct bearing on Lucy? It would make an appropriate ending to the interview. But the ex-senator only held up a detaining palm.

"Perhaps you consider me a parvenu, with more tenacity than brains? Don't underestimate me, Doctor: nothing could be more dangerous."

That's his dare to me, thought Julian swiftly. I can still call him out tomorrow, and—with luck—blow out his brains. He felt the old, unreasoning rage boil in his brain and suppressed it resolutely, forcing his tone to match Sprague's.

"My motives are the best, sir. I must ask you to believe that, at least."

Sprague bowed, with his ironic stare unchanged. "It's a bit hard, Doctor—but I'll try. Men seldom act from other motives than self-interest. That's why I'm in Nassau, where self-interest is thickest. That's why I must remain. It's a duty to my country——"

"And to yourself?"

"And to myself," said Sprague blandly. "At the moment I'm the tenth richest man in America; I intend to raise that rating, thanks to the war."

"Few of us can hope for that much."

"Few of us indeed. Naturally I need a wife here: our entertainment, as you can see, is continuous. Fever or no fever, I must insist that Lucy stay."

"I gather that sums up your case?"

"As well as I am able."

"What if I warned Lucy privately?"

"Lucy is devoted to my interests. She would refuse to listen."

Eye to eye with him now, Julian felt hate stab from Sprague's narrowed lids. Once again he acknowledged defeat. It was, of course, unthinkable that he should attempt to frighten Lucy into leaving Nassau. Lucy did not frighten easily—and Lucy really kept her bargains. If Sprague needed her to preside at his soirees, she would refuse to budge.

"My compliments," he said at last. "I hope you won't regret your attitude."

"The compliment is accepted, Doctor. So is your zeal in Mrs. Sprague's behalf. *Now* will you come up and meet our guests?"

"If you'll forgive me, I must join Mrs. Chisholm at our hotel."

Julian turned, with the words still on his lips. The voice that had just drifted down the stair well was unmistakable. So, for that matter, was the tremolo accompaniment.

> "A hundred months have passed, Lorena,
> Since last I held thy hand in mine . . ."

"Your wife has been entertaining us for the past hour," said Sprague. "Lucy sent word to the Victoria, inviting you both. We wondered what had detained you." He stepped back from the doorway, offering Julian that fixed and bitter smile. "After you, Dr. Chisholm."

As they went up the stair to the drawing room, Jane's voice poured down to meet them in a caressing, golden flood. He wondered why the threat of Lucy Sprague seemed only a half-forgotten nightmare now. Why nothing seemed important beside the urge to reach his temporary bride. . . . Certainly Lucy herself was unchanged as she stood waiting to receive him at the top of the stair. The hand she offered him was still a warm invitation in his own, even if her eyes were coolly modest. She was wearing one of the gowns she favored, and her breasts were proud as ever above the prodigal ruching. Julian felt his heart turn over once, after all. But it had resumed its normal beat as she slipped an arm through his and led him among her guests.

"Your wife is singing, Julian," she said. "Need I add that you have chosen well?"

And then the crowd parted and he saw Jane at last. She was seated at a spinet in the midst of the wide, shining floor, with a British naval lieutenant lolling at the music rack. Intent on her flying fingers, she seemed as unaware of the young god's ogling as she was of Julian. Unaware, too, that every man in that crowded, glittering room was envying the husband who came forward to greet her now.

> "Our hearts will soon lie low, Lorena;
>   Life's tide is ebbing out so fast.
>   There is a future, oh, thank God!
>   Of life this is so small a part!
>   'Tis dust to dust beneath the sod,
>   But There—up There—'tis heart to heart!"

The last note died: she looked up, smiling at the applause and at Julian. Much later he would understand what had passed between them at that moment. Now, as their eyes met and locked, he knew only that he was seeing her for the first time. As a woman, not merely as his deliverance. Lucy and her salon faded to a whisper as he bent to kiss Jane's cheek and blessed her for being.

vi

"Are you always this quiet—when you're in love?"

Their carriage had just rolled out of the Spragues' garden and into the pitch of George Street. Jane's voice was soft and faintly teasing. Now she moved closer to Julian and leaned forward to wave good-by to her British lieutenant, a mere bright silhouette under a street lamp.

Behind them the voices of departing guests met and blended in the dark; around them was the soft whirr of carriage wheels in sand. By night Nassau's slightly sinister charm was intact. But it was only background now: a burst of Negro laughter, the far-off throb of a guitar, somewhere in that amorphous dark. . . . He turned to smile at Jane's pale profile and knew he had no need to speak. His secret was still safe from her; he would keep it safe, if he could.

"Probably she's at a window," said Jane. "Watching us drive out of her life. Asking herself if you've really escaped. I think we came close to convincing her that you've done just that."

I hope you're right, he thought. It was a bitter admission, but he realized that Lucy had been much too sure of him tonight to give him any real attention. A month ago he would have eaten his heart out, watching her divide her smiles—like a model hostess— between the governor of the Bahamas and the Yankee consul. Tonight he could afford to smile inwardly at Lucy's confidence.

Jane said, "We gave a good performance. Won't you agree with me?"

He found his voice at last. "Someday I'll thank you as you deserve."

"Don't, pray. I enjoyed every minute. Naturally we should have arrived together: I did my best to make your visit at that hospital sound important."

"It was," he murmured. "I needed the breathing spell."

He saw no reason for telling her what he had found at Windward Point: it would only alarm her needlessly. At this moment he felt brave enough to turn his back on death, even if death was grinning at them from the darkness. His hand was steady as he slipped an arm through his bride's, bringing her face to face with him at last.

But Jane was following a thought of her own: if she noted the intimacy, she gave no sign.

"On the whole, we've used our time well," she whispered. "We've met everyone worth knowing; I'm established as your wife; our marriage is down in Nassau's visiting book. For good measure, you've put an old flame in its place, even if you haven't quite put it out."

"So we can sail for Georgia tomorrow, with a clear conscience?"

"Speak for yourself, Julian."

"Is that all tonight has meant to you?"

Her eyes were wide in the translucent dark. "Isn't it enough?"

It's more than enough for now, he thought. Yes, it is enough to sit beside you in this ancient British surrey and draw a tranquil breath. Enough that you'll be with me tomorrow, when we go aboard the *Sewanee*.

He tried to fasten his mind on what lay beyond—when they had reached Georgia, when they prepared to go their separate ways. That, too, was part of their bargain: from Jane's point of view, it was the most important part. Picturing the good-bys he would speak, he knew that he would make no effort to stop her, that he could never spoil the strange game she was playing. In that same sad moment of perception he knew why. If Lucy had been lust, uncomplicated by tenderness, Jane was love.

Since he loved her (and it was too soon to say how or why), he could only give her what she asked of him.

The surrey turned into the water front. Pondering the certainty of this new bondage—glad that Jane had fallen silent, too, and had let her head rest lightly on his shoulder—he watched the moonless bay open before them. Far out (where the town merged with the pine barrens of the West End) he could see the lights of Steed's pesthouse winking on the Point. They seemed oddly bright: for no reason at all he remembered the matching brightness in Victor Sprague's eyes when they had crossed wills in the latter's study.

The bizarre likeness was enough to bring him back to the present, just before the glare of a bar drenched the carriage in a hard yellow glow. Jane sat up primly, though her eyes were still twinkling.

"Impressing the Government House coterie is one thing. We needn't let all Bay Street know we're bride and groom."

He moved to his corner of the surrey and managed to return her smile. "I thought you enjoyed pretending."

A drunken sailor rolled away from their wheels and staggered into the bar; their driver, making a vicious circle with his whip, sent the carriage through the wall of darkness beyond. A long, tin-roofed warehouse loomed on their left. A British warehouse, to judge by the quiet. The hulls on this quayside were loaded with eastbound cotton and waiting for the tide. It was only the westbound blockade-runners that slipped out like dark fish with the sunset.

"Our pier is next," said Jane. "It seems the *Sewanee* is still loading."

He heard the rough chant before he saw the runner herself, outlined by flares at the dock's end. Black hands were tossing the flat rifle cases from dock to gangway. The crude glare picked out pools of brilliance on sweating ebony shoulders, on the brass of a supercargo's visor, on the enameled name plate of the Sheffield forge that had shaped these tools of war.

"What are they singing?"

"It's an old Easter hymn," said Julian. "In Balearic Spanish. The language of the Florida Minorcans."

"However did you know that?"

"One of our hands brought it up from Augustine years ago. When I was still a boy."

They had chanted those rich minor notes often in the quarters at Chisholm Hundred. He found that he was singing, too, as the surrey idled past.

> *"Disciarem lu dol*
> *Cantarem aub' alagria*
> *Y n'arem a dá*
> *Las pascuas a Maria!"*

"A Minorcan hymn," said Jane. "I should have guessed. Most of our crew comes from St. Augustine."

"It's my turn to be astonished now."

"Captain Nichols told me as much when he called on you this afternoon," she continued. "Here in Nassau he's known as Adam Nichols. Actually his name is Don Amadeo Menendez y Vega. His ancestors, I might add, were settled in Florida when Carolina was a wilderness."

"Why did he unburden himself?"

"Many of the runners are sailing under other names," said Jane. "Why should their captains be an exception? And why shouldn't they give their right names to us? Remember, you're a distinguished passenger. So am I—as your wife."

"Never mind the compliments. How did you make friends so easily?"

Jane smiled. "You needn't look so startled. Whit brought the good captain up from the bar and stayed while we talked. Don Amadeo gave me his right name fast enough—when I handed him a hundred dollars, all for himself."

"But I settled with Jarvis for our passage."

"Whit said it was always wise to give the captain something. Naturally I paid him in your name. I said you insisted we sail on time——"

Julian tossed up his hands. "It's your money, Jane. But I still don't understand."

"I wanted to spare you from Mrs. Sprague. I thought she might be still—dangerous. It seemed the least I could do."

"Suppose I insisted that I've outgrown my——" He hesitated, groping for a word that would not offend her ears.

"Intoxication?"

"You might call it that."

"You see? You had to face her one more time. Otherwise you might never have known." Jane considered that implication. "Just *how* did you know?"

"How does any man know he's in love—or out of love?"

"Is that a question to ask a lady?"

"You asked me first," he reminded her.

"It wasn't too fair of me," she agreed gravely. "Still, we've always discussed things so freely——"

"Everything," he admitted. "From state sovereignty to woman suffrage. And back by way of Voltaire and America's role in history. I've enjoyed your views, Mrs. Chisholm, even when I couldn't subscribe to them wholly."

She accepted his somber teasing quite seriously. "That's why I chose you as my temporary husband. So few husbands are willing to treat their wives as equals."

"Of course there is a subject we haven't even touched."

"If you mean me——"

"Who else would I mean?"

Despite himself he moved closer to her as the surrey swung up the rise to their hotel grounds. "You know all there is to know of me. Every virtue I was born with—and every prejudice. If you walked into Chisholm Hundred tomorrow, you could name every medal on my great-grandfather's waistcoat——"

"Chisholm Hundred isn't you," said Jane. "It was never you. Depending on your viewpoint, that's your tragedy—or your salvation. . . . If you do return someday—and I suppose you will, out of sentiment—you'll find it belongs to its ghosts."

"Perhaps I belong with them too."

"You belong with tomorrow," she said. "I've known that much since we saved Captain Shea."

Julian smiled. She had turned their talk away from herself—and turned it rather neatly. "I'm pleased that you think there's hope for me."

"Would you think me forward if I admitted I'll be sorry to say good-by at St. Marys? I've learned a great deal from you, Julian."

And I from you, he thought. Thanks to you, I know there's a difference between love and wanting. Between the hunger for another's flesh and the hope for another's happiness. But how can I wish *you* happiness if you won't tell me where you're bound or why?

"I've learned that a Southern gentleman can really be a gentleman," she said. "I've learned that you aren't all spoiled animals posing as princes——" Her voice broke, and he saw that she was crying. For a moment he was too amazed to comfort her.

"Is it something I said, Jane?"

"It's what you haven't said, Julian." Already her voice had steadied. "What you didn't do, that first night out of Glasgow."

He bent forward to touch her hand, as gently as he could, and prayed that he would not spoil his record by taking her in his arms. The coachman swung his whip again, urging his team up the last grade. Rain began to star the sandy roadway—a strange, warm rain that seemed to come from nowhere, to drift in the dark. Only the thunder, sudden and vicious behind the wall of night, convinced him that the soft downpour was real.

"We've come home just in time."

"Just in time," said Jane. "I was beginning to talk about myself, after all."

"Won't you talk a little more?"

But the surrey had already swept into the curve of the porte-cochere. She stepped out to the carriage block without waiting for his hand.

A Negro page met them under the white bell of an umbrella. Vaulting to the driveway, Julian hesitated in the teeming rain as his bride walked into the light. Then he fumbled for his composure and offered her his hand as they ran toward the latticed hotel porch together. The rain drummed down in earnest as they gained its shelter. Lightning split the night with a green sword, and he felt her shrink against him at last. Just in time he remembered he was her husband and put his arm around her waist.

Despite the magnificence of its Turkey carpet and white-enameled panels, the hall of the Royal Victoria seemed gloomy tonight. The storm, rattling a devil's tattoo on each of the close-drawn jalousies, seemed to be biding its time before bursting through—and with each crash of thunder outside he felt Jane's answering tremor. Marching straight down the apparently endless carpet, he did not risk words. Both of them were watching the small Negro page who danced just ahead, swinging their room key on its brass number plate.

"They gave us a suite," said Jane at last. "I—hope you'll like it."

He knew that she was talking against a growing agitation that had no bearing on her fear of storms.

When the page unlocked their door at last and whisked in ahead of them to turn up the lamps, she paused in the doorway and glanced at Julian imploringly. Supplication was a new note from Jane; so, for that matter, was the tremor in her voice as a monstrous white flash lit the room with nightmare day.

"Wait, Julian, I'm afraid of *that* kind of dark."

"Our second bedchamber," he whispered. "Shall I carry you over this threshold too?"

She made no protest as he lifted her in his arms and walked into the room. The page had already drawn the curtains snugly over the two wide windows; with the lamplight shining on the flower pattern of the carpet and the wine-red valance of the bed, the room was no longer sinister. It's ours, he thought: come what may, we're together now as we've never been.

Then, as he put Jane on her feet, he smiled at his own poetry. The page had already opened a connecting door; it swung wide, showing him a second bedroom, also complete with flowered carpet and bed with wine-red valance. He guessed that his own portmanteau had been neatly unpacked in there by a hotel valet—that the nightshirt of puce-colored linen, which he had bought in

London, was lying across that opened bed, just as Jane's nightgown case covered this turned-back sheet.

The Negro caught the flipped shilling and whisked out as nimbly as he had come. Julian found that he could wait for the hall door to sigh shut after all. His arm was still around Jane's shoulder, but she had made no move to leave his light embrace. She did not stir now, not even when he bent slowly until his lips all but brushed hers. For a moment of almost unbearable tension he thought she would break free. Instead she lifted her mouth to meet his own.

It was a dream kiss she offered, the lips full and firm on his, with no hint of passion. When she left his arms he saw that her composure had returned completely.

"Was that good night?" he said.

"If you like, Julian."

It was her voice that broke him. This time his mouth clung to hers for a heart-bursting eternity. Tomorrow, his kiss said, you'll sleep alone aboard the *Sewanee*. A few more tomorrows, and we'll say good-by. This is for all the tomorrows we can never share. This tells you, without words, what I've no right to say.

"That was really good night, Jane."

He went resolutely to the door that divided reality from romance. There he paused to make his meaning clear. "But I'd bolt the door to be sure."

She had not stirred from the spot where he had left her. He saw that her head was high; two spots of color glowed at her pale cheeks. But she was quite calm as she answered; if he had stirred her at all, her voice was in control, at least.

"Perhaps you're right, Julian. About the bolt, I mean."

He closed the door behind him as he stepped into his own bedroom. For a moment he stood with his hand still on the knob—smiling, despite the tumult in his brain, as he heard her skirts whisper across the floor. He knew that her hand had closed on that some doorknob. He heard her catch her breath, and guessed that her whole body was pressed against the thin cedar panel that separated them. When he heard the bolt slide home on her side, he choked down a cry just in time. Despite his good resolves, it was a tonic to know he had stirred her at last.

Then he walked across the room to his own oversized bed and saw the note propped against the night light. A squarish note, with his name in neat block letters—as though block letters could disguise the hand he would have recognized anywhere. Lucy had written eleven unsigned words, and he knew them by heart long before he could break the seal.

She had summoned him like this before, across half a continent. It was only fitting that she should use the same magic to call him one more time.

I'll be alone tomorrow, at three. Shall we say good-by—properly?

"At least we can say good-by," he remarked, to no one in particular, just before he blew out his lamp. At least I can settle our account in good order, he added silently, and lay down fully clothed on the splendid candlewick spread. Listening to the rain squall blow itself out in the hotel gardens, he told himself that he would not sleep tonight. And yet, once again, his eyes had closed ten seconds after his head touched the pillow.

When he opened them again, hot, staring daylight was beating at his lattice, and Jane's voice, tranquil as ever behind the connecting door, was ordering breakfast for two.

vii

The bell clamored again under his impatient hand; he heard it echo down the silent hallway behind the doorframe and felt an answering echo in his own brain.

All morning he had cooled his heels in the anteroom of the American Consulate while he waited to transmit his findings at Windward Point to someone in authority. When the consul had received him at last, the interview had been shockingly brief. . . . The harried man was quite as obstinate as Steed: clearly, he would never go beyond his authority; just as clearly, he was profoundly suspicious of advice from a Southern source. Yellow jack might come and go, Julian gathered; the slow poison of protocol was endemic in Nassau.

Somewhere in the siesta-hushed town a clock boomed three. He yanked the bell cord one more time and cursed himself impartially for answering Lucy's note. It was something to know that his things were already aboard the *Sewanee;* that Jane was now on her way to the pier, with Whit Cameron as a competent escort. He had insisted on this much before he came to this final rendezvous. . . .

"Don't be a fool," said Jane. "You didn't say a dozen words to her yesterday. If you avoid her now, you'll tell yourself afterward that you were afraid."

"I thought you'd appointed yourself my guardian."

"At the moment I don't think you need my protection. Prove I'm right, and meet us aboard."

He had pondered the ways of women as he climbed the heat-drugged slope of George Street. Now, as he fidgeted on Lucy's porch, he glanced down that same steep pitch and felt his heart rise when he saw how brightly the harbor beckoned across the white-limed roofs below. Was it possible that Lucy had repented her summons? The impassive, high-galleried house seemed empty as the moon; he wondered if its silence was a rebuff—or a warning.

Still wondering, he turned the massive wooden doorknob. His mind began to plumb the silence when the door swung open under his hand, to show an empty sweep of hall, a stairway spiraling up toward the dim sheen of a skylight high above.

"Is that you, Julian?"

Her voice was no more than a whisper, but it drifted down the stair with all its remembered lure. He followed it, taking the first flight in long-legged strides. As he paused on the landing, he heard her call again and realized she was in a room to the right. The door—it was really no more than a half-opened lattice—stood invitingly ajar. Here, at least, was precisely what he had expected to find.

Lucy was lying on a wicker divan, her pale hair streaming across the nest of pillows; he knew it was Lucy, though the room was filled with the dusk of drawn blinds. She was in flowing negligee. Without moving a step nearer, he could name every thread. The same hot, drowned light had outlined her body in the summerhouse at Chisholm Hundred. The same half whisper had drawn him down to find her waiting lips.

"I think I've done this rather well," said Lucy. "Especially on such short warning. Didn't you know better than to ring?"

"We're alone?"

"Quite alone. I sent the servants to a fete in shanty town. Victor, praise Heaven, has decided to go to Key West for a meeting."

"He's already sailed?"

"This morning, on the mail packet. Isn't it providential?"

It's almost too providential, he thought. Not that it was like Lucy to set traps. . . . Still he remained carefully in the frame of the doorway. Every line of her lazy abandon told him what she expected. If he refused to budge—as he must—she was quite capable of crossing the room to claim him. He spoke quickly, to cover that conviction.

"I came to say good-by to you both, Lucy. Will you—convey my parting wishes?"

Lucy stretched her long, slender legs. "Don't talk nonsense. You came to make love to me."

Her directness staggered him a little, as always—even as he strove to press his advantage. "Surely you remember I'm married by now?"

"I've been married for over two years," said Lucy. "Have you ever remembered it?"

"You married for money, I believe?"

"And you for love? Do you expect me to accept that?"

"You may accept what you choose. I've still come to say good-by."

"Then say it properly."

She was on her feet with the words, moving toward him with lazy certainty. "Naturally I can't ask you to delay your sailing. Especially when your bride is so lovely. I merely want to be sure —that this isn't the end—for either of us."

She spaced the words carefully, and her voice was not even a whisper now.

Despite his resolution, he found he had taken a step within the room. At the moment he seemed to stand behind his own brain, watching another Julian take over there. A Julian whose reactions, from this point on, were all too predictable. Given a free hand, that other Julian would have crossed the two yards of carpet long since. Already he was straining at the leash.

"Be human," said Lucy. "You can't help yourself—nor can I."

The robe she was wearing—he knew all too well how frail was its connection with the vibrant flesh beneath—had already begun its slow journey to the floor. An Ixion on his wheel, he watched it fall, and felt himself turning toward her, like steel to its magnet. A bare shoulder shrugged, flicking the swelling breasts into full view. They were proud young victories still, throbbing even now with a shameless anticipation.

Remembering, he felt the two Julians fuse in a single purpose. He watched his hands rip Lucy's negligee—from shoulder to thigh, from thigh to knee. She moved into the circle of his arms before he could fling the shards of silk aside. When he lifted her at last and carried her toward her nest of pillows, he felt the hard hammer blows of her heart and knew they matched his own in eagerness.

It was only then that he heard the footfall outside the door, and turned to face Victor Sprague, with Sprague's naked wife held like a shield between them.

The grotesque pantomime seemed even more fantastic when he saw that the ex-senator sagged rather than walked—that he was groping for the doorjamb with one trembling hand even as the fist that held the revolver wavered upward. The man's face glowed like a yellow moon. In the gloom of the hallway it seemed to diffuse a sickly light of its own. Julian felt Lucy go limp in his arms and guessed that she had fainted. He flung her across the wicker divan—out of Sprague's line of fire—and faced the muzzle of the ungainly Colt alone.

"Nymph and satyr," said Sprague. "A pleasant tableau, Doctor. Am I too late to savor it fully—or too soon?"

The voice was weak and drained of color despite the surface venom; only the will to murder remained. Sprague ventured a step within the room, thought better of the effort, and steadied himself against the doorway. "Too bad of me—isn't it? Deceiving my wife—playing the eavesdropper——"

Julian tried to speak, but his voice died in his throat. This was Victor Sprague's moment: he had no right to spoil it. But even as he waited for the crash of the gun, he could not help counting his chances. A quick move to the left would take him into the ambush of an overstuffed armchair; even at point-blank range, the wadding might deaden the punch of a bullet. . . . He took a tentative step in that direction, watching Sprague pivot shakily. The muzzle of the revolver was weaving in earnest, but Sprague was too close to miss, whenever he chose to fire.

For a long moment he stood immobile, while his enemy's sick eyes murdered him in advance. Then his nerves cracked and he flung himself behind the chair, even as he lifted it from the floor.

Sprague pulled the trigger long before he could complete his plunge for cover, but there was only a sharp click in place of the expected report. Julian teetered on his knees. The chair wavered shoulder-high, until his muscles gave under the strain. There was a double crash as the chair turned a heavy somersault on the carpet and Sprague himself crumpled in the doorway.

He heard Lucy cry out behind him and knew she had not fainted after all. His foot snarled in the revolver as he leaped forward, and he kicked it aside to kneel beside Sprague. The man's face was ashen now; his lips worked, as though he were trying to speak, but not even an anguished breath escaped them. Instead a red trickle stained the shirt front beneath as the head lolled forward.

Julian's fingers were already on the pulse, though he knew that there would be no pulse now. The hoarse rattle in Sprague's throat could mean but one thing—the relaxation of the laryngeal muscles that comes with death.

His mind raced as he lifted an eyelid and peered at the conjunctiva. The deep tinge of jaundice was unmistakable: it went with the yellow skin tone that he had already observed. Was there a further connection with a collapse obviously caused by cardiac spasm? His hands worked by instinct as they took out Sprague's handkerchief and wiped away the show of red at the lips. This was no edema that went sometimes with a sudden failure of the heart. Rather, it was pure blood, already congealing from contact with the air.

Julian rose with the picture complete. Yesterday Sprague had been bright-eyed with fever; today there was definite jaundice and sign of an internal hemorrhage. Only one thing gave the picture of fever, jaundice—and a hemorrhage that could kill in seconds.

"The *coup de barre*," he said slowly to the silent room. "Yellow jack."

Then he remembered Lucy and turned sharply toward her just as she rose from the divan. He stood a little aside while she knelt beside her husband. He watched her as she rose calmly and went to the decanter stand against the far wall—naked still, and unconscious of her nakedness.

"I need a brandy, Julian. So do you."

His voice broke in earnest then. "Can't you understand that he's dead?"

"I understand perfectly. Drink this, and you'll understand *me* too."

He took the glass she offered him with such a steady hand and drained it. Something in his eyes must have reached her then, for she stepped coolly into the hall and returned with her torn negligee wrapped sketchily about her.

"You're sure it's yellow fever?"

"I'm positive. Do you see what that means, at least?"

"Perfectly, Julian." Lucy sat down on the arm of the divan and balanced her glass on a bare knee. "My mother died of it when I was only nine." Her glance strayed incuriously to the body on the carpet. "I warned Victor some time ago that he had contracted the disease, but he wouldn't listen. Especially when Steed insisted it was only a touch of sun——"

Julian's voice ripped through the matter-of-fact recital. "What about yourself?"

"I always think of myself first," said Lucy. "I've had yellow fever and recovered—the year my mother died. As a doctor, you know that makes me immune."

She held out her empty glass, and he filled it wordlessly. "So you see, Julian, you were wasting your breath yesterday when you tried to frighten Victor. Yes, he told me all about it afterward— as a prelude to one of our best quarrels. When he stamped out to take the Key West boat, I half suspected he'd return to spy——"

"And you took this—this chance, regardless?"

Lucy was still quite calm. "I don't take chances. Look in the breech of that revolver; you'll see that there's no powder in the caps."

Julian picked up the gun and stared at it for a moment, if only to gain time. He could see the pattern of her life—and Sprague's— much too clearly. Undoubtedly her husband had suspected her for some time; he guessed that she had taken other lovers in this same room, with the same casual ardor.

He pictured Sprague, lurking in the empty house as the bell shrilled—an avenging demon who refused to admit, even then, that he was fatally ill. He saw the man fumble in his desk downstairs for the loaded gun. Burning with the twin fevers of hate and death, Sprague would hardly have paused to check the priming. It would never cross his mind that his wife would tamper with a revolver: he had bought Lucy for a plaything, without noticing that she possessed a brain, without suspecting that her will was quite as ruthless as his own.

It was a macabre picture, but he made himself face its implication. *Nymph and satyr.* Sprague had coupled them in that phrase —and it had the bitter ring of truth. No doubt it had also fitted the figure on the carpet: if there is a satyr in every man, it was Lucy's evil genius that brought it to rampant life. Sprague had erred only in striving to keep her for himself. Lucy (and Julian saw it now, with terrible clarity) could belong to no man for long.

He looked down one more time at the body. It was no good reminding himself that Sprague was already marked for death when he climbed the stairs. At the moment he could only wish that they had faced each other at twenty paces and shot out their quarrel, as convention demanded. . . . And yet there was a fearful rightness to Sprague's end, too.

Lucy's voice brought him back to the room and the grim problem it contained. "Must we send for a doctor?"

"Make yourself decent," he said brusquely. "You know what you have to do. Go to Steed. Tell him your husband dropped dead on the threshold of your boudoir——" He broke off abruptly. "Of course you'll be quarantined for a time—there's no help for that."

There was rough justice here as well, he thought. Steed could no longer hide the fact that there was yellow fever in Nassau when the news of Sprague's death reached Government House. Even the American consul would have to face the threat.

"You can go now," said Lucy. "I'm not afraid to be alone with Victor. I never was."

"You mean that?"

She stepped deliberately over the body, by way of answer, and into the hall. Julian hesitated, with the revolver still in his palm. Then he dropped it into a coat pocket and followed her. Going down the stair, he could not down a final question.

"Are you his only heir?"

"Of course. Why do you think I married him?"

He drew in his breath sharply; he had expected just such an answer, but it hurt nonetheless. On the last step he paused and watched her cross the lacquered dimness of the foyer. It hardly surprised him when she spread both arms wide, as if to embrace her new-found freedom. At the moment she was a pagan Lilith—

a temptress older than time, exulting in her greatest victory. He stared at her for a space before he turned his eyes away and told himself his emancipation was complete, now that he knew Lucy Sprague for what she was.

At the street door she laid a warm hand on his. "May I wish you luck, Julian?"

"I won't return the compliment."

"If you'll let me, I can really help you now. Help you in ways you never dreamed of——"

He felt his senses drown in her nearness one more time, and wondered if he could ever still that blind hunger after all. But the door had already opened under his hand, letting in the hot, sane breath of afternoon.

"Good-by, Lucy—and it's really good-by."

"Don't be too sure," she said. "And don't you think you should leave by the garden gate?"

He forced himself to look at her directly. "It would be safer—but hardly proper. One must observe the amenities in a house of death."

But his gesture was pointless after all: George Street was still drowsy with siesta when he faced it again. He would always remember how the hibiscus flamed in the yard across the way, the green, metallic whisper of banana leaves above a pink coral wall. For all its sleepy detachment, he felt that Nassau was watching him from a thousand eyes.

He walked away from Lucy's doorstep without looking back, just as a clock boomed somewhere in the town. It had been a long time since he had heard that clock strike three—an eon since he remembered that Jane was waiting for him, just around the corner on Bay Street.

Julian quickened his step. Beyond the spent heat of the town, the breath from the sea felt clean and bracing. He knew now that Jane had been right to send him back to Lucy, despite the ghastly outcome of that meeting. Just in time he had turned his back on the past. Out there beyond the harbor's mouth his future was waiting..

ST. AUGUSTINE

ACES over kings. Julian picked up the card Whit had just dealt him and saw that he had filled. Judging by the pot on the scarred forecastle table, the betting would continue to be heavy after the draw—too heavy, in fact, to make a full house more than an aggravation.

He kept his poker face intact as Captain Nichols made the first wager: the skipper of the *Sewanee*, hunched above his cards like a contented colossus, flashed a brilliant smile around the table and pushed a stack of blue chips forward. Mr. Rembert, the Savannah cotton broker, saw the bet instantly and raised—but Mr. Rembert did not smile. The gentleman from Georgia (who resembled a steel-bright pen behind one of his own clerk's ears) had smiled but seldom on this voyage from Nassau. . . . Whit was unsmiling, too, as he saw all bets and pushed his entire winnings into the overflowing pot.

"Table stakes, and no hard feelings. Are you with us, Julian?"

Julian tossed his hand into the discard and rose with a prodigious yawn. He guessed that there were fours against him in both hands; that Whit (who was surely seated behind a straight flush) would win the final pot of the night—though the gray chink at the door told him it was night no longer as he stepped from forecastle to deck.

It was good to breathe the sea-washed air, good to pause at the hatch amidships and hear a businesslike vibration from the engine room. The *Sewanee* was ready for sea again, even if she could not crowd on a full head of steam after her last bout of dirty weather.

The runner had stayed snug in this anchorage since yesterday's dawn, while the crew had swarmed along the water line to make doubly sure that their long job of caulking had left the hull bone-dry. Nichols had planned to take cover here from the first; he had also planned to make this part of their run by daylight, fetch Matanzas Inlet in the dusk, and pass St. Augustine by dark—their last major hazard south of the St. Johns. No one among the captain's four passengers—save Mr. Rembert—had complained too much at the day's delay. Mr. Rembert, as Julian gathered, had already made a fortune in cotton this past year—and banked it in London, like a practical businessman. Time was precious to a Georgia speculator whose reason for being might even now be rotting in a Savannah warehouse.

Even from her own deck the *Sewanee* seemed one with the tall marsh grass that hemmed in her mooring. To the east the ghosts of dunes on the sandspit shielded her neatly from the ocean side; to the west the flat, sick-green marshland was obviously empty of hostile eyes. Florida lay deep in stillness as the day brightened; across the stippled water mirror of the anchorage a school of mullet flashed golden in the first hot thrust of sun from the Atlantic. In that instant the tidal marsh changed from pale green to gold; the dunes, knife-edged silhouettes against the flamingo-bright dawn, gleamed in the fast-mounting tide of light.

It was a commonplace miracle after all: Julian had watched several of these flaming dawns as the *Sewanee* played her hole-in-corner game along the coast. Sleeping by day (when the hot winter sun beat down on their anchorage), crowding his luck by night in the endless poker games (while the runner bounced in the offshore swell), he had begun to take their topsy-turvy life for granted. It still seemed incredible that these prodigal sunrises could be real—or that any shore could be as lonely as these gull-haunted beaches.

So far they could thank Captain Nichols (known impartially now, to both passengers and crew, as Don Amadeo) for these lonely vistas. Captain Nichols had sailed his course by memory since their daring push across the Bahama Passage. Choosing the inshore route as the safest—since most of the Yankee gunboats were hunting in the Gulf Stream itself—their skipper had preferred to make haste slowly and take his chances with sand bars after dark.

Julian had been disposed to doubt Don Amadeo at first, for

their oversized captain had been content to manage his ship from an armchair nailed down amidships. But Captain Amadeo's mind moved faster than his ponderous body; though he could talk by the hour with Jane as they ran through the moonless nights, he was aware of every order whispered down the deck, of every vibration from his overworked boilers. He might seem to doze under his sunshade by day, but Julian knew that this Minorcan from St. Augustine slept no more soundly than a cat. Even when his lazy lids drooped shut, he scanned the sea beyond their anchorage with a sixth sense all his own.

Now and again a smudge of black vapor had shown along the horizon, to remind them that the Yankee hunters were not too far away. For the most part the sea offshore was empty as the day the Spaniards came. It was empty and inviting now, as Julian walked forward to watch the day grow beyond their tidal estuary.

A black stoker, stripped to a pair of greasy pantaloons, heaved up like Cerberus from the forward hatch to whisper at the forecastle door. (The crew had the habit of whispering, even when there was no need.) Don Amadeo, with his poker hand still hugged to his chest, put out his head and nodded. The *Sewanee*, shaking like a fevered witch, had already begun to nose her way through the marsh-grass ambush; the wild trembling steadied as her screw bit into deep water, though the boilers were pounding in earnest now. A linesman, straddling the bowsprit, began to chant soundings as they wallowed in the first blue roller beyond the tidal reach. . . . Any other skipper, thought Julian, would come on deck to con his ship to deep water. Don Amadeo—whose crew obeyed without visible orders—could afford to linger in the smoke-fouled forecastle and lose yet another hand to Whit Cameron.

It was a strange way to handle a ship, yet it seemed to fit the moment. It went perfectly with the *Sewanee's* cluttered decks (the brace of cannon lashed down under tarpaulins, the sheet iron doubling as carpet in the chartroom), with the crates of shoes that all but blocked the companionways, with the sacks of bacon that lumped every mattress in the forecastle itself. Even the tiny cabin where Jane was sleeping now was padded with goods. A dozen bales of raw silk. An express package of gowns that bore a label famous on two continents—and was consigned direct to an equally famous name in Savannah.

He chose a shady corner of the deck, where a space between two crates offered an unobstructed view. He had slept here before, through more than one hot noon, while they lay at anchor; he could do worse than settle now (while the *Sewanee* thrust into the open sea) and think awhile of Jane and the strange peace she had brought him.

ii

Tonight he had been more than a little shocked when she asked permission to join the poker game. It had shocked him even more when she rose from the table and retired to her cabin one hundred dollars the winner. Like everyone else aboard, Jane had fallen into the habit of sleeping by day. Now he felt an odd comfort in resting here, a few yards from her cabin door—a watchdog who asked little of life. Like a good watchdog, he would doze later, knowing that he would waken to her step when she crossed the threshold.

The sense of high adventure, of hide-and-seek with death, had failed to materialize so far: for that he could thank Don Amadeo's seamanship. His sense of shame (when he remembered Lucy and what had once been Lucy's husband) had lessened, too, with each sea mile: for that he could thank Jane and her acceptance of the story he had offered her. Even though he had not quite dared to tell her everything, when he hurried aboard in Nassau. There had hardly been time for a word as they ghosted down the crowded harbor.

"I'm glad you sent me there," he whispered. "We said good-by."
"Permanently?"
"Permanently. Lucy doesn't know it yet, but——"

Whit had come up then, to join them at the rail: they had stood in silence while the *Sewanee* made her turn at the squat white lighthouse on Hog Island. On the port bow Windward Point had begun to wink its own windows in the growing dusk. Julian shook his fist at Steed's hospital, as a kind of parting emphasis. It would have been worth lingering to see the Englishman's face when he found that he had lost a really valuable patient.

But the anger he had wasted on Steed seemed all but childish as Nassau dropped away in the night. So, for that matter, was the anxiety he had felt for Lucy's welfare. He could trust her to handle the business of widowhood admirably; his own part in creating that same widowhood had already begun to seem a bit less shameful.

Twelve hours later (as the *Sewanee* eased into her first hideout, a nest of mangrove cays within easy running distance of the Passage) he had told Jane enough of it to ease the weight on his conscience. How Victor Sprague had died—if not precisely why.

"Will you be blamed?"

"He was dead when he walked up those stairs. As a doctor, I can say that much truthfully." Julian looked away. "I've no right to tell you this, of course. It's just that I—*had* to tell someone."

"Isn't that what a wife is for?" She offered him a smile that forgave him in advance. "After all, I sent you there. Somehow I never expected you to meet an avenging husband: I thought your ladylove was shrewder."

"She isn't my ladylove now. Will you believe that much?"

Her eyes had sobered then; she studied him carefully before she answered. "I believe you. From what you say, it was an expensive lesson—and worth the cost."

"I can even feel sorry for Sprague."

"Don't," said Jane quickly. "Some men *are* pure evil, you know —even if the rest of us won't admit it. Nearly always they outlive the best of us. Why shouldn't we rejoice if one dies in his prime?"

It was precisely what he hoped she would say; he protested only for the sake of form. "D'you call that a Christian attitude?"

"It's profoundly unchristian; I know we must love our enemies if the world is to move. But I still say the world's a better place with Victor Sprague out of it. . . . Every cent he ever made was used to keep hate alive—to put men at each other's throats." Once again he noticed the deep bitterness in her tone; her eyes were blazing as she faced him again. "Of course *she'll* misuse his millions: women like Lucy always *do*."

"I'd no idea you were so well informed on Sprague."

"Does that shock you too? Would you be happier if I'd merely wept at your escape?"

From that moment they had abandoned the subject, by tacit consent. Lucy had merely ceased to exist as a barrier between them. Lucy (and this was the greatest miracle) had even ceased to haunt his dreams. His sleep had been dreamless since they left the Bahamas. It was enough that Jane was beside him—that **his** acceptance, as a comrade in danger, was now complete.

He had not told Jane that he loved her: there was still time to put that fact in words—if, and when, it seemed likely that she would hear him out. For the present he was content that she had accepted him as an equal.

Once again he smiled at his strange tranquillity. Another day (or two, at the most) would shatter it. Time was still a dream, and this blue morning endless. It was enough to know that she slept quietly in her tiny cabin. Enough to keep its door in view as his own lids fell in slumber. . . .

He knew it was not the rain that had wakened him; he had slept through rain squalls before on the open deck, as the *Sewanee* lay at anchor. Then the strange sound repeated, insistent as a dull, submerged thunderclap, and he sat bolt upright, uneasy because he could identify neither the disturbance nor the direction from which it came.

The runner was moving at top speed in a sea smooth as dark oil; the skirts of the rain cloud had already lifted ahead to let in a sweep of sun-drenched Atlantic. He sensed that much, even as he realized that he had slept like a log through the better part of the day; so, it seemed, had Jane, for the door of her cabin was still closed tightly.

Amidships, Don Amadeo slumped in his armchair with his watch open in his hand and his eyes on the horizon ahead. He seemed no more alarmed than the helmsman leaning easily on the wheel above him, or the two lookouts conning the rain scud astern. The sea was still black as night to the south; the orange flare, and the rumbling report that followed, seemed to split the murk like a fiery fist a few seconds after the round shot made its own futile geyser a safe hundred yards astern.

"Observe, Dr. Chisholm," said the skipper, without turning from his torpid vigil. "At this moment he marks his range. When we are in open sunlight he will give chase in earnest."

"How long has he followed us?"

"For perhaps three hours. The rain was a godsend. I prayed it would last forever. Now I pray for a brilliant sunset to blind him."

"Why didn't you waken me?"

"I have few rules in life, Doctor," said Don Amadeo. "One of them is never to disturb a bridegroom's slumber—even when he rests on his lady's threshold. The two other gentlemen still snore in their bunks. We must expect such annoyances in our trade."

Julian stared at the amorphous horizon astern. Their pursuer was no more real, so far, than that orange flare; now that he had watched it rise and die, the small waterspout in their wake did not seem too terrifying. . . . Curiously enough, it was the Yankee's standard that appeared in the murk before the Yankee himself. Thirty-odd stars of union, wet but vibrant on a mizzen spar. Julian stared at it thoughtfully before his eyes moved up to their own flag. The Stars and Bars, on their blood-red field, seemed garish in the clearing sunlight. He wondered why he had never noticed them before, and realized that Don Amadeo had neglected to advertise his allegiance, in any way, until this moment of crisis arrived.

"Should I warn Mrs. Chisholm to go below?"

"Let the lady sleep, Doctor. She's safer in her cabin. Don't forget we've munitions under hatches." The skipper did not even look up from his watch. "If we're hit, everyone topside has a chance to burst free."

"Can't you crowd on more steam?"

"Not without shipping more bilge. Don't be alarmed: my nose will tell me to come about any minute now."

Julian went irritably to the taffrail. The Yankee gunboat was a disturbingly solid mass now, against the southern horizon. He snatched up the captain's glass and studied the position of the swivel gun in her bows. It looked as competent as the vessel beneath it. So did the half-naked gunner who was sighting lovingly down the barrel at the moment, with one eye cocked toward the officer at his side. . . . Julian let his eye run along the water line and saw, to his relief, that the gun ports were still closed. Evidently their pursuer hoped to frighten the *Sewanee* into submission with a well-placed shot and had no thought of wasting more powder at the moment.

Remembering Don Amadeo's reliance on his sense of smell, Julian turned the telescope on the land. Florida lay like a black smudge against the westering sun, a good league away; there was no visible break in the surf along the endless brown-white strand, no hint of a tidal estuary where the heavier side-wheeler behind them would not dare to follow.

"Don't tell me you can smell an anchorage three miles away?"

"I refer to the fresh-water spring that bubbles up offshore near the Matanzas Inlet. Here in Florida we call it sulphur water: to a stranger's nose it smells like rotten eggs."

Julian turned sharply. Matanzas Inlet, as he knew from poring over the *Sewanee's* charts, was the tidal estuary that opened to St. Augustine Harbor from the south, behind the seaward-facing bulk of Anastasia Island. With Union troops in St. Augustine, it did not seem a likely haven.

"Won't that approach be guarded?"

"There is an old Spanish redoubt within the mouth of the inlet. The Yankees have posted a force there. But there are safe anchorages above and below the fort, well screened by dunes——"

Something wailed by overhead, not too close; there was a dull boom behind them as the round shot plunged, well off their starboard bow. "He plans to lay the next in my lap," said Don Amadeo. "As you see, he has us boxed in his sights. Breathe deep, and pray that we can put the sun in his eyes before he loads again."

Julian sucked air into his lungs and stared hard at the skipper. The sea ahead—peacock blue, now that they had cleared the last skirts of the rain squall—was bubbling with a milky exudate: the stench that Don Amadeo had mentioned was unmistakable, a hydrogen-sulphide gas that welled up from most artesian springs along this coast. This one, he gathered, mushroomed into the Atlantic from the sea's floor; the *Sewanee* bounced all along her keelson as she ran over it. Julian had just time to lean over the rail and watch the vast milk-white mushroom roil up from the blue depths below.

"I have charted a course by that stink, even at night," said Don Amadeo. He glanced up at his helmsman and nodded just once; the *Sewanee* had already heeled sharply, to head straight for the blinding sun that hung just above the coast. Once again Julian tried to sweep the beaches, and found that his eyes were dancing with spots as he lowered the glass.

"In the crow's-nest, with the sun behind you, the estuary would be visible to the naked eye," said Don Amadeo. "As things are, we hold our nose due west to fetch the sand bar. Watch the Yankee, Doctor. He is stubborn enough to try again."

Julian swung the glass toward their pursuer. The gunner on the foredeck was clear-etched as a statue now; even the thin wreath of smoke seemed painted against the backdrop of sky. This time the shot roared into the sea a good hundred yards to port: precise marksmanship was impossible, now that the *Sewanee* had become a silhouette etched in blinding motes.

"Will they try a broadside?"

"Undoubtedly."

The skipper glanced at the gunboat astern. "Unless she's changed her paint, that would be the *Susquehanna*. Captain Prescott. I've matched him for drinks in Cuba—and outrun him from here to Albemarle. A thoroughly pleasant Yankee, Doctor—but he was born stubborn. He knows he can never follow me across the sand bar at the Matanzas; and he knows I'm not afraid of round shot."

Julian's glance strayed to the closed cabin door. It seemed incredible that Jane could be sleeping through their first cannonading. Perhaps, with a closed door to muffle those distant reports, he would have done the same.

"Surely I'd best waken Mrs. Chisholm now."

"As you wish, Doctor. Believe me, she is safer behind that bulkhead. It would please me better to tell her of this—when it is over." Don Amadeo spoke a low-voiced command to the helmsman. The runner promptly broke her course, cutting a zigzag wake across the gunboat's threat.

"You'll put to sea again when it's dark?"

"*Exactamente*," said Don Amadeo. "Providing Prescott's gunners miss me now."

Despite her game of touch-tag, the *Sewanee* was now well inshore; a sand bar foamed with white water not too far from their starboard bow, and a puff of gulls' wings marked the sunset as the birds rose in fright at the throb of the engines. The *Sewanee's* captain watched their pursuer narrowly. When he saw that the gunboat was gaining slowly—and that the swivel gun was now deserted—he nodded again to his helmsman, who pointed their bows true and ran like an arrow for the land.

"If I had time," said Don Amadeo, "I'd tease him into running aground." He looked at his watch and snapped the case shut. "But he knows as well as I that there is not five minutes more of daylight. . . . Prepare to lie flat when I give the word, Doctor. We may expect a broadside at any moment."

Julian nodded absently. Though his heart was pounding in his throat, he felt curiously detached. Watching the first ground swell rise under their bows, hearing the wave crash on the beach that now seemed only a cable's toss ahead, he could not feel himself an active target. Even a landsman could see the course they would follow now—a narrow slough that opened in a green tongue of marsh grass, with a sheltering half-moon of dunes beyond. He had watched Don Amadeo play this hole-in-corner game before—with no more sea room. Despite their panting, soot-smudged pursuer, his confidence in Don Amadeo was unimpaired.

"You're sure they can't follow us?"

"We can wallow through, Doctor—the Yankee would stick fast. He has one choice only—to blow us out of the water."

The gunboat was far too close for comfort when Julian looked again. She had already spun on her ungainly heel, and danced broadside now to the *Sewanee's* flying stern. On each side of her paddle box the ports yawned wide; the fat snouts of her guns seemed trained by a single hand, though he could see a half dozen pairs of white-duck legs scurrying behind them. A long, glassy roller creamed ahead, and the *Sewanee* all but coasted down its length before the helmsman could steady her. At that moment the gunboat came about completely. Riding easily beyond the last ground swell, she lifted her guns with lazy assurance. The sun struck a blinding spark from the gold flanges of her bows. Julian read her name plainly under that ornamental scroll. . . .

"Now, Doctor, if you please," said Don Amadeo.

Sand screeched under the runner's keel as Julian pancaked on the deck beside the skipper. For a moment he felt sure they were aground, but the helmsman had judged his soundings with inches to spare. The *Sewanee* danced over the bar with the next push of the changing tide, trailing a white whorl of sand as her screw bit into the dead water beyond. Marsh grass parted magically in the slough, to show the snug depth of Don Amadeo's chosen anchorage. In that instant the sun vanished completely behind the skirts of the pine barrens to the west. The light changed with its vanishing, clamping a curtain of grayness on the coast, merging the runner's outlines with the grassy banks as she nosed for cover.

The crash of the *Susquehanna's* broadside and the banshee scream of the round shot smote his eardrums almost in unison. The runner trembled, like a thoroughbred under her first lash; there was a sound of rending wood along her port quarter before she heeled violently and all but grazed the bank of the narrowing slough. On either side the marsh grass flattened under that blanketing volley; another shot, aimed low, merely roiled the mud along the bank before it buried itself harmlessly in the bottom. Then silence clamped down on the marsh, broken only by the pant of the *Sewanee's* boilers. Astern a haze of smoke had swallowed the gunboat to her topsail spars.

Julian bounced to his feet ahead of the skipper as the *Sewanee* righted slowly. Even now, he saw, her decks were not quite level. Black ruin smudged her port gunwale like a giant's thumbprint; two of Don Amadeo's men had already gone overside with buckets to douse a thin trickle of flame beginning to creep up the runner's flanks. Underfoot the deck trembled unnaturally; it was only when he took an instinctive step toward Jane's cabin door that Julian realized their speed was halved. Canted as she was by that near miss, the *Sewanee's* screw was half out of water. Though she still had way enough to round the last corner of her anchorage (and vanish from her pursuer's sight in her nest of dunes), the runner was a cripple now.

His mind had no time to shape the thought as he wrenched open the cabin door. Jane was just groping her way out when he put his arm about her. Even in the confused release of the moment, he saw that she was more excited than afraid.

"Why didn't you call me, Julian? I'd have given the world to see it."

Clinging hard to her shoulders now, he scarcely heard. It was enough to marvel at the fact that she was unhurt. Another yard to the right, and that near miss would have made matchwood of the tiny cabin amidships. And yet, as Don Amadeo had reminded him, a direct hit would have ended all their troubles instantly. He heard Whit and the Georgia cotton broker fumble their way out of the slanting door of the forecastle and forced himself to take Jane's hand instead. He had only begun to understand his fear for her—now the danger was over.

iii

An hour later that fear was hardly lessened by Don Amadeo's almost beatific calm.

The *Sewanee's* skipper was throned in his chartroom, touching a map with an alert pen point. Whit and Rembert sat flanking him; Julian, who already knew the map by heart, stood in the doorway to watch night fasten in earnest on their narrow anchorage. Jane had left them long ago to pack. Jane, he reflected, was behaving much more rationally than he.

"Four hours of steady rowing will take you to safety, gentlemen," said Don Amadeo. "The tide is with you, as I have just explained. Once you have passed the mouth of the inlet, there is no risk whatever: that much I swear, on my grandmother's honor. What can you lose by trying?"

Whit's eyes had not left the map, which showed the grassy estuary in which they were now anchored, and the reach of the Matanzas, as far north as St. Augustine. He pointed a forefinger at the town.

"Don't tell me we can walk in here without being stopped."

"You can do just that, Mr. Cameron, if you follow my advice." Don Amadeo's pudgy finger joined Whit's on the map. "Here, as you see, is what remains of the city wall. Here is the Maria Sanchez Creek, a tidal arm of the Matanzas. It is not to be missed on a clear night. It will take you to a boat landing at the foot of Bridge Street. A hundred yards to the east—where Bridge and St. George streets join—is the house of my wife's people, the Menendez." The skipper's face relaxed in a still wider smile. "The aristocrats of my family. I, as you observe, am but a Minorcan upstart. Their blood goes back to the founder——"

"Never mind your family tree," said Whit. "How do we know they'll take us in?"

"I give you my word again, gentlemen. Be wise, and accept it. The doctor's wife will risk the journey. Why should you hesitate?"

"Why can't you spare us a man to each boat?" snapped Rembert. The gentleman from Georgia was pale in the chartroom lamp; his fox face looked even sharper in that uncertain light. "How do we know you aren't planning to make a run for it after all?"

"Observe my situation," said Don Amadeo patiently. "I am in a box tonight—with a watchdog at the open end. It is true that I hoped to run past him in the dark. Tomorrow I must limp out and surrender; if I linger, he will have me taken from the land side. You may stay and be taken too, Mr. Rembert. As a civilian, you will be released in time. So will I, when my prize money has been paid. . . . For a man of affairs like yourself, the wait will be long and costly. That is why I offer you a ship's boat and suggest that you row north to safety."

Rembert banged the chart with one fist. "I still say we should have kept to the Stream—taken our chances——"

"I do not apologize for my seamanship, gentlemen. Only for my luck. Even so, admit our luck could have been worse."

Julian shrugged as the skipper's eyes sought his. He had already agreed in principle to Don Amadeo's plan; he turned now to the deck and walked slowly forward, reluctant to hear Rembert go over the same craven objections.

It was a reasonable plan, with only a minimum of daring; he could even smile when he saw that the two ship's boats were already lowered, that the Georgian's portmanteau already lay against one thwart, cheek by jowl with Whit's London bandbox. Don Amadeo had taken their consent for granted, from the moment he had dropped anchor here.

He stood in the bow and stared across the anchorage at the wall of marsh grass to the north. Even in the faint starlight the curve of the slough was plain enough, as it opened a lane through that green maze. If he could take Don Amadeo's word, the rising tide would see them through easily, until they reached the open inlet, a scant half mile to the north. Here they must move warily: it was only prudent to assume that the Yankees had garrisoned the ancient Spanish bastion that overlooked the mouth of the Matanzas. But it would be easy to quarter across the current, hug the far bank, and slip up the inlet with the tide. From that point they need only coast—and wait for the ebb. As the tide fell, it would still be their ally, drawing them toward the northern opening of the estuary, which ended in St. Augustine Harbor.

So far the plan had the virtue of simplicity. Once they were safely in St. Augustine, it would be just as simple to establish their civilian status. The town had been in Union hands for some time now, but there had been no reports of violence on either side. If Don Amadeo's relatives accepted them, it should be easy to arrange for transport to St. Marys, the nearest point in Confederate hands.

Of course the Yankees might question the sudden appearance of four strangers in a community as small as St. Augustine: if martial law prevailed in the vicinity, travel might well be restricted. But these were problems that could be solved as they arose. Or so Julian reasoned as he stared across the black water mirror of their anchorage and waited for Jane to close her last box.

Her calm acceptance of Don Amadeo's offer had put him on his mettle from the start. He was still her husband—until they reached St. Marys. Here, at least, were two certainties: Jane was willing to risk a rowboat trip into the night, and Jane assumed he would be beside her.

Julian heard a light step on the deck behind him and turned eagerly. But it was Whit Cameron who joined him in the bows. For once the gambler looked almost subdued, despite the rakish boat cloak he was wearing, the fabulous Scotch cap that all but obscured his bony profile.

"I gather you're one of us?"

"So is Rembert," said Whit. "If he's still arguing, it's only for the sake of form."

He glanced unhappily at the two small boats, the Jacob's ladder shivering in the tide. "How long since *you've* rowed four hours?"

"The tide will be with us all the way. I'm enough of a sailor to know that."

"It's exercise, nonetheless," said Whit. "And I abhor exercise, especially after dark. However, I don't relish incarceration at Key West."

Once again he glanced at the wilderness of marsh grass beyond their bow. "It's a choice *you* might ponder, Julian. After all, Rembert and I can row Jane to St. Augustine."

"Are you suggesting I stay aboard?"

"And offer your services to the Surgeon General in Washington. Why not?"

"You made that suggestion before. Do you recall my reply?"

"Such nobility of purpose has less point tonight," said the gambler. "You've fulfilled your bargain with Jane: you've delivered her to the mainland as Mrs. Julian Chisholm. In all events, she'll be on her own at St. Marys. Why not say good-by tonight —on this deck?"

Julian turned away to hide his anger. He guessed that Whit was only prodding him lightly, for his own amusement; but the suggestion was no less distasteful. The fact that it was also quite sensible did not lessen his unhappiness. Hopelessly in love with a woman who did not even seem aware of it—clinging to any excuse that might keep them together—his was a less than heroic role. As Whit said, he had every right to resign that role tonight. To thrust Jane from his mind firmly, while there was time.

Why—when he could face that alternative so clearly—did he stand here in the dark and let his heart race with a contentment greater than he had ever known?

"Thank you, no," he said. "If you don't mind, I'll stay with my wife to the end. Even if she doesn't need me any more."

"And offer your scalpel to the Confederacy?"

"Like a born romantic." Julian found he was smiling again. "Remember, it's a cross each Chisholm must bear."

"So be it," said Whit. "Try to bear yours with *élan*."

He skipped lightly down the Jacob's ladder and spread his boat cloak on a thwart. Julian leaned on the *Sewanee's* rail and watched the phosphorus wink in the dark water when Whit feathered his oar. Don Amadeo, he gathered, had reserved the other skiff for the bridal pair: a man of Don Amadeo's prescience could do no less.

Tonight, he thought swiftly, we'll be alone as we've never been. Tonight we'll borrow time from the moment when we must say good-by at St. Marys. Reveling in that prospect, he knew why he had accepted this dismal ending of their voyage so joyfully.

It seemed quite logical that the skipper should come down the deck with Jane on his arm. That his men should whisk ahead to pass hatboxes down to the empty skiff and stow his own portmanteau and instrument case among them. No one stirred for a moment as Rembert stalked out of the chartroom and dropped into the forward skiff, without seeming to notice the skipper's proffered hand. The Georgian's rudeness was a minor annoyance. Julian had eyes only for his bride.

She was wearing a dark carriage suit tonight, with a wide pelisse and a small halo bonnet. He noted these details automatically, even as he wondered at the formality of the huge belled skirt that seemed to slow her progress to a queenly walk. It was hardly a costume he would have chosen for a rowboat, but there was no time to question it.

"Thank you, my dear," said Jane. "I'm sure I can climb down alone. If you'll just go first to steady the skiff——"

He was in the rowboat instantly, his legs braced wide. Jane hesitated as Don Amadeo offered her his most florid bow Then, with a sailor at either elbow, she eased her hoops gingerly over the *Sewanee's* rail and set both feet on the Jacob's ladder. In the starlight he saw only a white froth of lace as the rope ladder sagged beneath her weight. Then, as one foot touched a thwart, he caught her beneath the arms. The skiff teetered dangerously as she groped her way to a seat; Julian steadied her with an oar in each lock and shoved off firmly from the runner's side. The skiff that held Rembert and Whit was already circling impatiently, betrayed only by the iridescent gleam of its wake.

"I'll take an oar, Julian," said his bride.

"Really, my dear——"

"But I insist. It'll steady the boat."

He agreed instantly as he took his first stroke. The skiff was spinning crazily, even in the dead water of the anchorage.

"Perhaps we should trim ship. What have you loaded into those boxes?"

"It isn't the boxes." Her voice was a whisper now, for his ears alone. "It's me."

"Will you repeat that?"

"When I've more time, Julian. Just give me an oar."

He passed a lock into her hands without another word. Don Amadeo's bulk still loomed against the stars. He saw that the skipper was shaking with laughter as their combined efforts steadied the skiff at last.

"I fear I cannot save what you have left aboard, Mrs. Chisholm."

"The ladies of Key West are welcome," said Jane.

"One thing more," said Don Amadeo. "Can you still hear me, Mr. Cameron?"

"Perfectly." Whit's voice sounded almost petulant in the gloom.

"If you are delayed for any reason, wait out the day on Fisher's Island."

"What could delay us?"

"Nothing, I hope. But it is well to remember. A low island, in the Matanzas, just where the harbor opens to Augustine. Marsh as you approach from the south, high dunes on the seaward side. There is a palm-thatch hut. Saltmakers lived there before the Yankees came."

"We've enough to remember now." Rembert's voice was thin with nerves—and no less precise, now that Rembert himself was all but invisible. "Let's start moving, for the love of God!" The Georgian remembered he was a gentleman just in time. "Your pardon, Mrs. Chisholm—I was carried away."

"Swear all you like, gentlemen, if it'll make the trip easier," said Jane. "I quite agree, it's time we were starting. Go with God, Don Amadeo."

"Go with God, Señora!"

Whit's skiff had already swung away. Julian leaned hard on his own oar, not at all surprised to note that Jane was rowing as easily as a man, despite the costume she was wearing. He glanced back just once before they nosed into the slough. Don Amadeo was still a massive silhouette against the stars—and still trembling with laughter.

iv

Whit spoke for them all as their gunwales grated. "Fort Matanzas, well on our left. The inlet on the right. Open water dead ahead. Is my eyesight good?"

"The tide's running strong," said Julian. "I think we can risk it."

"Suppose the Yankees have good eyesight too? Must we stop if we're challenged?"

"By no means. But one of us should lie flat until we fetch the far shore."

They fell silent on that, letting the words sum up the risk they must take. Fifty feet beyond, where the marsh ended, the Matanzas rippled darkly in the swell of the tide; to the east the inlet opened to the Atlantic, marked by the pale half-moons of sand bars that still boomed with surf, even at full tide. The Yankee gunboat rode at anchor not too far beyond: Julian could mark her slender masts easily against the clear night sky. The low bulk of Anastasia Island, which sheltered the Matanzas estuary from the sea, vanished into darkness to the north. With the tide behind them, they could reach its shore in short order. Once in that shadow, it would be simple to run past the old Spanish redoubt without being seen.

He studied the fort carefully. Squatting like a gray toad on a point of land to the west, it all but blended with the lifeless landscape around it. But it commanded the inlet and the sweep of estuary beyond; and a cold square of light at a doorway told him that the Yankees had garrisoned it. Running with the tide, they could cross the inlet's mouth in a matter of minutes and gain the safety of the estuary beyond. In that interval they ran the risk of being challenged, if a sentry was on duty.

"Do you think the *Susquehanna* sent in a boat?" asked Whit.

"It's more than likely. They'd want some explanation of that offshore firing."

If the Yankees knew of Don Amadeo's presence in the anchorage to the south, they would probably force him to put to sea tomorrow. Perhaps they were preparing to move down on the *Sewanee* now. . . . Julian considered that dire possibility and put out a hand to steady Jane. But she was leaning easily on her oar.

"We're a bit lower in the water than you, Whit," he said steadily enough. "Suppose we go first?"

"You'll do the rowing, of course."

"Of course."

Julian took both oarlocks. "Lie down, Jane—and, no matter what happens, don't be curious."

"I can row as well as you," she said.

"Lie down, please."

He saw her eyes flash in the dark as she obeyed, pillowing her head on her folded arms. Her hoops belled briefly upward before he forced them below the gunwale level. Her eyes, calm as ever, continued to watch him gravely.

"I'll back out and go with the tide," he said. "Follow me when you're ready, Whit. Just give me time to clear."

Rembert spoke hoarsely out of the dark. "Who's to row for us?"

"You pull a first-rate oar, sir," said Whit. "However, I'll be glad to toss you for the honor."

Julian shoved off for open water without waiting to hear more. For an instant the skiff, still badly trimmed, danced wildly in the full wash of the tide. He felt his heart jump as the bow spun toward the old coquina fort and the cold yellow eye of the doorway. Then the boat steadied, with the current behind it. Already they were in the inlet's mouth, a low, scudding silhouette against the stars; if their progress was gratifying, there was no denying their excellence as a moving target. He dug hard on the oars and waited for the shot that did not come. . . .

Jane's whisper reached him from the forward thwart. "Wouldn't it be safer if you stretched out beside me?"

"Much safer," he whispered back. "Unfortunately, I can't steer with my toes."

The shadow of Anastasia was only a hundred yards away now: a cluster of dunes, covered—on the land side—with a thick growth of yuccas. The boom of surf at the inlet's mouth was behind them, tapering into the night like a dying threat. Julian tugged on his port oar and prayed the tide had scoured a channel inshore; if only he could run close to the island, he would be invisible in another moment.

Someone shouted from the inchoate gray mass of the fort; he saw a shadow block the doorway briefly, before he heard the scrape of feet on the terreplein. He rowed with all his strength, careless of the splash. The skiff, turning its nose to the east, grazed a sand bar and bounced safely to deep water, with the tide still pushing it like a mighty hand. His heart gave a leap as he knew they were safe, with ten miles of open water ahead.

"Who goes there?"

The voice, with a fine New England twang in the consonants, bounced across the widening gap that separated them from the Spanish redoubt. It was only then that Julian realized the sentry had hailed Whit's skiff and not his own. Yet he pushed Jane firmly back beneath the forward thwart as she struggled to rise.

"Speak, or I fire!"

He had a nightmare glimpse of the other boat, bouncing in a tide rip. Of a thin silhouette against the stars, struggling to bring the bow into control. Even at that distance he guessed that Rembert was at the oars, not Whit.

"*Speak, or I fire!*"

A drowned splash was the answer to the sentry's shout. Julian never knew if Rembert crumpled before or after the rifle crack. Resting on his oars in the shadow of the land, he noted only that the gentleman from Georgia had pitched overside, to vanish instantly in the dark swirl of the tide. The skiff, relieved of his weight, skimmed over the last of the open water like a homing gull, bounced easily against the shore of Anastasia, and whirled past him, missing his own bow by inches. Whit, his composure unshaken, had already heaved up from the bottom to take the oars.

"Fortunately, I won the toss," he said. "Shall I lead the way— or would you prefer we separate?"

There were no more shots, no stir of life in the coquina mass behind them. Julian offered no protest as Jane struggled to a sitting position again and reached for an oar.

"Don't go back," said Whit. "There's nothing to go back for."

"Are you sure?"

"As sure as I'll ever be. He was hit between the eyes."

No one spoke again as they leaned on their oars in unison. Already Julian realized that there would be no pursuit from the fort. Mr. Rembert of Savannah, a man of few words, had died without a sound. He guessed that a Yankee officer was stumping the redoubt now, peering into the blackness with his glass and cursing a too-zealous private for wasting lead on a drifting palmetto.

Whit spoke from the dark as their gunwales touched in the shadow of the island. "Lucky for you he wasn't watching when you crossed over. You were rolling like a tub, and just about as slow. How is Jane bearing up?"

"Perfectly, thank you," said Jane. "And you'd roll, too, if you had a fortune in gold sewed into your hoops."

Whit chuckled softly. "I guessed as much when you left the *Sewanee*. Want to divide the burden?"

"Not unless Julian objects."

Julian cut in quickly. He knew that she was not deliberately callous in her acceptance of Rembert's demise. The fact that she could keep her voice level showed merely that she had recovered more quickly than he.

"We're riding easier now. I think we can manage."

"Ten miles of open water," said Whit. "Fisher's Island, and Maria Sanchez Creek. Sure you can find them in the dark?"

"We can hardly miss the island," said Jane, still quite unruffled. "On Don Amadeo's chart it's a wedge in the Matanzas, just before it widens into the harbor. Perhaps we should hide there, after all, and wait till morning——"

"Suit yourself on that," said Whit. "Now we've passed our hazard, I'm going in."

Julian spoke again, vaguely resentful that they should plan so calmly around his silence. "Why can't we go in together?"

"I'd vote against that as well," said Whit. "One skiff alone could pass for a fisherman coming in after hours. Two close together might remind the Yankees of an armada." He spun an oar in the fast-running tide, and Julian saw the flash of his grin in the dark. "Think where we'd be now if we'd run across that inlet together."

"Shall we shift to one boat?"

"Use your wits, Julian," said the gambler. "As your bride has rather more than hinted, I'm to go on first and make sure the coast is clear—while you prolong your honeymoon under the Florida stars. No gentleman can object to that."

He looked at Jane and saw that she, too, was smiling in the dark. He could only hope that the darkness masked a blush. Certainly his own cheeks were flaming.

"Thank you for understanding so quickly," said Jane.

He tried to make his own voice cold—and knew, in advance, that he had failed. "You prefer to wait on Fisher's Island, then—until Whit reports?"

"Don't you think it's wiser?" she asked, and picked up her oar before he could answer.

Ahead a faint glow of phosphorus was all that remained of Whit. Julian dug his own oar into darkness, retreating to the sanctuary of silence, and rejoicing that the rhythm of Jane's rowing did no more than match his own.

v

"Who are you, really?"

Now that his lips had framed the question, he knew that he had asked it a hundred times without words. He let it sink into the silence that had grown between them—into the cloudy dark that pressed down on the Matanzas, a gloom so absolute that he could not see even her face.

"Who are you, Jane? Why are you here with me?"

It was well past midnight now. He could guess that much from the weariness in his arms. They had rowed for hours, it seemed, here in the slack water of the ebb. Now the outgoing tide had begun to draw them slowly toward the northern end of the estuary and the port of St. Augustine. He could afford to rest for a moment on his oar—and guess, without turning, that Jane had done likewise. No girl, he told himself firmly, could have rowed this long without tiring. No girl could sit in silence forever and let such a challenge go unanswered. . . . And then he remembered that Jane was like no girl he had ever known.

"Shall I take the questions in order, Julian?"

Her whisper was firm in the dark, for all its deceptive softness. He whirled as she feathered her oar, lifted the lock quietly, and placed it in his hand. Backing the skiff to midstream, he leaned on both oars. They coasted smoothly toward St. Augustine, one with the threat of rain pressed down on the Matanzas. For the moment the silence of the wilderness almost matched their own.

"I'm waiting," he said at last.

"You've waited a long time, Julian. Should I thank you for your patience?"

"I'd prefer enlightenment to thanks."

"You ask me why I'm here—that's obvious. And who I am: I've told you that. The night we met in Glasgow."

"You still ask me to believe that story?"

"You've no other choice. It's quite true."

"So you're the widow of a Confederate major——"

"A widow with a legal ax to grind," Jane said slowly. She leaned across the thwart; even in the dark he knew that her eyes were seeking his. "A widow who needed a husband badly in Glasgow —and acquired one, on her terms. Aren't you willing to let the terms stand?"

"Is that all you care to tell me?"

"Accept that much," said Jane. "You can fill in the details. I'll correct you if you stumble."

Julian drew a deep breath. "Is this still a game to you?"

"Can you think of a better game, while we ride with the tide?"

He refused the dare. Instead he said, soberly enough, "Don't accuse me of prying, I'll admit it. But——" And then it was out at last. "Do we still say good-by when we reach St. Marys?"

"When and if," said Jane. "How do we know we'll even reach St. Augustine?"

He shrugged off the question. "Tell me this much: how can you sit there with a fortune in your hoops and laugh at me?"

"I'm not laughing."

"How can you row for hours without tiring? Yes, and see a man shot without collapsing?"

"I told you once that I wasn't a lady. Perhaps you'll believe me now."

As though that mattered, he thought savagely. As though anything mattered but the need to take you in my arms. Tell me your troubles, Jane. Let me share them. Tell me the fight you've come home to win, and we'll see it through together.

Aloud he said only, "By now you must realize I'm not just curious."

And she spoke in the same breath, as though she had not heard. "I'll tell you this much about me, Julian Chisholm. A lady in *your* book might row this far—if she'd worked on a mountain farm since she could walk. And she could watch a man die without fainting —if she'd seen her own father shot for poaching."

His heart gave a great leap at her unbending, but he kept his voice colorless. "Are you telling me you were once a—a poor white?"

"The night we met, you guessed I was mountain-born. I admit that much now. I'll also admit that I refused to be a peasant from the start." Her whisper was vibrant with feeling. "And don't tell me there aren't thousands of white peasants in America. Particularly in your romantic South——"

"It's yours too, Jane."

"It was, until I had the strength to run away from it. At sixteen, if you'd like another milestone in my career."

"When did Major Anderson overtake you?"

"At Oberlin College. Where I insisted on earning myself an education. Does that confession of independence shock you?"

"I'm still filling gaps," he said. "Of course, if you'll fill them yourself——"

"Haven't I explained myself now? I thought I was in love with him when I ran away from my mountain; I was sure of it when he followed me. He was out of the deep South—visiting at an estate in the valley——" She hesitated, then went on firmly. "The same estate where my father was killed for poaching. Kirby had ridden up the mountain to find me. Of course I refused him then, when he offered to marry me. I didn't refuse when he followed me into the North and found out my—my hiding place. I even believed him—when he said I'd been hiding from life and from myself."

Julian steadied the skiff in midstream and made no answer. Her whisper lashed him in the dark. "Say you believe every word. Say you don't blame me—or my story ends here and now."

"I believe you, Jane."

"His plantation empire was all he'd promised me, and more; he made me its first lady, in spite of his sisters and a few other dragons. I could have lived the dragons down if"—her voice broke, but she went on, firmly enough—"if there'd been hope for his way of life. Or for Kirby himself. But he'd burned himself out long before: only a handsome shell remained. I was too young to see behind the shell, until I'd married him. Too naïve to bear the sight of him when he'd drunk himself blind to forget the fact that he was nothing . . ."

Her voice trailed off in a muted sob. She was crying, there in the dark—and he did not move to comfort her. At the moment the fact that she had dared confide in him was too precious to be spoiled, even by a gesture of sympathy. What could he say to defend a pattern that had always seemed as inevitable as breathing?

"It was easier when I found that he'd stopped loving me," said Jane at last. "And easier yet to leave him when I found he had a quadroon mistress he loved more. I went North again. When he made no move to follow me, I thought that I was free of him and all he stood for. The war came then—and the news of his death. At first I was shocked when I heard he'd left me everything. I was abroad then, seeing what I could of the world while my money lasted. . . . I hadn't minded selling his jewels for that; when I thought it out, I saw no reason why I shouldn't claim his estates, too, since they were legally mine. Do you blame me for that?"

"Not at all," he said, and wondered why his voice rang so hollow in the dark.

"It's a man's world still," said Jane. "No woman can last out her time in it, if she insists on being sentimental—or naïve. As you know, when we met in Glasgow, I'd engaged a London agent and pressed my claims for the estate. Unfortunately, Kirby's sisters had already filed similar claims. I was in the position of an adventuress abroad, fighting for my rights through an international lawyer——"

"So you decided to fight for them at home."

"Precisely as I told you, in Glasgow. Do you believe me now?"

"Implicitly, Jane."

She was laughing a little now, though he guessed that her eyes were still wet. "They'd have moved heaven to keep me out if I'd come back as Kirby's widow. Believe that too: it's the reason we're in this boat together."

"Your servant, Mrs. Chisholm," he murmured. "And my apologies for doubting you."

"I accept your apology, Dr. Chisholm."

The skiff rocked as she moved her unwieldy hoops and leaned forward to press his hand. "Does it depress you too much—to learn that I'm like your Lucy after all?"

"You couldn't be——"

"Surely my scramble for power is no less shameless. And remember, she stayed with her husband to the end. I ran away."

"You're running away from me now," he said.

"We've never been closer, Julian."

"You've told me nothing that really matters. All this is the past. Apparently you're quite as determined as I to live your past down. Why can't we help each other with the future?"

"My future is my own battle. So is yours. I can't go to war with you. Nor can you join me in an Atlanta courtroom——"

"Thank you for that much geography," he murmured.

"Promise you won't follow me." Her voice was troubled now. His heart sang at her blunder, but he did not press his advantage.

"You say I'm lonely," he whispered. "You've called me a stranger in my own world. I'm beginning to see why you understand me so well."

"But I don't really."

"You've been lonely from the start," he insisted. "All women are when they insist on fighting their century."

Jane laughed aloud. "I knew you'd blame me most of all for that."

He refused to be sidetracked. "You hated your youth—I endured mine. You hated your husband—as much as I hated Lucy. Now you hate this war, but you're going back, nonetheless, to claim your rights. Men and women have shared loneliness before, for worse reasons. If you ask me, Jane, it's the real reason marriage was invented."

She did not answer for a long time. When she spoke, her voice had changed. There was no attempt at sparring now; he exulted wildly as he guessed her defenses were falling, one by one. "Are you proposing marriage, by any chance?"

"We're married now."

"What are you asking of me, Julian?"

"Let me be your husband. Let me help you. I'll promise to

stand aside until you've recovered your estates. Surely you'd have use for me later . . ."

He let his voice trail off against silence, and was all the more startled when she rose suddenly, nearly capsizing the skiff as she stepped across a thwart and settled in the curve of his arm.

"Just to prove I'm honored by your proposal," she said. "After all, it was I who suggested our first marriage. This makes us even."

"Do I gather I'm refused, nonetheless?"

Her hair was warm against his cheek now; despite the grotesque heaviness of her hoops, he could sense the pliant body beneath—and knew that her heart was beating in time with his own. So far it was a quiet, confident beat, with no hint of passion. For the moment he accepted her nearness gratefully, without asking more.

"Won't you even answer my question, Jane?"

Again she hesitated visibly. "Every word I've spoken tonight has been true," she said. "Don't make me hide in half-truths to refuse you. Just agree with me when I insist we can't stay married."

"You'll have to tell me why."

He felt her body go tense in the curve of his arm, but she did not draw away. "I might say that you'd ruin my—my inheritance, if you claimed me as your wife. That would be a half-truth: actually, as you've just said, you could stand aside until the estate is settled. I might say that a Chisholm would never marry a mountain girl—would you let that stop you?"

"That isn't even a half-truth," he said.

Jane let out her breath in a contented sigh. "I think you mean that, Julian. But I must still decline your proposal. Gratefully—and quite firmly."

"I'm still asking why."

"And this time I'm refusing to answer."

"Do you think I'm a fortune hunter?"

"I think you're sweet," said Jane, and raised her lips to his. His head spun as he accepted the offer. Like the kiss she had granted him in Nassau, this one was friendly, with no invitation to venture further. When it was over at last, she rested her head on his shoulder and nestled deeper in the curve of his arm.

"I'll say more," she murmured. "You're an experience I wouldn't care to miss."

No one, he reflected, had ever been so frank with him before.

No one but Lucy—and Lucy had never seemed more remote. But he let the contented silence lull him, without pressing the point he had won. True, Jane had just refused him with finality—but no woman's refusal is final. Especially when that woman is your legal bride, he added with an inward smile; especially when she offers you her lips unasked.

As Whit had said, this was their honeymoon, and the night was before them. He could wait while that magic implication unfolded, in its own rhythm.

vi

Their bow scraped in sand and he roused from a half-waking dream. Jane lay quietly in the curve of his arm, with her eyes on the clearing night sky. He guessed that she had dozed no more than he, in the last stage of their journey. Even before he could step overside and draw the skiff up the shelving beach, he knew that he had never been more vibrantly alive.

"Fisher's Island, Mrs. Chisholm. Will you come ashore?"

He lifted her in his arms, hoops and all, and found she was much too heavy to carry far. Her smile matched his as he set her down ruefully on the slope of the first dune.

"I can't walk in these, Julian."

"Wait here," he said. "I'll climb the dune and see where we are."

"Let's look at the map first. Make sure we *are* on Fisher's Island."

He stood back, with no particular surprise, while she drew a sheet of folded parchment from her bodice. This was no time to resent the fact that it was Jane, not he, who had thought to bring a map of St. Augustine Harbor.

"We'll have to risk a match," she said.

He struck a lucifer, cupping the flame in his palms as they bent their heads above the parchment map. Fisher's Island, he noted, lay at the southern end of the harbor, with the Matanzas estuary to the east. Anastasia—the large island that had stood between them and the open sea—now tapered into marsh against the pale immensity of the Atlantic. Directly opposite the beach on which they stood, the Matanzas opened to the sea itself. Even by starlight Julian could note the spout of surf on the inevitable sand bar, the dark line of deeper water that marked the channel. Standing where they were, on the island's eastern shore, they could see nothing but sea and sky—marked to the south by the line of scrub cedar where the marshy point of Anastasia rose to higher ground.

Their own small island, Julian gathered, was mostly marsh. Only where they stood did the ground merge with a nest of hump-backed dunes, thrust into the harbor's mouth like a wedge. He saw that he had been wise to beach the skiff: with the tide running at its peak, it would have taken hard rowing to hold their course without being swept into the open sea.

"Don Amadeo spoke of a palm-thatch hut——"

"Here," said Jane. Her finger touched the map just as the flame of the lucifer died. "Marked with a cross, like treasure."

He smiled at her above the last spurt of flame. "Someone was very thorough."

"Whit has a duplicate," she said calmly. "He'll have no trouble finding us tomorrow."

"Suppose the hut is occupied?"

"In that case, Whit promised to wait here and warn us."

Julian whistled softly; this time he was sure that he had not missed the twinkle in her eye. "Between you, it seems, you've thought of everything. What about breakfast tomorrow?"

"There's bacon and corn meal in my smaller bandbox," she said.

He turned without a word and brought their luggage up from the water line. Jane waited on the slope of the dune. "I could help, if you'd turn your head," she remarked as he put the last box at her feet.

"I beg your pardon?"

"Bring the skiff up beyond the tide mark," she said. "And don't look back while you're about it. I'm not prudish, Julian—but I do want to surprise you."

He obeyed her wordlessly and tried hard to ignore the steady urge to turn as he dragged the skiff from the shallows to dry sand. Her feet were noiseless. When he faced up the slope, in answer to her call, he thought at first that she had vanished. Her carriage suit, standing upright on its hoops, seemed all but animate in the starlight, as though the shell of its former occupant still had the power to mock him. Then he saw that she was seated on top of the dune, a slender silhouette against the night. Barefoot, with her

hair knotted in a handkerchief, she could have passed for a boy.
"Whit loaned me the shirt," she said. "The unmentionables are my own inspiration." She came down the side of the dune to join him, and patted the dress-dummy rigidity of her hoops as she passed. "Admit it's a better costume than this, for a night in the open."

But Julian was still staring. He had never seen a woman in trousers before. Much less a girl like Jane, who could take trousers in her stride.

"Where did you——"

She extended a leg for his inspection. "I had them made in London—for just such an emergency. Do you find them becoming, Dr. Chisholm?"

"I'll answer that by daylight," he said, still groping for his aplomb.

"Don Amadeo's hut is just over the dune," she said. "It looks both empty and livable. Shall we——"

He bowed (it was idiotic to bow to another pair of trousers, but habit dies hard) and picked up her bandboxes without another word.

"This time," said Jane, "I can really help."

She proved it by following him lightly up the slope of the dune, with a portmanteau balanced on her shoulder.

"What about your dress?" he asked, looking back. From a distance the grotesque garment seemed even more lifelike. An elderly relative, pouting at her abandonment.

"Leave Aunt Charity to her own devices," said Jane. "She's an upright lady—I know she'll be safe." A barefoot sprite against the stars, she paused for a second on the summit of the dune before she led the way into the hollow beyond. Julian followed her doggedly, and tried hard not to pant under his load as his booted feet slithered in the sand.

The palm-thatch hut, he saw, was precisely where the chart had indicated, in a nest of dunes not more than three hundred yards from high water. Stout palmetto posts lifted its floor a good six feet above the flat, sandy hollow; the palmetto thatch, sunfaded but unbroken, was woven tightly to make a three-sided wall, with a wide opening facing south. He struck another lucifer and peered cautiously inside: the floor was clean and bare, save for a small stone hearth at the enclosed end, with a ragged opening in the roof to let out the smoke. Judging by the stone foundations that surrounded the hut (most of them were sanded over now), the place had been a primitive saltworks not too long ago. Those broken brick stumps had once served to support kettles and drying pans.

It was only when he swung up to floor level that he noticed the note pinned to the cedar sapling that served as a support to the ridgepole. He struck another match and saw that it was in Whit's spidery scrawl:

I have explored carefully—the island is deserted. *Bonne nuit*, my friends, in your private Eden. With luck, I shall return tomorrow—to tell you how the land lies beyond.

Julian touched flame to the white square of paper. The dark was deeper within the hut, and faintly scented with the dry aroma of the palmetto thatch. He saw Jane's silhouette against the stars at the open end, and guessed that she had scrambled up promptly to watch him while he read.

"Why did you burn it?"

"Too many people are thinking for me tonight," he said.

She took a step toward him in the dark and put a hand on his arm. "Do you mind that much?"

"You've all but admitted that you *planned* to spend the night here from the first."

"Isn't it wiser, Julian?"

"I'm not so sure," he said.

"Are you afraid, Julian? I'm not. Please believe me."

"If it's not too much to ask," he said, "may I plan by myself for a change?"

"Would you have stopped here with me if I hadn't suggested it?"

"Never in this world. And don't ask me why. You know why."

"Tell me anyhow," she whispered, though there was no need to whisper now: as Whit's note had remarked, this was their private Eden. He never remembered taking her in his arms. Perhaps she had simply walked into them, and found him waiting. This time her kiss was a white flame in the dark, burning away the last of his doubts.

"Does that answer your question?" he asked.

"Aunt Charity will be getting lonesome," said Jane. "Besides, I think this hut needs a duenna."

Neither of them spoke again as they returned to the beach. The carriage dress awaited them on the seaward slope, looking no less grimly human. "She won't be shocked if you take her waist," said Jane. "I'll manage the hoops."

It was all they could do between them to carry their unwieldy burden. Again he did not trust himself to speak. The presence of the whaleboned garment between them was both repelling and soothing, as though Aunt Charity had an actual personality, capable of keeping them in bounds. . . . He made himself speak at last, when they had hoisted the dress to the floor of the hut and placed it, still primly upright, in a corner.

"How could you walk in that?"

"I'm not so frail as I look," said Jane. "When I sewed in that gold, I planned to stay inside. . . . It's distributed to be carried from *within*, not from without."

He leaned against the center pole of the hut while she moved quietly among their luggage. Apparently the task of transporting Aunt Charity had given her a measure of calm. Watching her spread their boat cloaks on the rough pine floor and produce blanket rolls from a bandbox, he found himself accepting this shelter as his home, without question.

"Shall we risk a fire, Julian?"

"If it's a small one."

There was driftwood among the broken stones outside, and scattered splinters of fat pine. He gathered three heaping armfuls, without letting himself think at all. Jane did not turn as he swung up beside her again. Working deftly in the dark, she had already arranged bacon and corn meal in a skillet and set a small coffeepot beside their impromptu hearth.

"Will you eat now or in the morning, Doctor?"

He built her fire without looking at her. "Why not do both—if our supplies hold out?"

"Suppose we're marooned?"

"With Whit as our advance guard, I'll chance that."

It was oddly soothing to sit back and watch her prepare their supper. Her hands were quick and sure above the dart of the flames: he guessed that she had prepared meals like these from childhood. A new Jane was emerging against that goblin fire dance—a girl who compelled attention in her own right, quite aside from the worldly trappings she had so casually discarded. There was something reassuring in the way she tossed back her hair as she offered him his plate; something deeply friendly in the smile she offered him as she took up her own and sat down across from him, hugging her knees.

"Say you've tasted better coffee, if you dare."

He found that he could manage a lightness he did not feel. "If this is a sample, I could stay here forever." Waiting quietly, just outside the circle of firelight, he watched the flames strike highlights in her hair as she bent to refill his cup. Whit Cameron will spoil this tomorrow, he thought—simply by rowing over from the mainland and telling us that we can go on to the Georgia line. Tonight it's all ours. Jane made it, out of a map, out of an impulse she'll explain in her own time. Let her enjoy it her way, he warned himself. If this is to be our prothalamion, let her sing it in her own costume, against this backdrop of firelight and stars.

Jane gathered the plates and tin coffee cups in a stack beside the hearth. "When I was a girl, we washed up at once. Will you think me a poor manager if I wait till morning?"

"This is your home, Mrs. Chisholm. Manage it by your own rules."

"It's *our* home for now, Julian. Is the prospect too unsettling?"

He made his voice light, with another effort. "It's wonderful to have a home again."

She kept her eyes on the fire. "Even if it's only for a night. Even if you're sitting in a Yankee prison tomorrow."

"Is our position quite that dramatic?"

"It could be."

"Surely we're safe, as civilians——"

"Not after tomorrow," said Jane. "It's quite likely that they know all about you in St. Augustine. Including the fact that you were aboard the *Sewanee* with your bride——"

He looked at her narrowly, wondering why she had escaped into this bizarre notion. But Jane was quite serious as she continued—a conspirator, now, who was thinking aloud, not too happily.

"You're a Chisholm, on your way to take a valuable commission in the Confederate Army. They'd stop you if they could." Her eyes dropped for the first time as she stared down at her hands. "Now do you agree it was wise to let Whit go in first?"

Something in her manner had built a wall between them—at the very moment when he had expected the last barrier to fall. He controlled his mood as best he could. "You're making me sound much too important, I'm afraid."

Jane rose abruptly and left the dying fire. When she spoke again, she was standing at the door of the hut, with her eyes on the stars. "You're important to me, Julian."

"Thank you again, but I still don't——"

"Has Whit ever suggested that you offer your services to the Union?"

"More than once." The question had unbalanced him completely. Apparently asked at random, he sensed that it was in deadly earnest. "He even suggested I'd come out of the war a general, instead of a bankrupt——"

"Tonight," said Jane, "I could almost wish you'd listened."

A moment before, he had known he could take her in his arms when he liked. Now she was only a shape against the sky, remote as a cloud. He let the astonishment of that discovery build in silence. When she spoke again, her voice was as distant as her manner.

"I planned our marriage in Glasgow; I planned this night on Fisher's Island. You've forgiven me that, I hope. Will you forgive me if I half planned to give you to the Yankees?"

"You'd better finish that before I answer."

"Whit would have arranged everything, if I'd asked him," said Jane. "A word to the commandant, telling him you'd come ashore——"

Something in her tone wiped out his anger instantly. "Do I gather you wanted to save me from myself?"

"They'd have interned you for a time," she said. "When you gave your parole, they'd have made you a contract surgeon. You said you wanted no part in this war. Why shouldn't you save lives on their side? Why shouldn't you be safe?"

He saw the pattern clearly now. Whit's offhand questions, as they stood at the clipper's bow and watched their first Yankee gunboat drop down the horizon. Whit's suggestion that he stay aboard the *Sewanee*, permit himself to be taken to Key West. Even now it was hard to believe that the gambler had spoken for

Jane. Harder still to face the fact that she had played with the idea of betraying him.

"Damn me all you like," she said. "It was a hard temptation to resist."

"I'm glad you think me worth preserving," he said at last.

"And don't despise me," she said. "As you see, I conquered the temptation quite firmly."

He found he could join in her laughter now. "Perhaps you're the born romantic, not I."

"Just because I tried to arrange your life for you?"

"How do I know you haven't? Perhaps this island is surrounded by the enemy now."

"Perhaps," she said. "It's still ours."

So we're back where we started, he thought. Husband and wife, enjoying a moment of belated honeymoon. "Ours till morning," he said, "thanks to your planning."

"Don't say I didn't plan well."

"I'm eternally grateful, Jane. Even if Whit marches over that dune in the morning with a squad of Yankee marines."

"If I know Whit, he'll come alone," she said. "What's more, our transport to Georgia will be waiting on the mainland."

"Barring accidents, I'm disposed to agree. Does it still mean we say good-by at St. Marys?"

She nodded slowly, her eyes troubled. "Would you have forgiven me if I'd had you detained here?"

"Never," he said. "Especially if you'd gone on alone."

"Stop me if I'm wrong," said Jane, "but are you in love with me?"

"Hopelessly."

"For how long?"

"How long have you known?" he countered.

"Since Nassau."

"Nassau will do for a beginning."

"It was the night I helped you outgrow Lucy," she said. "The night you made me lock that door between us."

"Admit I was wise," he said.

"And you want our marriage to last—is that it?"

"You know everything now," he said. "Perhaps you'll tell me what comes next, when I've lost you."

"You'll get over me," she said. "Just as you got over Lucy. Tell me truly, Julian: was loving me too big a price to pay for that?"

"Far too big a price—if it means losing you tomorrow."

"I'm still here," she said, and dropped her eyes at last.

"Does that mean you—love me a little?"

"If I didn't, would I plan to have you arrested? Or maroon you on this sand bar like a hussy?"

They were on their feet now, face to face. Any other woman, he thought swiftly, would have dropped her lashes on such a declaration. Jane met his look firmly, and the blaze of her eyes more than matched his own.

"So you're my wife for tonight?" he said. "May I hope for that much?"

"You may indeed," she said calmly.

"Do you think I'd have a wife I must lose tomorrow?"

"I think you would, Julian—if you couldn't help yourself." She took a deep-drawn breath. "I think *I'd* take a husband on those terms, if I could offer him no others."

Still he held his ground. "We made a bargain in Glasgow——"

"Now we're in Florida, I release you."

"Admit I kept it to the last."

"A Southern gentleman could do no less," she whispered. "Even when he learned his wife is no lady."

Once again he did not pause to ask himself how she came into his arms or who began their kiss. But it was all he needed to sweep his doubts away.

vii

He wakened once in the night and saw Aunt Charity, still prim in her corner, looming above them like virtue made visible. But he did not stir from his impromptu marriage bed. Deep in his arms, Jane sighed in sleep, and her breath was warm against his tranquil heart. He knew that a touch of his lips would end her slumber—that he needed only a whisper to mold her body to his again. This time he did not waken her: at the moment memory was more precious than the need for renewal. . . .

He wakened in earnest with a hot chink of sunlight teasing his drowsy eyelids and the aroma of coffee pungent in the air. The hut was empty: he sensed that much before he could lift himself on one elbow and blink resentfully at the morning. A new fire crackled on the stone hearth; Jane's hand was evident, too, in the neatly scrubbed plates that waited to receive their breakfast. Jane herself had vanished while he slept.

He was on his feet now, shouting her name and pausing with a dazed grin when he saw the note she had pinned to the doorway.

> Swimming before breakfast. Will you join me?

Swimming before breakfast. It was the last thing to expect of a wife on her first real wedding morning, but Jane had stopped surprising him long ago. He was out of the hut and halfway to the beach before he remembered that he was naked as Adam. He laughed aloud and ran up the side of the dune.

Her clothes lay in a heap just above high-water mark; he heard her call good morning before he saw her, casual as a Nereid in the lazy surf. Sprinting to join her, he felt that his heart would burst with happiness. Last night—even at the height of their ecstasy—he had feared the disillusion of wakening, the reality that comes with every dawn. This morning reality was clean and bracing as the sea into which he plunged.

Jane offered him salt-wet lips between two waves. They kissed for a long, blind moment, letting the second wave roll them in its trough before they broke apart. Only then did he realize that she was naked as he—and just as unconcerned.

"Why didn't you waken me? We could have done this together."

"You looked so peaceful, I hadn't the heart."

She swam with the easy grace of a boy, tossing her red mane against the next wave and fighting her way to still water beyond. He followed with his own heavier stroke. The sea, apple green in the ground swell and translucent as glass, gave back all of her to his eager eyes: the high, white breasts (foam-flecked, now, as one round shoulder dipped and rose), the fluent thighs tapering into the dimness as she trod water and laughed back at his staring.

"Well, Doctor, are you enjoying your honeymoon?"

He answered her question adequately, without uttering a syllable. She was panting in earnest as she broke free and swam hard toward shore. He followed at a discreet interval, dropping his toes to find bottom as she rose, waist-high, behind the crash of a wave.

"We must go in now, Julian. It's really morning—and you can see the town clearly beyond that sandspit."

"Let's hope they can't see us."

"I think we can breakfast in peace."

Breakfast, and Jane. He walked up the beach with her in utter contentment, refusing to let his mind explore beyond. It was only habit that made him pause beside the little heap of clothing just where the dry sand began.

"Aren't you afraid of catching cold?"

"In this sun? Or are you ashamed to have your wife pose as Eve?"

He stepped back wordlessly to let her go first, offering her the adoration of his eyes; and Jane accepted the invitation with her head high. To his dying day he knew he would remember the sunlight on her long slim legs as she breasted the dune. He ran up the slope to join her and put both arms around her waist, just as she recoiled with a little scream.

"What is it, sweet?"

"There's a snake in Eden—even before breakfast. Or should I say a man in our hut?"

He dropped to hands and knees just below the summit and peered through the screen of wire grass, while Jane scurried to the beach for her clothes. There was no doubt that the hut was occupied, though all he could see from that distance were the trousered shanks of the occupant, who had evidently seated himself just inside the door and let his legs dangle.

"Breathe easily, Jane," he said. "It's the Cameron tartan, and I gather he's come alone."

"Will you talk with him, or shall I?"

"I think you'd better dress," he said, and strode over the top of the dune without giving himself time to think.

The elegant broadcloth legs did not stir as he approached, though a hand emerged to flick the ash of a cheroot to the sand. Julian recognized the hand instantly and let out his tension in a long, easy breath.

"What do you represent?" asked Whit. "The dawn of time?"

"Never mind me. Explain yourself."

"Don't accuse me of indiscretion," said Whit. "Though I came early for the sake of prudence, I knocked before I entered. Once I saw Jane's note, I sat down like a model best man and waited.

". . . Shouldn't you be a model husband and dress for breakfast?"

The gambler was holding a tin cup in his free hand; he inhaled its aroma gratefully as Julian fumbled into his clothes. "Do you always scowl like that before your coffee? Let me pour you some now. If Jane wants to dress here too, we can walk down to my skiff while we talk." He drew deeply on the cheroot. "It's moored in marsh grass on the land side. A cove my friends in town defied me to find unaided. Perhaps I've a talent for smuggling, after all."

"Perhaps you've a talent for keeping me waiting, too. We'd be safe in St. Augustine now if——"

"If is a big word sometimes," said Whit. "As it turns out, it was an inspiration that I went in first. I do not merely refer to your honeymoon, Julian: I refer also to the friends I made."

Julian knotted his cravat with steady fingers. "Tell this your way, Whit. I've learned to be patient."

"Rest assured on one point," said Whit. "We leave tonight for Georgia. Wagon train to Picolata, on the St. Johns. Thence by water to St. Marys. Unfortunately there is just one condition. I have agreed to it, in your behalf." He took Julian's coat from his hand and tossed it across a portmanteau. "Don't bother with more clothes. You're to go back at once, disguised as a fisherman."

"And you?"

"Jane and I will wait here until dark and cross in your boat. Believe me, there's not the slightest risk. Not if you'll take off a man's arm in the meantime, and the man still lives."

Julian stared hard at the gambler. For once Whit's artful aura of mystery failed to stir him to impatience: he was still swimming in apple-green surf, with Jane beside him. Only the surface of his mind had grasped the fact that this island idyll was ended, as strangely as it had begun.

"So you've found me a patient in St. Augustine?"

"A rather important patient. Have you heard of John Jackson Dickison?"

Julian nodded. Dickison was a guerrilla leader who had harried the Union invaders from the beginning. Thanks to his raids, the Yankees had been unable to extend their coastal holdings, so far. Operating from a base in the interior of the peninsula, he had fought a dozen bloody engagements with their patrols and driven them back to base.

"Don't tell me he's a prisoner?"

"On the contrary. But we can hardly expect him to let our party pass until we save his lieutenant's life."

Whit pointed across the harbor. "A youngster named Broussard, with living fire at each nostril. Two of his men brought him in yesterday, with a smashed arm. They've been holed in at a house on Charlotte Street while Menendez looked for a surgeon he could trust."

"Apparently you *have* made friends in Florida," said Julian. "Of course it'd help if you'd identify them."

"Where's your memory, bridegroom?" Whit got up and stretched out a yawn. "Or do you wish I'd waited until evening to disturb you? Believe me, there wasn't time. That boy's arm won't keep."

Julian picked up his instrument case and vaulted down to the sand. "Then you'd better come to the point. Menendez, as I gather, is Don Amadeo's relative in St. Augustine. On St. George Street. Why did you tell him I'm a surgeon?"

"As it happens, your fame has preceded you. I had no choice but to offer your services."

Whit still sat comfortably in the shade of the palm thatch, dangling his legs. "Don Amadeo's map was accurate: I found my way up the creek and landed with ease. His brother-in-law's house was on St. George Street—precisely where it was supposed to be. Don Carlos himself was the soul of courtesy. . . . But he had promised to find young Broussard a surgeon, and he knew you were aboard the *Sewanee*——"

"When did the accident occur?"

"It wasn't exactly an accident: the guerrillas and a Yankee patrol shot it out near Palatka, and Broussard stopped a bullet. His men brought him straight to Menendez; Don Carlos sent him to the house of a friend——"

"Didn't the Yankees in St. Augustine object?"

"The Yankees in St. Augustine are using most of their brains to hold on. They control the town, of course: they're in no danger of attack by sea. But they need every man in the garrison, to watch Dickison. Or so Menendez tells me. . . . We'll have no trouble leaving town with a wagon train: smuggling still goes on openly. That's how they brought young Broussard in: it was the only chance to save him. They hoped to bribe a Yankee surgeon, but there are only two in barracks at the moment. One happens to be honest. The other is a butcher."

Julian stood in the hot morning sunlight and frowned up at his friend's aplomb. It was like Whit to take this tangled skein of war as a natural thing: to the gambler there was nothing odd in the fact that a man should lie desperately wounded in an enemy town and not dare to ask for aid.

"Show me where your boat is hidden," he said. "I'll go over at once."

He stalked toward the harbor side of the island without looking back. Whit would have time enough to explain his absence to Jane when she returned to the hut. As honeymoons go, this one had been short enough. It had also been worth the risk; it was even worth this sudden wrench of separation. Remembering her half-formed plan to surrender him to the Yankees, he all but laughed aloud. At least it was appropriate that he should begin his army career—a bit ahead of time—by operating on a secesh guerrilla under those same Yankees' guns.

Whit kept pace with him easily as they climbed a notch in the dunes that faced the harbor.

"There's one point to bear in mind, of course. This operation can hardly fail——"

"Any operation can fail. Especially if it's performed too late."

"I was only thinking of our welfare. Dickison will be furious if he loses his lieutenant; Don Carlos will be twice as furious if they cut short his smuggling career by way of punishment. He'll probably begin by turning you over to federal headquarters—as a doctor operating on the enemy without a license."

"I'll take that risk," said Julian shortly. "Where's your map?"

But he saw that no map was needed as he looked down on St. Augustine Harbor at last. The old town dozed in the morning, across a mile of open water: a cluster of sun-faded coquina walls and bright, heat-drowned gardens, with the mass of the Castillo dominant on the low skyline. The flag of Union floated above the highest sentry box, but there was no sign of a sentry at this hour: evidently the commandant considered the two squat gunboats protection enough, as they rode easily at anchor beside the sea wall. Save for a catboat or two, the harbor was empty of other craft. At the distance, St. Augustine seemed a toy town, forgotten in the sun—ready to vanish any moment in the encroaching green of the marshes, the sad, gray-brown wall of pine barrens to the west.

"Follow that point to the south, where the town ends," said Whit. "Maria Sanchez Creek begins just behind it. It's really only a tidal lane in the marsh, but it flows straight to the town's back door." He led the way to his skiff, which was neatly ambushed in a grass-choked slough. "There's a dock at the end of St. George Street. You can't miss the Menendez house after you tie up. Coquina, like the others, but there's a spray of flowers at the gate and the only real slate roof in the block——"

"Suppose I'm stopped?"

"You won't be, if you remember you're an honest mullet fisherman; once you're tied up, it won't matter. Don Carlos assures me that there isn't a Yankee lover in his neighborhood."

"How do I know your Don Carlos isn't setting a trap for us all?"

"You don't," Whit said cheerfully enough. "Just remember they can't do worse than intern you for a while. You aren't yet in uniform, and you're bound on an errand of mercy——"

Julian looked hard at the gambler, but Whit's manner was unruffled; if there was guile behind it, the gambler had concealed that guile magnificently. He tucked his instrument case under the stern sheets and sat down gingerly in the skiff; as Whit had said, it was a flat-bottomed mullet boat, complete with neatly folded nets and a pervasive stench.

"There's an old straw hat under the seat," said Whit. "Pull it over your ears and you'll do."

Julian drew the broad-brimmed hat over an eye and took up the oars. He had already rolled his sleeves above his elbows, and blessed the tan he had acquired aboard the *New Providence*. Even to Southern eyes he could pass for a native now. Whit stretched out in the shadow of the dune and cocked his cheroot at the sky.

"Any message for your bride?"

"Tell her I'll be back by noon."

"I wouldn't count on that. Don Carlos will insist you stay awhile with your patient."

Julian began a protest and thought better of the impulse. He had lost enough time now, with a wounded man waiting across the bay.

"Where do we meet?"

"At Don Carlos' house, not before sundown. Shall I take Jane your love?"

"Take it now," said Julian. "Before she has time to wonder." He dug an oar viciously in the marshy water, spinning the skiff's prow toward the open bay.

It was pure anticlimax, driving the boat across the Matanzas alone. The harbor was a millpond in the ebb; the sea wall and the staring gun ports of the two Yankee ships already seemed uncomfortably close when he turned to check his course. Realizing that he was rowing with far too much energy for a native, he settled into a lazy pace, quartering across the roadstead with the town on his right.

A half hour's steady rowing brought him abreast of the point to the south; beyond a clump of wind-harried cedars he saw the creek's mouth, curving in a lazy arc amid the marsh grass that hemmed in the settlement to the west and south. He made the turn with his heart in his mouth, waiting for a hail that did not come. On one of the anchored catboats a tall Negro stared back at him without seeming to notice him at all; a cart creaking on nightmare wheels beside the sea wall was the only show of life ashore.

Julian had expected shots, a scurry for cover—anything but this lazy pull from shore to shore. Once he had gained the shelter of the marsh grass on the mainland, he rowed with all his might until he saw the crumbling shoulder of the old city wall thrust up from higher ground ahead. The timeworn coquina surface was all but drowned in vines and broken in a score of places. Already he could make out the shape of the town beyond, the straggling line of a roadway that became a street at the next crossing. The same lazy stillness hung over the morning, though the smoke curling from a dozen chimneys told him that St. Augustine was awake at last.

Someone shouted a greeting from the far bank, and he found himself staring at a pair of Yankee soldiers fishing from a rowboat in the shadow of a flowering oleander. Both of them were little more than boys. Their flat forage caps sat cockily on their heroes' curls; their uniform coats, open against the heat, were dark blue and gleaming with newness. If this is the enemy, thought Julian, he has a friendly grin. He remembered to wave just in time, as he coasted by.

"Any luck?"

"Not even a catfish, brother."

Had he broadened his drawl enough to pass for a Floridian? Apparently these boys had no thought of questioning him. Just as obviously, they were off-duty and lazing the morning away. But he did not breathe easily until he had turned the next bend in the creek and saw the dock leaning drunkenly in the lazy tide.

St. George Street—it could be no other—climbed the low bank, in a pair of sandy ruts that joined a makeshift pavement on high ground. The house of Don Carlos Menendez was in its place, behind a yellow curtain of jasmine—a grave, blank-faced house, with a bright copper knocker waiting for his hand. He tied the mullet boat up hastily and scrambled for his sanctuary, using all his self-control to keep from running.

Yet he was strangely calm before he could raise the knocker. This was America, after all. Even the enemy had waved a greeting.

viii

"I say it should come off, Doctor. Don't you agree?"

The young firebrand on the bed had had a convincing grin when Julian entered his sickroom; he was no less convincing now, as the surgeon sat at his bedside and began the examination. Only the hard line of his jaw betrayed him, the quick dart of the eye that followed the slowly unwinding bandage.

Julian let his own eyes rove about the room as he exposed the wound. Don Carlos Menendez had already settled into the one available easy chair with a gentle sigh: a monster of a man in white linen who might have passed as Don Amadeo's twin, with manners to match. The gaunt orderly who stood at his officer's bedside was a ramrod in homespun, with a stare that never wavered, despite the deceptive modesty of his bearing. A pair of warlocks who would rather kill than eat, thought Julian, and managed to smile at Broussard after all. The boy had been stripped to his waistband long ago, and the bed on which he lay was drenched in sweat. For all that, he seemed to belong to the gray uniform coat that hung smartly across a chair back.

"Tell me I'm right, Doc. I don't scare easy."

Julian's fingers continued to explore the exposed wound. Here, he saw, was a job to test any surgeon's skill. The bullet had entered the arm almost in the center of the elbow joint and smashed through. The bones of the elbow had splintered; when he tested the drum-tight skin, it was as though his fingers were manipulating a bag stuffed with wooden blocks. Under the hot swelling, the skin was stained with blood. Julian's hands moved along the muscles, feeling for evidence that the inflammation had spread higher up the arm. But there was no trace of telltale nodules in the armpit—those swollen glands indicating a suppuration draining into the body itself.

Young Broussard had youth and good blood on his side. His life was not yet in jeopardy, despite those two days' neglect. Julian considered his next move. Time had raced since he knocked at Don Carlos Menendez's door. He had been a lover at sunrise, swimming with his bride in apple-green surf. A cracker fisherman, waving a greeting to the enemy as he sculled into town by the back door. A conspirator who could whisper his name in a shadowed patio and follow a hog-fat, cheerful Spaniard through enemy-held streets without turning a hair.

Now, at long last, he was himself again—a surgeon with life and death balanced neatly on his palm. He made his decision swiftly and met Broussard's eyes.

"Could you stay here for several weeks without being captured?"

"Reckon so, Doc. But I don't *want* to stay. I belong with the general."

"I could do an excision—remove the bone fragments and try to save the limb. Isn't it a risk worth taking?"

Broussard scowled and raised his head. He was one of the handsomest boys Julian had ever seen: the clear-cut hawk's profile could have been cast in bronze without changing a line. Julian could almost see the hot pulse of the brain beneath as the lieutenant-aide of General Dickison weighed his chances.

"How soon would you be sure?"

"It might take months for full recovery."

"And if you take the whole arm now?"

"With good care, they could send you back in three weeks."

The boy glanced at Don Carlos Menendez, who beamed with the eyes of a contented tomcat. "I'll get that care, all right. This *hombre* owes us more than enough. Suppose you start taking it now—the arm, I mean."

It was a simple request, made without bravado. The boy's grin was still unchanged. Here, thought Julian, was bravery in its purest form. A devil-may-care bravery that lacks the imagination to be afraid. Much as he would have liked to save the arm, he knew that he must yield. Excision might well bring gangrene and death in its train. This was the only way to be sure that Lieutenant Broussard would live to dodge another bullet.

"Can I operate here?"

"Why not? The light's good—and I promise not to yell."

Julian glanced again at the high latticed window above their heads. The room in which he sat was a second-floor bedroom; below he could hear the noisy stirring of the Minorcan family that had accepted this patient so casually. A cart creaked down the street outside, the sound deadened by the thick walls. In Vienna he had heard screams drive through a hospital wall far thicker than this. . . . Once more he forced himself to smile at Broussard. On the way he had told himself that he must operate without anesthetic: he faced the actuality now, as calmly as he could.

Don Carlos spoke for the first time. "Around the corner, at the Treasury, the Yankees pay their troops today. One sound they do not understand will bring a musket butt to this door——"

"Shut up, hogshead," said Broussard. "I'll give you five dollars for each time I squawk, Doc. Five gold dollars out of *my* pay. Do you want me on a table, or will this bed do?"

"Stay where you are," said Julian. He made his voice crisp as he peeled off his shirt. "Have you any extra bandages?"

"Open my kit, Roy."

The orderly favored Julian with a piercing glance, then lifted a carpetbag that stood beside the bed. Clearly he was suspicious of any surgeon who wasted too much time in preliminaries. The bag contained no instruments but a razor-sharp bowie knife, a half-broken probe, and a forceps for removing bullets, stained red by rust. But there were several squares of browned, soft linen —suitable for sponging cloths and for tampons to cover the wound. Julian opened his own case on the night table and began arranging the equipment.

"Roy will help you," said Broussard. "So far he's done most of our cutting in the field. He was a pill pounder in my home town before we enlisted together."

"I was a doc too," Roy said affably enough. "Leastways old man

Sawyer promised me his practice when he died." He favored Julian with another of those level stares. "I could have took this off myself, neat as a whistle."

"Today," said Broussard, "you'll take orders from a real sawbones. No matter what he does to me. No matter if I faint, which I hope I can manage."

Julian, already placing a tourniquet on his patient's arm, murmured an amen to that wish. Then he twisted the knot and anchored it: protected from hemorrhage, he could cut quickly and mercifully, keeping pain at a minimum. Of course there must be moments of agony when he clamped and tied off the blood vessels in the stump, but that was unavoidable without chloroform.

A small brown girl came up the stairs with a steaming basin, and he went to wash his hands, prolonging the ritual as long as he dared; in time the pressure of the tourniquet would dull Broussard's nerves, perhaps save the patient from a fatal twitching as the knife cut deep. At the same time he kept an alert eye on the watch he had propped on the bed table: deprived too long of blood, the stump would not heal properly. Roy's dull hostility told him that hesitation would be fatal.

"*We're* ready," said the orderly. "Why don't you wait to wash up?"

Julian glanced at Don Carlos, but the fat Spaniard did not stir. Like a lardy symbol of inertia, he seemed to doze in his chair, without even watching the boy on the bed. As for Broussard, Julian saw no outward evidence of tension as he bent above the injured arm.

"Make it fast, Doc," he said. "That's all I ask."

"It's a promise, Lieutenant."

But his fingers were strangely reluctant as they closed on a scalpel. He had never performed an amputation without anesthesia; even aboard the clipper there had been the dulling effect of the whisky Captain Shea had consumed. Here there was nothing but dogged young courage to stand up against the knife, to control nerves already pulled taut by fifty hours of agony.

Across Broussard's body, the orderly watched like an alert lizard; when Julian brought the blade down at last, Roy's hands fastened on the lieutenant's arm. With that gesture Julian felt his own mind fasten—like another vise—on the job ahead.

He set the scalpel to the skin, outlining the contours of the flaps he would use—a long one at the back, a shorter one in front. He heard the voice of his dissection master again, as clearly as though old Dr. Frick stood in the same room.

"In the amputation, gentlemen, it is important always to make the posterior flap long. The muscle must cover the bone stump. Otherwise the extremity is useless."

The blade bit through flesh, bloodless now from the pressure of the tourniquet; it swept up in a curving line, making real the contours of the flaps he had outlined in his mind. Julian did not risk a look at Broussard; the boy had gasped just once at the first flick of the knife; he lay quiet now, in the iron grip of his orderly.

Pushing the superficial tissues aside, he exposed the bulging red surface of the muscles beneath. The next slash must shear through muscle to bone; he must make it at a slightly higher level, to ensure that the layers of tissue would fold and heal evenly across the cut end of the bone itself.

Again the knife cut through, this time with less pressure, since the muscle offered less resistance than the tough outer integument. Julian could see the cut mouths of several large vessels gaping in the depths of the incision; a trickle of dark blood was already seeping down across the cut surface. He did not stop to clamp: that could come later, when the present torture was behind him— and his patient.

The scalpel whispered against bone, and Julian modified the pressure instantly: scalpels would be precious where he was going. He nodded quickly to Menendez, who heaved up from his chair to assist; without waiting for that reluctant behemoth to reach the table, he moved on, letting the steel sever the last remaining shred of muscle tissue, until the blade had circled the bone, leaving its white surface bare in the depths of the wound.

"Linen, please."

For all their finicky puffiness, Don Carlos's hands were deft enough as they passed a brown strip across the table. Julian wound it around the bone and, seizing the two ends, pulled muscles and skin upward, exposing about two inches of bone. Again the bone must be cut shorter than the other tissues or it would project and cause a painful stump.

"Will you hold this—as tightly as you can?"

Don Carlos gripped both ends of the linen thong and held them in an even, upward pressure. Julian had already lifted the surgical saw from his case; now he set it against the bone, flush with the great, pouting lips of the retracted muscles. He felt the same reluctance that had hampered his fingers when he first took up the scalpel. The act of sawing, he knew, would be most painful of all for this young stoic—when the steel cut the outer periosteum, and again when it bit through into the sensitive marrow cavity. But he could not hesitate over that finale. Setting his jaw, he put out his strength and bore down. Saw bit bone, the sharp teeth—set precisely to cut the right depth—making a harsh, muted cacophony in the red cavity. The room seemed to fill with the pungent mustiness of bone saw dust.

"God is good," said Menendez. "He has fainted, our handsome fire-eater. It will go easier now."

Julian did not answer: he was driving the saw with all his skill, in a concentration too complete to pause at details. The muted scream of the steel stopped abruptly on a splintered note; he stood aside, letting the boy's forearm and ruined elbow fall to the floor. Don Carlos stared at it for a moment, then lifted it, quite casually, and carried it from the room.

There was time to look to Broussard now. His head lolled and his wax-pale cheeks glistened, but there was no hint of collapse as Julian tested the pulse at the one remaining wrist. He exchanged a quick glance with Roy, shrugged away from that uncompromising hostility, and began to clamp.

The tempo of the amputation offered him his first reward: thanks to his speed, the cut ends of all the major vessels were still in the operative field, with no sign of retraction. He clamped each separately, mindful of the dangers of suppuration later.

"Will you hold the forceps?"

Roy's scowl deepened, but he obeyed fluently enough, grasping the instrument in the approved manner, a thumb ready to release the ratchet when the surgeon had made his first tie. Julian cut his knot as closely as he dared, and held his breath as he nodded; Roy flicked the forceps smoothly aside and moved to the next without being asked.

When the last major bleeder had been tied off, he nodded again to Roy, who eased the tourniquet. A few vessels—hidden beneath the cut surface of the muscle—announced their presence with an angry spurting; he clamped these too and tied them off with the orderly's aid, feeling his tension ease with each smooth knot.

With the bleeding definitely ended, he shaped the flaps, ligating the cut ends snugly and bringing the cut tissue together in a compact fold. A continuous fold, without tension; once more old Frick's voice echoed in his memory. "In surgery one must always avoid tension. Where there is tension, there is slough. Where there is slough, gentlemen, there one finds gangrene as well."

"Compress, please."

Roy placed a folded linen square in his hand; he spread it evenly across the stump. "Keep this wet—with sea water."

To his surprise, the orderly nodded his approval. "Sea water it is, Doc. I've used it before. Keeps swelling down."

Was this his accolade? Julian's eyes met Roy's again, to seek an echo of that grudging approval; but the orderly's stare was still coldly appraising. He turned back, to bandage the dressing into place; then he dug deeper in the instrument chest until he had found a small phial of opium. He was glad now that he had overlooked the drug. It would dull the pain when Broussard regained consciousness. He would have preferred tablets of concentrated morphia and that startling novelty, the hypodermic syringe—but this would serve.

Broussard's eyelids fluttered while Julian was still measuring the tincture in a stone mug; a deep sigh escaped the boy's lips as he struggled to rise from the bed, only to be restrained by Roy. Julian watched his eyes flick down to the place where the injured arm had been; he watched Broussard fight the first full knowledge of his loss and win the victory. The grin was weak but definite when he looked up.

"Sorry to go out on you so soon, Doc. Reckon I didn't think of that bone saw."

"Don't try to talk. Just drink this."

Broussard swallowed the tincture of opium without argument; his remaining hand closed over Julian's as the latter held the awkward stone mug to his lips. The fingers were icy, but Julian knew that was only an aftermath of released nerves. He stood by the bedside and watched the languor of the opiate steal over the boy's relaxed body. A long, dreamless sleep was all he needed now: the will to live—and go on killing—would do the rest.

For a long time he sat at the bedside, counting the pulse and the regular breathing, and rejoicing that both were normal. When his watch told him that he had stayed for a postoperative hour, he checked once again on the wound, but there was no ooze of blood about the amputation. When he got to his feet he realized that Roy, too, had sat unstirring on the other side of the patient. Somehow it had been easy to forget the orderly in the quiet satisfaction of his accomplishment.

"I'll leave the phial here," he said. "You can give him more if he's restless."

"Sit quiet, Doc," said Roy. "Take yourself a nice long rest. You're not going anyplace."

"What do you mean?"

"Just what I said. I ain't trusting you to leave, not yet awhile."

"The operation's over; from what I've seen, you're quite competent to care for him. Where's Menendez?"

"Gone to see about those friends of yours. Until they fetch themselves to his house, you're staying with me. How do I know you aren't a Union doctor? The Yanks have good sawbones too."

For the moment Julian was too surprised to be angry. "I'm Julian Chisholm. Doesn't that name mean anything to you?"

"Of course it does—if that's who you really are. You can still be a Yankee—walking into the Menendez place this morning, pretending to be what you ain't. How do I know you won't go straight to the fort—and come back with the provost guard?"

Surgeon and pill pounder faced one another across the sleeping patient. The suspicions in Roy's eyes went far deeper than his words: here, thought Julian, was the ageless hatred of the rootless adventurer for the man of property, the camp doctor replaced by the professional. Roy was the poor-white South in person, insisting on its rights. The Roys of the Confederacy knew in their hearts that they fought for those above them, yet they fought like wildcats nonetheless. It was probable that Roy had never asked himself why. Perhaps, like the sleeping lieutenant he served, he enjoyed war for its own sake. Certainly he was enjoying the anger of Julian Chisholm now.

"I've my passport here," said Julian. "Would you care to see it?"

"No, thanks, Doc. I'm a poor hand at print. Maybe you're all you claim to be. We'll know when Menendez comes back tonight. Try to go out that door ahead of time, and your back will stop a knife."

Julian walked over to the high window and peered through a chink in the blind. The narrow street below was empty; but even as he looked a Union officer swaggered out of the square coquina building at the corner, paused to admire the sheen of sunlight on his new boots, and strolled away in the direction of the plaza. He had the look of a man who had just drawn his pay and was at peace with the world: for all that, a shout could bring him to this house on the run.

Julian hesitated with the words on his lips. It would mean a tussle with Roy, of course, but he rather relished that prospect. It would also mean capture for both Roy and Broussard, and internment for himself. Eventually he might hope to pursue his profession, probably as a contract surgeon for the North, far from any active theater of war. It was the fate Jane had visioned for him. In a sense it would be as fitting as the course he had planned.

He turned away from the window as the mood passed. It was unthinkable that he should betray Broussard—or himself. Like Roy, he was dedicated to a cause he did not even understand. He had chosen his side, though he could give no reason for that choice.

"Since I'm to stay awhile, do you mind if I rest?"

"Suit yourself on that. There's a bed in the next room." Roy was paring his nails with the bowie knife. He leveled the blade at an open door to the right.

Julian walked through without another word. The smaller room was dimly cool, empty save for a truckle bed and a prie-dieu in a corner. Only when he had settled on the neat quilt, and kicked off his boots, did he realize how tired he was.

"Call me if there's any change," he said to the open door.

There was no response—unless he could call the lazy scrape of Roy's knife an answer. He was asleep in five minutes, with the sound of that razored steel in his ears, and Jane was in his arms again, floating with him in a secure limbo somewhere between earth and sky.

ix

He opened his eyes to the dusk: the candles on the prie-dieu had been lighted, and the small brown girl from downstairs stood at his bedside with a steaming platter in her hands.

"Shrimp pilaff, señor. Will you eat?"

His watch told him that twelve hours had passed since his sketchy breakfast on the island. Taking the plate from the girl's hands, he saw that the room beyond was lighted: Roy's shadow was an immobile threat on one whitewashed wall. The rice stew on his knee was more important than that fanatic watchdog now. He was finishing his second plate, and pouring wine from a long-necked wicker bottle, when Don Carlos Menendez appeared in the doorway, his monstrous bulk all but blotting the light behind him.

"A thousand pardons, Doctor—but I had no choice. While you slept he saw your friend Señor Cameron. He is now convinced you are one of us."

So Whit had brought Jane safely across the Matanzas. Julian got up from the bed and asked himself again how he could have slept through that event.

"Where are they now?"

"Señor Cameron and your lady? They went to my house to prepare for their journey; you may go there when you like."

Julian led the way to the other room and sat down at Broussard's bedside to examine the wound. Roy still sprawled in a chair; if he repented his mistake of the morning, the repentance was not on the surface.

Broussard slept peacefully, and Julian found no change in the appearance of the wound. No surgeon could have asked for a more promising patient—or (he added grudgingly, with a glance at Roy) a more devoted nurse.

"I, myself, will see that he lacks nothing," said Don Carlos. "His friends in the scrub will make your journey easy. Go with God, Doctor."

"Don't tell me I'm dismissed this easily?"

"It is better you go now, while it is still light. Surely you can find my house alone?" The Spaniard opened his hands in a grotesque benediction above Broussard. "For me, it is better to remain: we have things to settle when he wakens."

Julian nodded: wars may come and go, he thought, but smuggling goes on forever. When the guerrillas control the back country, the smugglers must be on their best behavior. Don Carlos Menendez had gambled heavily on his skill today—he was glad that the Spaniard had won.

"Suppose I'm stopped on the street?"

"You will not be stopped, Doctor. The Yankees are still enjoying their payday. But it is well to be indoors before their curfew."

At the door Julian paused to exchange a final glare with Roy. For a moment he considered offering the orderly his hand, but he resisted the impulse. The gulf that separated them was too wide to be bridged by a casual handshake.

Charlotte Street was already deep in shadows when he turned south toward the plaza: in that light the ancient houses, with their balconies and high, shuttered windows, seemed to belong to another, more ordered world. This was a street from Seville, lacking only a booted hidalgo to make it complete: it hardly belonged to this little frontier town, dozing on the edge of a war. He forced himself to stroll, as a native would, ignoring the throb of an imaginary guitar beneath a lattice. . . . As a bridegroom (who had no notion of his bride's plans at the moment), he had every reason to hurry. As a Confederate doctor in enemy territory, he must merge with the growing shadows.

Whit, he gathered, had not waited until dark to cross the Matanzas; judging by his own experience, the risk had not been too great—especially if Jane had been shameless enough to stay in trousers. Yet they would hardly have come by daylight without a reason. Don Carlos had promised transport to Picolata by dusk: Jane had every excuse for haste. Could he blame her too much if she chose this painless way to tell him good-by?

St. Augustine's plaza was drowned in dusk as he turned the corner by the slave market and cut boldly across under a canopy of live oaks. His steps rang hollow on the flagged walk, but he could not resist running now. St. George Street, as he recalled, opened at the plaza's western end; the Menendez house stood at the next corner.

Julian made himself stroll again as he passed the lighted portal of a grogshop. If his fears were justified, there was no need of haste, no way under heaven to preserve the marriage he had made on Fisher's Island. If the house of Don Carlos Menendez was empty now, he could do worse than turn in here and quench his despair in advance. He smiled as he ignored the impulse. He had drowned Lucy Sprague in drink, after a fashion; the woman he had married was another problem.

Soon enough—at St. Marys, or beyond—he would face other gray evenings with no wife to welcome him. His fumble at happiness would then be worse than a memory. Perhaps he should rehearse that moment now, if only to dull the reality. Perhaps—

and here he yielded to desire again and began to run in earnest —reality was waiting for him at the next corner.

"*Jane!*"

It was no more than a whisper in the dark, but he dared to utter it as he walked under the great puff of jasmine at Don Carlos's gate. The house stared back at him emptily. He did not pause to knock, guessing that the servants were engaged in more profitable business at the moment. Even before his hand closed on the knob, he knew that the gate would open under his hand. He stood in the shadow of the vines, breathing their fragrance like a remembered dream, making the indecision prolong itself deliberately as he walked into the loggia.

The dusk was deeper here; for a moment he did not recognize his own portmanteau as it stood forlornly at the entrance to the patio. A fountain whispered, and he walked toward the sound as a man might walk through his own waking nightmare. They've loaded and gone, he thought. By now they're halfway down the road to the St. Johns. This is her way of telling me that I can leave tomorrow—with the next batch of contraband.

"*Jane!*"

Whit spoke out of the dark. "Straight up the stair to the bridal chamber. Don't bark your shins at the turn." The red eye of his cheroot glowed in the dark; a cloud of smoke drifted between them as he breathed his next words. "You might even take your portmanteau; it seems we stay till morning."

The gambler was seated in a deep wicker chair beside the fountain; there was a faint sparkle as he raised a glass to his lips. "Don't linger," he said. "Don't feel you must be polite and talk to *me*."

Julian was already on the stair, remembering, just in time, to grope for the sharp turn that gave to the upper loggia. A candle was burning here, in a hurricane lamp: it showed him the way to the tall door beyond, and he opened it without pausing to knock.

There were the men's clothes she had worn on the island, tumbled in a heap on the floor; there were her boxes, standing in a neat row at the foot of the four-poster; there was Jane herself, asleep in bed, with a night light shining on the aureole of her hair.

He stood in the frame of the bedroom door and waited for his heart to find its normal rhythm. Tonight her beauty was all the more precious, because he had found it again so suddenly. Yet he was beside her in another moment, and the tumult of his heart was more insistent than ever as he knelt to bury his face in her hair.

Jane stirred in sleep, and her hand moved to stroke his cheek before she could quite open her eyes.

"Good evening, dear. You didn't wait long to leave me."

He laid his cheek against hers, letting all his questions ebb away in that fragrant warmth. "I'd leave you for just one reason. That was it."

"War," she said sleepily. "Man's oldest reason for leaving woman——" Her voice was still foggy with sleep.

"My work," he murmured.

"Yes, Julian. I'm remembering now."

She sat up against the pillows and blushed becomingly. "That's why I'm here. In this room, I mean. I was—pretending."

"Pretending?"

He had never heard her use that word before. Somehow it touched him more than any avowal.

"Pretending we'd been married for years. That this was—our home."

She was wide-awake now; her eyes were lowered as modestly as the world's model bride. "I was waiting for you to come home from a case—and I fell asleep. . . . By the way, was it successful?"

He brushed the question aside and took her hands. "Then—you did want me back?"

"That's why I waited," she said simply.

So his suspicions had been justified after all. She had planned to go north with the first wagon; for all he knew, Whit had bribed Broussard's orderly to detain him at the house on Charlotte Street. It was a discovery that hardly mattered, now she had changed her mind.

"You and your war," she said. "Me and my lawyers. We forgot them last night, didn't we?"

"Magnificently." This was the Jane he remembered, the girl who could offer him her love without shame. "I'll always treasure our wedding night, darling. Five minutes ago I was quite ready to lock it in my memory book——"

"You thought I'd run away."

"Admit you almost did."

"I tried hard," she said. "I found I couldn't. Not tonight——"
"Or ever," he said.
"Or ever, Julian. I can say that tonight—and mean it."
"In spite of war and lawyers?"
"In spite of everything," she said, and gave him back his kiss with interest.

When he released her, he saw that her eyes were shining in the pale half-light from the night table. But she stopped him, with a gentle pressure of her fingers, when he bent over to snuff the candle.

"Not yet, my dear. I've something to tell you first."
"Tell me tomorrow—or the day after."
"It'll be harder to tell each day——"
"Keep it a secret forever. I won't mind."
"Until St. Marys, then."
"Forever's a better word," he said.
"Forever's a lovely word," said Jane. "If you don't take it seriously."
"If it's something you've done, or something you mean to do——"
"Tomorrow is better," she said firmly. "This is no night for secrets."

It was she who leaned forward to blow out the candle. With no sense of transition, his mouth found hers in the dark.

ST. MARYS

THE shrimp nets, hung on wide frames to dry, still dripped with the heavy morning dew: spread as they were across the dock's end, they framed the town like a parabola of gray lace. Muffled to the eaves in mist, St. Marys seemed to consist of the one wide street that began at the river's edge only to lose itself in the pine barrens a few blocks beyond. From where they were standing Julian could see only a few shacks straggling away into dimness. Negro children, playing under a chinaberry tree in a back yard, were the only sign of life; somewhere in the mist a hound bayed mournfully, to answer the side-wheeler backing into the fog above Cumberland Sound. . . . Florida was somewhere to the south, across the glassy water. Julian wondered if the Yankees in Fernandina had heard them pass in the dawn.

"I, for one, am sitting here until I'm wide-awake," said Whit. "That takes care of the luggage, pro tem. Why don't you two go exploring?"

The gambler had already made himself a nest of sorts among the boxes piled at the dock's end; he looked as contented as any night owl could at this early hour. Jane had walked down the stringpiece to watch their transport vanish in the mist; Julian steadied her, with an arm about her waist.

For a moment they stood in silence as the ancient side-wheeler merged with the cotton wool as casually as she had come. It was a fitting exit for a vessel that had bulled up the St. Johns, ignored Yankee-held Jacksonville without even striking her colors, and proceeded to her destination with the same shabby unconcern. The audacity of General John Jackson Dickison, Julian gathered, was not confined to the Florida backwoods. No man could have shown his gratitude more promptly—or more tangibly.

"Shall we take Whit's advice, my dear?"

"Why not? We're to look for a livery stable run by a Dr. Medford." Jane took his hand as they walked down the dock together and dodged under the shrimp nets. "It shouldn't be hard to find."

Two days ago he would never have believed that he could enter the last lap of their journey with such insouciance. Here, after all, was Confederate soil; here was the spot where they had planned to part company, from their first meeting. If Glasgow was an eon away, the threat of that parting seemed only slightly less remote. Neither of them had mentioned the word since they left St. Augustine. He refused to dwell on it now.

The street, they found, was little more than a sandy wagon track that seemed to have more affinity with the woods than the sleeping houses that fronted it. St. Marys was clearly a dying town, but Julian felt strangely at home in it. As a boy, hunting and fishing through the Cape Fear country, he had ridden down a dozen such lonely Main Streets—each with its tin-roofed general store, its clapboard church staring down the saloon across the way, its weedy yards open to the wilderness. Dr. Medford's establishment was part of the picture: its board sign, "Livery and Supplies," seemed on the point of dropping to the dust from sheer lethargy; its adjoining barn, leaning at a crazy angle, would surely do likewise in the next high wind.

Strangely enough, the small shingled house beyond—with the doctor's name plate on the door—was both spruce and respectable. The vines on the porch trellis were well pruned; the row of poinsettias that bordered the walk, cut waist-high, raised their heads proudly to the first wan sunlight that flickered through the mist. Jane had already taken a quick step to the front door; she drew back now and smiled at Julian.

"Sorry, my dear. The lord and master should do the knocking."

He came to earth with a jolt on that, and guessed, from the sober look she offered him, that she had made the remark deliberately. But he refused to surrender his high spirits, or his hopes, as he raised his hand to knock.

A gray-haired woman with gentle eyes opened the door—so promptly that he surmised she had seen their approach from her kitchen window. At least it was obvious that she had come straight from her stove: the air behind her was redolent with the aroma of baking bread.

"Is the doctor in?"

"Not at the moment, Dr. Chisholm. I'm Mrs. Medford. Is this your wife?"

"How did you know my name?"

Mrs. Medford looked mildly puzzled. "I had a letter from you a week ago, saying you'd be coming up from the South——"

Jane spoke quickly. "Don't you remember, dear? I said I'd write from Glasgow."

He recovered his aplomb. "Of course, I'm glad the letter got through ahead of us."

Incredible as it seemed, they were expected in St. Marys—precisely as they had been expected in Nassau. Jane had planned her journey well: even their detour in St. Augustine had not spoiled its pattern. Dr. Medford was this little town's synonym for transportation: he could hardly doubt that their transport had been ordered in advance. He put the question mechanically, if only to complete the picture in his mind.

"Has your husband reserved a carriage for us?"

Mrs. Medford looked even more puzzled. "Your letter said you were to stay here until——"

"Until our escort called for us," said Jane. "My husband has had his breakfast, Mrs. Medford—but he isn't wide-awake."

Julian took back his authority smoothly as the doctor's wife bustled to get them chairs. "Escort or no escort, we'll still need a rig. Don't forget the gowns you brought through the blockade."

"We have nothing but the doctor's buggy," said Mrs. Medford. "All our carriages are—busy." She had barely hesitated on the word; now she smiled at them like friends. "Some folks would call it smuggling, but Georgia has to live in wartime. We still don't understand why the Yankees haven't crossed the sound and taken St. Marys too. Maybe they don't think we're worth capturing."

"Surely there's something on wheels in the neighborhood."

"We still have two horses in the stable. You could ride along the road if you liked, Doctor. Maybe some farmer would let you buy a wagon—if you could pay in gold——"

Julian threw a quick look at Jane and spoke without quite waiting for her nod. "We'd pay in gold—gladly."

"Then take your pick of the stable," said the doctor's wife cheerfully. "Your wife can sit and visit through the kitchen door while I tend to my baking."

But Jane had already risen from her chair as Julian stepped down to the yard. "May I have a look in the stable too? I might take a ride on my own——"

"*Can* you ride, dear?" he asked.

"And jump," she said. "I've jumped fences since I was ten."

They were out of earshot of the porch now. Julian stood aside to let her precede him into the stable.

"You might jump out of your ambush, to begin with," he said. "What's this about an escort?"

"South Georgia has always been a near wilderness," said Jane. "Don't you think an escort is safer?"

"You planned to be met here—is that it?"

She stood just inside the stable door, watching tranquilly as he investigated the two stocky cobs in the stalls. "Put it that way, if you insist."

"I insist on nothing, my dear," he said, keeping his eyes on his work. "I'd just like to sing in key, if I can."

"But you did beautifully—even when you improvised. As you say, we can always use a rig——"

He threw the saddle he was inspecting across the straw-littered floor and whirled on her. "So it's still *we*, Jane?"

"For a while, I hope," she said. "Don't ask me how long." She was in his arms then, stilling his next question with her kiss. "I'm glad you thought of hiring a rig, Julian. Find us one, if you can. I'll have Mrs. Medford send for Whit and the luggage——"

"We leave together. Promise me that much."

"If you wish it," she said, and kissed him again. A long, hard kiss that brought back all their shared midnights. For an instant they swayed together in the dusty gloom of the stable before he released her.

"I'll remember that, Mrs. Chisholm," he said, and turned to the business of saddling.

It was a relief to blunt the tumult of his mind on details. To observe that Dr. Medford's livery was in excellent shape, despite the apparent bareness of the stable. To verify the fact that there was stabling for at least a dozen wagons—that the barn, for all its outer disrepair, was snug as an empty armory inside. Jane did not stir as he worked. Hugging her knees in the hay, she seemed thoroughly at home, and just as determined to let him ride out alone.

Yet she rose promptly enough when he swung into the saddle and held out his arms. It was absurdly easy to lift her from the floor for a good-by kiss. To cradle her in his arms as he braced himself in the stirrups and ride with her toward the square of sunlight framed by the barn door.

"Suppose I kidnaped you, just as you are?"

"It might be simpler," she murmured.

"Suppose we forgot my war and your lawyers—and just rode back to Chisholm Hundred?"

"Will you ride back to Chisholm Hundred—ever?"

"Only as a visitor, I'm afraid."

"There's your answer, Julian," she said, and slipped from his arms to the ground.

He looked back just once, as he kicked the cob into a shambling trot, and saw that she was standing in the frame of Mrs. Medford's wistaria, shading her eyes against the sun to watch him go. He swung in his saddle to face the road ahead and wondered if he was seeing her for the last time. Somehow his love deserved a better finale than a stolen kiss in a smuggler's barn.

ii

Much later, when he could hold his thoughts at arm's length and weigh them soberly, he knew that he had ridden through several miles of Georgia without seeing it at all. His mind, struggling to shut out a dark certainty, had shut out the landscape too.

Jane Anderson—the woman he had married so cavalierly in Glasgow a scant two months ago—was a widow bound for Atlanta to fight for her legal rights. That much he believed implicitly. Holding that belief before him like a shield, he plowed on to the next corollary. . . . Her purpose in marrying the Chisholm name, she said, was to smooth her entry into the Confederacy: that plan had certainly been worth the investment. It was obvious that she would plan her actual entry with care, identifying herself as his wife in Nassau, yet arranging to land in a forgotten corner of Georgia, where her subsequent movements could scarcely be traced.

For all he knew, the escort she had mentioned might be a brace of lawyers—or an even more tangible bodyguard. Certainly he had no right to object, or even to question her arrangements. Jane Anderson's future was her own. It was neither her fault nor his that their marriage of convenience had been consummated with a vengeance. Their wedding night on Fisher's Island and the nights that had followed were simply beyond their control. Or so he argued, riding bareheaded in the hot winter morning and cursing its brightness to the limits of his vocabulary.

He was still cursing, fluently enough, and the sun was at the zenith, when he turned in at a farmer's gate to water his horse. As he had expected, there was no wagon, either for sale or hire. The farmer himself—a gnarled jack pine of a man, with a mustache like a discouraged sin—offered him a less than cordial welcome.

"Came up from Augustine, eh? Why didn't you make a run for Savannah?"

Why not indeed? thought Julian, not without bitterness. If we were playing a simpler game, we could face the world as man and wife—with an item in the *Gazette* and a railroad outside our hotel door. And yet, despite his forebodings, he was not too unhappy to find himself in this corner of nowhere.

"How far is the nearest railhead?"

"That I can't answer, stranger. Brunswick is the nearest town that calls itself a town—and I hear we've evacuated *that*, 'cause we figure we can't hold it against the Yanks. If and when they decide to move in——" The man spat on his bone-dry doorsill. "I'm sure of one thing: it's hard to keep from starving, with your three boys at war, and a government that tells you to raise food for the army 'stead of cotton——"

"D'you mean to say there's no railhead in miles?"

"All I can say is head north and hope. There's no tellin' what you'll find on the roads."

"Don't tell me you have raiders even here?"

"Bushwhackers, mostly." The man spat again. "They call themselves Yanks, but they steal from friend and enemy alike. Don't *you* ride too far from town, mister—they might hold you for ransom." The farmer turned to the harness he was mending, and his worn face cracked into a smile for the first time.

Julian took the road back at the cob's best gait. At Picolata, just before they had boarded the side-wheeler, he had observed some of General Dickison's finest, who had been detailed to escort them to the landing. Rednecks to the last man, with the gleam of pure larceny in their eyes, they were also nominally soldiers of the Confederate Army. Yet Julian had guessed that they had been restrained only by loyalty to Dickison himself—and Dickison was a *condottiere* of the first rank. Obviously there was no substitute for such iron authority in this corner of Georgia. . . . What if Jane had yielded to impulse and gone riding alone in his absence?

St. Marys seemed almost as empty at high noon, as he urged the unhappy old horse down its rutted street. At first view there was no sign of life about the doctor's premises; then he saw the doctor himself, unharnessing his buggy in the shade of the barn. Even at a distance there was no mistaking Medford—or his profession. A plump little gnome in rumpled drill, he was the country practitioner from his untidy boots to the perpetual smile that peeped through his lazy-man's beard.

"Introductions quite unnecessary, Chisholm," he said, and offered Julian a small, fat hand. "Sorry I wasn't here to welcome you this morning. Your friend Mr. Cameron is napping before dinner; will you join me in a drink while we wait?"

But Julian's eyes were already searching the empty stable behind them. "Did my wife go riding?"

"Left an hour ago, I believe. Took the road to the cypress hammock." Medford gestured vaguely toward the east. "I shouldn't worry, if I were you—she'll be back for dinner."

"Didn't you warn her that there are bushwhackers about?"

"I did indeed, sir. But she's a plucky little lady. Said she could take care of herself. What's more, I think she meant it."

"Is there only one road to the hammock?"

"Can't miss it, sir. Just give old Toby his head, he'll take you there."

The doctor's eyes crinkled as he stared up at Julian; evidently he was about to add something to his directions and thought better of the impulse. "Don't ride too hard: my guess is you'll meet her on the way."

Julian was off, without waiting to hear more. The road to the cypress was easy to find; as Medford had said, the old horse took the turn without urging and plodded across the barrens toward the sad yellow wall of trees that blocked the horizon to the east. This time Toby's gait could not even be called a trot: like the doctor, he seemed to feel that this ride was worse than futile. Could it be that Jane had ridden east on Medford's own suggestion—that she might even resent his appearance now?

He put the thought aside and urged the cob to greater effort. Already, as the land dipped toward the hammock, the stand of pine had yielded to water oaks and dwarf cedar; a tangle of wild grape in the bright green underbrush gave the wall of foliage the look of a sub-tropic jungle. The earth was damper here, and he could see the imprint of a single horse's hoofs. For over a mile he drove Toby to his best speed, ducking more than once when a swaying gray beard of moss all but blocked his path. In the heart of the hammock the roadbed was squdgy under Toby's hoofs; despite the dry midwinter, there were pools of black water between the gaunt cypress knees. The trees themselves looked more like ghosts than ever in this hot green dimness.

He reined in and listened to the silence. Jane had been mad to ride this far; was his attempt to find her even more fantastic? The rank Georgia wilderness stared back at his question, unmoving and strange as a plate in an encyclopedia. He lashed at a head of dog fennel with his riding crop and opened his mouth to shout his wife's name. At that moment he heard the crunch of horses' hoofs on the road ahead. He saw the flame of her hair—more vivid than ever in that swamp—before he could make out Jane herself. She was riding the rawboned country horse as though she had been born to the saddle; the smile she offered him was a classic in unconcern. Then she rode up beside him and offered him her lips as well.

"I was afraid you'd worry," she said. "Believe me, I can take care of myself."

He saw that she was wearing her trousers and riding boldly astride the ancient hack; the pistol at her belt fitted the costume perfectly. He leaned across her saddle and took the weapon from its holster. It was the latest make of percussion-cap revolver, with a London label.

"Can you handle this too?"

"Well enough," she said coolly. "Not that I needed it, Julian. I'm wearing it for show, now that I command my own detachment."

She said it quite casually, and her eyes dared him to question her further. "If you're referring to that mysterious escort——"

"Stop me if I'm wrong," said Jane, with a soothing hand on his arm. "You came to rescue me from the bushwhackers. You're furious, in fact, because I dare to ride alone. But how would I get us an escort if I didn't go to them?"

"You mean you rode deliberately into the swamp to meet——" He swallowed hard, then went on firmly. "I'm beginning to see why you wanted to get rid of me this morning."

"Dr. Medford arranged everything," she said calmly. "All I had to do was ride to their camp and talk terms with the leader. Don't look so surprised, Julian—I assure you I was in no danger."

"Where is this fellow now? *I'd* like a word with him myself."

"He's gone on ahead, to round up the others. We'll rendezvous at Medford's in an hour." She urged her mount to an easy trot. "He assigned two of his men to guard me."

"So we're being watched now?"

"Look to your left," said Jane.

He swung in his saddle as she raised her hand and signaled the wall of jungle on their left. A lean horse and rider materialized in the leaves, as casually as a phantom taking form. The guerrilla stared for a moment, unblinking as a statue carved in yellow marble; horse and rider moved as one, though the fine gray gelding was obviously a recent acquisition. Julian gathered that the same could be said for the hunting saddle and the shotgun thrust into the boot.

Jane dropped her arm, and the fellow swung into the road behind them. When she signaled to the right, a similar apparition emerged from the hammock and galloped briskly ahead.

"Please overlook the melodrama," said Jane. "But it's my first command, and I'm really enjoying it."

Julian rubbed his forehead. "Did you say *command?*"

"And meant it."

He stared hard at the homespun back jogging down the green tunnel ahead. "Wouldn't it be more seemly——" He took the word back and tried again. "Surely these rascals would respect you more if——"

"If *you* had dealt with them, Julian?"

"I'm still your husband," he said. "If you need bodyguards, I should do the hiring."

Her eyes met his steadily, but there was a veil across them now. "I suppose it's too much for any man to understand. Believe me, it was the only way."

"Are you planning to use them later?"

"I was afraid you'd ask me that," she said, and kicked her horse into a sudden gallop.

The rider ahead, hearing the rattle of hoofs, nudged his own mount into a faster gait and led the way from swamp to pine barrens at breakneck speed. Old Toby, snorting his derision, was content to eat Jane's dust as the little cavalcade swept toward town—and Julian made no attempt to overtake her. The barrier that stood between them now was wider than this flying dust cloud and much more durable.

iii

The hammock was farther from St. Marys than he had realized; the afternoon shadows were already long in the rutted main street when they rode up to Medford's barn again. A dozen horses were tethered outside; a dozen riders lazed on the grass, obviously awaiting their approach. Even at a distance his heart sank as he surveyed this motley crew. No woman under heaven, he thought, could give these ruffians orders. Yet he found that he could rein in, quite calmly, and let Jane ride into their midst. His jaw sagged in earnest as the bushwhackers came to attention, to the last man. One of them—he was obviously the leader—came forward with his hand held out. A scarecrow with a scar down one saddle-brown cheek, his was the direct manner of authority as he shook hands with Jane and favored Julian with a curt nod.

"We're ready when you are, ma'am."

"We'll leave in the morning," said Jane. "Early."

She was riding among the men now, with the captain at her side, shaking hands with each in turn. Julian stayed where he was, determined to hear no more. For all its informality, there was an air of ritual to the moment. No queen, he reflected, could have reviewed her troops with more authority.

Far off, to the south, the sound of a horn floated on the cool afternoon air. Jane lifted her head in the midst of her command; the leader snapped an order and swung to his saddle in a running lunge. The other guerrillas mounted with the precision of a cavalry troop. In another moment only a faint reek of dust betrayed their presence as they rocketed down the hammock road in single file.

The horn sounded again, nearer this time. With it Julian heard the thud of hoofs on the river road. Jane swung a trousered leg over her horse's back and slid to the ground before he could dismount to help her.

"It's a patrol," she said. "I hardly thought they'd warn us they were coming. Shouldn't I make myself respectable?"

He stopped her at the Medfords' garden gate with a crisp salute. "My compliments, General. That was an impressive review."

Jane appeared to accept the remark quite seriously. "I think we can depend on them to take us to the railhead."

"And beyond?"

"And beyond, perhaps."

He watched the slender figure vanish through Mrs. Medford's kitchen door. There was no point in blinking the change in her: it was a new authority that went with slender, booted legs, the proud tilt of her head. A note of almost reckless confidence—an aura of *command*. It was the only word for Jane at the moment.

He stabled their horses and fed them from the doctor's bin. Granted that the roads of backwoods Georgia were anything but safe in this winter of war. Granted, too, that Jane's return had been prepared with all the care of a military campaign. There was still much more to this rendezvous than met the eye. He refused to face the implication squarely as he walked out into the blue evening. The question that had formed like a threat in his mind could be answered only with absolute proof.

He was just in time to see the patrol gallop into town, with a final operatic flourish of its horn. At a distance they seemed to ride almost as raggedly as the bushwhackers, though their uniforms made a brave show in the dusk. The officer at the head of the column looked astonishingly young despite the magnificent blond beard that spread like armor across his pale gray tunic. A medallion soldier, thought Julian, missing only a sweep of ostrich plumes at the hatband of his cavalryman's sombrero. The men behind him, however, lacked most of their officer's splendor. As the troop reined in before the barn, Julian saw that few of the uniforms were complete. More than one pair of farmer's jeans replaced the regulation pantaloon. Grimy toes peeped through the cracked soles of a dozen nondescript boots.

The officer dismounted and tossed his bridle to an orderly. "Lieutenant Paul Harris, sir. Georgia state militia." The hand he offered Julian was firm and deeply tanned. Mars himself thought

Julian, could hardly have created a more dashing envoy. He took the proffered hand and shook it cordially. He had come a long way to make this gesture of alliance; why did it seem to belong to comedy rather than to high drama?

"Dr. Chisholm, Lieutenant."

"I thought as much, sir. The Medfords have expected you for some time."

So Jane had made no secret of her arrival. Evidently a Chisholm was expected to enter his homeland with a certain ceremony, even in this forgotten corner of Georgia. And yet Jane had contracted with a guerrilla troop to shepherd her journey. What would this beau sabreur say to that? Julian smiled to himself: if the Medfords could keep that secret, so could he. Tomorrow, when Jane's rag-tail escort rode up, this same beau sabreur would probably be snoring in his bed.

Harris drew off his gauntlets and folded them into a stupendous belt that supported his side arms. A word of command sent the troop on its way; the orderly was already leading the lieutenant's mount into the stable.

"Weren't you at the University of Virginia, Doctor?"

"For a brief time, I'm afraid."

"Your fame has lingered. Perhaps you've forgotten that my brother was a second at your duel with young Raleigh? Is it true that you broke his pistol deliberately, when you could have had him through the heart?"

Julian smiled: he had all but forgotten that bizarre proof of manhood. "I'm afraid it was a lucky hit."

"Permit me to correct you, sir. Our armies will gain a surgeon; they have lost a soldier."

The compliment was offered with a fine flourish; Julian could merely bow—and blink.

"Are you stopping at the Medfords', Lieutenant?"

"I am indeed. Wait till you sample Mother Medford's biscuits; you haven't tasted their like abroad." Harris betrayed his youth with the widest grin his whiskers would allow. "I trust your wife won't be too fatigued to join us."

"On the contrary." Julian matched the lieutenant's grin in warmth. It was ironic that this representative of the military police should choose to rest his head in the house of St. Marys' most adroit smuggler. At the same time it seemed oddly natural to stroll toward that same house with Harris, as though they had been friends for years.

The doctor came out to the porch as they climbed the steps. In fresh white linens, he looked more like a well-scrubbed cherub than ever; the untidy gray beard and the cheroot smoldering in its midst were only afterthoughts.

"Inside, both of you," he said. "Mr. Cameron is pouring our drinks. Besides, the mosquitoes will soon be out in force, and it's a well-known fact they cause malaria."

Harris boomed with laughter and slapped at an insect that had somehow circumvented the ambush of his own whiskers. "Well known in this house, you mean," he said. "I'll wager there isn't another in St. Marys that's screened."

Julian glanced at the windows and saw, for the first time, that they were protected by a thin cloth netting. "Is this part of an experiment, Doctor?"

"Call it a private hunch, sir. I decided long ago that intermittent fever has wings. Ma and I have kept the mosquitoes out, so we never have malaria. Naturally we take a little dram of whisky and quinia now and again, to make certain. May I offer you part of that prescription right now?"

Unlike most country parlors, the Medfords' seemed both lived-in and cool. Whit stood at the sideboard, measuring bourbon into four tumblers. The gambler appeared to be thoroughly at home, and as brashly comfortable as a cat on a strange doorstep. But as he came into the room, Julian noted that Whit swayed a little and realized that his friend was quite drunk.

He had seldom seen Whit drunk before. Was it only an antidote for rustic boredom, or had Jane paused in this room, on her way to dress, to throw a cloud on his future? Once again he faced the fact that Whit knew quite as much of her plans as he, and wondered why he could face it so calmly.

Harris, he noticed, had responded to the introduction with less than usual warmth, though his punctilio was perfect. But Whit merely continued to stare at the lieutenant with icy disdain as Medford handed the tumblers around. It was a duel of looks without rhyme or reason, and Julian was not surprised to see the Confederate officer come off second-best.

"I'd toast the bride and groom," said Harris, "but I see we must wait for the bride."

"Permit me to offer a substitute, gentlemen," said Whit, and his diction was far more precise than his gait as he strode to the center of the worn carpet, like an orator on his platform. "I give you our Confederate Union—it must and shall be preserved."

"Your servant, sir," said Harris. "But I cannot drink to a paraphrase."

"Why not—if it's from the heart?"

Something *has* upset him, thought Julian. He's baiting this boy deliberately, to cover his own unhappiness. Aloud he said, "Lieutenant Harris is right, Whit. Since we drink to the Confederacy, let us ignore the ghost of General Jackson. Our Union cannot be preserved; let us drink to our armies and the cause they champion."

Harris clinked glasses with him, his eyes flashing his appreciation of this martial music. "To its glorious conclusion," he said.

"Spoken like a pair of bloody owls," said Whit into his glass. He had turned his back deliberately as he drank; Julian hoped that he had not spoken loudly enough for Harris to hear. But the lieutenant's good humor had been restored. He put down his glass and leaned easily against the Medfords' mantel—another attitude that set off his martial slimness to perfection. Evidently he had realized that it was beneath his dignity to quarrel with a civilian.

"You speak like a Southron, sir," he murmured. "Surely you do not question our destiny?"

Whit turned like a boxer on the points of his varnished boots: it was evident that he had lured Harris into the open deliberately. "Destiny, Lieutenant? It's a large word for a section that defies its government."

"Our defiance has succeeded. The Yankees have yet to win a major field."

"What about Antietam?"

"Sharpsburg, sir? We were the victors there as well."

"Not with the dead you left behind," said Whit. "It was considered a victory in Washington. A prelude to Mr. Lincoln's proclamation of freedom for the Negro. Your death knell abroad, sir, if I may make so bold."

"Must I accept the 'you' at face value, Mr. Cameron? Are you not one of us?"

"I am a citizen of the world, Lieutenant. However, you'll find my passport quite in order."

"Permit me to verify that for myself."

"By whose order?"

"Perhaps you aren't aware that this district is under martial law."

Whit glanced at Medford and Julian, favored them with a wink, and tossed his passport on the table. Despite himself, Julian stepped forward to read it over Harris's ramrod-stiff shoulder. Whit's birthplace was listed as a remote county seat in the Tennessee mountains; he had given himself the profession of pedagogue—which, Julian reflected, was a quite appropriate fiction. He himself had learned a great deal from Whit, even if some of the lessons had been hard to swallow.

"Well, Lieutenant, do I pass muster?"

The light in the gambler's eye was cold with hate: something about Harris had infuriated him from the young man's first appearance. Reading his friend's glare, Julian remembered Broussard's orderly back in St. Augustine. The steady venom in Roy's face was echoed now in every line of Whit's studied contempt. Was this another instance of the mountain white baiting the aristocrat and reveling in the aristocrat's righteous anger?

Roy's hate, thought Julian, had been rooted in blind instinct; Whit's was deeper and far more complex. Roy struck back at his betters out of an atavistic despair; Whit struck from the firm knowledge that these same rulers had driven their section to the brink of ruin—and would finish the job, with the stubborn thoroughness only the die-hard knows.

"Do you vouch for this man, Doctor?"

Julian heard his own voice. "Of course I do, Lieutenant. Mr. Cameron's character, like his credentials, is above reproach. His political opinions are his own."

"*That* is your passport, Mr. Cameron," said Harris with clipped emphasis. "As for your convictions—let's hope you don't find them an expensive luxury."

Whit favored the lieutenant with a deafening belch and picked up the bottle. "Don't speak to me of luxuries, sir. Even money says I come out of this gamble richer than you." He stalked from the room on that, pausing in the doorway to bow to Medford. "My apologies, Doctor: I seldom insult guests on a man's own hearthrug. . . . And while I'm about it, Harris, my apologies to *you* too.

Fact is, it wasn't you I was addressing: it was the system that produced you."

No one spoke as the front door slammed behind the gambler. Julian went to the window and saw that Whit had already seated himself under a tree in the yard. A splinter of sunset broke on the bottle as he tilted it skyward in the growing dusk.

"Believe me, Lieutenant, I never heard him talk quite like this——"

There was no time for more. Mrs. Medford's voice had already stabbed deep at his brain. A high-pitched call for help, from the stair well outside the parlor door. Even before he took the stair in a dozen long strides, he had guessed the meaning of the soft thud overhead.

iv

Jane—her stays half laced, her petticoats a wild white billow on the carpet—lay against the footboard of the four-poster in the upstairs bedroom with her head in Mrs. Medford's lap. He saw at a glance that she had only fainted, and knelt beside her to take her pulse. The rhythm was racing; the skin of her forehead seemed to burn under his hand.

"Fever," said Mrs. Medford. "I guessed as much when I came up to help her dress. But she insisted she was——"

Jane's eyelids fluttered. "I *am* all right, Julian. I've got to be."

He murmured a soothing affirmative and lifted her to a more comfortable position on the bed. "Have you felt badly long?"

"My head was aching when we rode in just now. But I thought it was the sun."

"It was more than that, I'm afraid."

He stood back, making room for Dr. Medford. The old man's voice was a soothing purr as he bent above the bed: his lips framed the one word "ague" as his eyes met Julian's. A word that covered a multitude of sins in the Atlantic lowlands.

"Both of you go out while I undress her," said the doctor's wife.

Julian fidgeted on the stair landing, doing his best to take heart from Medford's apparent calm, his rumblings of constant and intermittent fevers.

"Both are all too common in these latitudes. We can control it easily."

"I hope it's no more than that," he murmured. A picture of Steed's pesthole in Nassau—and the crash of Victor Sprague's body in Lucy's doorway—invaded his mind, with all the black overtones of doom. He pushed both memories aside, fighting for professional calm as Mrs. Medford summoned them again to the bedroom.

Jane was lying in the bed with her eyes half closed, her pallor heightened by the flame of her hair against the propped-up pillows. She was breathing quickly; her eyes, when they opened wide at his approach, were clear and bright. "I've got to go on," she whispered. "I've got to——"

"You'll go on, darling. We'll both go on."

"Both of us, Julian. Both of us——"

He stepped back to let Medford perform his examination. Even for a country doctor it was surprisingly thorough. Julian felt his confidence return when the other produced a thermometer from his bag and registered the temperature, even though the reading was one hundred and four degrees.

Medford had scarcely closed his notebook when Jane began to shake in the hard rigor of a chill. Julian hastened to her side at the doctor's nod and cradled her in his arms while the old couple wrappd her expertly in blankets. It was a bone-shaking chill, and her lips were blue before it ended. Medford was ready at the bedside with a glassful of pale yellow liquid.

"Time for whisky and quinia, Mrs. Chisholm. It will give you the strength you need."

They lifted Jane's head to help her drink: she gagged at the bitter dose, then downed it dutifully. Julian tried to ease her head into the nest of pillows again, but she clung to him like a child: he made another cradle of his arms and held her there, feeling her body relax slowly as her eyes closed.

After a time her deep breathing told him that she was asleep. He made her comfortable in the bed and wiped the perspiration gently from her forehead. It was cool and damp now, and the racing pulse had slowed to its normal beat. Magically, the fever had fallen with the chill, but he knew that this was not the end. Whatever had struck her down had sent her into a fever of one hundred and four degrees—and a rigor as severe as any he had ever observed. This was no infection to be taken lightly.

He looked about him, a bit startled to find the bedroom empty:

the old couple had evidently tiptoed out as the crisis lessened. Julian tiptoed out in turn: it was safe to leave her for a while. He found Dr. Medford alone in the parlor, deep in a book.

"Your supper is waiting in the kitchen, my boy."

"Thank you, but I'm too concerned to eat."

"She's sleeping now?"

"Between attacks, I'm afraid."

"It is still a good sign."

"Do you think it's malaria?"

"Fever is difficult to diagnose at its beginning. Any of them may begin with such a rigor. Nevertheless, malaria is the most common on this coast. It may very well be that."

Medford's manner was reassuring, but Julian found he could not respond. He sat at the table and buried his face in his hands, hesitating to reveal his fears. Yellow fever was rightly regarded with terror in the South. Not too long ago it had raged up and down the coast, literally decimating such great cities as Savannah, Charleston, Baltimore. If this were yellow fever, Medford would probably be forced to quarantine both of them—so rigorously that he could not obtain even the ordinary comforts which could mean life and death in such a case.

He glanced up, realizing that the old doctor was studying him benignly. "Believe me, son," he murmured, "there's nothing you could have done to stop this. Surely you know that yourself."

Julian walked to the door and stared out at the wide street. The moonlight had softened the gaunt bareness of St. Marys. It was hard to believe that he had ridden down this same street with Jane only a few hours before—and met a squad of hard-riding rednecks, waiting to take her orders. She had been so alive then, and so sure. Now she was utterly dependent on his judgment, perhaps already attacked by a foe against which he had no weapon.

He faced Dr. Medford firmly. His responsibility as a physician demanded that he tell the older doctor what he knew.

Medford listened in silence as he poured out the story of their brief stay in Nassau: the cases he had examined at Windward Point, the grim climax of Victor Sprague's collapse.

"You were quite right," he said. "Nassau is facing an epidemic. Let's pray the runners don't bring it to us before this business ends."

"Perhaps we've brought it to you now."

Medford smiled. "Your frankness does you credit, Dr. Chisholm. May I reserve my judgment?"

"Do I understand you've seen a great deal of the disease?"

"I've lived with it ever since I can remember. This town knows the yellow sickness as perhaps no other town in America."

"I recall no reports of an epidemic here."

"It's an old story, Dr. Chisholm—and it begins when I was a boy. At the time, I had a mild attack and recovered."

Julian breathed a deep sigh of relief. "Then you're immune?"

"There have been other epidemics, and I've outlived them. But the first was something I'll never forget. It began early in the century, when a sloop put in here from Baltimore. Our people didn't know at the time, but the *coup de barre* was raiding our seacoast cities like the Assyrian of old. Two men were dead on that sloop—and unburied. The others were prostrate. We took them in and nursed them until they joined their shipmates. Weeks later the disease struck. Death everywhere—and no way to fight back. At the end there were hardly enough well to nurse the sick. When it ended, most of us were buried in the cemetery behind the woods: you can read the headstones now and see how many died in a single day. A few lived on, but the town itself had died; it has never really returned to life."

"What carried the epidemic away?"

"Who knows? It could have been the frost. It was heavy that year: I remember, for I used to hunt rabbits to make broth for my brothers. All of them went with the others."

"You must hate the yellow sickness, even now."

"I have no hatred for disease, Dr. Chisholm. Only a wish to know its secret—so I can fight it. Perhaps, like malaria, it comes on wings; perhaps the frost killed the mosquitoes that year—and saved what was left of our town. Others have guessed as much and been called mad; who am I to raise my voice?"

The old doctor had spoken quietly; now he leaned forward to tamp his pipe. For the first time Julian noticed the noble plane of his bald forehead. In that light Dr. Medford had more kinship with Socrates than with cherubs.

"I only wish I knew," he murmured. "Of course I never will. Science moves slowly. I've learned not to be impatient."

"Suppose we've brought the fever to St. Marys again?"

Medford's hand was gentle on Julian's shoulder. "Don't worry about keeping your wife here. We'll give her all the care we can. I'll see that gossip doesn't spread——"

"Then you think she has it?"

"No. It's simply that we can't tell now. Science has deserted us: the verdict is in God's hands. We can only nurse her—give her what medicine we can—and pray."

Julian got up slowly. "Thank you, Doctor. I'm glad we're in good hands."

"Let me spell you awhile. Are you sure you won't have a bite of supper?"

"I'm afraid I couldn't. But I will have a breath of air."

Outside the cool night was almost bracing. He stood for a while in the unearthly white bath of moonlight before he moved toward the barn. It was hardly the moment he would have chosen for a ride to the cypress hammock. Yet someone must warn Jane's escort that there had been a change in her plans. With Harris and his patrol camped just beyond the town, there was danger enough of an armed clash.

At the doorway of the barn he breathed the reek of whisky and took an instinctive backward step. Whit Cameron heaved up from the feed box in which he had been reclining and offered the bottle with a solemn flourish.

"Friendship has its limits," said the gambler. "But I share this freely."

"How long have you been here?"

"Since Jane was taken. Since our gold-medal lieutenant stamped out to join his command—after refusing to break bread with a bombproof." He gestured toward the moonlit street. "You should have seen him ride away—head high, whiskers flying. Tonight he bivouacs with his men. Here's hoping he doesn't wake up with cramps."

Whit's craggy profile thrust forward aggressively, and Julian steadied him just before he fell. "Aren't you going to ask me why I'm disgracing myself—I, who never brood?"

"Later, perhaps. I've an errand now."

"If you're planning to ride to the swamp, forget it. I rode out myself an hour ago. Our friends are well warned. They'll wait."

"How long?"

"As long as they're needed. Bushwhackers aren't always so patient, I'll admit. But these are more loyal than most." Whit stared at Julian owlishly. "Jane told you that much, I hope?"

Jane told me enough, thought Julian. I guessed enough to fill in the gaps, even if I don't dare put my guesses into words. Strange how unimportant those suspicions seemed now that she was lying in the Medfords' bedroom, now that her future was in his hands and not her own.

The gambler wavered out into the moonlight and leaned against the trunk of the first pine tree; teetering against this solid support, he flung the empty bottle into the street. "No more of that medicine," he said. "I'm resigned, Julian—and getting sober fast."

"You don't look it."

"I'm sober enough to be sorry. For you. And for Jane too, while I'm about it. Remember, I lured you into this."

He knows everything, thought Julian. For once he's discovered that he has a conscience—and the shock of that discovery has driven him to drink.

Aloud he said, "What's so unusual about hiring an armed escort?"

"Have you any idea how long these guerrillas have been waiting for us? *Why* they're so willing to take orders from a woman?"

"Are those questions rhetorical?"

"Rhetorical—and useless," said Whit. "Being a romantic, you've guessed the answers long ago—and refuse to face up to 'em. Being a realist, I can see what'll happen to you both. Being tenderhearted, I take to drink."

"Never mind your tender heart. Make sense——"

"It's no use, my friend. People of my habits don't explain Jane Anderson to—people like you. You've got to grow up to her yourself."

Whit swayed in the moonlight, weighing that cryptic statement. "Someday you'll know that's gospel. When you're old enough. . . . Just lending her your name isn't enough. Or loving her. Or telling yourself you'll stand by her, come what may. You've got to grow up to her too."

"You said that once."

"It bears repeating. Maybe it's just as well we let you get this far—without turning you over to the Yankees. Maybe it's going to take a year of war to make you see how young you really are. And how far away you've been from things that matter."

"Like Jane, for example?"

"Like Jane. Suppose I told you that she's the best thing that could happen to you? Would you stand by then? Or would you be a Chisholm to the end?"

It was more a plea than a challenge. Julian took it in that spirit, realizing, at the same time, that Whit was not nearly so drunk as he seemed. "She's had no cause to complain so far."

"Right, my friend. You'll nurse her through this fever—and eat your heart out with worry. Even when you see it'll take more than fever to kill someone like Jane. Then you'll stand aside like a gentleman and let her go her way." Whit's voice rose in wrath. "You *knight-errant!* D'you think a woman enjoys that kind of treatment?"

"I'm sure it's what she wants."

"You mean it's what she *says* she wants. In her way she's just as stubborn as you—and carrying just as many ideals in her baggage."

Whit turned away, so pointedly that he almost measured his length in the Medfords' yard. "Go about your business, Doctor. Nurse your wife—and thank God she still is your wife. You'll look a long way before you find another."

"Are you telling me to stay with her, when I promised——"

"Back to the house, Galahad. I'll never explain you to each other."

But the gambler stopped Julian with his voice, from the shadow of the pine. A sepulchral voice, weighted with impatience and mockery.

"People with a mission. People who won't let the world find its own level, and have to build cofferdams of their own. Even when I make friends with 'em, they're beyond my ken."

"I'll accept the compliment," said Julian.

"You'd better. Because you *are* my friend, whether you like it or not. I'd enjoy you more if you were a little less noble——"

The gambler swayed from dark to moonlight, and Julian saw he had opened a fresh flask of whisky with his teeth. He drank deeply before he leveled a trembling finger at the house, as though he were lecturing Jane with the same gesture.

"Why can't you be happy the easy way? *Don't answer that, Galahad! Your lady is calling you!*"

Julian went into the house on the run. Halfway up the stair, the silence said that Whit had dismissed him with a hoax. He entered the bedroom on tiptoe. Medford smiled from an armchair.

"She is resting quietly. Why don't you lie down awhile yourself?"

"That chair looks comfortable enough for me tonight."

"As you will, Doctor."

Together they bent above the sleeping form in the bed. Jane lay as he had left her, but her cheeks were no longer so pale. A layman would have said that she was in perfect health, but Julian knew that the fever was still lurking in her blood stream, ready to pounce again at any moment. He followed the old doctor to the stair and stopped him with a hand on his arm.

"She'll have another seizure before morning."

"I'm afraid so. There's quinia on the night table when you need it."

"Assuming the best, how soon could she leave here after the fever breaks?"

"A week's convalescence is indicated, at the very least."

A week seemed a long time to wait; he wondered if Jane's escort would be patient that long. Perhaps they would vanish into the pine barrens as strangely as they had come; perhaps he could take her to the railhead—and whatever lay beyond. Knowing in advance that this was a futile hope, he held Medford in the hallway for yet another question.

"This escort she's hired—what do you know of them?"

"Only that they rode down from Atlanta, with orders to wait indefinitely."

The candor of the reply threw Julian off balance for a moment. "Why didn't you mention the fact to me this morning, Doctor?"

"Mrs. Chisholm said the men would expect her," said Medford soothingly. "She didn't want you to worry—"

"Suppose Harris learns that we've arranged for an armed guard?"

"Lieutenant Harris' patrol ends at the county line. The authorities are supposed to maintain order here; everyone who travels far must make his own arrangements if he hopes to travel in safety."

"How do we know these fellows won't cut our throats on the road?"

It was dark on the landing, but he saw the twinkle in Medford's eye. "I'd trust your wife's judgment there, my boy."

He went quickly down the stairs, with the cat-foot tread of age, before Julian could speak again.

v

Back in the bedroom, Julian drew the armchair close to the four-poster and settled for his vigil. Already he regretted the impulse that had made him question Medford. As Whit had said, questions were futile when one knew the answers in advance.

But none of it mattered as he stared at his sleeping wife and felt panic press down upon him like a visible threat. This morning she had planned to ride out of his life with her ragged escort; tonight he might still lose her to another and more terrible host. If this were yellow fever, his years at the greatest clinics in the world would mean nothing: something else must intervene if Jane was to be saved.

It had been a long time now since he had thought particularly of God. He was not irreverent by nature; he had simply immersed his mind in the material study of the life process—forgetting the immaterial essence that was man's soul. In Vienna they had stressed the body: nowhere had he been reminded that in sickness another doctor often directs the course of the disease.

He groped his way toward the imponderables of belief. With his cheek against his wife's, he forced his lips to frame unfamiliar words again.

"Dear God, let her live. Let her live for me. If not for me—dear God, let her live——"

He felt better as he rose from his knees, with his first prayer of years behind him. Whit Cameron would have scoffed at any man who asked a favor of God; the gambler would have added that Jane was too strong to die. . . . It comforted Julian, nonetheless, to confess his helplessness. This was his wife, no matter what wild plans she had made; this was his reason for being. For him the marriage they had made would endure so long as he drew breath. She might die tonight or leave him on the morrow—the tie would still endure.

Closing his eyes on that conviction, he slept fitfully through the night. As he had feared, Jane's next seizure came just before dawn.

She was already twisting the bedclothes and murmuring in delirium when he started up from the chair. He sponged her burning forehead and tested the racing pulse again. The skin of her arm was hot and dry under his fingers; when he poured her a tumbler of water, she drank it avidly. Her eyes stared at him, bright with fever—and he realized for the first time that she did not know him.

"Whit," she murmured.

"Lie still, Jane."

"I love him, Whit. I love Julian. Don't laugh at me—I mean it."

"I know you mean it," he said, understanding, all too vividly, why her mind had swung to the gambler now.

"He'll hate me when he finds out. Sometimes I think I can't do it to him . . ."

Sobs racked her body as her voice trailed off. Then she relaxed in his arms and seemed to sleep, though she continued her incoherent babble.

"Got to—go to Atlanta. Promised—country . . ." The whisper died, and then she spoke quite clearly. "The Union—it must be preserved!" Despite himself, he shook her shoulders gently.

"Jane—don't you know me?"

He remembered Whit's crazy toast, only a few hours ago. Jane's delirium seemed only a grotesque echo, but even as he held her in his arms and waited for her to quiet, he knew that it was no echo.

For several moments her voice went on, rising and falling as she struggled in his soothing grasp. None of her words had meaning now; he sighed with relief when he felt her skin grow moist under his hands and knew that the crisis had broken.

"Is everything all right, Doctor?"

He looked up dazedly and saw that Medford had come to the bedside. The old man was wearing trousers over his nightshirt; Julian wondered how much of Jane's delirium he had heard.

"She was feverish, but it's broken now."

"I'm glad of that. Shouldn't we administer more quinia?"

Jane roused a little when he lifted her head, and swallowed the bitter dose without protest. Almost at once she slipped back into a deep slumber; Medford nodded his satisfaction as he counted her pulse.

"I think you've earned your rest tonight, Dr. Chisholm," he said.

"Of course it's too soon to be positive—but all signs point to tertian."

"Intermittent fever, you mean?"

"Endemic in these regions. Weakening—but not dangerous. Your wife's a fine, strong girl, Doctor—give her a week and she should throw it off completely."

"Thank God it isn't yellow jack."

"I'll join in that, my boy."

Julian felt a great calm descend on him as the old doctor tiptoed out. But he had no desire to sleep, now that the die was cast. Now that he knew just what he must do when she recovered, he found that he could make his mind stop at will.

For a long time he stood at the window, watching the pale day grow along the rutted streets of St. Marys. Lieutenant Harris rode toward the river with his troop and saluted the house in passing, unaware that he was being watched from the shadowed bedroom. A little later Whit staggered out of the barn and entered the house by the kitchen door, like a homing tomcat that fears the light.

Time seemed to stand still in the little Georgia town as the river mist shut out the sun. From the bed behind him Jane sighed in her sleep, reminding him that the world turned, even here. Now that he had come to this moment at last, he knew that it was inevitable. The reality was no easier to face as he sat down beside her on the rumpled bed and took her relaxed hand in his.

vi

Dr. Medford's diagnosis was accurate, almost to the day. Thanks to generous doses of quinine and Julian's careful nursing, Jane mended rapidly: eight days after the seizure she was able to move from the bedroom to a wicker lounge on the porch; the following afternoon, when she walked across the garden unaided, Julian knew that her recovery was certain.

It was almost a relief to let her doze a day away while he walked through the barrens or fished from the boat pier at the foot of the street. Tired by the sun, he found that he could sleep well enough after an hour of cribbage with the doctor, even though his bed was now only a cot besides Jane's. If the nights were hard to get through sometimes—if he wakened to her quiet breathing and discovered that he was standing at her bedside like a mournful ghost—it was easy to slip out of the house and walk again beside the river until the dawn.

Ten days after her illness he returned from an afternoon's fishing and filleted his catch on a board behind the woodshed. Scrubbing at the cistern pump, he found himself rebelling, for once, at the strange, almost animal sloth that had crept over his spirit. Sun motes still danced before his eyes, thanks to those long hours beside the river, and his head ached dully as he mounted the stairs to the bedroom.

Jane was seated at the old-fashioned bureau mirror, combing her hair. She was wearing a loose peignoir knotted at the waist. Absorbed in her ritual of brushing, she turned to him only when his image joined hers in the glass.

"You're looking well," he said.

"I *am* well, my dear. Just a little weak, that's all. You've been a wonderful doctor."

"Without a practice, now you've recovered."

"In another fortnight you'll have more practice than you can handle."

He saw that she was keeping her voice impersonal with an effort. Remembering the revelations of her delirium—and the bittersweet happiness they had brought him—he could afford to match her tone.

"Will you be seeing your lawyers, then?"

"I hope so, Julian," she murmured, and hid her face in the copper cloud of her hair.

"This time it's really good-by?"

"We can ride together to the railhead."

"I think it's better if you went alone," he said.

Jane tossed back her hair. His heart gave a great leap when he saw that her eyes were swimming with tears. For an instant she sat looking at him, and her lips trembled, as though she was exerting all her will power to keep back the words. Then she gathered her peignoir about her and walked out of the room.

He heard the plash of water down the hall and guessed that Mrs. Medford had prepared a bath for Jane in the small room above the kitchen. The ache in his head had increased steadily while they talked: it throbbed behind his eyeballs now, insistent as a triphammer—a warning that this was no mere touch of sun. He groped his way to the bed and started to stretch out, but

Jane's clothing was in the way: the muslin she was apparently going to don after her bath, her nightgown beside it.

He pushed the latter garment aside. Something dark and flat slipped from the folds and fell to the carpet. Hardly knowing what he was doing, he bent dizzily to retrieve it.

His head was spinning now, but he stared at the flat leather object in his hand: a small leather letter case, stamped with her initials—J.A. Did they stand for Jane Anderson after all?

He began to curse himself in a low, even voice—and knew why, before his thumb flicked up the leather flap that closed the case and its contents. A folded paper slipped easily into his hand, and he stared at it without seeing it at all. Something was written here in pen, in a fine-grained clerk's hand. The seal in the corner was vaguely familiar; so, for that matter, was the name signed beneath it.

The room turned a solemn somersault, and he stared back at the wall to bring it into perspective. When he looked at the case again, he saw that his hands had restored the paper to its place and closed the flap, quite without orders from his brain. He sat remote, watching those same hands fold the leather oblong into Jane's nightgown, precisely as he had found it.

Stretched on the bed at last, he fought the sickness that was creeping over him like a gray miasma. His forehead burned and his limbs ached, but there was not a drop of perspiration on his body. Jane came into the room again, and he struggled to open his eyes as she sat down at the mirror and began to wind her hair into a long coronet braid. She did not look at him as she worked. Even in that fevered moment he saw that she had brought her mood back with her, intact.

When she spoke at last, her voice seemed to come from a great distance, though the words probed instantly at his heart.

"I hoped we could stay together for a while longer. Why have you changed your mind?"

"Do you think I can bear this forever?"

She kept her eyes on the mirror. "Bear what, Julian?"

"The fact that you hold the whip hand," he cried. Though his brain was spinning, the words came clearly enough. "The knowledge that you've run our—our romance by your own rules from the start. The fear that I'll wake up tomorrow, or some other tomorrow, and find you've gone for good. Don't forget that's the last rule you made. Don't think you won't enforce it when you're ready."

She was on her feet now, with the peignoir whipped tight about her slim figure. Lifting himself to one elbow, he saw that she was naked beneath it. To his amazement, her voice was a bizarre contrast to her amazon pose.

"I'm not ready to leave you yet, Julian," she said in a whisper. "And if you must mention rules—well, there were times when we had no rules at all. Do you remember them?"

"Much too well," he said.

"And do you regret that we've still today?"

He let his silence answer her, and exulted as he saw the rich color mount to her neck and cheeks. Then she turned from him with a low moan and loosened the ties of her peignoir, letting it drop in one quick gesture to her feet.

She had turned to him before he could surge up from the bed to sweep her into his arms. But he never reached her, despite the invitation in her eyes. Instead he stood for a moment, swaying in rhythm to the crazy whirligig of walls and ceiling. He remembered her voice calling his name through the sudden blankness as he crashed to the floor.

vii

For a long time—much longer than he could measure—day and night were one, lit by endless dull-red rockets that exploded behind his eyes without sound. The eons of pain seemed more than he could bear at times—when his head threatened to burst, when every bone in his body was racked by the fearful shaking of the ague. Intermittently he was conscious of Jane's voice, or the doctor's, urging him to drink incredibly bitter potions. And there were times when he moaned for water, and knew that he was too tired to make his voice heard above the hard hammering of his pulse.

Then, as abruptly as the room had lost itself in the vortex of his fever, walls and ceiling took form again. He knew that he was lying in bed, naked save for a shirt, and drenched in sweat; he knew that it was dark beyond the circle of the night light and that the darkness was real.

For a long time it was enough to stare at the ceiling and revel in the discovery that he was both alive and sentient; when he tried to marshal his thoughts, they refused to place themselves in any familiar pattern. The last thing he remembered was the way Jane's robe had glided about her body, the warm light in her eyes as she turned to give herself to his embrace.

Turning at last, he saw that she was lying on the cot across the room—the same cot he had occupied when he had nursed her through her own sickness. She had evidently been dozing lightly; the noise of his turning in the bed, faint though it was, had wakened her instantly. Even as he watched, she sat up sleepily, then groped her way toward him. He watched her face come alive as she saw that his eyes were open and clear of delirium.

"Julian—do you know me?"

He nodded slowly. Even that little effort taxed his strength. The caress in her voice had filled him with a greater happiness than he had ever known.

"Have I—been sick long?" He could get the words out by spacing them. "Have you—been with me always?"

"You've been ill for a week. I slept here every night——"

He tried to smile and found he could manage it after all. "How are *you*?"

"Completely well."

She poured water into a tumbler and held it to his lips; the touch of her hand on his cheek, as she held the vessel, was quiet ecstasy. He prolonged the act of drinking as long as he dared, to keep it there.

"Would you like some broth?"

"No—don't go, please. I'm too tired——"

She smoothed the pillows expertly and stood back. "You must sleep—and so will I. It's almost midnight now."

"But that pallet." He forced another twisted smile. "I remember —how hard it is——"

"I don't mind it, now you're out of danger."

"You could lie on the bed beside me."

She looked down at him with luminous eyes. "Would that help you to sleep, Julian?"

"Don't ask—foolish questions, darling," he whispered.

But Jane was already streched full length on the rumpled sheet; an arm moved gently beneath him, turning his face toward her until his head rested against her shoulder and breast. Through the thin silk of her nightgown he could hear the steady beating of her heart. Sleep began to steal over him like a healing drug; he fought his drowsiness as long as he could and clung to her with the little strength he had. . . .

The sun was warm at the window when he wakened at last and knew that he was well again. He felt the quiet in the room even before he could open his eyes, and guessed instantly that he was alone. Her boxes were gone from the corner, and the dresser was bare; the boat cloak she had worn on their wedding night had vanished from the open armoire. He put out his hand to touch the pillow where her head had rested, and smiled, even in the first shock of her absence, for the pillow was wet with her tears.

Mrs. Medford nursed him for the next few days; the doctor, she explained, had been called away on a distant case. Julian never knew if the old man had ridden out with Jane and Whit on the first stage of their journey: somehow he could not bring himself to question the gentle white-haired woman who helped him from bed to armchair, and from chair to his first tottering steps in the fresh spring sunshine.

Jane had left him—that was all that mattered. He had known that she would go the moment his recovery was assured. Reality left his mind spent, his will power dead. He felt that he could sit here forever, with a rug across his knees, in the dappled shadow pattern of the veranda vines and stare back at time with eyes that asked for nothing.

When the old doctor returned at last, Julian was able to walk to the gate and back; his mind had begun to stir faintly as his body mended, though constructive planning was still beyond him. There was a man in Richmond named Clayton Randolph who would take care of his future, neatly enough. General Randolph would be only too delighted to send him to his first baptism of fire: an uncle on headquarters staff was an asset in time of war.

He would always be grateful for Medford's casual greeting as he stepped out of his buggy; for the easy pressure of the old man's hand on his shoulder as he turned from veranda to kitchen door; for the offhand way he dropped a newspaper in his lap.

"Maybe you're well enough to read the news, son. Shall we take a chance?"

Julian stared for a while at the flamboyant masthead of the journal as it lay half open across his knees. The Charleston *News and Courier*—already ten days old, and creased from many hands. Still, it was a link with the outside. He forced himself to read.

His eye strayed first to an editorial that proved, beyond a doubt, that prisoners from a South Carolina regiment had been used for living targets in a Yankee prison pen. Beside the editorial was a schedule of steamer landings: apparently the runners still came into Charleston harbor on schedule. . . . He remembered the starlit nights aboard the *Sewanee*. If Don Amadeo's luck had held—if he had insisted on remaining aboard—they might have reached Charleston too. Or Savannah. Or even Wilmington. He could have taken his wife to Chisholm Hundred—if Chisholm Hundred was still standing in this second spring of war.

Once again he forced his mind back to the smudged text. A triumphant headline met his eye:

GUNBOATS FAIL TO
REACH VICKSBURG

Stanton Reported
Angry with Grant

Stanton. The war secretary in Lincoln's cabinet. He felt a dull red light explode in his brain, and feared, for an instant, that his fever was returning.

The paper slipped from his hand as memory stirred, and pounced, with terrible finality. That afternoon in the bedroom upstairs, when Jane had gone to the next room to bathe . . . When his fingers had fumbled with her letter case and a paper had slipped out . . . His fevered eyes had read the name then, and it had registered somehow on his brain. The paper in Jane's case had been signed by the Union Secretary of War. The impression on its corner was the great seal of America.

The woman he had married—the only woman he would ever love—was an agent of the United States Government.

Now that the fact was proved beyond a doubt, he knew that he had guessed it from the beginning. He had known, just as surely, that he could never betray her—or rest until he had found her again. He sat for a long time with that quiet certainty, feeling his heart pound with a new purpose. The hot, leaf-dappled sunlight that fell across his knees was a challenge now. He had lingered too long on the edge of this war; at last he had a reason to plunge into its turbulent heart.

VICKSBURG

IT WAS cooler in the cave—and quiet enough, save for the low, bubbling groans of the lung cases. Julian stood for a moment in the entrance while his nurses transferred his last patient from the crude operating table that stood under the tent flap outside. Then he turned back wearily to the paper work that always crowded these intervals.

The boy whose femoral artery he had just probed out and tied would surely live. So would the lank naval officer they had brought up from the river's edge that morning with most of his foot blown clean away. The lung cases would probably go by morning, to join the six ramrod-stiff bodies that lay in the hollow below their dugout, awaiting the next burial party. Six dead, after steady hours of operating, two dying, five doubtfuls sleeping off their first postoperative shock under morphia. It was a respectable average for any surgeon working a mere hundred yards behind his lines.

He wiped the sweat from his forehead and stepped into the glare of the declining sun. It had been almost as hot under the tent flap, but he had learned long ago that it was safer to work in the open air. From where he stood—their hollow cave was halfway up the face of the bluff—he could see most of Vicksburg, a mere mass of rubble now, from which the populace had moved long ago. To the west the Mississippi lay serene as a tan prayer rug in the lengthening light. At any moment a breeze would move over the face of the town and the skeletons that defended it. He had looked forward to that breeze for an hour, ever since his last hopeless case had screamed under the chloroform as his scalpel probed a smashed pelvis for the shell fragment that would not be dislodged.

Six dead, two dying, five doubtful. He had had a month of general surgery at Richmond and five weeks in this doomed bastion. But he was still unable to think of his cases as statistics. Eyes still begged for mercy out of the red fog; a boy from Texas, born to sit proudly in a saddle, still cursed him blindly in dreams as he stared down at the place where his legs had been. . . . Then there was the bearded artilleryman (another leftover of the navy that had smashed itself against Porter's ironclads) who had kissed his hand when he emerged from the anesthetic and knew he would live. Strangely enough, you never dreamed of the good cases, only the bad.

Yet he was sure that his results had been good: the volume of work that funneled into this small hospital was grim proof. Many died: that was inevitable. Wounds of the abdomen were generally fatal, and chest wounds were a close second. The legion of compound fractures was the most heartbreaking: even now he yearned to treat them by excision and splinting, but there was never time. Operating under constant pressure, handling incredibly large numbers of wounded in a single day, he had learned the first stony lesson of war: to sink the good of the few in the good of the many. Vicksburg under siege was no place for detailed surgery, the complex operation that might force another case to wait.

He turned back to the canvas flap as his head nurse—muscled like a gorilla, and quite as hairy—came out to scrub the table. The ground shook under their feet as the man worked; a peal of muffled thunder assailed their eardrums. Neither of them spoke; Grant's sappers had been exploding mines for a week now, as that patient brown bear tightened his ring about the town.

Vicksburg fought back, even today—though trenches caved in beneath the fighters' feet, though the new and ever-narrowing circle of fortifications must sometimes be dug with bayonets and sharpened boards in lieu of mattocks. For the hundredth time Julian asked himself why Vicksburg insisted on starving itself into submission. His own uniform, which had fitted him so perfectly when he had purchased it in Atlanta six weeks ago, now hung on him in folds when he troubled to wear it. Like most of the surgeons operating in the shadow of the guns, he found it simpler to work stripped to the waist. It was even simpler to work without thinking, when he could; but from the day of his arrival there had been too many pauses, simply because essentials were lacking.

The lack of essentials: when the history of the Confederacy was written, it would do nicely for an epitaph. Always there were shortages—of food, ammunition, dressings. There was no embargo on human misery that comes from festering wounds, from the fever that racked men's bones and threatened daily to become epidemic because there was almost no quinine left to combat it.

"Next man's ready, Doctor."

He turned to the operating table, glad enough to put such thoughts aside. Automatically he checked the chloroform: the supply was low, but there was enough for a few more days if the casualty lists did not increase. He picked up the scalpel. Always it was the scalpel. Destroy, do not save—the doctor's maxim in wartime.

"He's ready, sir," the anesthetist repeated.

Julian studied the wound. It hardly looked serious on the surface—a long, jagged laceration of the buttock, laying open the skin and tearing through muscle. But these injuries were always troublesome to the surgeon. He had seen dozens these past weeks. Often he could recognize the trademark of the missiles that had caused them. This one had been plowed by a conical musket ball, the so-called "minié," which had struck tangentially. A few inches deeper, and it would have splintered the spinal column, lacerating the great nerve tract. He had worked over too many of these cases. They were worse than dead—the body without feeling below the waist, reeking with its own uncontrolled excreta as it came in on the stretcher.

The present case had, fortunately, escaped such a fate. Julian cut down through the tissues, seeking for the scrap of uniform, the fragment of projectile which so often lay in the depths of such wounds, ready to set up a center for inflammation, erysipelas, and death. He found the minié ball at length, with the inevitable bit of blood-soaked cloth pinned to its point, and opened the wound a little wider to make doubly sure there were no blind pockets. Then a quick application of forceps to a spurting vessel, a compress to stop the oozing, a bandage to anchor it. . . . . Their supply of the new adhesive plaster had long since vanished.

The patient joined the others in the dugout, and another took his place. Julian took up the scalpel once more. It was really late now: he could gauge the time, to the quarter hour, by his own state of weariness, the dull throb of his head, induced by the heat the reek of chloroform, the stench of unwashed bodies. Three more cases, before the lull that always came at dusk. At last he turned away from the table, washed his hands in the bloody basin, dried them on the much-washed flour sack that hung beside it.

"It's my turn to go down the lines," he said.

Walking into the cooler evening air, he breathed deep of the freshness, ignoring the sickly aura that already hung above the pocket where the dead lay waiting for the burial party. He picked his way slowly down the scarred face of the cliff until he reached a sandbagged path that skirted the river's edge. It was a dangerous short cut, since it was in direct range of the Yankee gunboats that sometimes ghosted by in the half-light of dusk, but he preferred it to the arduous climb.

A short walk brought him to the communication trench that gave directly to their own front lines. The surgeons working in his unit had arranged to patrol this section in turns, to deal with any cases that might require attention on the spot. Tonight, he found, the area was quiet; so, for that matter, were the enemy trenches that faced their position on the lip of the next ravine. Even the nightmare pecking of the sappers' picks were silenced underfoot. Perhaps it's another truce, he thought. Terms had been offered and rejected before now. . . . He searched the gray waste of the slope below for a sign of a white flag, but nothing stirred in that ominous limbo.

After he had made his turn he paused by rote for a moment in the front-line observation post to drink a cup of coffee with the officer in charge, or rather the anonymous liquid that had long since passed for coffee in Vicksburg. He had just put the tin mug to his lips when the explosion came—a bone-shaking crash that seemed to split the weary earth below them. Julian was thrown back against the wattled support of the rampart and felt the scalding chicory water spray his chest as he scrambled on hands and knees in the dirt. The force of the blast in the trench was a tangible thing, as actual as the punishment of a bludgeon. He had worked over men who had been too close to such blasts—men who had died without apparent wounds, purely from the force of rushing air.

On his feet instantly, he found he was running with the others toward the focal point of the explosion, almost before the monstrous mushroom of dirt and smoke could settle earthward. It was soon apparent what had happened: a mine, exploding prematurely between the two lines, had carved a deep gash between the facing hillsides, toppling a gun emplacement into its maw. Crouched where the parapet ended in a jagged opening, he could look directly down into this man-made crater. At the moment there was no sign of life. The men who manned that gun, it seemed, had been blown to bits, along with their own magazine.

Someone shouted on the far side of the pit, and every eye turned in unison to a writhing dark form that shook off the dirt like a broken earthworm, struggled to rise, and fell back with an unearthly scream. When the earthworm moved again in the landslide far below, Julian saw that it was human after all. The face and torso of a man, both arms feebly waving, lungs bellowing another of those calls for help. . . . Once again the mud-daubed figure fought with all its strength to rise—and this time he saw why the effort was hopeless. The broken gun carriage lay across one leg, burying it to the knee in earth.

No one moved in the trench beside Julian. No one could while Yankee fire enfiladed the walls of the new-made crater, denying it to the Confederate engineers who might seek to shore up its walls and prevent their whole line from collapsing. Already the pit was more than half filled with the water seeping from several of the subterranean springs that honeycombed the hillside. In another moment it would lap the man's free foot as it slithered in the crumbling earth.

Julian found that he had risen without conscious thought and entered the nearest gun mount. There was a coil of rope in an embrasure of the trench; he tossed it over his shoulder, ignoring the sputter of the gun crew as he ran toward the lip of the crater, waving his white pocket handkerchief as he went. All day that handkerchief had served as a sweat rag on his streaming forehead. If it doesn't show white to the Yankees, he thought, I'm done before I start. But he went down the side of the parapet regardless and continued to wave it wildly.

"I'm going after that man," he shouted. "Will someone anchor me?"

A murmur spread down the line of watchers behind the parapet; a dozen hands thrust forward to seize the rope as the firing slackened somewhat. With a belay steadying his left shoulder, Julian found he could descend the wall of the crater easily enough if he kept his mind away from the bullets that still spattered his face and arms with dirt. As he worked his way down he groped with his free hand for the small kit that all army surgeons carried in the lines. It contained nothing but a scalpel and an artery forceps, but he had saved lives with it before.

The earth was softer now as he moved deeper; he crept rather than walked, putting all his weight on the taut rope, placing his feet like a cautious crab to avoid landslides. The shots seemed fewer now. He saw that most of the firing was concentrated on the rim of the crater: evidently the enemy was waiting for a general movement from the Confederate trenches and considered him more of a decoy than a threat.

His foot touched a smooth knob of rock. Striving to brace himself against this support, he felt the rock give under his weight; in a flash he swung free of the pit wall and dangled for a while in space, like an oversize puppet in a magician's hands. The twisting pressure of the hemp seemed about to slice his shoulder from his body, and he shouted to the men above him, begging them to swing him back to a purchase in the earth. The whine of bullets built to a crescendo as a black-bearded face thrust around the parapet. He heard a shouted order and felt himself dropping fast; the flooded bottom of the crater, black as a midnight tarn, rushed up to meet him.

He sank above the knees before his feet touched bottom. There was a strange silence here. Sound waves did not penetrate immediately, and only the angry spat of bullets, well above his head, reminded him that there was a full-scale war a few yards above. He loosened the rope and breathed deeply; feeling his nerves steady again, he anchored himself to the slipknot and began to flounder toward the mass of debris where the imprisoned gunner lay.

The man watched him come with unbelieving eyes. In places the water rose almost to his waist; in others his feet plunged into a bog that seemed to have no bottom, and he tugged hard on the rope support to swing himself clear. It seemed hours before he seized a splinter of the gun mount and swung down beside the prisoned victim. Actually it was a matter of seconds.

"Thank God you made it, Doc."

The man's lips were blue, but his mind seemed clear. His hand closed on Julian's arm, as though he feared the surgeon might vanish in the smoke that hung above them.

Julian bent over the leg. It was wedged immovably between the gun and the rocky outcrop at the bottom of the pit. Blood oozed wetly over the smooth curve of the barrel and stained the cloudy clay-brown pool below; he could almost see the water creeping higher as he leaned his whole weight against the caisson. It was a futile effort. Almost a ton of dead weight was crushing leg against rock. Even if he could have freed it, Julian knew that the bloody pulp would be useless.

The clay-daubed figure moaned under his hands; when he looked into the man's eyes again, the pupils were wide with fear. But it was evident, too, that he understood his predicament clearly.

"Take it off, Doc!" he cried. "What are you waiting for?"

"I'm afraid it's the only way."

Julian had already whipped off his leather belt. It would do as a tourniquet: there would be no time to clamp off vessels here. A few slashes of the scalpel freed the man's knee of clothing; he rolled the muddy trouser leg well above the joint and slipped the belt buckle tight as he fitted it into place. Leather bit flesh, and he felt the victim shiver.

"It must go tighter," he said as calmly as he could.

The water had begun to lap his waist as he slipped the buckle into the last hole, putting his foot against the leg and pulling with all his strength to force it home. There was no place to lay out his instruments on the slippery crater wall; he took the scalpel handle between his teeth and restored the case to his hip pocket. Then he fitted the knife handle to his palm and marked the spot for his first incision. He remembered the bedroom in St. Augustine and the strange reluctance that had all but paralyzed his hand. There was no time to yield to it now.

"Take it off, Doc." The man's voice seemed to come from the tomb. "I'll drown if you don't."

The words released his nerves, and he cut across the skin below the kneecap with a firm stroke. Thank God for anatomy, he thought: a knee disarticulation was a simple operation—he had performed dozens in the Vienna clinics. The knife grated against bone, and he heard a soft thud as his patient's head slipped back against the mud in a dead faint. For an instant he wondered if the face would be covered by the rising flood. But the water, though visibly higher on the bank, did not quite reach the soldier's nostrils. There was yet time to complete his work.

The steel entered the knee joint deftly, cutting down and around, severing the ligaments which bound the complex of bones. They dropped apart under his steady pressure; already the cartilage that covered the bone ends glistened in the wound, unbelievably white against the giant mud pie that served as his operative base. The water was lapping his hands as he considered his next approach. With the joint only partly separated, there was no way to work beneath the knee. The scalpel must cut between the bone ends—a space hardly larger than the thickness of the blade itself.

He held his breath and cut downward again, making the stroke as clean and deep as he could manage. Blood vessels parted under the steel; the tough cartilage of a ligament snapped like a broken fiddlestring. Then the knife was biting through skin, and it was over. He stared down, astonished as any raw interne, as the amputated leg stayed where it was and the stump swung free.

There was only a light ooze of blood; he tested the tourniquet to make sure of the buckle and saw that it would hold under punishment.

Someone shouted a question above him as he reeled out into the open; the question merged with a ragged cheer as he signaled an affirmative, but he had no time to hear plaudits now. The water had reached his armpits when he lifted the man's inert torso, slipped the rope beneath his body in a rude sling, and waved to the hands above to haul away. Flattened against the crater wall, he eased the soldier's body into the clear and watched it skid grotesquely in the mud before it wavered free of the watery muck and spiraled upward.

He floundered beside it, to make the journey as painless as he could, then stood back and awaited his turn. For the first time he was conscious of the silence. The firing had stopped while he worked; from the lip of the enemy trench a white flag wavered on a bayonet.

A flag of truce. The Yankees had answered his signal after all, though the answer had been a trifle tardy. He breathed another prayer of thanksgiving, knowing he had dreaded, more than anything, a return through that vicious hail of bullets.

The body moved upward easily enough as a swarm of gray-clad figures straddled the parapet to lend a hand. In another moment it had disappeared through a gun port, and the rope snaked down again. A great cheer roared over the crater's mouth as Julian stepped into the sling and slithered up the walls to the level of his own trench. To his surprise, he saw that the Yankees were cheering too. He sat astride his parapet and stared across the narrow void that separated the two trenches. It seemed strange to face a solid wall of blue bodies, all of them standing breast-high behind a mud wall that usually seemed empty as the face of the moon. . . . Somehow he felt better when he saw the white flag vanish at the precise moment he dropped behind his own breastwork.

Bullets were droning like angry hornets before he could walk down the communication trench. Those cheers still vibrated on his eardrums, but the truce was over.

ii

He followed the victim's litter to the main field hospital—a barn that stood in a rock-ribbed angle beside the river and had been spared most of the punishment visited upon Vicksburg itself. By the time he had scrubbed the worst of the clay from his body, the man was on an operating table and his own anesthetist was waiting. Revising the amputation with care, he could take pride in the risk he had surmounted. The patient's condition was excellent. It was necessary only to cut back, achieving tissues which had a better blood supply and would have a better chance of healing.

By the time he had stepped back from the table and watched the amputee moved to a cot in an already crowded ward, the whole episode seemed curiously remote. He was conscious of nothing but bone-deep weariness, of the ever-present hunger for sleep. Thank God there would be no more operations before dawn, he told himself as he shrugged into his too-large uniform coat and felt his way down a darkened alley to his quarters. By mutual consent, night fighting was almost a thing of the past in this siege. Both sides had learned to their cost that skirmishing by dark resulted too often in sharp exchanges between one's own troops; a respite after sunset was one thing a surgeon could count on.

His bed was a makeshift trestle in one of the caves; his orderly had improvised a mattress of sacking stuffed with leaves and rigged a strip of burlap for privacy. With his arms behind his head, Julian surrendered to weariness. This was the only time he let his mind return to Jane: after a month under fire, he had trained himself to observe that discipline.

Tonight, for the first time in weeks, he could not re-create her image: there was only an angry buzzing in his ears as he closed his eyes and summoned her. . . . He knew that he had dozed, and, as he dropped off, his mind had spun down into the black hell of that mine crater again. The buzzing in his ears was only the aftermath of that deadly hail of lead through which he had passed.

He sat up with a cold sweat on his forehead; wide-awake and trembling, he faced the fact that he had been desperately afraid. There had been no time to think while he worked, waist-deep in gumbo, driving a scalpel with all his skill. . . . The walls of the cave shook with yet another explosion even as his mind shook with the memory. The inverted cone of the pit was crystal-clear now, oozing into the black void; he felt the slime on his cheek and winced at the remembered whine of bullets.

He gripped the boards of his bed to still his trembling. Was he a coward to yield to fear, now that all danger was past? The question answered itself, out of his own brief taste of war. He had treated too many soldiers who had admitted that their worst hours had been those when they recalled a narrow escape or wakened in the night with a dream like this pressed like an incubus on the brain. . . . Remembering those others, he felt his own heartbeat ease. In another moment he was deep in slumber.

Jane was beside him instantly in the soothing dark; he felt the warm satin curve of her breast against his cheek as he slept, and counted her steady heartbeats out of the depths of his contentment. His contentment deepened as the dream changed, effortless as a magic-lantern slide. They were swimming in green surf again, riding the back of a roller, tumbling waist-deep in the creamy backwash as they scrambled hand in hand to reach the shore. A slim Venus rising from the Florida sea, his wife offered him her salt-sweet lips in a long kiss, then broke free of his arms to run toward the dunes. She ran lightly, teasingly—pausing just once to look back at him with the sun making its own glory in her hair. Her white, naked body was etched vibrantly against the sunrise before she ran on—to blend (as dreams will) with the endless white curves of the dunes.

He followed her with a choked cry. For a moment his feet slithered in sand. Then even the dunes vanished as the tempo of his dream changed once again. . . . He was still running—charging, head-on, into the photographer's studio in Richmond where he had met General Randolph a scant three months ago. His uncle Clayton intruded but seldom in his dreams, and the effect was usually comic rather than nightmare. This time the general sat erect and proud: an aged firebrand brandished in the face of history. Even in the dream Julian remembered how he had paused to gape at the stairhead.

The photographer clucking under his black hood, the iron clamp that held Uncle Clayton's neck steady for the three-minute time exposure were mere impertinent details. In his fine gray regimentals, with the stars of his rank gleaming dully at the collar tabs, General Randolph faced posterity with a flashing eye. The hands, folded negligently on a brand-new sword hilt, were mottled with liver spots, to match the apoplectic red in Uncle Clayton's cheeks, but touches like these were not for posterity. Nor, for that matter, was the well-bred belch that Uncle Clayton released as the photographer whisked out from behind his camera at last and bowed his compliments.

"Forgive me for making our appointment here, Julian. A busy man cannot always choose his own moments."

"I only wanted to thank you, Uncle, for helping me to enlist——"

"Say nothing about it. We need every man nowadays. I'm glad you came back to us at last, Julian. . . . I trust your commission is already in your hands? You should be in uniform——"

"It's been promised, sir, but there's been some delay. I hoped you could use your influence to——"

"Order that uniform now. You can put it on tomorrow if you wish. What service did you have in mind?"

"I've heard something of a plan to organize small field hospitals along the front. If I could head one of those——"

"An excellent idea, Julian."

"A word from you to our Secretary of War——"

"I will speak that word today," said General Clayton Randolph as he somersaulted neatly out of Julian's sleeping brain. . . .

Perhaps the word had been spoken on time, after all. It was something he would never know, as he cooled his heels for nearly two months in Richmond, operating as a contract surgeon at the hospitals; working for ten-hour shifts in that sweltering spring, as the wounded came back from Chancellorsville by the hundreds, as every tobacco warehouse on the James became an impromptu ward, to groan with its complement of agony.

But his dream followed no such precise chronology tonight. Atlanta filled the next lantern slide in the fluid theater of his mind. A canopy of leaves at a sunlit corner, a face laughing from the ambush of a pertly tilted bonnet. He had followed that bonnet for a city block, sure that he would find Jane's face beneath it, but only the girl's flaming hair reminded him of Jane as she laid a hand on his arm.

"Looking for a friend, soldier?"

He was breaking away from that sultry invitation, feeling his heart thump with thwarted rage. The new uniform still choked him as he watched the girl vanish into the crowd. . . . But he was seated in the anteroom of the corps commander's office now, hating his cousin for his insouciance. Captain George Randolph, no less, who could lounge at ease in a stiff-backed chair and look immaculate as a cavalryman on dress parade.

If it had been a minor miracle that Julian's orders had brought him through Atlanta en route to the Mississippi, it was no less shocking to find himself face to face with George. Clayton Randolph's son was an authentic replica of his father's splendor, with this difference: young Randolph had shot eighty-odd Yankees from their saddles since the war began. He had raided behind Union lines from Pennsylvania to the Ohio, and no man had dared to question his courage save at pistol point.

Julian saw him clearly now as his cousin sat admiring his narrow, handsome face in his own polished boots. Though their relative rank was the same, George could afford to stare with the disdain of the veteran who had smelled powder and enjoyed it.

"Don't fidget, Julian," he murmured. "And try not to *sit* at attention. No one doubts that uniform is real. You'll look well enough once it seems part of your skin."

"I'll feel happier when I've lost the crease."

"Your rank entitles you to a valet."

"But I don't want a valet."

Julian heard himself speak the words aloud and sat up in his rickety bed. His hand had already fumbled for the box of cigars at the bedside: it was another of the small luxuries he allowed himself when he could not sleep.

George Randolph had been quite right about the valet: many of the officers took more than one slave to war, even with the prospect of active fighting ahead. That morning in Atlanta he could hardly tell George that he had refused to submit to the pattern that his rank—and the Chisholm name—demanded. The memory of Macalastair's face was still too fresh.

His father's overseer had come up to Richmond while he was operating there, long before the War Department had put through his surgeon's commission. He could still feel the pale, unbelieving stare of those honest Scotch eyes and hear the man's sputter.

"Twenty slaves is enough, sir. A man who owns that many is exempt from service if he chooses——"

"Just because I happen to be an owner, under my father's will?"

"Asking your pardon, Doctor, but don't you owe a duty to your four hundred darkies?"

"I can trust you there," said Julian slowly. "I'm sure you're caring for them well enough. Just as you always have, Macalastair. Far better than I ever could—even if my heart were in it."

"What's to become of them, sir—when this war is over?"

Overseer and owner exchanged a long look. "What do you think of the South's chances?"

" 'Tis not for an outlander to say, Doctor."

"Say it anyhow."

"The South is fighting the future," said the overseer. "Those who fight the future are always doomed." He spread his big-knuckled workman's hands on the brim of his planter's hat. "A feudal dream in this young country—in this young man's century: it is beyond my ken why you fight for it. . . . But that is not my business. I am here to save you money—if I can."

"Are you suggesting we sell the slaves?"

"Before this madness began," said Macalastair, "they would have brought you a quarter million on the open market. I could still dispose of them for a sizable sum."

"Tell me this much: are they still well fed?"

"Well enough, sir. As you know, we have stopped the cotton crop this spring. From this planting on, we produce entirely for the commissary, under army orders." The Scotchman's lips curved in a humorless smile. "They pay us well enough—in Confederate paper. Almost enough to turn a profit on the books——"

"We'd better go on as we are, then. It sounds like a full-time job for you. If you like, I'll see to it that you're paid in gold."

"I've arranged that already, Doctor." The pale eyes all but twinkled. "The money goes direct to my agents in Glasgow."

Julian nodded his approval: he had learned all he wished to know. Macalastair could be counted on to give his four hundred Negroes the same care a good husbandman would bestow on any blooded stock: in these times he could hope for no more.

"Will you be coming to the river for a visit, Doctor?"

"I'm afraid there won't be time."

Actually he could have returned to Chisholm Hundred whenever he chose. It seemed better to stay on in Richmond, operating on a bone-breaking schedule, while he waited for the mills of the War Department to grind out his commission. Too many ghosts were waiting to reproach him in the Cape Fear country.

iii

Weeks later, when he sat facing his cousin in the general's office in Atlanta, he could remember his overseer's remarks with only a wry aftertaste of irony. It had been quite like Macalastair to mention the fact that a large slaveowner was exempted from actual war service—and the corollary that a fortune still awaited him if he moved fast. How could he explain to that shrewd Scotch brain that he no longer considered the slaves his property? Or tell George Randolph now that he had applied for active service in Vicksburg solely because it meant he must pass through Atlanta first?

Of course he had known it would be a footless errand, but he could not rest until he made at least one effort to find her.

Atlanta, a brash young railroad town mushroomed into a city by the demands of war, had stared back at him cockily as he stepped down from his train: a town of jerry-built stores and mud-daubed sills, its windows black with the soot from brand-new factories, its plank sidewalks swarming with clerks and walking wounded, with harlots and bombproofs, with sleek government factors and their even sleeker ladies, with grim-faced boys in ragged uniforms. . . . He had walked the length of Peachtree

Street, staring into a thousand faces; he had stood in three jammed barrooms with an untasted bourbon before him, hoping at least to rub elbows with Whit Cameron.

Even then he had admitted that he must trust to luck—and hold his tongue. A newly commissioned surgeon in the army of the Confederacy could hardly adn.it that he was the husband of a Union agent, or that his best friend was undoubtedly her accomplice. Still less could he risk inquiry anent Mrs. Kirby Anderson, presumably in Atlanta now to settle a lawsuit.

Eventually he had stopped a brigade runner and asked the whereabouts of his commanding officer's headquarters. As he had expected, George Randolph was there to greet him. George was recuperating in Atlanta, after a slight wound suffered in the Tennessee campaign. He had already promised, by letter, to do what he could to speed Julian's orders.

George grinned up at him now from the depths of his armchair. The grin of a wolf cub who had learned to enjoy life long ago, in war or peace.

"You still insist on being a hero, then?"

"I've applied for work in a field hospital," Julian said patiently. "If that means Vicksburg, so much the better. Your father thought that my training abroad would—"

"Your training abroad should have taught you common sense," said George. "Why can't you win your kudos sawing bones in Richmond—or right here?"

Julian weighed the temptation. If he established himself with an Atlanta hospital unit, he could count on a long stay: the trains were bringing a steady stream of wounded from both Tennessee and Mississippi these days. Swollen though Atlanta was with a wartime population, he would hear of Jane eventually. . . . He smiled inwardly at the romantic hope, knowing that he had already abandoned it.

"I'm afraid it's still Vicksburg, George."

George glanced at the door of the private office, through which a magisterial voice still boomed in dictation.

"Your orders are on Old Thunder-Mug's desk now," he said. "I saw to that myself this morning. Frank Pinckney's his aide—and Frank owes me three hundred for poker. If you insist, you can go out tonight."

Julian nodded soberly. He had hoped, in his heart, for a longer respite; now that his orders were almost in his hand, he could be glad that his stay in Atlanta was short. It had been heartbreaking enough on Peachtree Street this morning, pounding the muddy sidewalk like an unwanted ghost, staring under a hundred bonnets like a humorless Casanova. Being in love with Jane was one thing; realizing that his presence might distress her was another. Yes, he was grateful to fate—and a fire-eating cousin—for settling the matter in advance.

George said sourly, "I've never quite made you out, Julian. At the university you pretended to be one of us: I don't think you really were, underneath. Now you come into this war, hell-bent to get your head blown off. Granted you came in late—must you take yourself so seriously?"

"You're the official hero in the family, George. Don't confuse my role with yours."

"Hero, hell," said the cavalryman. "I fight because I enjoy it. So do more of us than I'd care to name. Yankee-killing is just more fun than shooting squirrels—even if they are easier targets."

George spoke with a wide grin, but his eyes were stone-cold above it. Julian stared at his cousin with a new interest; in that candid admission George came crystal-clear, like a gadfly imprisoned in wax. Julian understood now why this steel-bright youth could lie for hours in a muddy duckblind to wait for one more shot at a flying wedge of mallards; why he could ride for hours in the rain for one more running duel with a blue-coated patrol; and why he had had to thrash George soundly, when they were boys together, for beating his small body servant until the Negro could no longer stand.

"Maybe I should operate on your brain, George," he said slowly. "Maybe I could stop war altogether if I could take that hate outside your skull and see what makes it tick."

"Don't blame *me* for the war," said George. "Professional soldiers don't make war—no more do talented amateurs like me. Look out that window at the real warmakers. If they had their way, it'd go on forever."

Julian nodded grimly. From Nassau onward the bombproofs he had counted had all but outnumbered the army.

"They're fat enough now," he said. "But can they keep it?"

"Every Yankee bond issue has been bought out so far," said his cousin. "D'you think all the money comes from the North?"

He took a quick, nervous turn of the anteroom and spat casually through the window at the sidewalk beneath. "Before Sumter, every firm of importance in the South had banking connections in New York or Boston. Most of them are still investing through the border states——"

"Hedging their bets, you mean?"

"Backing their judgment on the outcome. It's only the old-line aristocracy that believed in this war and forced the issue. It's they that will suffer, when it's over. Including idealists like yourself, who still won't sell your slaves and cut losses."

So my talk with Macalastair is no secret after all, thought Julian. He wondered if George despised him for his decision. But his cousin's eyes were still cold with a bitter wisdom as he paced the office.

"We went into this war with a flourish. Chivalry against the shopkeepers. Look back on that crusade clearly—listen to the trumpets of our cause: you can't miss the tinny note in *that* battle cry of freedom. Since when has there been any personal freedom in the South—except for the few thousand dandies on top? Answer me that, Julian; then tell me why the farm boys and the poor whites go on fighting. . . . When you've answered that, explain why our smartest bombproofs are already deserting to Europe, when we've nothing but victories behind us . . ."

He paused and spat again at the open window, as though he were daring the busy town outside to protest his sacrilege. Nothing stirred in the anteroom but the panel of the office door, which seemed to vibrate gently under the compulsion of the booming voice within. A lieutenant general, far from a fighting front, proving the invincibility of his larynx; a cavalry captain, who had swung through most of the battlefields since First Manassas, voicing a bitter counterpoint of his own. . . . Here, thought Julian, was a pattern old as war itself.

He had talked with many fighting men since his return: few of the veterans had much real faith in an eventual victory, now that the last hope of intervention had gone glimmering. Those who had fought longest, like George, were the gloomiest. It seemed incredible, with Chancellorsville still screaming its triumph in the headlines, with General Lee girding the Army of Northern Virginia for an invasion that would smash the Union forever.

"Why do you go on fighting, George?"

"I've told you why—I'm a born Yankee-killer." George favored his cousin with another of those ice-cold grins. "Granted it scares me a little sometimes—watching them jackrabbit into my rifle sights. Shoot one of 'em—and there's two more coming. Even if they've Irish or German names. . . . Did you know that the Yankees are enlisting their immigrants by regiments? That they've charged us, in line of battle, yelling in languages no white man could understand?"

George sank into the armchair again and crossed his knee-length boots with a gesture of pure despair. "You can't go on killing that kind of sheep forever, Julian. After a while you find you're on the defensive. Pulling in your flanks and yelling for more ammunition. Caving in from sunstroke and skitters, because the commissary has bogged down with your rations and there's nothing but green corn to eat. Next thing you know, the sheep have turned your flank and are trampling the home front. Then the bombproofs make peace behind your back; the Yankees move in with their factories, and you starve to death because you never bothered to learn a trade. I still say it's fun while it lasts—if it doesn't last too long."

He broke his soft tirade in the middle and snapped to attention as the office door opened at last. A moment later Julian had marched in, ahead of a ramrod-stiff orderly, to salute rampant optimism again.

That same night he had entrained with his orders in his pocket. The trip to Vicksburg was a long and dusty boredom, enlivened only by his fear that he would be afraid at his first real smell of powder. Actually the last lap of his journey had been a strange anticlimax, with none of the expected fireworks.

Nothing about it had equaled the melodrama of the supply train itself. The roof of each coach dusted with a gray carpet of sharpshooters, the cabbagehead locomotive puffing defiance as it roared down the straightaways with its throttle wide. The flat gray swamplands along the right-of-way had echoed their passage, but there had been no sign of the enemy that afternoon: Grant, he learned later, had had more important business beyond the Mississippi. Jammed, not too uncomfortably, in a corner of a freight car packed to the doors with cartridge boxes, Julian had played cribbage for a while with a sleepy major of ordnance.

When the major's head had sagged in slumber, Julian had found, to his surprise, that he could sleep too, without even troubling to stretch out on the floor of the wildly dancing boxcar.

He had not heard the thunder of the artillery as their train pulled into Vicksburg that afternoon. Tonight in his cave—as he doused his candle a second time and turned on his side to sleep in earnest—he knew that it would take more than the rumble of the land mines to waken him. If there had been a baptism of fire after his arrival, he was too tired to recall it now. That one stark moment of terror had been lost in the procession of wounded flesh that had passed beneath his knife.

iv

The orderly's hand was insistent on his shoulder, calling him back to the reality of another dawn. He shook the sleep from his head as he swung his feet to the dirt floor of the cave. Only then did he remember that his sleep had been dreamless after that midnight awakening. He felt a moment of panic as he fumbled his way to the crude washstand in the corner: there would be little left to him indeed if he lost Jane in his dreams.

"Couldn't you wait till reveille?"

"Sorry, sir. Colonel's orders."

"Colonel Withers?"

Julian found that he was suddenly wide-awake. Withers was his commanding officer, in complete charge of the complex of trenches covered by his field hospital. A busy man with the reputation of a martinet, he had hardly spoken twice to his surgeon.

A perfect summer's dawn was just breaking over the bluffs as he stepped into the open air: a quiet dawn, still waiting to be smudged by the dirty thumbprint of war. He climbed the corduroy road that twisted up the side of the hill to the farmhouse at its brow, pausing to stare incredulously at a rambler rose in full flower above a shattered doorway. From where he stood, that shattered doorway was the only jarring note: the farmhouse itself, protected by the hilltop, had been miraculously untouched by Grant's artillery.

He found his colonel at breakfast on the veranda, watching the river with a pair of binoculars as he sipped his coffee. Withers pointed to a chair and continued to study the flashing yellow-gray immensity of the Mississippi. A string of Yankee barges, shepherded by an ironclad, swam brazenly downstream in mid-channel, ignoring the shore batteries. For some time now the Yankees had known that Vicksburg must hoard all her ammunition for her land defenses.

"Sit down, Chisholm," said the colonel. "I hope you haven't breakfasted." Julian saw that two places had been set on the board trestle that served as regimental table. "Depressing, isn't it, to have targets to spare—and nothing to throw at them but bad words?"

Withers swung back to the table on that and devoted himself to the Vicksburg coffee. Julian joined in the meal without further ceremony: the dreary protocol of salutes belonged to the home front. While he ate he studied his superior. Withers, he knew, was a West Point man who had returned to support the South in its bid for independence. In the full glare of morning he resembled nothing so much as a weary hawk—bold-beaked, steady of eye, and vaguely sad. . . . Julian wondered if he still fought for patriotism—or for the glory of it, as George Randolph did. Or simply because war had always been his trade.

The colonel laid down his fork at last and spoke without further warning. "I'll begin with a compliment, Chisholm. All of us have been more than impressed by your work since you joined us. The medical director tells me that you have excellent surgical judgment. Better, in fact, than any man on his staff."

"Thank you, sir." Julian watched the other man narrowly, but Withers's face was empty of expression.

"You're a valuable property, Chisholm. I intend to keep you in one piece, if I can. A number of lives may depend on your skill today—or tomorrow. Perhaps even mine. A field colonel can't expect to live forever."

"I hope you're mistaken there, sir."

Withers ignored the compliment. "I don't take chances without reason, but one never knows. That gunboat in the river could blow us to kingdom come, if she cared to spend a broadside on the effort." He brooded on that thought awhile. Julian did not interrupt: he guessed that the colonel was suffering from the worst malaise of war—the knowledge that he was beaten and could not strike back in defeat.

"I intend to keep you with me when this business is over. I'll tell you in confidence, it's only a matter of days. But I won't have a surgeon in my command who exposes himself needlessly."

Julian began to see the light. "If you refer to my operation in the crater——"

"Precisely, Chisholm. Had you been shot during that descent, I might eventually have lost the lives of dozens of my men."

"I see what you mean, sir, but——"

"Naturally you're dedicated to serve humanity. But there's always the question of where the most good can be done. You know the military principle: sacrifice the one to save the many."

"I've modified my surgical treatment on those lines."

"You must model your own life on those lines too. Without exceptions. It's my business to win battles—or, failing that, to hold my ground. It's yours to stand behind me and heal my wounded. When you needlessly expose yourself, you're guilty of an operatic gesture I won't tolerate. You saved a Yankee's life yesterday—nothing more. You might well have done the South a great deal of harm."

"A *Yankee?*"

"Didn't you realize you were saving one of the enemy?"

"I'm afraid not, sir. Both of us were too muddy."

Withers looked at him curiously. "Suppose you'd known in advance? Would you have gone down into the pit regardless?"

Julian got slowly to his feet. "I'm afraid that's part of my—dedication, as you call it. I don't like the word, but it'll have to do. Are you asking me to resign my commission?"

"I'm asking you to stay alive, if possible," said the colonel. "This war has too many heroes now to suit my fancy." He just escaped a smile as he held out his hand. "God knows you doctors don't often get credit for the job you do: to my mind, you're hero enough every time you pick up your knife."

"I accept the rebuke, sir. Next time I'll try to stay with my operating unit."

"See that you do. You can call me selfish, if you like, but at least admit I've common sense. We may have better luck when we go into battle the next time: I'd like to know I've a good surgeon behind me."

Julian walked down the corduroy road again. This war was indeed a strange business. He had risked his life to save that of an enemy, not knowing that he was an enemy. He had operated under fire, without ever knowing that he was afraid. And he had just received a reprimand which sounded oddly like a compliment.

The first dull boom of cannon split the fresh morning air. He watched the lazy plume of smoke drift back from the gun emplacement that had sounded the first defiance of the day and quickened his step. Judging by the tempo of that broadside, the stretcher cases would be arriving at his dugout almost before he could strip for action.

He began to shed his tunic as he ran toward the hospital cave, and followed it with his shirt. The sun was hot on his back now; it would be hotter still as he bent above his table in the clammy heat of noon. For all that, he was glad for the magnet that drew him back: those bloodstained boards, and the ragged canvas that sheltered them, had become his world.

v

During the next week night seemed to merge with day. There was still little fighting after dark; but the press of casualties was so great that Julian was often forced to work by lamplight until the gray trickle of dawn, or the last case, sent him reeling to his pallet for a few hours of broken rest. Even in the depths of his weariness he could not sleep through the cannonading, the burst of the mines, as the Union sappers worked deeper into the defenses of the stricken city.

He knew that his hospital was almost at the battle line now, for the nights were hideous with the moans of the wounded left between the two facing trenches. But he remembered his promise to Colonel Withers and stayed at his own operating table. At least he could take pride in the fact that his hands lost none of their skill, even when utter exhaustion threatened to strike him down in the midst of an operation. The notations on his logbook were heartening evidence of that. Inevitably such a record meant more work: he guessed that the stretcher-bearers were bringing cases to his hospital that should have gone elsewhere, but he could not turn them away.

He knew that they had turned the corner into July—July of '63. Rumor hung thick above the town, and each rumor was only an echo of doom. Terms had been offered—terms had been refused.

Grant had repeated his famous phrase and demanded an unconditional surrender; Grant and their own commander in chief had met between the lines and agreed on a parole.

Withers settled matters for Julian when he summoned him to another conference. Once again they faced each other on the veranda of the farmhouse in the flawless morning. This time the colonel handed his surgeon a mug of coffee to which a dram of whisky had been added. Julian swallowed the life-giving potion without speaking. He was too tired for thanks.

"Grant has given us terms," said Withers. "General Pemberton has accepted them. Richmond ordered us to hold out till the end, but even Richmond will be satisfied now."

The colonel had a broad Texas drawl; Julian could guess his opinion of the "Virginia mind" that had concentrated on spectacular victory in the east and permitted the Confederacy to be severed in the west. "There isn't a whole roof in Vicksburg now—or a live rat in the cellars."

"We're to be prisoners?"

"No. General Grant has taken our parole. He will let us leave Vicksburg unmolested."

Julian nodded. At the moment he did not know whether he was glad or sorry. Tired as he was, he would almost have welcomed the stockade of a Yankee prison camp. Withers would not fight again; Dr. Chisholm would move on to yet another scene of blood and hopeless screaming, to the sweet death smell of gangrene, to louse-ridden bodies and maggot-white wounds. . . . The picture was dim in his mind, like a faded daguerreotype that has lost its meaning with age. Already he could hardly remember when he had lived or breathed apart from war.

"We ride out on the fourth," said Withers. "You'll go with my column, of course."

"By railroad, sir?"

The colonel smiled thinly. "By hospital wagon, if you're lucky. The Yankees have other uses for our railroad now. It's understood that we'll make contact with General Johnston somewhere to the east." Withers's smile faded in his lined face; his sad hawk's eyes stared at Julian moodily. "A first-rate commander, Doctor. I'd be proud to serve with him, if I hadn't given my parole."

Back in his hospital cave, Julian listened to the quiet for the first time. He had prayed for this moment: now that it was upon him, he felt no emotion whatever. There was only an overpowering urge to sleep—and he needed all his will power to fight it down as he supervised the packing of their meager equipment. A few bottles of chloroform remained, his own chest of instruments, a little morphia and quinine; another day of fighting would have swept his medicine chest clean. His patients would be better off when the Yankee surgeons entered the town.

The first of these surgeons came in as he worked—a dapper young man in an incredibly clean uniform, a handsome young man who smelled of soap and macassar oil and good cigars. It was evident that he was competent to his finger tips, and equally evident that he was struggling to hide his scorn of this makeshift hole and its hollow-eyed occupants. Julian grinned as he saw the hands flinch when they touched the blood-spattered covers of his record book.

"Shall we go the rounds now, Dr. Randall?" he asked. "Or would you prefer to see me fall asleep on my feet?"

Walking down the aisles of the overcrowded main hospital, he revived a little as they discussed each case in detail. Randall was especially interested in two devices Julian had developed during the siege: an arrangement of boards and pulleys to maintain traction on broken legs, and a method of sealing off chest wounds with an adhesive mixture which allowed drainage through a tube which was always opened under water. The first had saved dozens of legs and assured their owners that they would walk again; the second had actually sent more than one chest case back to the lines—an unheard-of miracle.

Back at his quarters again, Julian dumped the rest of his belongings into a rucksack. When young Dr. Randall knelt on the board floor to assist, he knew that he had received the accolade after all.

"This is truly amazing, Dr. Chisholm," said the Union surgeon. He had an odd, precise way of speaking, as though he were reading from an invisible book. Julian had observed the phenomenon before, in his clinics abroad. "I have observed the work of your Southern surgeons, in towns we have taken. May I be frank?"

"Go the limit. I'm too tired to bark back."

"Almost invariably it has been inferior to our own. Don't think me unkind if I state a fact so bluntly."

"I agree with you. We haven't had much to work with. And good doctors have always been scarce in the South."

"But you have done better work here than I have seen anywhere—even at our headquarters hospitals."

Julian bowed his thanks. It was good to hear that his professional standards had not fallen, even in these appalling surroundings. Sometimes, when he was working in a welter of blood and grime, racing against time with a wounded man barely under chloroform to save the precious fluid, he had felt that all his effort was wasted. Praise from the enemy was sweet indeed—though it was hard to look upon this pink-cheeked, well-fed young man as an enemy.

"Where did you study medicine, Dr. Chisholm?"

"At clinics abroad. I took my degree in Vienna."

"Shake hands with a disciple of Virchow, Doctor. Who is your particular god?"

"Lister, I think—or perhaps Semmelweis."

He felt some of his weariness slip away as he recalled those arduous days of his apprenticeship. But it descended again like a drab blanket when he climbed into a hospital wagon at last and rolled down the blasted streets of Vicksburg to seek out Colonel Withers's column. His very bones ached now: he was half afraid that the ague was returning. There was a half pint of whisky in his ulster; he mixed it with a recklessly liberal dose of quinine and swallowed it without tasting it at all. Long before he could stretch out on the bare boards of the wagon floor, he knew that he was asleep.

vi

He did not know when or how the formalities of departure were carried out. Nor did he hear the cheering as the wagon rattled through the massed Union battalions and the Yankees paid homage to the surgeon who had saved their comrade's life in the crater. All through that night, and most of the day that followed, he slept the sleep of utter exhaustion. When he wakened at last, the wagon had bumped over the last of the corduroy roads east of Vicksburg and was bowling merrily along a turnpike only lightly scarred by war.

Somewhere not too far beyond, Joe Johnston's outposts were waiting to receive them. He learned later that most of their 'column had preceded the hospital wagons, to make liaison with that wily wolf, whose genius, so far, had consisted mainly of his murderous efficiency in retreat.

When he wakened in earnest in the late afternoon, he heard the sound of rifle fire in the ragged woods beyond. A brief, spiteful crackle that seemed to end almost as suddenly as it had begun. A little later, when they paused to water their team at a ford, an officer rode up and stopped to have a slight wound dressed. Julian recognized him as one of Withers's aides; most of the firing, he learned, had come from the carbines of Yankee cavalry, who had been driven back with respectable losses. Certain units of the command, it seemed, had already ignored their parole.

"What did the colonel do?"

"Rode down the lines himself to stop the firing." The aide accepted a nip from Julian's flask. "If you ask me, Doc, he wasn't *too* riled. Just had to pretend he was."

Julian climbed forward to sit beside the driver as the wagon lumbered on, oppressed by a vague sense of foreboding. The sunset was red on the gaunt pines that lined the roadway when a second aide came thundering down the line of wagons, leading a horse by the bridle. Even in the uncertain light Julian saw that the man's face was streaked with sweat.

"Colonel Withers' compliments, Doctor. Will you come with me at once?"

Julian's hands were already moving automatically, to collect his instrument case. Swinging down from the wagon seat, he turned back to stuff in whatever dressings he could find and the remaining bottles of chloroform.

"How many this time?"

"Only the colonel." The aide gave him a hand up to the extra saddle. "He stopped a stray bullet—just when we thought it was over."

"Is he badly hurt?"

"The surgeon in attendance has given up hope." The aide flashed a weary smile as they wheeled into the road together. "Colonel Withers ordered him from the room and asked for his own man."

He led the way, at the crashing pace of a born cavalryman. Julian followed at his own best gait. Strange, how he had expected this summons long before it came. At the moment he could only wonder dully what would happen if he fell asleep in this madly jouncing saddle.

Somewhere along the road, he knew, they must have passed through Johnston's picket lines: he remembered only a shouted word from a thicket as an arm waved them on. Already the light was almost gone. It was dark when the aide swung to the left and dismounted on the porch of a cabin just off the road.

"We brought him here, Doc. Go straight in: I'll carry your things."

Julian paused for an instant and blinked at the raw lamplight. A little knot of staff officers was gathered at the doorway of an inner room, where, he judged, the wounded colonel lay. But his path was barred instantly as he started in that direction: he found himself facing an irate butterball in spotless gray.

"Dr. Chisholm reporting."

The butterball tried hard to stiffen into a military attitude. Julian had a confused impression of bushy eyebrows, claret-red cheeks, in which two small eyes blazed with anger. "Surgeon Major Smart, sir."

So this was the doctor whom Withers had dismissed in his favor. Julian struggled to thrust affability through the fog of his weariness as he held out his hand. Surely there was no time for military protocol now—even though Smart, to judge by his rank, was probably medical director of the district.

"I am honored, Dr. Smart."

"Major Smart, if you please. Do you agree with me that a rupture of the spleen is hopeless?"

The man's voice had risen to an indignant bantam squeak. Julian felt every eye in the room turn in their direction.

"May I make an examination of my own, Major?"

"It is entirely unnecessary. My prognosis is already on the record."

"And I'm here under orders," said Julian, feeling his temper snap. "Colonel Withers is still living, I believe?"

"With a ruptured spleen. In my experience, that type of injury is always fatal."

"How many such cases have you seen, Major?"

The claret flush in Smart's cheeks deepened to an apoplectic purple, but he did not answer as Julian brushed past him. The colonel's adjutant had already detached himself from the group of officers and came forward with a hand held out.

"Thanks for hurrying, Doc." He favored Smart with a brief stare and did not trouble to lower his voice. "Seems they sent us a vet by mistake this time. It happens, behind the lines." He led Julian into the other room, ignoring Smart's furious sputter.

Colonel Withers lay on a pile of shuck mattresses in a corner of the smaller room; a trio of oil lamps, placed at the ends of the impromptu bed, seemed to confirm Smart's pronouncement. Testing the thready pulse and noting the extreme pallor, Julian admitted that he, too, would have marked this case as hopeless in advance. It shocked him all the more when Withers opened his eyes and spoke in normal tones.

"Good evening, Chisholm. Is the horse doctor right?"

"I've only just come, sir. May I see the wound?"

"It's all yours: just don't let that popinjay assist you. It's a joke on me—getting my ticket home after I've given my parole."

Julian had already turned back the covering on the colonel's left side and removed a temporary dressing. "Better not talk too much, sir."

He hoped that his voice was calm, and sighed his relief as the colonel closed his eyes. Only a soft-nosed bullet could have made so jagged a tear in the abdominal wall. The penetration was complete—so complete, in fact, that a purplish, pulpy object had protruded and lay exposed in the wound. His mind named the organ before his fingers could test its condition: Dr. Smart had been quite accurate when he had insisted the spleen was injured beyond repair. Watching the dark ooze of blood on the ruptured surface, Julian knew that he was facing the most difficult decision of his career.

Spleen injuries were nearly always fatal: even in Vienna he had never seen one saved. Yet he had read of such operations, read that the patient had lived. Cases were on record at the Krakenhaus: he had heard Rokitansky discourse on the subject, when that master had demonstrated the anatomy of the organ.

He studied the injury carefully. Rupture of the spleen, he had read, was accompanied by heavy hemorrhage: there had been only surface bleeding here. He tested the muscles of the abdomen and found none of the rigidity associated with internal hemorrhage; then he lifted the spleen itself, as gently as he could, to study the wound. The laceration extended for about six inches, and he could see the muscles lying bare beneath.

Suddenly he saw the reason for the lack of hemorrhage, and his pulse began to pound with excitement. The blood supply of the spleen (he had dissected it out a hundred times) lay along the stalk, or pedicle, of the organ. Prolapsed through the wound, as it now was, the pedicle had been firmly pinched in the retraction of the abdominal muscles: for the moment the bizarre position of the organ had saved the colonel's life.

"Can you operate?"

He looked up with a slight start as his patient's pale lips framed the question. "We'll operate at once, sir."

"The difference between a surgeon and a vet," said Withers. "I knew I could count on you."

Julian smiled grimly at the reminder that he must still deal with Smart. After all, the other doctor was medical director of the district—and his superior. He put a soothing hand on the colonel's shoulder. "We'll begin as soon as my wagon arrives, sir. Try to be quiet in the meantime."

"I could do with a little whisky," said Withers, and Julian noted a hoarseness in his voice for the first time.

"I'll order a hot toddy," he said with a glance at the aide. "Hot as you can make it," he added in a whisper. It was worth the chance, now that he was reasonably sure none of the other organs was involved.

Dr. Smart was still pacing the other room. Despite the cold clarity of his purpose, Julian found time to wonder if that turkey-cock swagger was perpetual.

"And now you've wasted your time and mine, Doctor . . . ?"

Julian spoke, loudly enough for the room to hear. "You were right. There's a wound of the spleen, prolapsed through the abdominal wall."

"Then you agree prognosis is hopeless?"

"Poor, but not hopeless. A splenectomy will save him, if there is no sepsis."

He had used the word on impulse, though he knew it would ring strangely in Smart's ears. "Do I understand you to suggest *removal* of the organ?" asked the older doctor.

"Precisely. I intend to operate the moment my assistants arrive."

"Colonel Withers will die on the table. He is suffering now from internal hemorrhage."

"I disagree. There is no generalized abdominal rigidity."

"Then where is the blood?"

He's barking now, thought Julian. When he struts, he resembles a pint-sized turkey; when he speaks, he's a lap dog trained to walk upright, as a parlor trick. Aloud he said, patiently enough, "The muscles of the wound have evidently compressed the pedicle. Fatal hemorrhage has not yet occurred."

Smart barked his triumph in earnest. "But it'll occur if you dare to enlarge the wound."

"Perhaps. I think not."

"And I insist it will. You have no right to take the risk."

"Why?"

"Colonel Withers is one of the heroes of Vicksburg. He has been cited repeatedly in dispatches. If he dies under your knife, you'll give our whole department a bad name."

"Do you think he'll live in any case?"

"I have already classified his wound as mortal."

Julian felt a hard white light burn in his brain and let his voice rip through his anger. "Then what difference does it make?"

"The Medical Department——"

"Damn the Medical Department, Dr. Smart—if you are a doctor!"

He waited for the challenge, but no words came. The small man's voice was deadly with venom when he spoke again. "I shall report this, of course——"

"Report away, sir. I still mean to operate."

"I'm your superior. I say you shall not. That's an order."

"I refuse to accept it."

"Major Smart!" It was the voice of Withers's adjutant, and the voice was cool with contempt as the lean lieutenant colonel stepped between the two surgeons. "Must I call you a horse doctor to your face, or will you clear out now?"

Watching the pompous medical director turn on a new enemy, Julian thought the man's eyes would pop from his head. His neck was swelling above his tight collar, red with the choler that threatened to burst the corded veins. He struggled to speak, but no words came.

"Your silence will do for an answer," said the adjutant. "If you aren't out of this cabin in ten seconds, you're under arrest. Dr. Chisholm is operating at the colonel's order."

No one stirred in the room as Smart stalked out with his dignity intact. But the tension relaxed when the thud of horse's hoofs came through the open window.

"Hell-bent for the next command post, to damn the lot of us," said the adjutant coolly. "If there's one thing I can't abide, it's a bombproof in uniform."

Julian leaned against the fieldstone fireplace and fumbled for a cigar. The adjutant offered him one from his own case and proffered a lucifer. "Of course, Doctor, you'll bear the brunt of this later——"

"It's worth the risk."

"What chance does the old man have?"

"Not too much. But he'll surely die without surgery."

They both looked up as an axle complained on the road outside. Julian hurried to the door and shouted a greeting at his wagon and its crew. The decks were cleared for action, now that his nurses were tumbling out into the yard and rushing his equipment to the cabin kitchen. He had only his own stubbornness to blame if he failed.

vii

Opening his instrument case on the stout pine table, Julian saw that the kitchen would do well enough as an operating room. The colonel's staff could hold the lamps: the light would be streaky at best, but he had learned to operate with very little light. For the first time he saw that his instruments were dirty—stained with wound discharges, crusted with dry blood. He shook his head in silent disapproval as he remembered how he had dropped them in the case at Vicksburg without even a perfunctory washing—something he had never done before.

He wondered if his deep weariness, which had caused him to skip that familiar routine, was distorting his judgment now. It was a temptation to proceed with the present task without pausing to clean his tools: he had watched other surgeons work all day without wiping a scalpel. He pulled his mind back to its standard groove and called to the smaller of his two male nurses, a pale youth with amazingly agile hands, who had been a pharmacist before the war and understood his surgeon's strange habits.

"Boil some water, Dick. These things must be clean."

When the water was bubbling in the kettle, Withers's staff had already brought him to the table. Julian watched the two assistants set up for the operation with impassive faces. At the side table he scrubbed each instrument in the scalding water, soaked and wrung out the dressings he would use, and washed each strand of ligature. The ritual gave him a sense of rightness that made the effort worth while: here, in this backwoods kitchen, he could be as clean as Lister himself. He wished vainly for creosote, but there was none to be had. He must rely on the water dressings that had served him so well in Vicksburg.

The colonel's pulse, he found, was a trifle weaker; the delay had not helped, but he could not regret it.

"Good luck, Chisholm," said the patient, and closed his eyes as the chloroform-soaked cotton folded about his nostrils. The drops fell rhythmically from the anesthetist's bottle. Julian stood back from the table, watching the involuntary struggle, waiting for it to subside as the deep gasps changed to a steady, quiet respiration.

With the scalpel already at the lip of the wound, Julian paused for thought. Enlarging the opening would release the pressure on the pedicle of the spleen. Why not control the expected spurt of blood in advance, by applying a tourniquet to the stalk itself?

He held out his hand for a ligature. His assistant, trained to obey instantly without comment, slapped a strand of whipcord in his hand and stepped nearer for orders.

"Lift the organ while I apply a slipknot."

The man obeyed, the mere pressure of his fingers causing the spleen to exude blood like a sponge. Julian dropped the loop and began to tighten it along the stalk below, as deep in the wound as he could force his fingers. When it could be tightened no more, he let the whipcord ends stream free and took up his scalpel a second time. At least he was protected against hemorrhage for the time being—unless, of course, there were damaged vessels still deeper in the wound. That was another chance he could not avoid.

The scalpel extended the wound in long, smooth strokes. At his nod, the assistant inserted a rakelike retractor to widen the operative field. Already Julian could see the whipcord knot he had just tied; his heart sank as he noted also the dark welling flood that was rising below it.

"Release the pressure, Dick."

Watching the muscles drop back into place, he knew that his

first guess had been correct, for the bleeding stopped at once. He fashioned a second slipknot, making his fingers fly.

"Can you retract and lift the spleen at the same time?"

"I think so, sir," said Dick. He shifted his hands, spreading his fingers to steady the retractor and still maintain traction on the damaged organ. As the steel rakes spread again, blood formed around them. Julian's fingers had gone deep into the wound, deeper than he could have gone with the first knot, forcing the whipcord noose down toward the base of the pedicle. The blood was warm on his fingers, and he knew that this could not last: every drop the patient lost at this juncture might spell disaster.

There was a bad moment when the second whipcord noose almost fouled on the knot he had tied to hold the first. Working entirely by feel now, he inched the strand past the danger point, letting his fingers hug the soft, friable tissue of the pedicle, making the improvised tourniquet bite home a good half inch below the original noose.

The flow of blood continued. Was the rent too low to reach? A desperate urgency filled him, yet he knew that his movements must be deliberate, lest he tear through the delicate tissue of the stalk and the walls of the great blood channels that throbbed beneath. Another half inch, and he tried again. This time the results were definite. He sponged away the excess blood, feeling the sweat run on his forehead, and smiling his thanks when an anonymous hand darted out of the penumbra to wipe it away.

He worked the ligature still deeper and tied off. The flow had ceased, but the danger was not over. His fingers were still involved in the wound; their pressure might be keeping back the expected hemorrhage. Slowly he eased his hand free of the pedicle and waited; but the wound was still dry, save for a slight red stain at the very depths. There was no time to pause for that now. He would excise the spleen and investigate that menace later.

Reaching for the surgical scissors, he cut just back of the ruptured organ. The spleen came away in his hand, a red-blue mass that felt like a bag of crushed raspberries. He tossed it in the waiting basin and forgot it instantly as he probed at that ominous ooze of blood that still clouded the base of the wound. He could risk deep retraction now in this search for some sign of internal injury. But there was no reflux of blood from the abdominal cavity, no gush of acid intestinal contents to signal an injured bowel.

The largest of the lamps circling the table came closer to the wound at his signal. Again he sponged clear and studied the field. This time he saw that the loop of intestine was injured after all, but not completely ruptured. This was the source of the oozing, and there was no choice but to place a suture.

He took one of the curved needles, the product of a century of family training in the German instrument makers' guild. Such wounds were still death warrants in most cases, but he refused to give up hope. He had removed the spleen, and controlled hemorrhage, by heroic, if unorthodox, means; he would improvise on this threat as well. It would be folly to close such a wound at once: the damaged tissue might slough through at any time, spilling its contents into the abdomen and ensuring death. True, this perforation was potential, rather than actual; but he refused to take chances now.

A length of suture, placed beside the rent in the intestinal wall, lifted the damaged loop into the area of the wound; a second loop anchored it firmly. He set the sutures in the muscles themselves and tied them firmly. The damaged section, now clearly visible, was foolproof until the process of healing was over. Even if it perforated, it would discharge in the open, safely away from the abdominal cavity.

"Stop the anesthetic. How's the pulse?"

"Weak, sir."

"Weaker than when we started?"

"Very much, Doctor."

Julian turned to the circle of faces outside the raw yellow glow of the lamps. "I'll need heated blankets——"

"They're ready now, Doctor."

It was the voice of Withers's adjutant. Julian turned back to his work, remembering that these men had faced death too, back in the holocaust of Vicksburg. Like himself, they had learned how to fight back with what weapons they had.

He worked quickly with a few more strands of suture material, pulling the muscles together in the wound but leaving room for access. Then he strapped a wet compress in place with a binder cloth and stepped back from the table. Willing hands had already brought the shuck mattresses from the bedroom and spread the heated blankets. He watched them transfer the colonel from table to bed, and knew that he was in ideal hands. The nursing job was all-important now: he could trust these veterans from the Mississippi.

Standing alone in the doorway at last, after he had scrubbed hands and instruments rigorously, he fumbled for another cigar and realized that the adjutant had transferred his own case to the surgeon's pocket while the surgeon was busy at the table. He turned to the table to murmur his thanks, but the adjutant was too busy to hear. At the moment it was simpler to go back to his instrument case and close the hasp with the elaborate care of exhaustion.

If Colonel Withers lived, he might need those instruments later. If he died, Major Smart would make sure that they were not used again in the Confederate Medical Service.

Julian took that thought into the night, behind the fragrance of the adjutant's best Havana tobacco. Suddenly he realized that he was not afraid of Smart. Come what may, he was free of this campaign: now that the regiment he served was dissolved by parole, he could only be returned to Atlanta for questioning.

Jane would be waiting in Atlanta; and this time Jane would not avoid him.

He lifted his eyes to the summer stars and laughed aloud at his romantic conviction. For all that, it was a belief that needed no proof. Jane—his dog-tired brain insisted—was in Atlanta; and he had earned this respite from war to seek her. He paced the dusty farmyard wildly as he schemed out what he would say to her; only the stars were witness when he reeled at last, asleep on his feet as he pitched awkwardly into a pile of corn shucks beside the barn.

ATLANTA

THE comfortable girth of Surgeon Colonel Cletus Townsend, and the way he lazed in his chair, had assured Julian from the first. After all, Townsend was merely the assistant medical director of the Atlanta area. Only the presence of Uncle Clayton in the place of honor (the magisterial swivel chair behind the director's own desk) reminded him that his reprimand was to be more than verbal.

He tried hard to focus his attention as Townsend rumbled on, and counted the row of uncut journals on a side table one more time, the calfskin library in a locked bookcase. The medical director's office was sad and flyblown; there was mud on the carpet, and the windows were too grimy to admit more than an echo of the bright summer day outside. . . . In its way, it was a final proof that the medical departments of armies were still minor units. There was no aura of glory here, and certainly little chance for profit. Watching Uncle Clayton make a fastidious tent of his hands to avoid the dust on the desk top, Julian realized that the general was still posing for an invisible camera, even in this dingy setting. Certainly he was devoting even less attention to Townsend than Julian himself.

"Consider this fact, Captain Chisholm," said the medical director's assistant. "What if Withers had died?"

"He would have died without my operation."

"That is not my point. You performed an abdominal suture and an excision of the spleen. Daring innovations, both of them. Need I remind you that belly wounds are synonyms for death in our profession?"

"Yet Colonel Withers recovered."

"Do you still claim credit for that miracle?"

"Not at all. My splenectomy merely gave him a fighting chance; from then on, it was a question of nursing. As you know, his own staff took on that duty, and performed it brilliantly."

Townsend looked pained. "My report has other black marks against you, Captain. When you moved on to Meridan with your patient, he was entered in the hospital there, with the commanding doctor's consent——"

"Dr. Tanner, sir. An excellent surgeon——"

"You persuaded him to wash the entire establishment, from porch to attic, with a solution of chloride of lime. When the commissary refused to issue more, Colonel Withers' staff—how shall I put it?—overrode all objections and removed a half-dozen barrels by force."

"The hospital was rotten with gangrene when we arrived. Dr. Tanner had just taken over and was desperate for a remedy. I had seen chloride of lime used, with excellent results, at Semmelweis' clinic in Budapest——"

"We can win this war without assistance from Hungary, Captain——"

It had gone on like this for a half hour.

Julian leaned back in his chair and let his eyelids droop; that fortnight in Meridan had been anything but a rest cure. His memory of Tanner was the only bright spot—and a living proof that there *were* first-class doctors behind the lines after all. A dour martinet in his own right, Tanner had backed the newcomers from the first. Julian still could smile as he recalled how Withers's staff had brought that chloride from the quartermaster's warehouse—which they had entered at pistol-point, keening the rebel yell as only Texans can. . . . He spoke out of that memory as Townsend paused to draw ponderous breath.

"Our results justified our means. There wasn't a new case of gangrene after that washing, sir. Dr. Tanner was commended by the Surgeon General himself, after his first report. And Colonel Withers is in San Antonio today—a well man."

"There, my dear Captain, you are rarely fortunate. Had things gone otherwise, you would have faced a court-martial."

The medical director was speaking for General Clayton Randolph's benefit now. We can discipline our own, the words said.

With no aid from Richmond. Even if you are a headquarters general who happened to be in Atlanta. Even if this hard-eyed cockerel happens to be your nephew.

"I still have the authority to put you under arrest, Captain," said Townsend. There was a petulant squeak in his voice now, and Julian was positive the case was closed. He had known as much in Meridan, as he labored beside his own orderlies to help free Tanner's hospital from the threat of gangrene. How would he have fared if he were not related to a general, if Tanner himself did not claim kinship with the Confederate Secretary of War?

"Aren't you interested in our findings at Meridan?"

"I'm more interested in the fact that you have exceeded your authority."

There, thought Julian, was the doctor's wartime dilemma, in a wormy nutshell; there was the cramping pressure of small minds upon every initiative, every improvisation to save life when life hung in the balance. Thanks to Tanner's liberal co-operation—and his own memory for an established prophylaxis—an epidemic of "hospital gangrene" had been stopped in its tracks. Properly exploited, the same treatment might salvage thousands of lives, on and off the battlefield. But the lardy mind that faced him took no interest in experiments. It was concerned only with the fact that discipline had been flouted.

"I'm afraid I can't apologize for saving lives, sir."

Townsend ignored the remark and heaved to his feet. "You will consider yourself confined to this area until further notice, Captain. When your commanding officer returns from Macon, a decision will be made as to your—future usefulness."

Julian smiled faintly. "May I consider this a furlough, sir?"

"You may not. Report to Major Bruff at eight tomorrow. He'll assign you to inspection duty at the railroad yards."

Julian managed a passable salute, which Townsend returned; the colonel then saluted the general, who accepted the compliment without rising from the desk. It was a ceremonious exit, somewhat spoiled when the floor boards creaked under Townsend's weight as he stalked through the door.

General Clayton Randolph spoke softly from the comfort of the swivel chair. "I'll spare you a second lecture, Julian. After all, as you say, you've saved lives for the Cause."

The Cause, thought Julian, was an abstraction that was rarely mentioned these days, until one was a safe distance from a fighting front. "I'm afraid I'd do the same again, Uncle."

"So am I," said Clayton Randolph. He rose pontifically, with his knuckles resting lightly on the desk. This time he seemed to be addressing a whole attentive Senate, in place of the reluctant nephew who still faced him at attention. "It's only fair to add that I can't protect you from your superiors forever."

"Do you accept their viewpoint, sir?"

"Townsend's a fat fool, my boy; so is that silly rooster Smart. But they both have friends in high places——"

"So have you, Uncle Clayton," said Julian, watching the general narrowly to see if his impudence had struck home. But Clayton Randolph merely inflated his chest and continued to address his imaginary audience.

"We must pull together, if the Cause we both serve is to triumph. All private quarrels must be merged in that effort."

"Do you think we've an outside chance, sir—now that we've lost at Gettysburg?"

Clayton Randolph broke his oration, with his bearded mouth spread wide, for all the world like a mastiff whose muzzle has miraculously frozen in the act of howling at the moon. When he spoke again, his voice was suddenly old, though the ghost of that forensic bellow still lingered.

"A doubter, Julian, is beyond my ken. How dare you even hint that we cannot rise above defeat?"

"Ask your own son, General," said Julian. "*He* was there with Stuart. He'll tell you the truth—if you can bear it."

Clayton Randolph's voice was icy now as he stalked toward the door. "Good day, Captain."

"Thank you for your intercession, sir."

"I refuse your thanks. In the future you may atone for your own missteps."

The door slammed, and Julian was alone in the flyspecked office. For an instant he stared at the red mudstains on the carpet and fought down an insane desire to bellow with laughter. Then, feeling that he would stifle in this forgotten corner, he followed the general into the open air.

Baiting a brigadier, he reflected, was an expensive luxury, even when that brigadier was his own uncle. Yet he had never felt so free, now he had burned his last bridge to the past.

ii

The barroom of the Atlanta Hotel, where he had left his rucksack, swirled with equal clouds of soot and tobacco smoke when he entered it: thanks to its nearness to the railroad yards, the Atlanta Hotel could be grimy indeed when the wind was right. But he forgot the soot, and his own cloudy future, over his second bourbon. If Townsend had made up his mind to knife him, he could count on only a few days in Atlanta. There was still time to convince himself that Jane Anderson had walked out of his life for good.

Jane Anderson. He thought of her by that name now: it was fantastic to insist that she had once been Jane Chisholm, his legal wife. The certainty that she was here was only a pale memory now. Even if the intuition was accurate, it was cold comfort as he stood alone in Atlanta and stared at its frantic bustle.

What could he say to her if they met again? And yet they must meet, if only to dissolve the torment in his heart. If he had really lost her, it was better to learn the worst. If there was still hope, he might learn to be patient.

A cloud of red dust swirled in the street outside as a company of infantry slouched through on their way to a train and the battle lines of Tennessee. Somehow the file of bravely whiskered boys—many of them swaggering in parts of Union uniforms, more than half of them barefoot—made a fitting postscript to his quarrel with Clayton Randolph. He had seen troops like these drop by the hundreds at Vicksburg; he had realized, long ago, that such courage could not endure against the lumbering North, a young giant that was only beginning to feel its power. Perhaps, if the war ended in a matter of weeks, his account with Jane could wait. Perhaps the mere sight of her would soothe away the worst of his unhappiness.

She was somewhere in the South, on Union business: that much was certain. The guerrilla cavalry that had met her in St. Marys was involved in her plans, and Whit Cameron had been hand in glove with her since they had left Glasgow. From Jane's viewpoint, these were ample reasons for their separation. . . . His mind spun on, in the familiar squirrel cage. He could serve her best, of course, by making their separation permanent, by baiting Cletus Townsend until the lardhead sent him up to Tennessee in sheer exasperation. But he would be less than human if he did not hope for a reunion, however brief.

He remembered his first stopover in Atlanta, the conviction that Jane was in town even then and would send for him. Perhaps there was a note in his letter box now: he had been registered at the hotel since morning, had read a mention of his arrival in one of the papers. Captain Surgeon Chisholm, of Chisholm Hundred and Wilmington, desires to establish contact with Jane, his wife—who happens to be a traitor. His brain refused to give the word shape or meaning. He knew only that he must see her again, at once.

The hotel lobby, like the bar, was thick with men in uniform. Julian elbowed his way to the desk; his voice was hoarse as he asked for his room key and letters. Already there were three envelopes in the pigeonhole: two notes from family connections, bidding him to dine; a card from some charity committee, for a ball.

"You're sure this is all?"

"Quite all, Captain. Let me ring for a boy to take you upstairs."

"I'll find my own way," said Julian dully. Just in time he remembered that he had offered this same clerk a sizable bribe when he registered. Rooms in Atlanta had been at a premium for months now. Surprisingly enough, the man only shook his head when he reached for his wallet.

"Thank you, no, sir. I've already been suitably rewarded."

"By whom?"

"By your friend, sir. Mr. Whitford Cameron. He's been upstairs since noon."

Julian took the stair in six long bounds, ignoring the sputter of a white-haired colonel he all but capsized on the landing.

The door to his room was ajar: he saw Whit's portmanteau before he saw its owner, elbowing his shabby rucksack with all its remembered elegance. Whit's London shoes stood between the two brass bedsteads, smirking at the dusty cavalry boots Julian had brought back from Vicksburg. Whit himself, immaculate in white linen and a prodigious silk cravat, lolled on one of the beds with a newspaper on his lap. As always, he seemed utterly at home—and utterly content. He looked up as Julian burst into the room, and smiled with no particular surprise.

"Beds are scarce in Atlanta, Captain. I hope you won't mind sharing this room with a civilian?"

The gambler had the same steel-fingered handshake: it welcomed Julian as no words could. We might have parted yesterday, he thought, and sat down on the other bed to stare at his friend in silent admiration. No one but Whit had the right to be this casual. The anger he had prepared to feel had already vanished. Whit *was* his friend still, no matter how oddly he proved that friendship.

"Will you tell me how this happened, or must I begin asking questions?"

"Don't I explain myself?"

"You look prosperous. But then you always do."

"This time it's more than skin-deep." Whit produced a card from his wallet. "A government contractor, dealing in army supplies, can afford good hotels."

"Since when did you give up the profession of pedagogue?"

"I still teach poker to amateurs. But it's only a side line now." Whit sat up with a yawn and adjusted his shirt cuffs. "I told you there was a fortune at this end of the table. Now I'm proving it."

"Who are your principals?"

Whit shook his head. "There, my friend, I must refuse to answer. I can only assure you that they've had no complaints. I earn my commissions—whether I'm selling blockaded shoes in Richmond or outguessing a Yankee cotton factor in Cincinnati."

Julian nodded his belief. He had heard tales of the cotton speculators who still traded with the North. Wild stories of bales that had been smuggled upriver on Yankee barges, of high-ranking officials who continued to make fortunes in this perilous game. Whit's offhand declaration merely gave the practice reality. It made trading with the enemy seem almost logical.

"How did you know I was here?"

"I, too, have friends in headquarters now," said Whit. "It's essential to my profession."

"Why didn't you stop me when I passed through Atlanta before?"

The gambler smiled. "I heard about your mad rush to be a hero; may I add that it's quite in character? Unfortunately I was in Philadelphia at the time, on a matter of business."

"How do you arrange these trips?"

"A trade secret, Dr. Chisholm. Of course, if you're thinking of changing professions, I might take you as a partner. I could use that honest façade on occasion—"

Julian's fist crashed on the brass footboard of the bed. "Never mind that now. Tell me what you've done with Jane?"

"Reverse that query, my friend. Ask what Jane has done for me."

"D'you mean it's *her* money that—"

"Draw your own conclusions there. As I say, my lips are sealed."

"You left me in St. Marys without a word. Isn't it time you told me why?"

"If I'd had my way, we'd have left long before we did," said Whit. "It was Jane who insisted on staying until you were out of danger."

Julian felt a warm glow at his heart. It was something, even now, to know that Jane had considered his welfare at the last moment.

"It was understood she'd leave you at St. Marys," said Whit. "Who are you to complain?"

"I'm not complaining. I'm only asking if she's well and happy."

"Jane's health," said Whit, "is as excellent as any rich widow could hope for. I couldn't say if she's happy. *I'd* be—if I were a woman, and you'd honored me with your love."

"We can do without that sort of humor."

"Can we, Julian? When you married, you were supposed to keep love out of the contract. I'd be easier in my mind if you had—since I'm your friend, as well as Jane's." Whit sent a fragrant blue smoke ring toward the ceiling; his eyes followed it wistfully. "As a citizen of the world, I can't blame either of you. I'd have married her myself, that night in Glasgow, if she'd considered me."

"You've known her a long time, haven't you?"

"Long enough to know she's one in a thousand."

"Do you both come from the same mountain in Tennessee?"

"I'll admit that much, without betraying a confidence."

"Are you both Union agents?"

Whit studied his cigar. "Do I look like a man who'd risk his neck for an abstraction like the United States?"

"I know the truth about Jane," said Julian steadily. "Why not make the picture complete?"

"You know nothing of Jane, my friend. Only that she's a widow who came to Atlanta to fight for her estates. A fight she won handsomely in the Supreme Court of Georgia, just two weeks ago."

"I know that she's still my wife."

"Try to prove that in Atlanta. Jane has the marriage certificate, not you. She'll make you a laughingstock if you so much as open your mouth."

"You don't understand, Whit. I'm in love with her. I can't rest until I see for myself that she's established here. If she's in any danger——"

"Why in God's name should she be in danger, unless the Yankees invade—or unless you make trouble? She's got what she came for: Kirby Anderson's estate. An estate, I might add, that was wonderfully liquid for these times."

Julian only half heard Whit now. The gambler's manner—a typical blend of frankness, cynicism, and poker-faced bluff—had begun to numb his brain.

His suspicions were strong as ever, but their direction was blunted. What if Jane's purpose had been precisely this—to recover a fortune in escrow and reconvert it into gold? Other Southern families had been just as wise, as bursting bank balances in the North bore witness. . . . Jane herself had no reason for loyalty to the feudal clique that had forced this war upon the Confederacy. Could he blame her now if she worked through Whit to make her future secure?

Then he remembered the paper that had fallen from her letter case in the bedroom at St. Marys. And he smiled to himself, knowing he could pierce Whit's glib ambush when he wished.

"You're a good agent," he said. "And a good liar—if I may use an old-fashioned word."

"Both compliments are accepted."

"One thing still puzzles me. If Jane is determined to be Mrs. Kirby Anderson—if I'm to remain an unrecognized husband—why did you meet me here?"

"I came at Jane's suggestion."

Julian's heart gave a great leap. "She wishes to see me again?"

"*See* is the precise verb," said Whit. "Don't think her desire goes further. For some time now we've realized that a meeting was inevitable. Especially when we learned that you'd applied for service in this area."

So we're back where we started in Glasgow, thought Julian. She wants to see me, right enough—on her terms. She still intends to give the orders, to play the game by her rules, until it's played out.

Aloud he said only, "Must I promise to behave in advance?"

"That won't be necessary," said Whit. "A Chisholm's behavior is always above reproach—even when the situation has no precedents."

"What does she want of me?"

"Need you ask? Surely you know how to conduct yourself when you meet a lady for the first time."

"So I'm to be presented to Mrs. Kirby Anderson all over again?"

"This afternoon, if you like," said Whit. "At the Warrens' musicale for the hospital fund. Mrs Anderson is one of the performers. Widows, as you know, may appear in society if it's for the Cause we all are serving."

The picture was complete now. They had said good-by without words at St. Marys. This afternoon Mrs. Kirby Anderson would make that good-by final. She would tell him that their love was a thing of stolen moments in the Florida dunes, a romance that had no relation to present realities. She would insist that he could only jeopardize his future by demanding his rights as her husband; and, as he bowed to the inevitable, she would offer him her hand to kiss in farewell.

It was a neat picture, and he would take joy in smashing it to bits.

"Will you present me to the lady, Whit?"

"Nothing could give me more pleasure."

"Then what are we waiting for?"

iii

The flower of the South, Julian reflected, was an accurate phrase. He could feel its presence in this tall white drawing room as Jane charmed her listeners with a bravura rendering of the "Fantasie Impromptu."

True, it was a flower that had begun to fade before its time. But there was no denying its shining beauty or its fragrance. He could sense it in the dedicated faces of the women (many, like Jane, were in flowing black, but there was a brave show of crinolines too). It was in the proud, cat-foot walk of the house slaves as they ushered late-comers to seats; in the tanned profiles of the three young officers who occupied the places of honor (alert young eagles, all of them, ignoring the fact that their legs were gone). It was a nameless thing, this rebellion in its last, full bloom

—fragile as the great spray of magnolias on the mantel, clarion as a bugle call. It was wistful yet proud. Haunted by its own phantoms, yet vibrant with a defiance all its own. . . . It was the flower of the South, holding its head high. Refusing to admit, even in its secret heart, that its life was ebbing.

Chopin's last bittersweet chords faded. Jane dropped her hands in her lap and bowed to the applause. He held his breath as her eyes sought him at last. A half hour ago, when he drove with Whit to the musicale, he had felt sure that he would betray himself somehow. It was incredible that they could face each other so calmly. That her eyes could move on, as though he were a stranger. . . .

Jane said quietly, "I have been asked to sing 'Lorena' as an encore."

Applause welled up about her with the first chord, and then a hush settled as she began the familiar ballad. Was he the only one in this crowded room who guessed that she was mocking them with this turgid sweetness?

He remembered Lucy's salon in Nassau, when Jane had sung that same ballad to a far different audience. Then, as now, he had felt that she was singing to him alone. He had known that he loved her when their eyes met over that piano in Nassau. Today her eyes were on the keyboard. Only the mockery was the same.

"Yes, those words were thine, Lorena;
They burn within my memory yet;
They touch some tender chords, Lorena,
Which thrill and tremble with regret."

He tried hard to hate her as she sang, and knew that the effort was beyond him. Like the hapless youth of the song, he had given his heart for all time. True, he was not quite so lyrically resigned to their parting; he was determined to speak out the moment they were alone. But he was still a member of this gathering, in a way that Jane could never be: "Lorena," for all its determined sweetness, could still strike an echoing chord in his heart.

Perhaps he had pictured this scene too well to be startled by it now; somehow he had always guessed that she would face him again across an ambush of strangers.

When she rose from the piano at last, it seemed only fitting that Surgeon Colonel Cletus Townsend should bustle up to offer his arm. And it was part of the ritual that she must sweep past him at last. His own careful bow had been rehearsed (deep in his mind) until it was perfect.

"May I present Captain Chisholm of ours?" Townsend's voice had a patriarchal boom. "A hero of Vicksburg, Mrs. Anderson."

"My felicitations, Captain."

"And mine to you, Mrs. Anderson."

It was over, as simply as that; but he felt the blood roar in his ears as he watched her sweep about the room on Townsend's arm. Her widow's black became her wonderfully. Such a wide bell of taffeta, he thought, could be bought only through the blockade in these times. It went perfectly with her cream-smooth shoulders, the flaming copper chignon. He closed his eyes, remembering how that skin had glowed beneath his lips, how that bright hair had cascaded about them both as their bodies met and merged in the Florida surf.

Apparently she knew nearly everyone in the room. He watched her pause for a word with dowagers and red-sashed staff officers, with a black-bearded cavalryman on crutches, with a swaggering dandy in puce-colored gabardine who—like Whit—could only be a government contractor. Several of the more magisterial guests were his own family connections; eventually, if he lingered in Atlanta, he would leave a card at their doors. . . . For the present he was content to bide his time and remain anonymous. It was enough to know that Jane had taken this society by frontal assault. A rich widow with her voice and manner could do no less.

But it was harder, by the minute, to believe that she had been his wife. Though his flesh still tingled at the memory of their shared rapture, she seemed remote from his own orbit as a star, and quite as lovely.

The crowd parted, and he thought that he had lost her. He was about to start forward wildly, when Whit Cameron laid a hand on his arm.

"Mrs. Anderson is leaving, Captain: I have the privilege of driving her home. Would you care to join us?"

"Where does the lady live?"

Whit looked mildly astonished. "At High Cedars, her late husband's estate. Where else would she live?"

The inner portico was full of late afternoon sunlight. Jane stood in a knot of officers, twirling a black lace parasol and chatting brightly. The group parted reluctantly to let her escape, just as a house slave came up with Julian's hat. He felt her eyes on him as he took the broad-brimmed felt sombrero, and wished that it could have been a trifle less dusty. He had bought that hat at a sutler's store just before he entrained for Vicksburg; the brave C.S.A. (in its laurel wreath on the pinned-up brim) was already green with tarnish.

"A soldier's hat, Captain," said Jane, and touched the gray felt lightly with the point of her parasol.

"The hat of a doctor in uniform, Mrs. Anderson."

"A soldier of the Confederacy, nonetheless," she said with a dazzling smile, and turned to the door. Her coterie of officers enveloped her instantly, and Julian let the group precede him into the open air.

Here, he found, Whit's carriage was already waiting under the wide green arch of a live oak. He felt his spirits bound when he saw that Whit sat at the reins, in lieu of a coachman, and felt them drop again when most of the officers reappeared on horseback, with a great jingling of spurs and compliments.

Jane spoke firmly. "You may escort me as far as my gate, gentlemen—and no further. No, Captain Hutchens—this seat is reserved for a hero from Vicksburg."

The dashing captain (who was only in a Home Guard uniform) made way for Julian with a crestfallen grin. Whit slapped the reins, and the phaeton moved out easily to the red dust of the street.

The mounted escort closed in with the precision of a cavalry troop, and spoiled the effect instantly as various cavaliers began to jockey for the right to ride beside the carriage. Julian saw at once that conversation would be impossible during the drive. A few polite inanities, no more. That, too, seemed part of this meeting; he could not doubt that Jane had planned it so.

"Do you live far, Mrs. Anderson?"

"A mile beyond Peachtree Creek, Captain Chisholm. I trust you won't find the ride too boring?"

"I've waited a long time for just this sort of ride," he murmured. "I can wait a little longer."

He settled in his corner on that, accepting the reward of her flashing smile, and keeping his mood intact as she turned that same smile on the officer cantering beside the phaeton, at the peril of his horse's forelegs. So far every word he had spoken was gospel. With Jane beside him again in the summer evening, he could afford to wait a little for the verdict on his future.

iv

High Cedars was a square red-brick mansion on a gently sloping hill, complete with eight *nouveau riche* Corinthian columns and a noble sweep of cedar-arched driveway. He had seen many such mansions in this raw, rich section of Georgia. Most of them dated back hardly a generation; the cotton barons who had built them sometimes moved West from their gutted plantations before the carefully planted ivy could give their walls the patina of age. . . . High Cedars did not quite belong to this parvenu class: he saw at once that it was an estate, not a plantation, a few acres of rolling woodland enclosed by whitewashed fieldstone fences. Evidently the owner had amassed his fortune elsewhere; just as evidently, he intended to set himself apart from the red-clay farm lands that surrounded him.

Major Kirby Anderson, Confederate States Army. Once again he tried to picture Jane's late husband, and lost himself in a feudal mist, without limits or meaning. This square silhouette against a pale evening sky should have given the man reality: he saw only a rich weakling who had burned himself out too soon, who had lost Jane from the first moment of their marriage, and atoned for that blunder by riding away to his death.

Once, not too long ago, those tall windows had glowed with light; this evening only a single lamp was burning above the portico, as befitted a widow's retreat. He smiled inwardly as he saw how well she had carried out her role.

At the driveway entrance Whit reined in and looked back for orders. But Jane was already waving back her would-be cavaliers.

"Remember your promise, gentlemen."

Julian felt the hostile eyes of a dozen firebrands; it was only natural for them to wonder why a mere civilian and a shabby medical captain should be so favored.

"Will you ride to Atlanta tomorrow, Mrs. Anderson?"

"Tomorrow I'll be nursing at the hospital," said Jane severely. "Must I remind you, Captain Hutchens, that I mingle in society only for charity's sake?"

The phaeton whirled away down the drive on that note, leaving the Home Guard's mount pawing the air. Jane settled back and closed her parasol.

"Thank you for your discretion, Captain Chisholm. Was the strain too great?"

"Do I seem under a strain, Mrs. Anderson?"

"On the contrary. Perhaps I've hoped for too much."

"Have you lived here long?"

"Since my return from abroad," said Jane. "As you may have heard, I returned to settle my husband's estates."

"Surely he left you more than this?"

"There were two plantations in south Georgia," she said. "There were town lots in Atlanta, cotton warehouses, a good part of a railroad. I say *were*, Captain, for my husband sold everything before my return. All but this house, and the cotton from the last crop. That is ginned, baled, and stored. I needn't tell a fellow Southerner that it's as negotiable as gold—if you can get it out."

"Your husband was wiser than most of us," said Julian.

Whit spoke irritably from the driver's seat. "Use your right names—these trees can't hear."

"Well, Julian?" she said.

"I'm still waiting, Jane."

"Wait a moment more," she murmured, and offered him her hand. He covered it with quick kisses as the dark green tunnel of the driveway closed about them.

High Cedars was no less magnificent on nearer view. Perhaps it was the very magnificence that gave the place a chill, untenanted look, even in the warm afterglow of the summer evening. Julian knew that there must be caretakers about, at least: there was a faint plume of smoke at a kitchen chimney, a stamping of horses in the stable wing. For all that, house and formal gardens faced them, empty as the moon. No stableboy ran up to gentle the horse in the phaeton shafts as Whit drew up at the carriage block; there was no sign of a black major-domo in the pale white cave of the entrance, though the door stood a trifle ajar between the towering pillars of the portico.

"Kirby sold his slaves when he joined his command," said Jane. "I've hired a few caretakers to keep the place up. Sorry I can't receive you with more ceremony, Captain—but this is wartime."

She danced down lightly from the carriage block as Julian sprang to offer her a hand. The entrance hall—neo-Greek to the last pilaster, the last spray of ivy at the stair well—received them with its chaste dignity intact. Like the silent house that surrounded it, the hall was aloof and timeless as a diorama in a museum. Only the whisper of Jane's skirts gave it life as she turned toward the archway that opened to the formal living room. As the dimness engulfed her, she seemed only a darker silhouette amid the shadows of furniture, the great hooded bell of the chandelier.

Then, as she turned up a lamp and touched a spill to the candelabra on the mantel, he saw that a corner of the great, gloomy room was lived in after all. A desk, neat with stacked papers in an alcove, a sofa on which a paper-backed French novel lay open.

"Won't you come in, Julian?"

He held his ground, still fighting the conviction that eyes other than hers were watching him. Hearing the whisper of wheels on the driveway, he turned to look through the half-open door—just in time to see Whit and the phaeton vanish down the cedar tunnel.

"There's a horse for you in the stable," said Jane. "You can leave it at your hotel livery when you return."

"So I'm to go back," he said, and moved toward her at last.

"I'm a widow," she said. "Would you ruin my reputation?"

"A horse from the hotel livery," he murmured. "Was that your idea or Whit's?"

"We thought of everything, between us."

"Everything but me, it seems."

Her eyes held his for a long moment without wavering. When she turned at last, she walked quickly to a pair of glass doors which gave to a small garden beyond the living room. Jane opened them in that same swooping retreat, as though the air of this formal room was too stale to be borne.

"I had to see you again," he said. "I had to be sure——"

"You knew I'd be in Atlanta. You knew it was madness to follow me."

When he did not answer, she took a step into the closed garden and breathed deeply of the evening. Once again he stood and watched her go, until her widow's gown had merged with the dusk and only the whiteness of her hands and throat reminded him that she was a living presence, waiting for his voice. Above her the leaves of a giant magnolia made a canopy that shut out the early starlight. The air was heavy with its sweetness. He had always hated the magnolia, that strumpet among trees, hated its heavy fragrance and the damp shade it cast. Tonight it was part of this dark garden, the symbol of the old and dying South.

Jane spoke from the leafy canopy: "You'll have to believe it was madness. You've no choice. I brought you this far so you could see, with your own eyes."

Her voice was quite matter-of-fact. Like a man emerging from a dream—and clinging to its shadow pattern to the last gasp—he refused to credit the evidence of his ears. Surely Jane's withdrawal was only part of the nightmare that encroaches on every dream. He had only to hold out his arms one more time, and she would give him back the magic they had created together.

But he did not stir as she entered the room. When he made himself speak, his voice was quite as cool as hers.

"Since we're here—and quite alone—can you tell me how it happened?"

"Whit gave you the facts."

"They'll bear repeating," he said.

She came back to the circle of lamplight, closed the book on the sofa, and sat down, spreading her billowing black hoops precisely. "The morning we left St. Marys"—her voice wavered, then steadied—"the morning you were out of danger, I knew I'd waited too long. Two days later we reached a railhead. It was only a commissary depot in the barrens, but Whit bribed our way aboard a boxcar."

"And your escort?"

She took the question in her stride, so easily that he knew she had anticipated it. "I dismissed them. Think what you like, Julian —but I had one purpose that morning: to reach Atlanta, and my lawyers."

Julian turned away from her and looked up at the mirror above the tall fireplace. It gave back the room to him, in all its muted elegance; he had only to turn his shoulder a trifle to see Jane's reflection too. At the moment he found High Cedars a better vis-à-vis than the girl on the sofa. Not even Chisholm Hundred had faced him with such dead immobility.

"Whit told you how the case turned out," said Jane. "Kirby's relatives had contested the will, of course. The court turned down the case when I appeared in person. His eldest sister died last spring: she was always the head dragon. The other dragons were willing to settle for cash—and agree to sue no more."

"So it's all yours now?"

"All mine, to do with as I like. It's a strange feeling, Julian. Like sprouting wings, or a sixth sense——"

Lucy Sprague had spoken thus in Nassau. He had never expected Jane to behave in the same fashion. Strange that she should remind him of the other at this time; stranger still that her gesture of emancipation should help him to understand Lucy. Perhaps all women reacted identically when they lost their shackles.

"Is Whit your agent?"

"You might call him that," she said. "Though he's done more for me than any agent could."

"I can believe that too. Is it true you're transferring your estate to Union banks?"

"Quite true. It isn't difficult. Most of it's in gold—or cotton." She looked at him without flinching. "Do you blame me, Julian?"

Never in this world, he thought. You weren't born in the shadow of this garden, as I was. I must linger, till the last wall is breached and the clean sun can heal our earth again. You must escape before it stifles you.

Aloud he said only, "I've no right to answer that."

"Of course I could donate every penny to our Cause." She offered him a tentative smile. "Others in Atlanta have melted down their plate and given their gates to the foundries. The rich Mrs. Anderson sends her gold to Boston and hoards her cotton for the highest Yankee bid. Why don't you despise me, Julian? It might help you to forget me."

"It's true I'm in this war," he said. "That doesn't mean I'm part of it."

"You could pass for a hero in this light," said Jane. "Don't be surprised that I haven't asked how you've fared. You see, I know already—thanks to Whit."

Do you know why I asked for active service? his mind cried wordlessly. Can you understand that it was agony to break off my search for you—to force myself to leave you in peace? Aloud he said only, "I am honored by your interest, Mrs. Anderson."

"I've seen your citations for Vicksburg," she said. "I know how you risked your career to operate on Colonel Withers. I even know you'll be sent to Tennessee tomorrow—for speaking out of turn today."

He let his bitterness break through for the first time. "Did you arrange that tour of duty, by any chance?"

"Believe me, no. But I'm glad you're going back. I think you'll be safer in the lines."

Was she about to confess everything after all? Tell him that her bushwhacker troop was stabled at High Cedars now—that the mission she had come here to perform was only beginning? But he saw her eyes cloud as she tried to continue, and knew that she had said all she dared.

"You're still in love with me, Julian. Even if I'm wrong, don't stop me."

"I'll always love you," he said. "That's why I'm here."

"And that's why you must go."

"Is that all you have to say, Jane?"

"I'm asking you to believe me. You mustn't come again. It's dangerous for me—worse than dangerous for you."

"Judging by what I saw at the musicale, you are firmly established in Atlanta."

"I've given lavishly to every fund; I sing at all the benefits and work hard in the hospitals." She offered him her bland smile again, minus the assurance. "I'm also one of the richest war widows in Georgia. Atlanta isn't Charleston or Wilmington, you know."

"Why shouldn't you go on being accepted? And why shouldn't an innocent army surgeon go on visiting you?"

Even now she refused to be pinned down. "I've told you it isn't safe. Can't you accept my word?"

"Do you expect social disgrace because you're sending your gold where it's safe? Plenty of our first families are doing just that, more or less openly; others would follow suit if they had agents they could trust."

"It's more than that."

"Don't pretend you're afraid of legal troubles. Even if it gets out that we're married. You've nothing to fear if Anderson's heirs have signed waivers."

She faced him on that, and her eyes were hard. "We made a bargain in Glasgow. We reaffirmed it at St. Marys. Must I remind you of the terms?"

"That won't be necessary," he said. "I'll admit that I'm breaking my contract by being here. But it's important to explain you've nothing to fear from me—even if you are a Union agent."

He let the statement sink into silence as a tall shadow fell across the archway that gave to the hall. A scarecrow of a man, who still retained an air of authority as sharply pointed as the carbine resting in the hollow of his arm. Even without the scar that zigzagged down one brown cheek, Julian would have recognized the bushwhacker leader instantly. He spoke quickly, before the man could step into the room.

"I'm glad he's in the open at last. How long has he been guarding you?"

The scarecrow spoke softly, without rancor. "From the start, Doc."

But Julian kept his eyes fixed on Jane. She had not budged so far: if his words or manner had surprised her, she gave no sign.

"Do you deny that he was the leader of your escort at St. Marys?"

"Why should I?" Her voice was part of her poise.

"But you said you'd dismissed the bushwhackers at the railhead."

"That's quite true. Amos turned up at the estate a while ago and asked for a job. I made him my caretaker." She all but smiled on that. "As you observe, Julian, he takes the work seriously."

"What about the others? Did they come too?"

"Several of them are quartered in the stable," she said. "We're deep in the country. This is no place for a woman to live alone."

"That depends on the woman's purpose."

Amos took a lazy step into the room, but Julian stopped him again with his voice. "My guess is that these men are loyal to the Union—and to you. Judging by this one's accent, he hails from the same corner in Tennessee that produced you—and Whit. Let's say he's one poor white who sees this war in the proper light. Let's say he gathered his troop, supported them on funds supplied by you, waited for you at St. Marys."

When Amos spoke, his tone was still quite casual. "You want to be a widow twice, Miss Jane? It's right easy to fix."

"Let him talk," said Jane. "He's earned it."

"Thank you, my dear," murmured Julian. "That makes Amos official. It also makes sense of everything you've done so far. Don't you want to complete the picture?"

"You're doing well enough," said Jane. "Not that I admit a word, but——"

"Then I'll finish for you. Either you're a spy, part of the underground railroad—or both. As you say, it's a dangerous game. If

256

I'm linked with it in any way, I'll be shot along with you. Do you think that will stop me from coming here again?"

"If it don't," said Amos, "I will."

"That's where you're wrong," said Julian. "If I know my wife at all, she rules her command. And she's well aware of the stir it would cause if I were found dead on her doorstep." He turned to Jane again, pleased to find that his voice could be as steady as hers. "Only one thing will keep me away: your word that I can't help you."

"How can you," said Amos, "with that coat on your back?"

Jane's stare was unwavering. "Will that do for an answer, Julian?"

"What about afterward?" he asked.

"Afterward?"

"He means when this cruel war is over, ma'am," said Amos, with a tremolo twang.

Jane spoke crisply. "I didn't know you were that romantic, Julian. Tonight 'afterward' sounds like forever."

He walked through the hall on that, and out of the house, without looking back. A horse was waiting at the hitching post, and he swung into the saddle, pausing, for a second only, to turn an ear toward the house he had just quitted, in the hope that she might call him back. But High Cedars was only a cold rectangle of stone against the stars; in the portico the widow's lamp burned serene as ever in the dark. For the last time he reminded himself that Mrs. Kirby Anderson had every right to keep her grief—and her plans—inviolate.

Riding down the tunnel of the driveway, he was hardly surprised to hear the rattle of hoofs behind him. On the highroad he did not even rein in to assure himself that Amos was trailing him to Atlanta. A widow who lived alone in these times could not take too many precautions. Amos would see to it that he arrived at his hotel—with no detours.

v

Surgeon Julian R. Chisholm, attached unassigned to this headquarters, will proceed without delay to Chattanooga, Tennessee, and report to the Medical Director.

By order of the Commanding General
C. M. WALTERS, Adjutant General

He crumpled the order in his fist as he climbed the hotel stairs. Cletus Townsend could move fast, after all, when the threat of a headquarters brigadier removed itself from his path; Cletus Townsend could brush aside such halfhearted penance as policing hospital trains in the Atlanta yards and send his erring subordinate straight to the front. For the moment the news all but banished the last bitter memory of Jane, until he recalled that Jane herself had predicted the order.

Undoubtedly Townsend himself had told her at the musicale that afternoon. A lady as highly placed in society as Mrs. Kirby Anderson could be entrusted with so minor a secret.

The hotel clerk had said that Mr. Cameron had departed on the night train for Macon. It was only when he paused at his door that Julian remembered he had forgotten to ask for his key. Hotel doors in Atlanta were usually locked in wartime, and he wondered why the clerk had not offered a key on his own. His wonder deepened to a gasp of surprise when he felt the knob turn under his hand and sniffed the aroma of fresh tobacco smoke in the brightly lighted room beyond.

The man in the armchair was a stranger, but he seemed utterly at home. At first glance he seemed a caricature of the small planter, from his baggy nankeen trousers to the cheroot clamped in his square, tanned jaw. But when he looked again, Julian realized that his visitor, in country eyes, could have passed as a city type with equal ease.

He let out his pent-up breath in a sigh of resignation, acknowledging his visitor, and his purpose, even before the man cupped a badge in one palm.

"Tracy Crandall, Captain. Counterespionage. No offense intended, but I thought it'd be simpler if I waited here."

Julian kept his smile intact. It was, at least, reassuring that Crandall had given his name so readily.

"Do you mind if I pack while I confess my crimes? I've a train to catch."

"Go right ahead. I know you've an order of movement in your pocket."

Julian found he could broaden his smile into a grin as he tossed the few articles he had unpacked into his battered traveling bag. "I gather I'm not to be arrested on the spot?"

"Believe me, this is only a routine questioning." The manners of the counterspy were as nondescript as his dress, but they were soothing enough. "Are you surprised to learn you've been under observation for some time?"

"Surprised and flattered. Why?"

"It's our job to investigate everyone entering the country."

"That seems reasonable. Did you think I was a spy because I joined the war late?"

"Your family connections would disabuse us of that notion, sir."

Julian returned Crandall's bow; it was a shock to realize that even this baggy nonentity (who was, actually, anything but that) could speak by the book as fluently as Clayton Randolph.

"Naturally we're a bit puzzled by your attitude toward slavery."

"I'm afraid I don't follow."

"You own over four hundred hands at Chisholm Hundred. Most men in your position would make sure of their property instead of trusting them to an overseer."

"You forget that I am a surgeon, not a planter. As I just remarked, I entered the war late: I wished to make up for lost time."

"You'll get that wish in Tennessee," said Crandall solemnly. "Shall we come to the point?"

"By all means."

"I'm here to investigate the credentials of a Mrs. Kirby Anderson—the lady you visited this evening."

So it was coming after all. Julian looked at the closed door that led to the corridor, the latticed window that gave to the upstairs veranda. If Crandall was in earnest, there was no way to warn Jane: the counterspy had chosen his time and place too carefully. He clamped down on his jumping mind and faced the other blankly.

"Now I'm really confused."

"You met Mrs. Anderson last fall, I believe. In Glasgow."

"True enough." If it was coming, it was coming fast. He would save his denials till later.

"You were married on shipboard, when you'd cleared for Nassau."

"Are you questioning the legality of the marriage?"

"On the contrary. I'm asking why you and your wife chose to separate after you reached the Confederacy. And why she no longer uses your name."

"Can I be sure that anything I tell you is in confidence?"

"Absolutely. Our files are never made public."

"I met Mrs. Anderson in Glasgow. We were married after a short but intense courtship on my part."

"I can understand that. Your wife is a very lovely woman."

"She was also a woman in difficulties at the time. Anxious to reach Atlanta with the least delay to recover the estates of her former husband."

"That, too, is a matter of record."

"We agreed that it would be simpler for us to separate until the legal matter was settled to her satisfaction." Julian listened to the timbre of his voice: it rang true enough in his ears. "Since I contemplated active service, there was no chance of an early reunion in any case. Tonight, in fact, was our first opportunity." He opened his order of movement on the table. "As you see, it was all too brief."

"My sympathies, Captain."

"Tonight we agreed that we might well be separated for the duration. My wife's contribution to the war effort—as you must know—has been magnificent."

"I am aware of that, of course."

"Unfortunately, it was made as Mrs. Kirby Anderson. For the sake of propriety, we decided that she must continue in that role so long as she remained in Atlanta."

He paused, and hoped that his smile did not resemble an afterthought. The silence seemed to echo in the room as Crandall's mild eyes weighed him. Once again Julian looked into those eyes and knew that he would not remember tomorrow if they were gray or brown. . . .

"May I say that I appreciate your frankness—and accept it? And will you admit that *we* had the right to be puzzled, especially in times like these?"

"By all means, Mr. Crandall." Why did he feel no elation at this easy victory? Why did those mild eyes still seem to probe his heart?

"You've a half hour before your train," said the counterspy. "And a soft bed to rest on. Don't let me keep you from it, Captain. It may be quite a spell before you find yourself another."

Julian knew his smile was growing strained, and knew, just as surely, that he could afford an anxious note now. "Do you expect me to rest after this?"

"Why not, sir? You're a soldier, aren't you?"

"Surely I've the right to ask why you suspect my wife."

"Suspicion is too strong a word. Let's say we don't take chances. There are many agents in both camps. Far too many for comfort. We are hampered in our search by too many conflicting interests —too many old loyalties——"

"If you're inferring that I——" Julian could even bristle now, and enjoy it.

"You have an old Southern name, Captain Chisholm—an excellent support for a secret agent. We don't say your wife is one: we simply make certain that she is not."

"Are you certain now?"

"As certain as I'll ever be," said Tracy Crandall.

He had a handshake that managed to be both soft and firm; Julian felt that he had left the impression of his own fingers in the other's palm. "Forgive me if I go as abruptly as I came. I'm a busy man these days."

Julian was still staring at the door Crandall had closed behind him when the step sounded on the veranda. He turned in time to see Amos glide through the lattice with the celerity of a blacksnake on the prowl. The bushwhacker was no more prepossessing in the full lamplight: the scarred cheek, Julian noted, throbbed with a nervous energy of its own. Amos sat down on the bed and laid the carbine carefully across his knees.

"Don't bother to look, Doc. He's on his way."

"How did you——"

"I'm right good at listening," said Amos. "Don't you fret, either. Tracy Crandall's got you ticketed as an honest man. As he says, you won't have much chance to behave otherwise for quite a while. Not where you're going."

Julian found his voice. "What right had you to spy on me? I should call the provost guard——"

"You should, Doc—but you won't. Fact is, you're *glad* I'm here —'cause I can report to Miss Jane now."

"What will you tell her?"

"Only that she was right about you—and I was wrong."

Amos offered this admission with an unexpected grin that split his saddle-brown face into a myriad wrinkles. "Course I had to be sure of you—just like Crandall."

"Did you know he'd be waiting here for me?"

"He's been snooping in Atlanta for a long time now. He's a smart hound-dog, Doc—only we're smarter. Don't let him worry you."

So I'm to be watched from both sides, thought Julian. So long as I keep clear of Jane, she has an outside chance to stay alive. At least there was no doubting the alertness of her lieutenant, nor his loyalty.

"What will you do if I try to see my wife again?"

"You won't," said Amos. "I can trust you that far."

"Suppose I'd told Crandall the truth?"

"You'd be a sieve right now—and so would he." Amos patted the stock of his gun. "This carbine's got two barrels: it was just six feet from your back while you talked."

"I'm glad we understand each other," said Julian. He suppressed an insane desire to roar with laughter. Certainly he had never felt less like laughing, as he faced the future he was entrusting to this lanky outcast. The fact that he had no real choice was no solace to him now. Nor was the more evident fact that Jane could handle her work—and the men who served her—far more smoothly if he stayed away.

"You'll do, Doc," said Amos. "I'll go further: you'll do nicely. Don't blame me for making sure. I've fought nabobs all my life. Since Bull Run I've just fought another way."

He stepped to the veranda lattice and put one cautious foot on the sill. "I'll tell her you're one of us," he said. "Even if you don't know it yet. Even if you go on hoeing your own row till the shooting's over." He was gone on that, so quietly that Julian could not be sure if he had imagined the last words.

When the whistle sounded from the freight yards, he was still staring at the rectangle of darkness through which the bushwhacker had vanished. Mechanically he swung his rucksack to one shoulder as he turned toward the stairs—and the troop train that would soon be taking on its human cargo.

vi

Julian walked down the neat row of cots as the orderly beckoned from the door of the operating room. The field hospital was rough but clean, as solid as it was complete. Even after six weeks he could not cease to marvel.

True, he was working largely with captured Yankee equipment; it was even luckier that he had been assigned to Tanner's area. Tanner was now in charge of his base, and Tanner was still related to the Secretary of War. Most important, Tanner's stock had soared with the Army of Tennessee since they had fought gangrene together at Meridan. . . . It was odd, in a way, to reflect that a man's medical career might turn on the theft of a few barrels of lime; that an impromptu partnership at Meridan could result in this compact operative unit, with the blessings of the medical director.

Cletus Townsend had done his worst to make this tour of duty a synonym for purgatory. But Julian had discovered once again that a man was accepted on his own merits once he reached a battle area.

The operating room was a sturdily built annex to the main hospital, open on four sides to the hot autumn sunlight that poured down this hillside. Many of the trees were splintered by Union cannon—the aftermath of a battle that had ebbed across this area in the summer. The front, Julian knew, was still fluid, though it had been fairly stable since he had taken his orders at Chattanooga. Tennessee would see another major battle before the snow flew in the mountain passes to the northwest. In the meantime it was the surgeon's job to clear his cases to the base hospital across the Georgia line.

He glanced briefly at the patient waiting on the table, then went to the basin to wash his hands. His two assistants were busy laying out his instruments: thanks to Tanner, he had even been able to salvage Dick, the ex-pharmacist, to act as his anesthetist. As he scrubbed he nodded approval of the instruments. Dick had ceased grumbling long ago at his orders to boil each of them between operations, even if it meant a slight delay in bringing men to the table.

The present case was a head injury fresh from an ambulance. Julian frowned as he noted the patient's youth. The fuzz of adolescence was still on the chin he cupped in his palm as he turned the injured area to the light. The lifeblood of the Confederacy was ebbing fast, to judge by this replacement. The boy's combat record told the rest of the damning story. Though he was down on the muster roll as sixteen, Julian guessed that he was a good two years under that optimistic figure. A Yankee's musket butt—with well-fed beef behind it—had written finis to his army career after a half day in the lines.

"We crossed him off, Doc," said the ambulance driver when Julian's husky male nurses had carried the case in. "Only brought him to you for a favor." The man's dirt-caked face had opened to show his own pleasure at his doubtful humor; beneath it was a puzzled respect at the ways of this mad surgeon who insisted on fighting death when any reasonable man would curl up in the shade and sleep.

The boy's pulse was full, the respiration slow. Dick had cut away the worst of the matted hair around the injury, leaving the great egg-shaped clot undisturbed. Julian's fingers outlined it gently, testing the bony table of the skull beneath. Here, in the left temple, a section of skull had been driven down for perhaps half an inch, to press upon the brain beneath. The area included the parietal lobe, the center for movement. It was small wonder that their patient lay so still.

Julian tested the muscular tone of the boy's limbs to balance his diagnosis. As he had feared, the left side was normal; paralysis was complete in the opposite members, which took their orders from this area of the brain. Again he nodded his approval at the array of instruments on the folded flour sack beside them. Dick had learned a great deal of surgery in these six weeks of hard but rewarding work: only a trained assistant would produce trephines and a Hey elevator without being asked.

"Hold him steady. I'll have to shave his head."

The wound emerged rapidly under the razor: an ugly gash in the scalp fully two inches long. When the operative area was outlined, Julian flicked away the clot with a linen pad and studied the depressed area in detail. Dick, with a nod to the second nurse, stepped away from the table to slit the neck of an ether bottle.

"He won't need much, sir."

"Just put him under, and stand by in case he moves."

The habits of that siege at Vicksburg were still with them: though the captured Yankee loot was plentiful now, they knew that it would be precious later.

When the boy was breathing deeply under the anesthetic, Julian enlarged the scalp wound to expose the normal surface of the skull beneath; Dick stood by to control the bleeding with individual forceps. A sponge revealed the damage completely, thanks to the enlargement. Julian saw that it would be best to trephine at the edge of the injury. Proceeding thus, he could slip the flat metal elevator into place, anchoring it on a sound foundation before he applied leverage. Pressure would vanish instantly if he succeeded, but it was still a nerve-tensing job. There was always the risk that the surgeon's own weight on the steel—or the trephine itself—might deepen the damage. Convulsion was the aftermath of carelessness: he had seen patients die in the clinics, the body jerking wildly in the nurses' grip as the surgeon tried in vain to compensate for his error.

Yet there was no other approach in a case of this sort. When the depressing of bone was sufficient to cause paralysis of half the body, spontaneous recovery was ruled out in advance.

The patient seemed in good shape as he picked up the trephine, placing the cutting end hard against the skull and applying a strong rotary pressure to take the first bite of bone. Progress, as always, was agonizingly slow: he counted the turns deliberately, forcing the toothed circle under his hand to bite ever deeper, gauging the depth by feel. It was almost a matter of instinct now: an extra half turn, as he knew only too well, could spell death, plunging that serrated steel deep into brain tissue instead of resistant bone.

Dick spoke as he was easing the pressure for the final thrust.

"His left arm just gave a jump, Doc."

"Anchor it, someone!"

A pair of huge hands swooped to his bidding: that, thought Julian, would be Fred Jonas, the colossus who had been his tower of strength at Vicksburg. Fred had anchored more than one patient to the table when they were sweating out an emergency without ether: he might need that strength before the present operation was over.

There was no time to investigate that ominous twitching now. If it was the prelude to a convulsion, as he feared, he would order more ether and risk the aftermath. Again he leaned hard on the trephine. Another full circle, and another—and still there was no lessening in the resistance beneath it. A boy who would run away at fourteen to enlist might be stubborn: he had no right to such a thick skull.

Fred said, "He's jumping like a monkey with fleas, Doc."

"Straddle him and hold fast. More ether, Dick."

Even where he worked, with the patient's head in a close hammer lock, Julian could feel the twitching now. Despite his care, he realized that the pressure of the trephine had moved the already depressed bone area deeper against the brain, setting up enough irritation to cause this overture to convulsion. Come what may, he must follow the present operative line—complete the trephining, lever up the bone.

Each turn of the saw-toothed circle increased the spasmodic jerking of the body just below his firmly anchored elbow; only the dead weight of Fred Jonas—a weight that made even the sturdy wooden trestles creak in protest—permitted him to continue at all. Another half circle, however, and he felt he had turned the corner: his trained fingers, testing the resistance beneath them, had detected a lessening of the almost unbearable barrier. A quarter turn, and the warning was definite. He took a half turn more and rocked the instrument gently in its bony well before he lifted it.

A round button of bone dropped out in his hand as he cracked the steel shaft against the table. Every layer of bone was represented in that precisely shaped disk. When he returned to the perforated skull he could see the glistening white membrane of the dura mater winking in the depths like a good augury. It was just as easy to locate the edge of the depressed fragment where it menaced the brain structure: here the dura was dark and discolored by hemorrhage.

The elevator came into his hand. Though the approach was established, the most dangerous part of the operation was ahead. For a few seconds he must lever beneath the depression, increasing rather markedly the pressure that had already brought on a near convulsion.

He moved in without giving himself time to think, trusting his hands to remember their task. The flat metal blade screeched for a moment, then eased deeper as it sought a purchase. When it was no more than half an inch beneath the edge of the depression, Julian saw that the boy on the table was in convulsion. There was no other name for that fearfully contorted rhythm that was constantly breaking into nightmare twitchings that seemed to have no relation to the human physique. The patient was simply thrashing away his strength, his muscles lashed into fury by the irritation of his brain.

There was no time to attempt a deeper penetration of the

retractor. Julian leaned hard on the handle, but there was no change; he increased the pressure until his whole weight seemed concentrated in that stubborn curve of steel. Then, in the depths of the wound, he felt the bone fragment loosen slightly. He fought to increase the steady leverage, knowing that he must keep it moving at all costs.

At first the half inch seemed adamant as time itself, but he knew the improvement was steady. One more effort brought the sweat to his back, but the bone was in place again, its edges locking with the normal skull around the trephine opening. The elevator came out easily in that last effort. When his fingers tested the fracture line, he was hard put to locate it, so completely had he relieved the pressure.

"He's quit jack-rabbitin', Doc," said Fred, and got down from the table without waiting for orders.

"Stop the ether, Dick."

Julian went back to the trephine opening. There was a slight ooze, but no threat of hemorrhage. A creosote compress came into his hand, and he placed it carefully above the opening. It was another procedure they had filched from the Yankees, who had obligingly left a considerable quantity of this pungent liquid behind. Left open for drainage, with a wet dressing, the injured surface could be trusted to heal in time. Later this would-be hero of fourteen could be returned to his home with a silver plate where the perforation had been.

It was Julian's last case, barring the sudden arrival of another wagon; for several days he had wondered at the lull. He forgot to wonder when the orderlies took the patient to his cot and he could stand for a few moments at the open wall of his operating theater. Sunset sparkled on the face of the first great mountain to the north. The Yankees were up there somewhere, sparring with Bragg: that much he had learned since Tanner had established him here. At the moment war seemed strangely remote from this little world.

It was a perfect moment that would not come again: that much he granted freely. From the admitting shed, where uniforms were treated to the unheard-of luxury of delousing and sweat-stained bodies were scrubbed for his operating table, to this airy room (where so many of those same bodies had been given a second chance at life), it was a field hospital to dream about. Willing hands had made it complete at his orders, but he knew that he could not keep it for long.

He faced the winding road at the base of his hill and saw with surprise that it was choked with a solid mass of infantry, a patient, homespun snake moving toward the blue-misted mountains to the north. The battle would be joined there, when it came: even a layman could say as much, after a perfunctory glance at the map. Bragg had outguessed Rosecrans, from the feints before Chattanooga to his selection of this proving ground. What right had a mere medical captain, flushed with the triumph of a ticklish operation, to cancel the coming struggle in advance?

Julian shrugged off the silent debate. The boy he had just saved was one answer—in this case a pleasant one. Once he had reported the case to the provost guard, he was sure that the stripling would be packed off to his farm with a reprimand that he would treasure forever. Of course, if the war lasted, he might grow up to the army after all. Dr. Chisholm—an amateur of battles, but a strategist nonetheless—refused to believe that the war would go beyond another spring.

That, too, was wishful thinking, and he faced the fact candidly. If the war ended in a sudden collapse, Jane might outlast it too— even as this boy he was sending out of danger. In Jane's case the danger was constant: not even a front-line hero like his cousin George (who had roared past this crossroad only yesterday, behind his cavalry guidon) could boast such incessant contact with death.

He began to curse softly in the dusk as the image of her mounted in his brain. If one of those wagons would turn in his gate, it might bring respite: standing alone, with the hospital ticking behind him like a clock, he was conscious of time and the loneliness of his dread.

Six weeks ago he had put it down with an iron hand, thinking he was riding out to war. The organization of this model field unit had distracted him for a time. . . . He knew now that his real work here was over. Only today she had whispered in his ear as he bent above his reports; she would whisper tonight without cease as he tossed in his cot and wondered if she were alive or dead.

The dreams that came with sleep were the hardest of all to bear. Tracy Crandall leered through most of them, of course: peering through a window at High Cedars like a confident vampire, leading an army of his fellows to surprise the estate by night, pacing a prison cell with a leaded whip in one fist while Jane stood before him, refusing to confess.

But sometimes Jane rode through his dreams alone—an Amazon who straddled a horse like a man, with a tatterdemalion horde of ex-prisoners behind her, daring a hail of bullets in their dash for freedom. Sometimes she was at a piano, in blazing evening dress, leading a throng in "Dixie"—a lively hymn that always conflicted with such Northern heresies as "John Brown's Body" and brought him awake in a flash.

Once, while a soft autumn rain whispered in the shattered trees, she had knelt beside his cot. But such dreams were rarities: ecstasy (as he was learning to his sorrow) must be renewed if it is to have meaning, even in dreams. The memory of their wedding night among the Florida dunes was a pale thing now. Even in the muted midnight he could not believe that the poised, and well-protected, widow of High Cedars, Atlanta, had belonged to him once, however briefly.

A bugle sang in the twilight, and a cavalry column rocketed past the plodding infantry with a brave show of patched tunics and freshly washed beards. The leader saluted the crude hospital gatepost, and Julian acknowledged the accolade. The dust of that martial meteor had barely settled when a hospital orderly turned in at the wagon yard, followed by an officer. Julian's eyes opened wide as he took the first rider's salute: he had been expecting Tanner for days, but his superior's arrival was a pleasant shock nonetheless.

"Inspecting, sir?"

Tanner tossed his bridle to the orderly and motioned to the man to wait. "Not this time, Dr. Chisholm. I'm taking over."

"I thought you were in charge of base, Doctor."

"*This* is base now. You're moving up. Haven't you heard that Bragg's beating hell out of the Yanks at Chickamauga?"

Julian kept the excitement out of his voice. "I've been too busy for rumors, Doctor."

"Tomorrow this time," said Tanner, "you'll know what busy means. Can you ride on now?"

"If you like, sir."

"Take my horse, then: he's good for ten miles before he lathers. There's a command post at Five Oaks where you can turn him in for another." Tanner came up the hospital steps, beating the dust from his gloves. "I don't have to ask if your reports are in order. Or your wagons. They'll follow you at once, of course."

Julian smiled faintly at the bustling gray back. "Might I ask where I'm bound, sir?"

"Rendezvous orders at Five Oaks," said Tanner. "If you ask me, you're bound for the battle line. See what comes of having a good name?"

So it was impending once again. The thing he had crossed an ocean and given up a love to find. The struggle to save life, within the sound of the guns. At Vicksburg war had been a cornered animal, snarling in its death throes. This was war in the open, the last romantic war, where men by the thousands charged a fully visible enemy, blunted the flower of their courage at the cannon's mouth—and re-formed to charge again. This (and every man in that slow-moving column knew it perfectly) was the Confederacy's dying bid for victory—and he, Julian Chisholm, was a part of it, with no weapon but his scalpel and his brain.

"You bring good news, sir," he said, and held out his hand. Tanner shook it warmly from the top step of the admitting room.

"See that you come back, Julian. If you live long enough, you'll make me famous."

Julian grinned down at him from the sweat-stained saddle. Then he sawed on the bit and cantered out the gate to catch up with the orderly's dust. He did not even pause to look back at the hospital. That belonged to Tanner now; it was a comfort to know that Tanner would use it well.

vii

Twenty-four hours later, honing the last of his scalpels in the flicker of a wagon lantern and listening to the bullfrog cacophony of snores in the woods around him, Julian knew that his romantic picture of the surgeon in battle was in need of revision.

True, they had been under fire twice today—once as the hospital wagons careened drunkenly down a log road on the shoulder of a disputed hill, again when they worked up this ravine to the sheltered dell that now housed his field hospital. But even then he had been far too busy to fear that dry-stick popping that meant a nest of snipers on a wooded knoll. Later he was to learn that the main battle had not been joined when his unit moved into the lines —that Bragg and Rosecrans, like two wary fighters who know each other's strength, were merely sparring while they awaited the arrival of their reserves. For all that, the litter cases in this mountain pocket had kept him working at top speed from early morning. Now, as always, the last-minute chores of preparing for the morrow would keep him awake until his mind spun down into the darkness of exhaustion.

They had come up with the infantry battalion that slept in the thick woods on all sides. Veterans to the last man, they had pitched in with a will to help the surgeon set up his workshop; now they were snug in their blanket rolls against the chill of dusk, ready to snore until morning, if they were lucky. These men had learned the trick of complete repose in odd moments—or odd days. Julian had learned it too, along with the bitter corollary that a surgeon never rests while a battle is joining.

A hundred feet from where he sat a mountain brook chattered on business of its own; when they had moved on, that brook would soon forget that it had run red with the dressings his orderlies had wrung out to dry on its bank in the scorching midday. He had been working under the tent flies at top speed then, red to the elbows and dripping sweat from a naked brown back. A chest wound on the table, betraying itself by its nightmare whine long before he could slash away the blood-caked uniform: sponge and compress, with a long tampon for drainage; there was no time for more. . . . A throat lacerated by a bullet that had coursed down the tissue that separated windpipe from esophagus: suture and pray that this boy's shattered youth could throw off the pneumonia that was almost inevitable with this type of injury. . . . A spurting artery, bursting its dike when the tourniquet slipped somewhere between the lines and his table: ligate and pray once again that the loss of blood was not too great. . . . A simple fracture, for a change: set with a temporary splint and risk yet another prayer that the splint would hold the jagged bone ends in place on the long hell of the journey to base.

The procession stumbled through his mind, a two-way march that split at his table—some to the groaning hospital wagon, some to the neat windrow behind the tent flap, to await the burial party. Soon that ghastly cavalcade would begin to dim around the edges, as his head dropped in slumber. It would not be the first time that his assistants had found him so. He had wakened often in Vicksburg, bundled into his own shakedown, with no memory of his arrival there.

Julian shook himself awake just as the hand touched his shoulder a second time. He was looking up into another pair of pain-haunted eyes. These, he noted mechanically, belonged to a lieutenant of cavalry who had apparently stumbled into the dell on foot. The man was swaying with weariness and loss of blood. Julian eased him to a blanket and turned to the banked fire to pour soup into a canteen cup.

The cavalryman drank gratefully. Julian watched his face compose itself. Another of those young medallion faces—stamped long ago with the quick-aging secret that only a soldier in battle knows. The boy waved Julian's hands aside as the surgeon started to unwind the dust-covered bandage at his temple.

"Not me, Doctor. It's the captain. Just got his ticket in the next ravine. No place for cavalry, those ravines. Said as much when we took on this action—and I say it again." The lieutenant shook his thoughts together and wavered to his feet. "This is the only field unit I could find. Captain said it was a field unit—Dr. Chisholm in charge——"

"I'm Dr. Chisholm. Who's your captain?"

"Cousin of yours. Name of George Randolph. Needs you right bad, sir."

So George's career had ended in this nameless wood, beside a brook that would be forgotten tomorrow. Julian's hands were already scooping instruments and bandages into a kit on the wagon seat.

"Is he hurt badly?"

"Bad enough, Doctor—else he wouldn't ask for you. Shell took his horse—and part of his leg."

Julian groaned: a compound fracture was always his most heart-twisting problem. He had faced a dozen of them today, forcing himself to reach for the amputation knife simply because there was no time for more.

A sleeping orderly stirred from the depths of the splint wagon as they went past. Julian paused to whisper his destination before he followed George's brother officer into the dark. They were expecting orders before morning; he would let the wagons move on without him and trust to luck to find them again.

"Is it far?"

"Only a quarter mile, sir. The Yankees are a lot nearer than you'd think."

It was a strange walk, but the cavalry lieutenant picked his way with the ease of a weary cat. Giant fireflies starred the darkness on either side as the stretcher-bearers worked with torches to hunt out wounded strays. Julian saw, with no surprise, that more than one foot soldier from their own ranks had joined in the hunt: almost from the beginning of the war a dead Yankee had been considered a legitimate gold mine, from the miracle of his unpatched boots to the greater miracle of a filled haversack. He stared back at these ghouls absently and wondered if he would still find mockery in George Randolph's eyes as George awaited his knife.

"Only a step now, Doctor," said his guide. "Mind those brambles—the path's to the right."

There was no mistaking the spot where the shell had burst. George was lying almost where he had fallen, though his men had risked carrying him a few yards' distance from the blasted bag of skin and bloody pulp that showed where his horse had stumbled and pitched his rider to the ground. A small smudge fire—too small to do more than light the knot of faces with an eerie glow—danced feebly at the edge of this man-made clearing. Beyond, the wall of darkness was absolute. Julian had no need to ask if he was standing on the battle line itself.

"When did this happen?"

"About two hours ago." The lieutenant's voice was bitter. "We'd been scouting positions all day, when the Yanks started moving. Our lines opened up to let us in, just before the burst——"

"Was there much bleeding?"

"Plenty—at first. Then it shut off by itself."

Julian frowned in the dark. Wounds that bled freely usually meant damage to smaller arteries. A large artery, cut clean across or torn in two, sometimes ceased to bleed with amazing quickness.

He bent over George and offered a greeting. But even as he spoke he saw that his cousin was beyond mockery now, though his rolling eyes lightened when he recognized Julian's face in the flicker of the firelight.

"Hello, Cousin. Glad—still alive——"

"Don't talk. I've something here for the pain."

A pair of hands emerged from the dark, offering a canteen. Julian dissolved a morphine tablet in the water, sucked the injection into a syringe from his kit, and jabbed the needle home. George had already begun to relax under his hands when he folded back the blankets that covered him and tested the heartbeat.

"Ticking like the general's watch," said a voice in the dark.

"It takes a lot to kill a cavalryman."

Julian nodded in agreement: men like George Randolph were always hard to kill, but George was on the threshold now. He folded the blankets away, forcing himself to ignore the stench: the wound had been soaked in the discharge from the horse's entrails as horse and ride wallowed under the first impact. He slashed the uniform aside, baring the wound from knee to thigh. He had fought against time with many such cases: he knew that he could not even pause to investigate the welter of blood and shredded flesh below.

Even now he could see the torn artery lying in the depths of the wound—if this macerated flesh could be described as merely wounded. George Randolph had escaped instant death only because this great trunk vessel had been torn in two by the first searing impact of the shell: nature, retracting the arterial walls in that initial agony, had made its own tourniquet. Julian's eyes moved along the bone. For perhaps a foot it had been denuded of all flesh: even in the ghostly flicker of the smudge the splinter gleamed horribly, a clean, unearthly white, a blanched harbinger of the grave.

There was perhaps a foot of uninjured thigh above the wound. What lay below must come off at once.

"Can you move him, Doc?"

Julian shook his head. "I must operate here. Build up the fire."

A heavy silence answered him from the dark. "The Yanks are on the next ridge, Doc. We'd all be sitting targets."

"Send out a flag of truce: tell them a surgeon is working——"

"It's bad weather for truces."

"Then you must spread your cloaks and stand together to cut off the light. I can't work without it."

There was a muttered consultation; Julian knelt beside the wounded man without waiting for the outcome. George's head had lolled back under the soothing balm of morphia; his lips were parted in a gentle snore. Julian looked up without surprise as Dick spoke at his elbow: he knew that Dick would follow him without orders and stay close, even in the clinging gloom.

"He'll need chloroform too, sir."

Julian nodded and stripped off his uniform coat. Behind him he heard the crackle of fresh flames: the black cave of branches expanded instantly, bringing the powder-smudged faces of a dozen men into focus. All of them stood in a rigid half circle, with arms laced: their tattered cloaks hung like shrouds from their shoulders as they stood with their backs to an invisible enemy. Julian hoped that the screen was perfect: save for an occasional rattle of musketry, far off to the right, the wall of darkness faced him silently.

He turned back to his work, his nostrils wrinkling to the familiar pungent reek of the anesthetic. He could trust Dick to give just enough to keep George Randolph under.

"Patient's ready, sir. I've put on a tourniquet at the joint."

Julian nodded: his assistant had prepared too many of these operative setups to waste time on details. The clothing slashed away to George's hip joint, the torso above swathed in blankets: how many such cases had they rushed from the table together? The fact that this job must be done on a forest floor, within musket shot of an enemy line, was only an irrelevant detail.

"Not too much room, Doc."

"We'll make it." Long since he had given up the accepted practice of cutting elaborate skin-and-muscle flaps when he amputated on the field. The practice, advocated in most surgical textbooks, was usually a soldier's death warrant, if there was a chance of sealing dirt in the wound. Julian merely removed the damage now, as quickly as possible, and left the wound open to drain.

Someone retched in the half circle above him as the scalpel screeched on bone. He wondered absently if either sound had reached the Yankee lines, but the wall of silence was still absolute as he continued. Here was the great femoral artery, still pulsing under his fingers. The forceps crunched as it gripped the arterial wall; he set the ratchet carefully before he cut the vessel beyond it and whipped a ligature in place. Two more knots now: his hands moved mechanically, spacing the tough whipcord and drawing the nooses tight. As always, he paused for a breath to see if the cut artery was snug, but there was no fatal spurting now. Only the steady, monotonous oozing that would control itself in time, now that the tourniquet was loosened.

The nerve fibers in the depths of the wound seemed to jump under his fingers: he knew that this was only reaction of the muscles they controlled and cut through them ruthlessly. Later— if George lived—these would be troublemakers of their own, pretending that the leg they once served was still there. He wondered how George Randolph would react to those messages, if he opened his eyes again.

Dick put the surgical saw into his hand; the glance they exchanged told Julian that he was making good time. He set steel to bone and whipped down. The low, vicious rasp seemed to fill the clearing; he braced himself for the sound of a cocked carbine in the dark, for the deadly chunk of lead against the unprotected human wall above him. The leg jerked under his hands, but he did not dare ask Dick to step up the chloroform; this patient was his cousin, but there would be others who needed chloroform tomorrow.

Instead he let his free hand anchor the splintered bone end a good foot below the operative field. Once again he noted its unearthly whiteness as he increased the tempo of the saw.

The bone came away at last; what was left of the lower leg dropped away into darkness. The half circle of cavalrymen seemed to draw a deep breath in unison; one of them broke away and stumbled into the woods, where he vomited with a sigh that was almost a sob. Julian pushed the shattered leg aside and studied the stump. The oozing had almost stopped now, and the muscles along the cut surface seemed red and healthy. Red as a piece of beef cut across the grain, he found himself thinking. . . .

"It'll kill him not to ride again."

Julian nodded confirmation of the anonymous whisper: it summed up George Randall as well as any formal eulogy.

"You can douse the fire now. And we'll need a litter."

"Got one ready, sir. If you hadn't come down here, we'd have brought him to you."

Julian nodded to Dick, and doctor and assistant stood aside in the darkness. Now that the stump was ligated and bandaged, their task was ended for the time. The business of bringing George Randolph to a hospital wagon could be handled by his own troop. They would only have resented the help of outside hands.

A rifle cracked in the night, and then another. In that flash the cavalry troop vanished as though it had not been: even from where he stood, Julian could not see a telltale gleam of flesh or eyeball. He knew that each man had picked his tree and frozen to the bark, that a dozen pistols hung ready on their lanyards, if the Yankees should follow that nervous stab with an actual advance. One of the bullets had whined past his own head with inches to spare. Evidently the enemy had noticed the fire after all and were trying to feel out its exact location before risking a move.

He felt the minutes tick by, but no more shots came out of the darkness. When George's lieutenant stepped into the open again, Julian saw that he was carrying the captain's saddlebags. In that same general movement two bandy-legged sergeants appeared with an improvised litter between them.

"George can use this as a pillow," said the lieutenant, as casually as though he were in barracks. "His pistols are inside, Doc. No matter what happens to him, will you see he gets 'em? George set powerful store by those pistols."

Their eyes met in the faint starlight as they moved out to the road together. Julian nodded and slung the saddlebags across one shoulder: he understood the unspoken meaning perfectly.

viii

The hospital wagons were moving up as they came down the road in the graying light of morning; to the west and north the mountains trembled with man-made thunder. Julian took the salutes of George's troop as they galloped ahead for orders, and praised Heaven that his own orders called for a halt this side of the shambles they would ride to meet.

There was no time to think of George again after he had made him comfortable in the corner of a wagon: all that blinding day, and for most of the night that followed, the wounded and the dying flowed through his field installation in a choking stream. Toward dawn there were repeated rumors of a general enemy withdrawal, though it seemed evident that the front they faced was still clinging stubbornly to its mountainside. When they received orders to move forward again, the guns still rumbled sullenly in the defiles ahead, but the wild rebel yell had begun to drown them out as the advance swept forward with the second dawn.

The battle, Julian gathered, was definitely won. His own battle with death seemed never-ending.

There was no time to visit George until their next advance post had been established and some of the more grievously wounded, who still waited evacuation to the rear, had been checked and made as comfortable as possible. When he stumbled back to his cousin's wagon at last, he would not have believed that a man could be so tired as he and yet walk upright.

George's hot, dark stare met him from the canvas depths of the wagon. The cavalry captain lay on a pile of straw, with his amputated limb propped on a blanket fold. Julian's heart sank with his first look: he had feared that George would prove a difficult patient.

"Why did you do it, Julian?"

"I'm sorry, George. But it was the leg or you."

"*Why did you do it?*"

His cousin's voice rose in a thin scream. There was a ghastly timbre to that scream, an echo of utter despair. Julian knelt on the wagon floor without answering and removed the dressing. There was no sign of inflammation about the stump so far, though the whole leg jerked spasmodically from time to time, as the muscles continued their inexorable contraction. George snarled again, though it was not a cry of pain. It reminded Julian of the warning of an animal that knows itself cornered, knows that it is hopeless to fight back, yet lashes at the enemy with all its strength.

"You'll come out of this yet, George. When the war's over we'll get you one of those newfangled English legs. I'll see to it you walk again."

"I'm through killing Yankees. You know that."

"Haven't you killed enough?"

"In Atlanta I told you it was a habit. That still goes. Where are my saddlebags?"

"In the supply wagon. I'll see they're kept safe."

"Let me have 'em now, Julian."

"You don't need them now."

"How d'you know I don't? Here I sit, half a man—with no way to pass my time. We're going toward action, aren't we? Suppose a stray Yankee should——" He broke off and clamped his teeth against the wild jerking of the blanket-wrapped stump.

"Suppose you tried them on yourself, George?"

"Suppose I did? Who has a better right?"

The boy's lips were blue when he settled back in the straw, and his forehead pearled with sweat. Julian poured a tin cup of whisky and offered it without a word: the decision his cousin had voiced could not be answered with words. He watched narrowly as George all but strangled in his effort to down the fiery draught.

"Hard to swallow?"

"Hard enough."

"Easy does it, George. You've let yourself get too excited. Try to rest a minute, while I examine you."

He was glad that his head was down as he percussed across George's midriff: knowing in advance what he would have read in his cousin's eyes, he could hardly have added the hammer blow of his own discovery. Beneath his searching fingers the abdominal muscles were rigid as a board. Taken with the tightly twisted mouth and the dysphagia, it could mean nothing but tetanus—an inevitable corollary of George's fall beneath his own horse.

"Use the right words," said George. "I've known it was lockjaw since noon."

As he spoke, his body gave a giant heave. Julian forced him back to the straw just before he pitched over the tailboard of the wagon. Even so, his neck remained slightly arched as the convulsion clung to those muscles. Julian knew that each succeeding spasm would increase in violence. Before too long, George Randolph's body would be bent like a bow—and bent again, until the strained muscles gave up the struggle.

"Now can I have those saddlebags?"

Dick was shouting for the surgeon. Julian felt his feet obey the summons even as his mind rooted him to the spot. He contented himself with a mute pressure on George's shoulder as the fit subsided at last and the weary body groveled in the straw again.

A half dozen cases were waiting in the early morning light. Beyond he saw a file of stretcher-bearers that seemed to stretch to infinity, though he knew it must end somewhere in the mist. He nodded to his anesthetist and stepped up to the table for his first case.

The greatest good for the greatest number. George was his

cousin, and George would die in agony, alone in his corner of a cluttered hospital wagon. There was no one to ease his pain in this harried moment. There wasn't even time to wonder if he should bring back the pistols from the supply wagon. . . .

When he heard the muffled report an hour later, he hardly looked up from the fractured arm he was splinting. Dick's eyes met his above the dressing without a flicker.

"Were there guns in those saddlebags, sir?" asked the ex-pharmacist.

"Two dueling pistols. I should have warned you."

"He asked for them when I was passing by. Of course I didn't know," lied Dick.

"Of course you didn't," lied Julian.

They worked in silence until the case was taken to join the walking wounded. "I'll see if he shot straight," said Dick, wiping his hands. "Cavalrymen generally do, but——"

Julian nodded and bent to examine the next wound. He was too tired to ask himself why the sound had brought him no emotion but relief. At least he was glad that it had been Dick, not he, who had ignored the oath of Hippocrates.

Fred Jonas came up on the run. "Litter case hemorrhaging, Doc—can't get him to the table."

They passed Dick on their way down the line. The ex-pharmacist merely nodded. Both of them had known in advance that George Randolph would shoot straight. As George himself had said, a world without Yankees to kill was not to his liking.

Perhaps, thought Julian, it was better that such a legacy of hate should blast itself to eternity. Even if that bloody stump had healed—even if George had hobbled home a simon-pure hero—the war had destroyed him in advance.

ix

The train of hospital wagons twisted down the stony roadway in the rain. On either side the woods were pocked by the iron breath of Mars; behind them the guns still quarreled in the mountain passes; ahead, in the lowering mist of evening, there was no sound but the screech of an axle, the keening moans of a man whose pain was beyond all bearing.

Julian plodded beside his own supply wagon in the return to

base. He was walking in a blind dream, too tired to raise his head to mark the next step on the slippery downgrade. One thought was fixed in his mind: George Randolph would find a hero's grave after all. He could do no less for the son of a brigadier. His own supply wagon was heavy with wounded, but the body of a Randolph was worthy of transport. Even if the bone-weary surgeon in charge must tramp in the rain.

Someone shouted from the roadside, and he turned to meet the inevitable babble for morphine. In this case the wounded boy was sprawled in the ditch, with ten grimy fingers spread fanwise on his swollen abdomen. Julian did not need to examine him to guess his story: the gray-blue loop that swung between his hands, like a pendulous smear on the dirty uniform, could be only a loop of intestine. Perhaps he had rolled from a passing wagon in his agony; perhaps he had merely crawled from a thicket in the woods and collapsed. There was no time to ask, no time to explain that the last grain of morphine had been used long ago, on cases quite as urgent as his.

For all that, Julian found himself kneeling in the mud to gentle a shoulder made knife-thin by hunger. The touch was all the boy needed: a reminder, however useless, that he had not been entirely forgotten. He was smiling as death supplied its own belated anesthetic.

Julian opened his mouth to curse, but no curses came: there was only the cold, flat taste of the rain on his tongue as he clamped his jaw down on screaming nerves. He began plodding again, without raising his head, without noticing that corduroy logs were underfoot now, instead of the stones of the roadway. It was a long time before the quiet reached his brain—and longer still before he looked up and saw he was alone with the finale of evening on a slope of cutover pine.

Somehow, in rising from the ditch, he had taken the wrong turn: his feet, fumbling on the bank, had blundered into a side road and carried him far from the moving column of wagons. He gathered as much in a hazy fashion, even as he noted that the surrounding woods were hash-marked by cannon, the underbrush trampled by the two-way surge of war that had moved to quarrel elsewhere not too long ago.

He continued to stare stupidly at the desolation, even after the first shots came. A short, hard burst, from a single rifle, whining about him like hornets gone berserk. A repeater, he thought: the Yankees are using repeaters now. Certainly no muzzle-loader could throw lead that fast.

There was a pause as he stood swaying drunkenly, his eyes piercing the shredded arabesque of branches ahead to seek out the origin of the fire. Probably a lone sniper in the woods, he thought. Afraid to give himself up, he's clung to his hide-out all through the day. Now, with evening, his finger itches for the trigger, forgetting that his personal war is over. . . . The second burst cut the thought in half; he turned toward the main road again, staggering rather than running, in a scramble to gain the shelter of the underbrush beyond.

Something paralyzed his right leg, just below the knee. He plunged numbly, striking his shoulder against a tree, and reeling yet another step forward before he pitched into the mud. He knew that his head would strike the rock, long before it rushed up to meet him. For a second he seemed to hang in space, awaiting the crashing impact that would wipe out mournful woods and the threat of death behind him.

He was unconscious only a few seconds. In the moment that followed he lay still while he canvassed the sensations that reached his brain. Head and rock had made only glancing contact, it seemed: at least, his brain was clearing rapidly. Save for his bone-shaking weariness, the rest of his body seemed intact—until his exploring hand touched his right leg below the knee, where feeling ceased to exist.

So this was what the wounded felt, he thought. This was the trap of pain into which so many had blundered. But where was the wound? He fought down panic as he tried to move the leg. At first nothing happened; then, as the message from his brain beat through the shock of the bullet, he felt the muscles begin to contract. The pain began with the contraction—biting, lancing agony that brought sweat to his forehead and set his whole body trembling.

He set his teeth on it and pushed himself slowly upright in the mud until he had assumed a sitting posture and could lean his back against a tree. He had fallen half in the shelter of a spray of evergreen; beyond, where the toes of his boots pointed, the corduroy road seemed wide as the universe. Somewhere in the tangle of branches to the north a rifle was covering that road, waiting for its living target to stumble into the sights again. He faced the thought as he faced the rain-pitted road and waited for the pain to ease.

When the first wave passed, he flexed his injured leg against the other to bring it close and pulled up the tattered uniform trouser. There was a neat hole through the fabric, about six inches below the knee. When he twisted the cloth for a better view, he saw another hole on the opposite side. So the bullet had gone through, after all. Was it a good omen?

Slowly he drew the fabric higher, until he could find the dark hole in the calf where the bullet had entered. The perforation looked smaller than he had feared, though there was a steady flow of red that seemed to pulsate a little as it trickled down to soak his sock and boot top.

His brain began to tick again as he refused to panic at the sight. The pulsation was steady: he refused to believe that the bullet had found either artery or bone. To prove the latter, he lifted his heel and jarred it against the ground. The movement brought a sharp stab of pain, but the leg felt solid; if the bone had smashed, it would have given a little with the impact.

The wound of exit, he saw, was larger than the wound of entry, but not unduly so. Again he had been lucky: the Yankee repeaters fired a more slender projectile than the muzzle-loaders. A minié, turning and twisting in its flight, would have made mincemeat of his calf at this range.

There was some bleeding at the exit wound as well: the whole perforation was beginning to come alive down its length, as if someone had thrust a red-hot probe through his calf and left it there to simmer. But he was calmer now, his mind moving ahead to what he must do, even as his hands brought a compress from the emergency kit in his side pocket. He placed it carefully against the wound of exit, steadying it with the pressure of his good leg as he applied a second compress to the smaller wound. A twist of muslin completed the bandage: he wound it snugly, splitting and knotting the ends with the dexterity of long practice.

There was whisky in his pocket flask, and he took a long draught without counting the swallows. He needed a clear head and courage, and he needed them fast. The woods behind him were a bog: his only means of reaching the main road was the corduroy trail that lay wide open to the sniper's sights. Yet, with a good hour of daylight remaining, he could hardly cling to his muddy ambush. In any case, he felt sure that the Yankee had marked his hiding place: it would be only a question of time before he moved down for the kill.

His fingers clawed at the bark of the tree, and he felt the sweat roll down his back in earnest as he pulled himself to his feet—or, rather, to his good foot, for he could not risk an even distribution of his weight. Hopping like an ungainly bird, he began to parallel the road, working his way back toward the clump from which the shots had come. Presently he was opposite the spot where he had stood when the first burst of lead had screamed past. There was no sign of life in the woods ahead: save for the patter of the rain, he might have been on some strange planet, moving through a landscape without meaning or end. . . . He pulled up sharp when a twig cracked underfoot; the thinly spaced trees gave only a poor shelter after all, if Yankee eyes were marking his advance. Somehow he must warn them first that he was a doctor and unarmed.

Then he saw the rifle barrel in the leaves at the bend of the road. It was trained dead on the straightaway he would have followed had he been rash enough to continue his retreat to the main highway—an immobile threat, strangely lacking in menace now that he had flanked the muzzle. For a long time he froze where he stood, wondering how any human hand could hold a gun so steady, and wondering, too, why the Yankee had not turned to mark his crablike progress through the woods.

The blued steel of the barrel shone with rain: even as he watched, a few drops glided from the front sight and dripped across the muzzle. He risked everything to shout a challenge and flattened against his tree trunk while he waited for a reply. When none came—when the rifle barrel did not waver in its vigil—he dared to hop nearer before he shouted again. The woods gave back his echo. This time he could see the Yankee himself—a flat blue shadow hugging the stock of his rifle, all but lost in the deeper green shadow of the leaves.

He burst into the open before he weakened, ran a dozen wavering steps on both legs, and collapsed against the bole of the tree in which the sniper lay. The force of his impact sent the rifle twisting earthward, where it plunged deep in mud and stood quivering like a poorly balanced spear. For an instant the sniper himself seemed to hesitate in his nest of green; then, like a great, inert crow, he tumbled after his gun. Somersaulting clumsily in mid-air, he landed at Julian's feet—sprawling there in the grotesque repose of death, his uniform coat blue-black with rain, a fragment of steel gleaming just below the left shoulder blade.

x

Julian stared at the steel splinter without seeing it at all. Like his insane dash into the open, the thing had happened too fast. It was only when he knelt to test his enemy's heartbeat that comprehension dawned. Trapped in this wood by the sudden backwash of war, the sniper had evidently been wounded by a shellburst—hours before, to judge by the great dried lake of blood that had spread beneath the tear in his uniform. Too weak to call for aid, he had merely clung to his nest, with his rifle still at the ready, his cheek still resting on the stock. . . . Blind with hate and fear, but not too blind to aim after a fashion, he had simply blazed way at the first gray silhouette to cross his sights. The effort had been his last, opening a fresh torrent of red in lungs that were already drowned. Perhaps he had died as he pressed the trigger. Certainly he was dead long before Julian approached his hiding place.

As the fact sank home, he felt his flesh shrink from the tumbled blue mass before him. The Yankee seemed a greater threat in death, though he could hardly have said why. He knew that he should pause to go through the pockets like a good rebel: the haversack on the man's back was heavy with food; these snipers were issued extra rations for their long vigils. But he could no longer bear to touch the body now that his work as a doctor was over.

Fifty feet down the road he felt his knees buckle and knew it was impossible to move farther without some solid support for his wounded leg. Already the muscles were stiff to the touch, and there was fresh bleeding around the compress. Any further disturbance might set up a real hemorrhage. Yet he must keep moving until he reached the main road and the shelter of a hospital wagon. Too many walking wounded had passed through his own field hospitals, after a prolonged exposure to bad weather: often they would be feverish with pneumonia long before they could find a bed at the base; pneumonia, in this season, was almost as great a scourge as the dysentery that seemed to sweep through the camps in any weather.

His head was heavy, and a dull ache had begun to pound behind his eyes. Perhaps the cold, plus the shock of the wound, had unleashed a fresh attack of ague in his blood stream. He had had a narrow escape when he moved out of Vicksburg; this time he might not escape so easily. He sank down by the roadside as a fresh wave of pain and nausea swept over him, feeling his spirits tumble with the physical drop. The dead Yankee was still too near for comfort. Despite himself, Julian found he was staring into the glazed eyes that were now open wide in death.

He forced his mind to be practical. A crutch of some kind was essential. He hobbled among the saplings at the roadside until he found one with a fork not too far from the ground. It took a long time to cut through the green wood with a jackknife, and the base had still to be trimmed to his height. Finally he finished by ripping a trouser leg to the thigh, hacking long strips of cloth to pad the fork of the crutch, and balancing himself precariously against a tree trunk while he fitted the improvised support under one arm. The activity steadied him somewhat, though he felt a fresh wave of nausea as he began to stump painfully toward the main road.

The muscles of his injured calf automatically put the leg into a position of flexion, so that his progress was slow but steady. It seemed a long time before he drew within sight of the ditch that bordered the highway—and saw that the log road he had followed made a kind of rough fork with the main route. Both roads were deserted in the twilight, save for the dead—who sprawled as before in grass and mud, where the hospital orderlies had tossed them to lighten their loads. The dead were the only human attribute: save for them, it was a landscape without pity, dominated by the dark whirr of wings as a buzzard rose languidly from its feast at the roadside and spiraled into a tree, where it perched with insolent ease.

Man and bird regarded each other for a silent interval before the man dragged himself painfully up to the wagon ruts. The buzzard, thought Julian, was precisely the cachet that the scene required. There was no doubting the hideous purpose that caused it to rise in slow, flapping flight. Julian forced himself to walk slowly, ignoring the bird's lazy parallel. He had seen too many of these winged ghouls above the field in Vicksburg, quarreling like harpies over the newly dead: thank God they were not so numerous in these mountain defiles.

As his mind swung dully back to sanity, he found that he was strangely calm. At times, in fact, he seemed to float gently above the road, suspended in a serenity of his own making; even when he felt the hard stones beneath his boot soles again, the stab of agony that spread from calf to thigh like living fire, his own ego seemed detached from the pain of that slogging journey.

Weighing his chances of survival (if night found him still alone in the rain and cold), he could shrug off his fear as easily as he ignored the carrion bird that followed him. Wondering how long he could walk without collapsing (as the next bone-shaking wave of fever all but engulfed him), he could pick a resting place in the wet grass, pause to look at it longingly for a moment, and stagger on, with a strength that went beyond his own will.

But the quiet emptiness around him continued to mock his half-waking pleasure in finding himself alive: the dead, huddled at intervals along the road like restless sleepers frozen at the moment of rising, were a constant reminder that he must keep moving or join them.

When he heard the rattle of hoofs ahead, he shouted with joy. For a moment he stood on his good leg in the midst of the highway, waving his crutch frantically to slow the breakneck approach of the dispatch rider. A lathered horse and orderly, sweeping down like doom, and swerving just in time to avoid riding him down. . . . He swayed and all but fell as the courier rocketed out of sight around the bend; it was hard to realize that to this messenger of Mars he was no more than an obstruction on the road.

Yet, as he continued his journey, he remembered how often he, too, had ignored the walking wounded when his own hospital wagons were packed with the last case they could carry. Those same wagons were miles away now. The battle they had served was over. Was he doomed to walk between two worlds until he dropped?

He told himself firmly that he would live through this aftermath of battle—that he would save himself for the search that lay ahead. Somehow he must find Jane, if only to tell her how completely they had misunderstood each other from the start.

He had found her, after all, an eon ago—and each word that

passed between them had deepened the gulf. Would he ever know if she was living or dead, if the house called High Cedars was still her sanctuary? He spoke her name aloud to the cold rain and stumbled on. When he saw the glow of a campfire through the trees, he moved toward it as a man who has walked in the shadow might approach life itself. Days later he remembered that the green sapling had split beneath his weight, while he was still a hundred yards away. But this time his hoarse call for help was answered. There was a sound of running feet in his ears as the sudden dark engulfed him.

xi

The straw in which his head was resting had tickled his nose for some time, but the effort to sneeze was beyond him. He looked up lazily at the swaying roof of the boxcar and focused his energy on linking the events that brought him here.

At first there were too many gaps. He was content to lie deep in this clean straw and stare at the flat gray back of the orderly seated on an upended pail at the far end of the boxcar. The man was one of a group of four, and all of them were deep in poker; there was no one else in the car, and he puzzled over that fact for a while. This train was Atlanta bound: he was certain of that much, remembering clearly that they had bowled through Marietta a good hour ago. Most of the southbound trains out of Tennessee were loaded with wounded these days: this one carried only baled hay and a few lowing calves in a pen—and even the calves had been dropped at a commissary depot en route.

It was Tanner's doing, of course—Tanner, who was a blood relation of the Secretary of War. Tanner himself had ridden with him to the railhead, after he had probed and dressed his wound at the field hospital; Tanner's own hands had poured his final potion of whisky and quinine and given the vial of morphine tablets to the orderly in charge. As for Julian, he had been too weak to protest such special treatment at the time. Racked by the ague that had blacked out the last few days in merciful grayness, he could only stare as his friend had arranged his transport. . . .

But he must go back to the moment when the cavalrymen had found him lying in the mud at the roadside—too tired to call again, though their campfire was a scant hundred yards away. He remembered how magically he had revived in that human warmth. The sheer joy of finding a world where men laughed and breathed and cursed in a language he could understand. . . . He even remembered the charred squares of meat lying on a grid across the coals —and how the fire had hissed and flared under the dripping grease. They had offered him one of those steaks, on a flat slab of rock, and he had devoured it with animal gusto, laughing with the others when someone mentioned the Yankees' cavalry losses.

Later he had ridden behind one of the officers, with his bad leg wrapped in sacking. The fever had returned to him then: he had all but fallen more than once on the long journey to the field hospital. That nightmare came back to plague him now, even in this tranquil moment: the wounded lying in rows in the rain, with only a few shreds of canvas for protection; the surgeons working with the celerity of butchers in lighted cabins; the hospital wagons rolling out of the cabin yard, each with a red stain to mark its passing. . . . A preoccupied doctor, whose very beard was matted with blood, had given his wound no more than a glance before he waved them on.

The first great emptiness came at this point: when the fog lifted, he was lying in a cot at the hospital he had built on the hillside. Tanner's own hands wavered into the foggy picture and out again, then steadied at his knee, as the expert fingers flicked the last of the field dressings aside.

"Looks clean to me, Captain," said Tanner. "Sure you weren't hit twice?"

He was taking Julian's pulse now, his eyes lowered. "Don't talk —I'm getting the picture without any help from you. Overwork, one part; two parts shock; three parts breakbone in your blood stream. The sort of fever no man can put down until he catches up on sleep. Which is precisely my prescription for you, Dr. Chisholm. Do you agree?"

His head had cleared then—enough to follow Tanner's lean finger as the other surgeon tested the skin tone around the wound. It looked clean enough: through-and-through bullet wounds did well with as little treatment as possible, if no foreign bodies were driven into the flesh.

"Brace yourself," said Tanner. "You know this will hurt."

But Julian had fainted under the probe, without shame. Still later, as his mind swam back to lucidity for another brief moment, he remembered the elder surgeon's words:

"You'll be walking in a fortnight, if you stay clear of hospitals. This one's clean as a whistle, thanks to you. I can't say the same for my esteemed colleagues at Dalton. Nor are you likely to fare better at Atlanta. You should convalesce at a private home."

High Cedars, with Jane to nurse him. He remembered how tenderly she had seen him through the fever at St. Marys. Every mansion in Atlanta opened its doors to wounded when the backwash of battle was at its peak: as an authentic hero, he had a right to choose his corner—and his nurse. But he clamped his lips tight on her name, just in time.

"I'm afraid I've no friends in Atlanta."

Tanner looked puzzled. "Don't be so modest: a Chisholm has friends everywhere. Or should I say relatives?"

"As a surgeon, I'll take my chances on a bed."

"As a surgeon," said Tanner, "you mustn't talk nonsense. You're much too valuable to risk a case of hospital gangrene just because some filthy orderly touches you out of turn. This wound will heal itself, if you give it rest. You've earned that last, God knows."

In the end Julian had agreed to convalesce at the home of Tanner's uncle. A letter crackled in his pocket now, addressed to that worthy gentleman's mansion on Whitehall Street, Atlanta. . . . He had been too spent to argue when Tanner had bundled him off to the railhead.

"What about this ague?"

"You can sweat it out in the straw," said the surgeon cheerfully. "I'm putting four furloughs in the same car. They'll keep you under blankets."

His teeth had drummed with chill as the journey began. All through the night that followed he had sweated and shaken by turns, as the fever ebbed and built in his blood stream. Staring at the flatlands of Tennessee, at the rivers swollen with the autumn rains, he had watched the sad-brown country melt into the hills of northern Georgia and wondered if this changing landscape was part of his delirium. The morning brought his first glimpse of cotton fields and the proud cedars that fenced a great manor house from the northern winds. He had seen cots on the porticoes and gray-clad figures hobbling on crutches under the trees. All that day the sight had repeated itself as the train rolled deeper into Georgia. The people of the South had opened their homes to their wounded now that the great victory of Chickamauga was a part of history. Why had he hesitated to give Jane's name when Tanner had questioned him? Who could be surprised if he used this means to force himself on her attention?

He remembered Tracy Crandall again, just in time. The orderly, hearing his name called, threw his hand into the discard and turned to the pale officer thrashing on his bed of straw.

"Time for your quinine, sir."

"Can't I shake this one out on my own?"

"Sorry, sir. Dr. Tanner's orders."

Julian swallowed the whisky and quinine without argument. Dr. Tanner, he reflected, was a competent magician. Had he been stronger, he would have protested this special handling—while hospital trains waited on sidings, packed to the engine cab. At the moment he could hardly lift his head from the straw to hold the bitter cup to his lips.

He dreamed he was in St. Marys and started up from the heart of the dream, only to collapse in the orderly's arms. The train had stopped in the hot shadow of a station: the sun, burning through a steamy mist, gave a miragelike quality to the country beyond the panting engine.

"Don't tell me this is Atlanta."

"Cavalry depot, sir. Atlanta's eight miles to the south." The orderly looked down doubtfully at his charge. "Dr. Tanner said you could go on by buggy, if you were well enough. This was where I aimed to leave you if——"

Julian nodded. He felt sure he could waver to his feet, after his long sleep—and proved it, with the orderly's arm about his shoulder. After all, the man was on furlough: he could shake out his misery in the seat of a buggy, if he was properly bundled against the coming chill of evening.

"I'll make it. Just get me a driver."

The orderly jumped to the cinder platform of the siding with alacrity.

"This is my bailiwick, sir. My father's overseer will take you."

The overseer, Julian discovered, was a one-armed veteran who wore his faded uniform with pride; the "buggy" turned out to be a buckboard, padded with straw and folded blankets.

"I'm sorry we couldn't get a rig, Captain."

"This looks even better."

"I'll leave you in Jordan's hands, then, sir. You'll sleep in Atlanta tonight, or he'll know the reason why."

I'll sleep before then, thought Julian. He tested the stopper of the vial nestled in one palm and found he could obtain one of the morphine tablets with a minimum of effort. It was something to look forward to, if the road ahead lived up to his first view. He offered the orderly his free hand as they nested him among the blankets of the buckboard.

"Enjoy your furlough."

"The same to you, sir."

The first jounce of the springless axle was all he had expected and more. Watching the shed of the way station merge with the piney woods, he gritted his teeth and kept the morphine in reserve. After the first mile he would ask the driver to halt while he fumbled in his instrument case for a syringe. Already his instrument case seemed a long way off, though he had seen the orderly tuck it safely under the front seat of the buckboard. Surely there was water in the canteen that swayed from a bowed gray shoulder above him. . . . He'd better ask to be sure.

"Jordan!"

The overseer turned. Julian realized dimly that he had interrupted a long harangue on the mistakes of the high command at Seven Pines.

"Anything wrong, sir?"

He felt his teeth chatter as he tried to frame an answer, and knew there was no controlling the deep coldness that had begun to creep to his finger tips. The overseer's whiskered face, the trees that bordered the wagon ruts, had already begun to turn in slow circles against the sky.

"Is the road this bad all the way?" He wondered how his voice could be so steady as the rigor neared its climax.

"We'll pull into the turnpike at Peachtree Creek," said Jordan. "It's easy riding from there."

Peachtree Creek, and High Cedars. So they were taking him to Jane's, after all; he must make some protest, protect her before it was too late. Perhaps he could reach the letter in his pocket—and explain that he was to be taken past that danger point and on to Atlanta. . . . He tried to pin the thought down, but his mind refused to keep pace with his crying need. He heard his voice trail off into an earnest gibberish and sensed dimly that the driver had stopped the wagon and climbed over the seat to fold another blanket about him.

"Easy does it, Doc. I'm taking you there."

"But you don't understand——"

"Sure I do. Everyone in the county knows the place. You're lucky we're so close."

Tanner's orderly, he reflected, was little more than an eager boy. Naturally he could not wait for an overdue furlough to begin. He had followed orders literally, without pausing for details. Turning Captain Surgeon Chisholm over to his father's overseer, he had also surrendered the responsibility of delivering Captain Chisholm to his destination. The captain had seemed well enough when he was lifted to the straw of the buckboard; the captain could be trusted to give Jordan precise directions. Apparently the captain had done just that, in the first flush of his delirium.

He fumbled for coherence one more time as his mind sank deeper in a whirling vortex of darkness.

"High Cedars isn't—that is, I——"

"An hour does it, Doc," said Jordan, and folded the extra blanket under his chin. It was the last thing he remembered before darkness claimed him.

Much later (though time had ceased to have meaning) he opened his eyes and saw they were in a dark green tunnel that seemed to have no terminus. He breathed deep of the fragrance of the cedars and slipped back into the dream. Above and beyond it he heard his own voice ranting. High Cedars, he told Jordan, was his only sanctuary in a world at war; High Cedars was the dwelling place of his heart. . . .

xii

When he wakened again—or seemed to waken—he knew that he was still dreaming. He was in bed now: a huge, wide bed with linen sheets. Overhead was a tester and a richly embroidered field canopy; the posts were squares of mahogany, solid as plinths in the dusk of the room. Away in the distance there were windows with white draperies: the curtains seemed to rustle in a lazy breeze, though he could not be too sure of that. He smiled wanly at his puzzle: dreams like these were always without rhyme or reason.

Actually, of course, he was still in the buckboard, jouncing on a rutted country road and fumbling with nerveless fingers to unstop a vial of morphine. . . . Only a moment ago he had been arguing with Jordan, the driver, insisting that McClellan could have taken Richmond in '62 with a little Dutch courage. Breaking that argument in the middle to insist, no less vehemently, that his destination was the Tanner mansion on Whitehall Street, Atlanta. . . .

His head still ached with each hard bounce of the axle. It was good of Jordan to stop the buckboard, to lift his head and offer him a drink. Only, the arm about his shoulders was soft and white; the hair that brushed his cheek was living gold; the voice was Jane's, and only Jane's.

"Drink this, Julian."

The liquid was bitter yet pleasant, like quinine and whisky. He swallowed it dutifully, even as he surrendered utterly to his dream. It was pure ecstasy to imagine himself in this comfortable bed, to let his thoughts float with Jane's phantom nearness. How long could he go on pretending she was really at his bedside—that her hand rested on his burning forehead as he settled among the pillows?

He turned his head a little in his dream, cautious even now lest he break the spell. But she was still there when he opened his eyes wide. Strangely enough, she was dressed for a ball. Though she was still in half mourning, her gown seemed to blaze with jewels. Or was it the gleam of bare shoulders that deceived him? He could not quite see her face, but he knew her lips were red and smiling. They had smiled at him like that, he remembered, when they had met his own for the last time at St. Marys.

In his dream her hand touched his cheek again. Her fingers were cool and soothing.

"Go to sleep, Julian."

"You'll be back?"

"Of course."

Had she said more? He would never know, for he had begun to sink through the big bed into the familiar abyss that shut out all sound.

When the dream came again, he saw that she was different. The ball gown was gone, replaced by a shimmering white robe. He could see the outlines of her body as she floated between him and the moonlight that now filled the window frames. He wanted to reach out and catch the folds of her robe, but he could not move his hands. He stared down at them as they lay inert on the counterpane and cursed them softly. A man had every right to curse his hands if they deserted him when he needed them most.

Then Jane approached the bed without a summons. Dream or waking, he knew that he would go on living, now that she had turned to him of her own accord.

"Drink this, Julian."

Again she was offering him a bitter potion, and he accepted it dutifully as before. When her hand touched his forehead, the burning stopped. Would she vanish again if he asked her to keep her hand there forever?

"Don't let it stop, Jane." Her eyes came alive at last, and he saw that they were bright with tears. "The dream, I mean. Don't let it stop."

"Lie still, Julian."

"But you're going away."

"Only to the next room. Good night."

"Good night, darling."

He heard her murmur softly in his dream as she took her hand away at last; he watched her float out of the room. Something soft and white drifted from her body to the floor. He saw that she had dropped a handkerchief and tried to call her back. Then he smiled in his dream and knew that he had believed her promise. Across the room he could just make out the dark rectangle through which she had vanished, and guessed that a door stood open between her room and his.

For a long time he lay quietly, staring at the white blur of the handkerchief as it lay in the bath of moonlight. Then, comforted by his wife's nearness in his dream, he put the dream away and slept in earnest. . . .

It was a bright, cool morning when he wakened with a head clear as a bell. He knew instantly that the fever had left him, that his body, though weak, was on the mend. His hand went down to his injured leg, and there was only the ghost of a twinge there to remind him of the wound. For a while he lay warily in the midst of the enormous bed, weighing these miracles with care. When he stared down at his body, he added yet another miracle: he had been bathed, dressed, and shaved—and the sprigged-muslin night-shirt he was wearing had never been a part of his wardrobe.

The homely detail held his mind for a while. When he ventured to raise himself on one elbow and glance about the bedroom, he saw that it was cool, white, and extremely bare: save for a mahogany highboy and a neat arrangement of his portmanteau and instrument case, there was nothing in the room but the four-poster and its night table, on which a light still burned in the full daylight.

How had he managed to get here? He waited patiently for memory to resume its full sway. There was a great blank between his last lucid moment—when they had lifted him from freight car to buckboard—and the tranquil present.

He reviewed his dream. Jane had walked through many of his dreams, but this time she had lingered in this very room—once in a ball gown, again in some sort of robe, as though she had paused on her way to bed to check on his welfare. He remembered that last white shadow best of all. For a moment he lay with his eyes closed, to enjoy once again the picture she had made by moonlight, the way she had drifted from moonlight to darkness, the flutter of her handkerchief on the carpet.

There was the spot where her phantom had vanished. There, on the carpet, was a small white square of cambric, as real as the sunlight that illumined it. And there—before the shock of that discovery had quite subsided—was Jane herself, poised in the doorway. She was wearing the same white robe, he saw, and her hair tumbled wildly about her shoulders.

"Even from here," she said, "I know you're better."

Her voice pinned his mind to reality again. It was a friendly voice, cool and precise. Despite her costume, despite the magic of last night's memory, he knew the tone. He was a guest in this house, and not a husband.

"Much better," he said. "Thanks to you, it seems. Stop me if I'm wrong."

She sat on the foot of the bed and leaned back against one of the massive posts. Julian watched her spread the lace of her sleeves until only the tips of her fingers showed. It was a natural gesture, without coquetry: there was no invitation in her nearness.

"You were here last night, weren't you?"

"Of course. You needed nursing, and my bedroom is next door."

"I thought it was a dream, until I saw the handkerchief."

Jane bent to retrieve the square of cambric. "Is it too great a shock to waken?"

"I'll try to bear up," he murmured. "Of course I'm still rather weak: will you make allowances if I don't quite——"

She lifted her eyes to his. "Aren't you going to ask me how you got here?"

"I'm beginning to remember, Jane." He offered her a tentative smile. "Perhaps I'll apologize when I'm stronger."

"You were delirious when they brought you in."

"Precisely. As a good Southerner, you had to accept me."

"A one-armed veteran carried you in on his shoulder. He insisted that you'd ordered him to deliver you here."

"I may have said as much. In my delirium, of course."

She rose from the bed on that and went to the windows to stare out at the bright autumn morning. When she spoke her voice was far away. "I thought we said good-by, Julian—once and for all."

"So did I, Jane."

"Then why——"

"*Le cœur a ses raisons que la raison ne connaît point.*"

"Is this a time to quote Pascal?"

"To my mind, it sums up my case perfectly. We made a bargain—with our heads. My heart forgot it promptly enough when I really needed you."

"I'm glad you're better," she said at last. "I'm glad I could help you. Naturally you must go quietly, the moment you can leave this bed."

"Naturally," he murmured.

She faced him on that, and he felt the tenderness in her eyes even before she could return to him and take his hands in hers. "Tell me about it, Julian. I'm sorry if I——" She groped for words, then began again firmly. "We had to—to understand each other first. Now I want to know everything."

"There isn't much to tell, really."

"I want it all. From the moment you left Atlanta."

"Including my visit with Mr. Tracy Crandall?"

She brushed that aside. "Amos told me about Crandall. He isn't important, really."

"Don't be too sure of that. He may be too important for comfort."

"Never mind that now. Tell me about you. How were you wounded? Why are you here?"

He told her everything then, prolonging the story as much as he dared. When he had finished at last, she let her hands rest on his a moment more, then she rose precisely and went to the night table to turn out the now useless lamp. Once more she spoke with her back to the bed.

"I'm glad your luck held, Julian."

"Are you glad I'm here?"

"We'll answer that later."

He sensed that she was keeping her voice steady with a great effort, though she seemed calm enough as she turned to him with a glass in her hand. He let himself go limp among the pillows: the recital had tired him more than he cared to admit, but her effort to feign coldness was reward enough.

"For the present," said Jane, "it's time you took your medicine."

"Is that wordplay, by any chance?"

She held out the quinine and whisky with a steady hand. "Is this literal enough?"

He struggled to raise his head from the pillow; again her manner changed instantly as she put her arm around him and lifted the glass to his lips. He drank obediently, smiling around the rim of the glass as he contrasted the perfume of her nearness with the bitter medicine she offered. Beneath his cheek he could feel the warm solidity of her breast. Her heart was beating wildly: he dared to guess why as he let his head return regretfully to the pillow.

"I think we should get a few facts straight, Julian."

"Go as far as you like," he murmured. "I'll answer truthfully."

She ignored the implication. "Does your commanding officer know you're here?"

"No one knows but the man who carried me in." His smile pleaded with her, but she did not budge. "Apparently I insisted on it in my delirium. But that's something I can't prove."

"Where did you plan to convalesce originally?"

"At a house in Atlanta. You'll find the letter of introduction in my coat."

Jane considered. "You're too weak to be moved at present; besides, I don't think it advisable now. I'll risk sending a note to Atlanta—saying your fever reached a crisis on the road and you had no choice but to stop here."

"Why should that be a risk?"

She hesitated, then went on resolutely. "You've guessed a great deal about me, Julian. So, for that matter, has a man in Atlanta named Tracy Crandall. Neither of you can prove your suspicions, so far."

"Do you think I came here to spy, Jane?"

"I've accepted your explanation," she said calmly. "The fact remains that Crandall will be suspicious if he learns you're here. He may even come in person to investigate."

"Would that embarrass you?"

"Not too much," she said calmly. "After all, you aren't the first soldier I've nursed back to health at High Cedars." Her eyes challenged him on that, but he did not dispute her. "It just happens you're the—last casualty we've cared for."

"You're a good nurse, Jane," he said. "I'll try not to spoil your record."

"We're in agreement, then? You'll stay here until you're well enough—then you'll leave the area quietly?"

"Where would you have me go?"

"You've a home on the Cape Fear, I believe."

"A home peopled by ghosts, as you once reminded me. Would you send me back to them?"

Jane looked down at her hands. "You can't stay indefinitely at High Cedars."

"You won't give me a share in your life," he said. "I've adjusted my mind to that. But I'm still in love with you. It means everything to me to be near you, even if——"

She finished the phrase for him, quietly. "Even if you're no nearer than this?"

"Why shouldn't I stay out my furlough here, if I promise not to ask questions?"

He watched her draw a deep breath on her decision. "Very well, Julian. You may stay—on two conditions. You must promise not to leave the grounds until I say it's advisable. Then you must go at once—without visiting Atlanta. Crandall must have no chance to question you again."

"That seems fair enough."

"Say you'll go when I tell you." Her voice had a hard edge now.

"I promise."

She got up on that, turned toward the door, then thought better of her abruptness and returned to his bedside. "You'll see things you don't understand, Julian. Things I won't be able to keep from you now. Promise you'll forget them the moment you're out of here."

He took her hand and kissed it. "Good luck, Jane," he said. "I wish I could be part of it."

She let her hand linger in his for a moment before she withdrew it gently. "The doctor should be along in a moment," she said. "He thought you could get up tomorrow, or the day after."

He forced himself to match her composure. "So you've a doctor in the house?"

"That's your first surprise," said Jane. "Sometimes we have need of one—even between battles."

She lingered a moment more, as though she wished to explain the remark, and her eyes held his steadily. When she turned and left him, he felt that an almost visible bond had snapped between them.

He lay back in his pillows, exulting quietly in his victory. When the shadow fell across the bed, he knew it was the doctor even before he opened his weary eyes. A moment later he was staring with mouth agape.

It couldn't be Louis Rothschild—but it was. A slightly older Louis than he remembered—clean shaven now, in lieu of the student's beard. But it was still young Dr. Rothschild of Vienna. The same Rothschild who had shared a cadaver with him on a marble slab at the Krakenhaus and a café table on the Prater. Brilliant Dr. Rothschild, who had slaved after hours to pay his way through medical school and graduated with the highest surgical rating of his class.

It was only when Louis offered his hand that he noticed the torn blue uniform coat he was wearing and the Federal insignia at the collar. Somehow the sight helped to cushion his surprise.

"Don't look so amazed, Julian," said the Viennese. "America is a country of miracles: therefore we meet again."

"But how on earth——"

"Examination first, report later," said Louis. "That was Virchow's routine, remember?" He folded back the bedclothes to expose Julian's bandaged calf. "First the wound, then the temperature. I will talk then—when you cannot talk back."

Julian watched the long, deft fingers unwind the bandage and test the incipient scar tissue at both ends of the punctured muscles.

Watching, he sorted his memories of Louis Rothschild, as rapidly as he could. They had been out of touch since Julian had left Vienna, but he recalled that Louis had dreamed of migrating to America. . . .

"You'll be on your feet tomorrow, plus a cane," said Louis. "Were I not a conservative at heart, you'd take a turn of the garden before your morning nap." He thrust a thermometer between Julian's lips and took his wrist between his fingers. "Being a doctor —and a good one, as I remember—you know that much yourself. What would you know about me?"

He held up a detaining hand as Julian mumbled around the thermometer. "My questions are asked to be answered—by myself, of course. Why am I here? For two years, now, I am an American citizen, with a practice in New York. Vienna, as you are aware, does not always welcome doctors of my race. . . . Being an American, I offered my services to the Union when this war began. I served as a field surgeon on two fronts: with McClellan at the Peninsula, with Rosecrans in the West, with Grant before Vicksburg. Yes, I was in trenches not a hundred yards from you. I was watching the day you went into the crater to save that wretched sapper's life——"

He snatched out the thermometer and glanced at it absently. Above the glass cylinder, Julian felt the probe of Louis Rothschild's eyes. He's gone as far as he can without betraying Jane, he thought, and spoke quickly to bridge the silence.

"Jane said she needed a doctor here, at times. Of course I never dreamed——"

"I have held stranger posts," said Louis. "Also I have lived through darker hells than your Confederacy, Julian."

"Was it Andersonville?"

"Your guess is excellent, my friend. I was four months behind that stockade until——" Again the Viennese made an eloquent pause. "Forgive me, Julian. I do not know how much I can tell you. As you see, I still wear the tatters of my uniform: it gives me a certain status to be an escaped prisoner of war. Perhaps it is wiser if you do not ask me why I am here—or how I came."

"Do I look like your enemy, Louis?"

"Of course not. We are both surgeons: our work is our life. How could we be enemies?"

"Then you'd better talk."

"Sometimes it is better not to talk freely—even with friends."

"Then I'll do the talking. This house is a station on an underground railroad: I've known that for some time. Jane and that troop of wild horsemen shuttle escaped prisoners through Georgia to the mountains. Since you're a doctor, you've been kept under wraps. More than one escaped prisoner is in need of repairs—especially if he's broken out of Andersonville."

He paused and grinned up at Louis as the latter whipped a scalpel from his sleeve and laid the steel against Julian's neck, with the razored edge nicking the carotid artery. "Thanks for telling me I'm right," he said, with a wary eye on the knife. "How did she get you out—by bribery? Or does someone else handle that detail?"

"I wouldn't know," said Louis.

"It doesn't matter, really. And you needn't cut my throat, for I won't say a word. The lady who ransomed you happens to be my wife."

"I know that too," said Louis. "She told me everything the night you arrived." He pocketed the scalpel and matched Julian's grin. "I only wondered how well you remembered."

Julian felt his whole body relax in the bed. It was a strange relief to know everything, to face the risks that Jane was taking. At least he could rejoice that men of Louis Rothschild's caliber were on her side.

"Where is she now?"

Louis leaned against the bedpost and thrust an unlighted cheroot between his lips. "Right now she's giving Amos his orders—and admitting she's a fool for keeping you here. Amos is agreeing heartily."

"Speak for yourself, Louis."

The Viennese surgeon stared down at him thoughtfully. "You always were a knight-errant, Julian. Knight-errants can get in the way in a crisis. It's my opinion that a crisis is overdue at High Cedars."

"You mean she's been found out?"

"It is an opinion, my friend, not a conviction. In Atlanta, of course, there are—how do you say it?—counter*espions* by the dozens. Most of them, fortunately, are amateurs at their trade. I do not think we are suspected directly, so far: Jane has been more than discreet——"

"How long have you——"

"I have been here since July. The post was already established. As you guessed, I have nursed many starveling souls to health here; others were strong enough to make their dash at once. All told, we have smuggled more than a thousand men to freedom, without a hitch. Such good luck cannot last forever."

So Jane had decided to tell him everything, after all: she had merely entrusted the task to Louis. The latter's elaborate approach was typical of Louis's own character. So, for that matter, was the sorrowful look that the Viennese surgeon offered him now.

"What would you have me do, Louis?"

"Do? There is nothing a husband can do for his wife when she is willing to risk her life for an abstraction."

"Meaning?"

"The abstraction, my friend, is democracy. A big word, even for these times." The lips of Louis Rothschild were full and red, but they thinned now in a bitter smile. "Like the Christianity of which you are sometimes too proud, it has never really been tried in this corner of America."

Julian opened his mouth to protest and then nodded a grim affirmative. Perhaps Louis had stated the purpose of a whole war in those words.

"Do you blame her for risking her life?"

"No, Julian. Do you?"

"I'd take her out of this if I could. You know that."

"But you cannot. She knows just what she is fighting for, my friend. That makes her stronger than you—for the time being. It is not a pleasant discovery for a man to make."

Louis stared down at his cheroot. "Nor is it pleasant to stand by —knowing that your wife may die tomorrow—and knowing that you could not lift a finger to save her. . . . I am afraid I must agree with Amos. You were a fool to come here; Jane was a fool to take you in."

"And now I'm here regardless——"

Louis Rothschild smiled again, and this time his lips were full and red. "I think we will put you to sleep for a while, until we get used to you. When you waken, you may eat what you like. Don't ask for me again: I've a broken leg in the stables that needs setting, and three pneumonia cases——"

Julian watched the long fingers flick a needle into his arm and closed his eyes as the other surgeon massaged the morphine into his blood stream with the ball of his thumb. Somehow the action fitted the moment. It would be well to sleep awhile, to let this picture of Jane, and Jane's future, sink deep in his mind and find acceptance.

And then, just before he slipped into the tropical repose induced by the drug, he realized that this was only Louis Rothschild's way of dismissing him for a while. Quietly but firmly, he was being put aside while High Cedars continued to do its work without him.

xiii

The gloomy conviction had vanished when he wakened. It was tranquil late afternoon, and a tall Negro in a Yankee uniform was sponging his body gently. He lay quietly and watched the man's hands move expertly at his task. It did feel good to be waited on, he acknowledged. Good to know that he could lie back, in this pleasant half doze, and hold thought at arm's length for a while.

The Negro, he gathered, was some kind of orderly, yet he did not resemble a servant. Julian had heard that the Yankees were using Negro troops these days; he knew that he should feel resentment at the other's nearness, and smiled wanly as he waited for a nonexistent hate to materialize. Either this man was a runaway or a freeborn citizen of the North. In any case, he had the right to wear the uniform of his liberators.

He smiled to himself, wondering what Clayton Randolph would say to such heresy from a Confederate officer.

The Negro saw his smile and echoed it. "Feeling better, Doctor?"

Julian stared in spite of himself. The black man's voice was free of accent and as well modulated as his own.

"Who are you?"

He had not meant the question to sound so curt. But he had expected the low-pitched slurring of the South in this man's speech. The eternal subservience (he added sharply) that was somewhere between a grovel and a whine. . . .

"Dr. Noah Heath," said the Negro. "Your servant, sir." There was no irony in that polite commonplace. This was a man born to be no man's servant. Julian weighed that fact carefully while he groped for his own composure.

"Did you say *doctor?*"

The Negro smiled. "You are quite right to be startled, Dr. Chisholm. My degree comes from the University of London; my practice is in New York—such as it is. Actually I'm Dr. Rothschild's assistant."

"Don't tell me you were captured together?"

"Dr. Rothschild was working at a forward post when he was taken; I was at the base." Dr. Heath had a gentle, heartbroken smile. "When I recovered from the news, I applied for transfer—as you see. As it turned out, I was useful here too."

Julian blinked: this was coming awake with a vengeance. The underground railway was a two-way affair, of course. Once he was in its service, it would be quite possible for a man like Heath to learn that Louis Rothschild was a prisoner at Andersonville and ask for work in that area. He tried to picture the devotion that would bring a free Negro across these miles of hostile land.

"You say you—worked together in New York?" It was a hard question to frame—and harder still to picture those dark hands and Louis Rothschild's sharing the same case.

"Why not, Doctor? We left Liverpool on the same boat, the year before Sumter." The Negro's smile was as gentle as before; his eyes seemed to dwell on a hard past, without regrets. "Neither of us had too much hope that year: too many friends wrote what we might expect in America. A Negro and a Jew——"

"And yet you prospered?"

"Yes, by trimming our hopes. Louis opened a New York office, in his name alone; as I said, I was his assistant—behind the scenes. The war, and his skill, brought him an immense practice, almost at once." Heath's chin lifted proudly. "I had my share in that, of course. Even before we enlisted I was beginning to have patients too."

"So you went to war together."

"Could we do less? Naturally I could only enter the Union Army as an orderly, but——" The black hands spread eloquently; for the first time Julian saw the power in the long, spatulate fingers. "If necessary, I would have gone as his body servant. When he was taken, I had no choice but to follow him. To wait for the day when we might work together again."

Julian nodded. At the moment he could not trust his voice. Slavery—and he repeated it firmly—was a moral blot on the South, a feudal anachronism. Yet the anachronism lingered, even in the most liberal Southern heart. Try as he might, he could not picture this black man as a doctor. . . . Was it possible that they could really be the white man's equal someday? That they could meet —over work, and after—as *friends?* Louis Rothschild, the Jewish émigré, had proved as much. Could Julian Chisholm, of Chisholm Hundred, accept that proof at its face value? Could he rejoice that a new wind of freedom was stirring, however faintly, in the heart of the enemy world?

"You're a brave man, Dr. Heath," he said.

"I'm loyal to my friends, Doctor," said the Negro. "Don't make me sound a hero." He offered Julian that ageless smile one more time. "Whenever I look out that window I'm so afraid it hurts."

He turned to the sound of footsteps in the hall. Both of them were silent as a tall blond boy in a blue uniform edged through the door with a tray of food. A boy with a farmer's gangling walk and a grin to match it.

The boy said, "You're wanted in the stables, Doctor."

Julian half rose from his pillow, thinking that the soldier was speaking to him: even now he could not believe that a white man might address a Negro with such obvious respect. He was still staring when Dr. Noah Heath went out with a quick nod. The boy felt the stare; he put the dinner on Julian's knees and followed the black doctor into the hall without a word.

There was a glass of milk on the tray and a bowl of soup that exuded a rich aroma. He ate and drank mechanically, feeling the strength pour into his body—and waiting hopefully for a parallel expansion of his mind. But his mind was obstinate. It simply refused to take in the example of social evolution he had just witnessed.

He wondered if Dr. Heath's visit was an idea of Jane's. Now that he had, so to speak, forced his way into High Cedars, she had promised him a series of revelations. Louis was a fair beginning, Heath a startling counterpoint: what other surprises did she hold in store? Not even her bushwhacker guard had startled him so much as this queer team of doctors. And yet he felt a strange confidence at the fact that they were helping in this hazardous game.

Languor was stealing over his muscles once again, so insistently that he felt sure the food contained some kind of sedative. He could trust Louis Rothschild for that: his friend had sensed instantly that rest, and more rest, was the only prescription he needed now. Just as obviously, Louis had decided to keep him on his back until his adjustment to this new world was complete. . . . He dropped into another doze with the conviction that Dr. Noah Heath was standing over his bed, smiling down at him with an understanding he could not match.

He sat up vigorously in his nest of pillows, knowing that he had slept away the dregs of his weariness. The room was pitch-dark now, save for a glint of dying moonlight at the windows. For an instant he glanced about wildly, to make sure he was alone. Then, hardly knowing what he did, he put one cautious foot outside the covers and then another. Just in time he remembered that the mattress stood a good five feet above the carpet, and lowered himself to that level by grasping one of the bedposts.

His legs seemed unrelated to his body, and the wound gave a warning twinge, but he made himself take three resolute steps in the dark before he paused to listen. The sound was repeated outside the windows, and he knew now that he had heard it before, at the tag end of his long nap: the unmistakable stamp of a horse's hoof, the muted rattle of bit and bridle.

The window frame was a long way off, but he felt steadier with each uncertain step. To his surprise, he found that he was looking down into the closed garden behind the formal living room. The leaves of the magnolia shut off most of the view: between them he could glimpse the garden itself—enough to guess that it formed a long rectangle between the wings of the house, with its far end enclosed by a tall hedge of oleanders and a grape arbor.

He could see the arbor clearly, just outside the encompassing shade of the magnolia; under the high green arch of vines there was a glimpse of a flagged walk that led to the open lawn behind the house. He heard the horse stamp again in the dark. A man's voice spoke gently to the animal, just as horse and rider came into view, moving under the arch of the arbor at a slow walk and entering the garden with an inch of headroom to spare.

At the same moment he heard the doors of the living room open directly below him. A rectangle of lamplight fell across the garden, splintering against the legs and hindquarters of a dozen mounts: now he realized that the unquiet mass beneath the magnolia was, in reality, a group of mounted men.

The lamplight brought the scene alive; he stared down at visible proof of the touch-tag Jane played with death. Perhaps half of the horsemen in the garden were in Yankee uniform. The others were the bushwhacker guard he remembered so vividly from St. Marys; the man who had just ridden through the arbor was none other than Amos, their saturnine leader. The light picked out the visor of a forage cap, the tanned plane of a cheekbone, the insignia on a shoulder strap that had had time to tarnish in some prison pen— and time to burnish itself bright again in this sanctuary. . . .

"If you please, Colonel," said Amos. "You too, Saunders."

An officer who sat his mount like a ramrod and the blond boy who had brought the tray that afternoon detached themselves from the group and rode toward the arbor. A third rider, who seemed less certain of his horsemanship than the others, followed suit. Amos held up his hand sharply.

"Not you, mister. You're still in sick bay."

"Dr. Rothschild said I'd be happier on the road." It was only a hoarse whisper. Julian could not see the man's face under the slouch hat he wore, but he could picture the ghosts behind the eyes.

Amos glanced toward the open glass doors and the invisible living room. "Right, Doc?"

Louis Rothschild's voice drifted out with casual emphasis. "He's as well as he'll ever be, Amos—till he's through the lines. On your way."

There were no more words as the three Yankees rode through the arbor on Amos's heels. A second bushwhacker swung into place as rear guard, and the little file of horsemen vanished soundlessly in the dark. Julian flattened against the wall to watch the next batch of riders fall into line. They would ghost through the night like this—following the back roads, clinging to each scrap of cover, riding at a hard gallop when they dared. Moving in small groups, with an experienced leader, they could cover sixty miles between moonset and dawn. Daylight would find them at their next hideaway, their horses stabled and groomed, their own tired bodies already deep in slumber.

Julian heard a faint sound behind him and turned warily. There was no one in the room as the sound repeated: the muted rasp of metal on glass. He saw now that it had come from the adjoining room, saw for the first time that a thick pencil of light lay across the sill. He guessed that Jane was stirring there. The sound he had just heard was the rattle of her lamp chain.

With no sense of transition, he found himself at the crack in the door; his bare feet made no sound as he inched it a trifle wider. If this was spying at its worst, he was not conscious of disloyalty: he forgot all scruples at the sight that met his eye.

Jane was seated on a bench before a cheval glass, whipping her hair into a knot and holding it snug with the gipsy bandanna she had worn at sea. The peasant handkerchief made a bizarre contrast to her nightdress; the slouch hat she pulled over it was even more startling. He held his breath as she bent close to the glass to make sure that no telltale wisp could escape. Already her fingers were busy at the drawstrings of her gown. When she rose from the bench, the garment slipped below her waist. Now she stepped out of it entirely and stood for a moment before the cheval glass— naked in the lamplight, her small, proud breasts lifted as she touched her weird headdress one more time.

Julian felt his bare toes grip the sill; in another second a force beyond his control would catapult him into her bedroom. But even as he hesitated Jane stepped free of the shimmering silken mass at her feet and vanished behind the open door of an armoire.

He heard a horse stamp in the garden and guessed that another group had ridden away. Someone might come into the room at any moment; Jane herself might return and find him, but he could not force himself back to the sickbed.

His eyes had already found the pistol on her dresser. He remembered that pistol, too—and how carelessly she had thrust it into her belt at St. Marys. The pattern was complete when she emerged from the ambush of the armoire door. Even so, he stared at her blankly: it was hard to believe that this was really Jane.

Apparently she had begun her costuming from the head down. She was wearing a linen duster now, which fell almost to her ankles; he glimpsed a man's shirt under it, the trousers she had brought from London, a pair of dusty boots that reached her knees. Even by daylight she could have passed for a slim boy— thanks to the loose linen coat which concealed her figure, the wide-brimmed hat that shadowed her face.

The whole costume should have been outlandish on a woman: on Jane it seemed as natural as the stride she took to the dresser, the way she dropped the pistol into one pocket and a fat wad of bank notes into the other. She might have been a planter going to town for supplies, he thought. Or a planter's son, intent on some escapade of his own. . . .

He pulled the door shut just before she turned from a final inspection at the mirror. He was back in bed, and fighting hard to feign the easy breathing of slumber, when the door swung wide and she came into the room on tiptoe. Watching her from under half-closed lids, he guessed that she had come to his room each night at this time, to make sure he was resting quietly. Last night she had been in full evening dress, bound for a charity ball in Atlanta. Tonight she was an intrepid Amazon, risking everything to ride once again with her own bushwhackers.

He clenched his fists under the covers and knew that his whole body was rigid as she bent above him. Her nearness was more than he could bear—to say nothing of the urge to hold her at his side, to force her, somehow, to give up this wild game that could have but one ending.

Louis Rothschild was right, he thought: this is a poor role for any husband. But Louis had also said that he was powerless. Jane would see this thing through to the end, no matter what protest he offered. Feeling her cool hand on his forehead again, he knew that he had deceived her, after all. She believed him asleep, believed that she could ride away unobserved. She could even bend closer, to cover his lips with a fleeting kiss before she whisked out of the room.

He was out of bed before he heard her tiptoe down the stairway. At the window again, he saw that Louis himself had stepped out under the canopy of the magnolia to hold her bridle: her mount was a deep-chested gray with the air of a born jumper. Louis led the horse toward the arch of the arbor, and the rest of the little cavalcade fell into place. Counting heads, Julian saw that the last group to ride out was by far the largest: Jane, it seemed, was willing to take the greatest risk.

It was heartbreaking to stand inert in the window frame and face the fact of her departure. His knuckles were white on the sill as he watched her swing into her saddle and lead the way through the arbor, but the shout died soundlessly in his throat.

Louis turned back into the house as the last horseman vanished among the vine leaves; the lights winked out in the drawing room, and the dark garden was empty of life and sound. Julian stood for a long time in the window frame. In the warm autumn night the white, bell-shaped blossoms of the magnolia seemed to stare up at him like drowsy eyes. When he crept back to the bed at last, his skin was cold with a malaise that went deeper than ague.

xiv

Dr. Noah Heath brought the decanter from the sideboard, placed it before Jane with a little bow, and resumed his place at the table between Amos and Dr. Louis Rothschild. Dr. Julian Chisholm (who was seated on the hostess's right) pulled his mind back to the conversation and tried not to stare at the Negro. All through the dinner his mind had not quite grasped the fact that he was breaking bread with a black. The fact that they would now drink together and the fact that Jane showed no sign of leaving the table were no less agitating.

It was his second day downstairs. The last trace of ague had left him long before, but he had preferred to keep to his room. Below him, as the Indian-summer days wore by, he had heard only the muted voices of Louis and Heath and guessed that High Cedars was empty of escaped prisoners now, save for the leftovers in the sick bay. He had not dared ask news of Jane, though it seemed obvious that she was still afield. Taking a few cautious turns of the carpet to test his game leg, resisting the temptation to open the door that separated her room and his, he had never felt so lonely—or so deserted in his loneliness.

Louis had been affable enough and Noah Heath's grave politeness had been unchanged, when one or the other brought his trays at mealtimes. But he had felt an invisible barrier, as though they feared more questions and were determined to turn them aside. When the pressure of four bedroom walls grew intolerable and he came downstairs at last, they had received him with professional courtesy intact—admitting him to the sick bay above the stables as a matter of course, insisting that he sun the afternoon away in the grape arbor. And he felt, once again, that they preferred to have him outside, in that sunny enclosure of vine leaves, that their small sickroom could function perfectly without his inspection. . . .

The same feeling had invaded his spirit last night, when he started from a troubled sleep and heard Jane ride into the garden below his windows. Watching her stagger with weariness as she entered the house with Louis's arm about her, he had been afraid to knock on her door when he heard her mount the stair. Instead he had listened in the dark like an outcast who had no right to comfort her. With only the door panel between them, he could hear her clothes rustle to the floor as she undressed, the deep sigh she gave as she settled into slumber. He had paced his own carpet for an hour after that, until the twinges in his wounded leg drove him to his own bed.

Now, as he sat at the table in Jane's dining room, his mind was still pacing that same carpet. Reminding him that he should have offered to leave High Cedars this morning—and wondering if the time of his departure was beyond his control now. Wondering, too, if there was more behind Jane's high spirits than met the eye. It was, in short, intolerable that he should sit in this group, like an interloper, while they continued to talk around his silence, in a language he could only pretend to understand.

Whit Cameron's eyes sought his across the cloth, and he saw that Whit, as usual, had read his mood perfectly. The gambler had driven out from Atlanta with the dusk; his buggy still waited at the carriage block. Julian remembered how cordially the company had received him—and his news (it was more than a rumor now) that General Sherman might well begin an invasion of Georgia before the spring.

Whit said, "Now that the brandy's before me, I'm in the mood for a toast. To our hostess, naturally. The only lady I know who could preside over such a gathering with tact, beauty, and grace."

He was on his feet with the words—a slender figure in his formal evening black, swaying a little from too much wine yet completely in control of mind and tongue. His eye traveled about the table as he spoke, and Julian felt his own eyes parallel Whit's stare. True enough, it was a bizarre quintet that faced Jane about the board. Amos, a sullen firebrand in homespun. Two Yankee doctors in their well-patched blue. Himself in a gray uniform only a trifle less shabby. Whit's own elegance was a sprightly counterpoint to this motley of a well-fought war. So, for that matter, was the leaven of his gaiety as he raised his glass in the candlelight.

"Gentlemen, I give you Mrs. Kirby Anderson."

The glasses rose in unison; even Amos beamed as he bounced to his feet and clicked his heels. Only Julian hesitated.

"The lady's name is Chisholm," he said. "But I endorse the sentiment."

He bowed deeply to Jane as he drank, then smashed the glass against the wall. Amos whooped again as he followed suit. Jane herself accepted the tribute with lowered lashes; no Southern belle could have improved on the moment. Tonight she was all white and gold; her gown, with its deep-cut bodice framing the jeweled cameo Julian remembered so well, was a far cry from widow's weeds.

She came back to the room swiftly as she offered them all her impartial smile. "I'll admit it's been a strain," she murmured. "But thank you all, just the same."

"Was that remark aimed at me?" Julian found that the words had escaped him willy-nilly: he could scarcely have recalled them.

"Need you ask?" said Whit.

Julian waited for Jane to speak, but she let the gambler's words sink into the silence without comment. "I'm sorry if I've been a—a jarring note," he said at last. "Unfortunately, I can't help my antecedents."

"Nor can we, Julian," said Louis Rothschild softly.

Noah Heath spoke out of the next silence, quite without embarrassment. "In Vienna today there are families who would not break bread with Louis. I'm grateful to *you*, Dr. Chisholm—for breaking bread with me."

"I assure you, Dr. Heath——" But Julian knew he was blushing fatally. "If this is part of my education, I, too, am grateful. I still can't help wondering what Tracy Crandall would say if he walked into this room now."

The tension relaxed in Amos's deep-bass chuckle. "Don't you fret about him again, Doc. I've lookouts on the job, if Tracy aims to visit us."

"It's worth a thought, nevertheless," said Julian. Interloper or not, he told himself, I'll make myself felt in this room. "What would *any* Southerner think if he saw the six of us dining together in peace?"

"I see your point, Doctor," said Heath. "Here I sit—the bone of contention in this war—accepted as an equal. Beside me is a man who has escaped the ghetto of an older world, to find his destiny in this. On my right is a mountain white who knows, even now, that the future of my people and his own are one."

313

The eloquent dark hands spread wide on the cloth; Heath looked down at them for a moment before he continued. "Facing me is Whit Cameron—gambler and self-styled cynic. Yet Whit Cameron has risked his all, more than once, to bring money and orders through the lines to us."

His gentle eyes rested on Julian. "You, Doctor, I cannot sum up in a phrase: at the moment you are too busy living down your prejudices, too deeply troubled by your wife's role in our group. . . . As for the lady herself—" He rose solemnly and offered Jane his homage in a quick smile. "I have already drunk a toast to her honor. No man can overpraise her devotion to the new world that must rise from these bitter ashes." He smiled around the board as he settled in his chair again. "Yes, Dr. Chisholm, I agree that most Southerners would be puzzled if they blundered into this room tonight."

"Thank you for excluding me," said Julian.

"You aren't entirely excluded. Admit that you're still a trifle shocked to find I can talk your language."

Julian nodded an affirmation and realized that his tension had dissolved, neatly enough, in the general laughter. Whit broke the moment sharply by slapping his palm on the table.

"This is a serious meeting," he said. "Even for you, Julian. I, for one, vote we tell him the news."

His eye roved around the table, collecting nods. Only Jane sat aloof. Glancing at her again, Julian saw that she was pale and withdrawn, a sharp contrast to her recent mood. This, he decided, is something that was agreed on long ago. *Her* vote was taken in advance.

"Point one," said Whit. "We're finished here. Amos takes out the last three men in sick bay this midnight. The rest move at dawn."

"May an outsider ask why?"

"You may indeed, Julian. Would it shock you to learn the Yankees expect to take Atlanta this summer?"

Julian shook his head. The capture of this nexus of railroads, as every Confederate officer knew, would mean the end of the war. He had seen the Yankee juggernaut roll back at Chickamauga, and feared it was only a breathing spell.

"The Confederates are preparing for the invasion now," Whit said calmly. "When it comes, there'll be twenty Tracy Crandalls working behind the lines to nip trouble in the bud. Therefore Jane and company have been ordered to move. Naturally I can't tell you where. I can only say that this good-by must be definite."

"I've already given my promise," said Julian, and added, with his eyes on Jane, "This time I understand why I must keep it."

Whit nodded briskly. "I'd take you back with me to Atlanta if I dared. But I'm sure Crandall will be waiting for me: we had a drink together in the hotel bar just before I drove out."

"Surely it's known in Atlanta that I'm convalescing here?"

"Precisely. Crandall has accepted the fact: he even sent you his regards." Whit twirled his brandy glass thoughtfully. "But it would be unwise for us to return together. Especially tonight, when Jane is planning to vacate High Cedars. We don't want Crandall calling to see if there's a connection between your departure and her future plans."

Julian looked around the table. Again he was conscious of a united front. The faces were friendly enough, but they were determined too. I'm part of their plans now, he thought. For the time being, at least. Whatever they've decided, I must accept.

"I must go somewhere," he said tentatively. "After all, I'm still on furlough."

Jane spoke with her eyes on the cloth. "If we can get away clear tonight—and I hope we can—you're to ride with us."

"May I ask how far?"

"As far as you care to go," said Louis Rothschild. "Through our lines, if you're willing to change sides."

Julian let his glance move slowly around the circle: the five pairs of eyes that met his own were still friendly and still unwavering.

"Do you think for a moment I'd change sides—any of you?"

Whit said, gently enough, "We can go on hoping, Julian."

And Louis Rothschild added, "You're on the side of humanity. Does it matter where you save lives?"

Julian said, "I'm still a Southerner."

"So am I," said Jane. "I'd prefer to call myself an American."

Once again he admitted that the reason for the South's rebellion—and the ruthless devastation that would be its harvest—had been stated in a sentence. The North, and all Southerners farsighted enough to join its banner, were fighting for an ideal, if you liked. So were the firebrands in gray. . . . But the North's ideal was rooted in common sense, in the heartbeat of tomorrow; the Yankee ideal could only expand with the times. The ideal of the Confederacy had blown itself to bits with the first whiff of powder; only the romantic ghost remained to lead its devotees to death.

And yet he heard his voice answer Jane firmly: "I'm still a Confederate officer. God helping me, I'll be one to the end."

"Does that make us enemies, Julian?"

"Only if you insist."

Her eyes narrowed, though she was still smiling. "I could insist you come with us when we ride north."

"As your prisoner?"

"I could send you back with Louis," she said. "We've arranged to rendezvous with Yankee cavalry across the Chattahoochee——" Amos stirred in his place, but she silenced him with a look. "A sizable raiding party, Julian: as you know, they've struck close to Atlanta before this. Amos thinks I'm giving away a secret. It'd hardly matter, if they took you back to Tennessee. Certainly I would rest easier if I knew you were safe in a Union prison pen."

"Thanks for that much," Julian murmured.

But her eyes had reprieved him, even before she spoke. "I couldn't, of course. My job in this war is to free prisoners, not make more. It's a temptation, just the same." She weighed the thought a moment, and he saw the sparkle in her glance. His mind went back with hers to a night among the Florida dunes, when she had threatened to surrender him to the Yankees in St. Augustine. He found he was smiling, too, as he remembered how that threat had ended.

"Give me my marching orders," he said. "I'll do my best to obey."

"They're very simple, Julian. We ride out together, this side of daylight. Five miles to the north we turn west on the river road; you continue east on the turnpike——"

"And then?"

Her voice was flat: he saw that it was an effort to keep it so. "And then, Julian—you'll remember you're a Confederate officer and gentleman and do as you like. I only ask that you keep clear of Atlanta, and Crandall, until we've made our contact."

"You haven't answered my question," he said hoarsely. They were facing each other across the table now; the others had receded into a dim background.

"And then, Julian, I'll go on with my work, as you'll go on with yours."

Her eyes were straight ahead, fixed on a distant point that only she could discern clearly. "I think you've a clear idea of its importance now; I think you'll grant me the right to continue—and save myself, if I can. Perhaps I should tell you that it won't stop with the war. Democracy is a long way off in America. There'll be other kinds of prisoners to rescue, North as well as South. . . . Will you help me in that rescue, if you're still alive?"

Her hand sparkled with jewels as she offered it to him across the table. A note of mockery crept into his voice as he took it and answered her. "When this cruel war is over? I asked you that same question long ago—and you said 'forever' was too short a word."

"I was tired that night," said Jane. "Now that Whit's brought the news from Tennessee, I'm daring to hope a little."

Whit spoke out of the heavy silence around the table, and Julian came back to his presence guiltily. "Jane has a cool half million in gold, where it can't be touched," he said. "She's planning to put every cent into community farming——"

"Negroes and poor whites," said Amos. "Share and share alike. It's the South's only hope, Doc. Without it we'll go back to what we were."

Noah Heath spoke softly. "I would work in such a community, Dr. Chisholm. So would Amos. So would many of the boys we have saved from Andersonville. Perhaps it will only be an oasis in a wilderness: it is still a beginning. Somewhere we must have such beginnings; the enemy will be back soon enough."

So this was the destiny of Kirby Anderson's fortune: the black sweat that had watered his Georgia acres, transmuted into gold, would buy new acres for new freemen, white as well as black. He opened his eyes wide to the vision, striving to encompass it.

"You say the enemy will be back, Dr. Heath. Just who is the enemy—myself?"

"Never *you*, Doctor," said the Negro. "Only the class from which you came. Until that class is only an evil memory in the South, the enemy will be always with us."

"All planters weren't evil."

"Many were among the finest men the South has known. But they did not decide the policy of the group—as you know, Doctor.

They did not lead their states to war—they only followed. When power is in too few hands, the brain of a selfish minority is always its evil core. . . . So I say again, the plantation economy, as we remember it, must be smashed—if this land is to survive. The men who made it—good and bad—must be ground in the dust of their own pride."

The Negro's voice was still soft with compassion; he looked around the table for his endorsement before he went on. "We have our freedom now—on paper. For a long time that freedom will do us more harm than our slavery. The men who owned us once will use every trick in the book to keep us in their power: we are much too useful to them just as we are. . . . The North will not really help us, when the fighting ends: the Union will be far too busy fulfilling its own destiny, as the richest nation the world has known. No, Dr. Chisholm, we must find our own salvation, on our own land——"

Julian broke in with a smile. "I'm glad you don't look on the Yankees as crusaders."

"You must see the North to believe it these days," said Whit. "New York, for example. I was in New York only ten days ago. Whole streets still black with fires the draft riots left behind them last summer. Alternates asking their weight in gold, and getting it. At first glance you'd say the whole population is shirking the war and making money—usually by swindling the government. Or riding railroad stock to a fortune. . . . Take your old friend Lucy Sprague."

He shot a knowing look at Julian and grinned as the latter turned his head aside. "If I told you what her mills have made in army contracts, you wouldn't believe me. Incidentally, I dined at her Fifth Avenue mansion—to discuss a deal in contraband cotton. She sent her regards——"

"Never mind Lucy Sprague," snapped Julian. "What about us?"

"But Lucy's important," said Whit. "Lucy's a horrible example. Lucy and a score of brand-new Yankee millionaires are already planning the greatest power grab in our history. Planning to freeze the power in their hands forever. To use their millions to make more millions—and less democracy." He bowed to Jane. "We're reversing the process, or trying to. Are you with us?"

"I'm with you completely. How can you ask?"

"Would you let us buy in on Chisholm Hundred when peace comes—and begin our experiment there?"

He felt the hush settle on the table: he felt Jane's eyes on him once again and knew they were warm with hope as she awaited his reply. Strangely enough, the question had not been in the least surprising. Now that it was in the open, he found that his mind had framed the answer long ago. If he hesitated to utter it now, it was only because he wished the words to ring true.

"Chisholm Hundred is yours for the asking," he said. "I'm sure its future couldn't be in better hands. But I'm still in uniform—and still at war."

"Thank you, Julian," said Whit. "It's nice to know the mold is broken at long last."

Jane did not speak; the warm pressure of his wife's hand on his was enough reward.

"We'll talk of this later, then," said Whit.

"Much later—if I'm still here to talk." He offered them all his best smile and knew it was genuine. "Naturally I can hardly sign my land over to the enemy——"

The enemy. The word had no meaning in this room. We're *friends,* he thought, and was amazed that he had taken so long to make that astounding discovery. Perhaps this war is being fought for a purpose, after all. If six people, from all corners of America, can sit down and map a common future, there may be hope for America, after all. For democracy—and more democracy. . . .

Then Louis Rothschild got up from his place. The lamplight made a blue shield of his tunic. The war was in the room again, and Julian let himself tumble back into the present as he took the other surgeon's hand.

"We'll meet again, my friend—at a better time."

Dr. Noah Heath shook hands wordlessly. It was only when he followed Louis from the room that Julian remembered he had never taken a Negro's hand before. That he had wondered, in his heart, if his flesh would cringe at the contact—and had rejoiced when it had turned out like any other handshake.

Whit cuffed his shoulder in passing, and bent to light his cheroot from one of the massive silver candlesticks. "There's no doubt we'll meet again, Julian. Just don't name the time. In New York they were betting the war would end by April. Odd, isn't it, that the Yankees should misunderstand the South even now?"

For a moment Julian thought that Amos would trail the gambler to the hall with his owl-eyed stare intact. Instead the bushwhacker paused beside him and all but crushed his fingers in a work-hardened palm.

"Glad you're with us in spirit, Doc. I guessed as much that night at the hotel. Now I'm sure of it."

The dining room seemed very still as Amos pulled the double doors shut behind him. Julian sat unstirring, waiting for Jane to speak, and wishing that the silence could last forever. The silence of acceptance, of trust—the seal on a future he could only pray for now. He realized that the others had withdrawn tactfully, to give them this moment. Would she use it to give a foundation to his hopes—or would she only dash them anew?

"It's nice to plan," she said at last. "Plans are such solace when you're living in a whirlwind."

"Is it as bad as that, my dear?"

She smiled wanly, and he guessed that her thoughts were far afield. She's glad I could meet her halfway, he thought: she's too great a realist to bubble over with joy, simply because I've made her a promise she could count on from the beginning.

"Tell me what you're thinking, Jane. It might help us both."

"I'm thinking where I'll be tomorrow," she said simply. "Or should I say—wishing I knew?"

The full import of the words sank into the silence between them. He felt her hand stir in his and cling there for an instant before she drew away.

"I'll quit if you will," he said. "I'll quit tonight. Get myself a sinecure in Texas and take you with me. Not even Crandall would follow us there. We could wait out the war together . . ." His voice trailed away against her tranquil stare.

"Do you know how many die each day in your prison pens?"

He nodded grimly. "And in yours, Jane."

"And in ours," she agreed. "I can't help that, of course. But I've no right to shirk my assignment here, now that the war is going into its climax."

"Surely you've done enough."

"Have *you*, Julian?"

"My work is different. I don't risk my life."

"You did at Vicksburg," she said. "And at Chickamauga. You will again."

"So will you, I suppose," he said wearily. "Let's not torture one another by—by dwelling on it."

320

"It's hard to think of anything else tonight," she said, and got up with the words. He sat unstirring, forgetting his punctilio for once, as she circled the table and stood behind his chair. Her hand touched his shoulder gently. It was not a caress. Rather, it was the touch of a comrade who was sealing a bargain—once and for all.

"Thank you again, Julian."

"For what?" he asked, keeping his eyes ahead.

"For understanding us so well—and so quickly."

She went out before he could turn, leaving the double doors ajar. He sat on alone, with his eyes on the half-burned candles, hearing the rustle of her skirt on the stair, the sound of a closing door in the hall above.

Watching his hand fasten on the decanter, he knew that he would not taste the first stiff drink of brandy he was pouring, or the second. His mind was still poised, heavy with unspoken words, moving warily about her sudden departure, trying to grasp its motive. Did she expect him to follow her, he wondered, or had she left him abruptly to forestall a more ardent farewell?

He was still frowning at the unanswered question when he heard Amos ride into the garden. Through the archway that gave to the kitchens he saw Noah Heath come across the grass with a worn carpetbag under each arm. Louis Rothschild followed shortly, bundled to the ears in a poncho, a planter's hat perched on his curls like a crown in some masquerade. . . . He wanted to go to the lawn, to shout a farewell—if only to break his inertia. But he sat on, even when the three pale Union prisoners rode into the shaft of lamplight—two boys like scarecrows grown old too soon, a veteran with a ragged, graying beard and an empty sleeve.

Someone muttered an order in the dark, and the troop rode out together. The house seemed quiet when they had gone, though he guessed that there were still horses in the stables, and riders in the loft above, snatching a last few hours of sleep before their own orders came.

Jane was sensible to retire early; Jane, as always, had planned a bit faster than he. . . . One more drink, and he would be too fuddled to care if he slept upstairs or rested here, with his head on his arms.

The chair turned over as he staggered to his feet, but he plunged into the darkened hallway without pausing to right it. His breath all but left him when he crashed head-on into the massive newel post at the foot of the stairway, and he glared at it resentfully, as though it were a living enemy. Beyond and above he could see the ghostly spiral of the stair well and the landing of the bedroom floor. Her own door was the first on the left, he remembered dimly; his own was the first right.

He had no recollection of climbing the stair, though he knew he had turned right by instinct. He was standing in his own bedroom now, with a hand groping for the solid support of a wall. Listening to the thunder of his heart, he wondered why the room beyond should be so quiet.

Perhaps she had already slipped into her riding clothes; joined Amos on the road while her lawful husband brooded over a decanter downstairs. It was more likely that she had locked herself in and was already deep in slumber. He found that his step was steadier as he went softly to the connecting door. In a way, the silence of that closed room was more wounding to his pride than her imagined flight.

Wounded—and hating himself for admitting the wound was real as the Yankee's bullet at Chickamauga—he raised a fist to smash the door panel, to claim what was his. Caution checked his hand in time, and he tested the lock instead; his breath caught in his throat as he felt the door swing open without sound, as though it had been set ajar.

The night light burned faintly beside Jane's bed. At first he thought the room was empty. Then he saw her silhouette against the dark rectangle of portieres that framed the window. She was standing with her eyes on the starlit sky; even before he could enter, he sensed that her whole body was taut with waiting. The white evening dress was a tumbled mass beside her bed: evidently she had decided to leave it when she departed. The negligee she was wearing now gleamed like a moth's wing in the dark, and her hair was the same living gold, even in that dim room.

He took in these facts mechanically as he crossed the room to her; his heart did not even miss a beat when she turned to him. Her voice was a whisper, so low that he scarcely heard.

"After tonight, did you think I'd lock you out, ever?"

He tried to speak as his arms closed about her, but her mouth had already sought his and clung there.

"Take me, Julian—I've waited so long."

The negligee slipped to the floor unheeded; she ran her arms inside his coat, as though she could not bear the feel of fabric between her flesh and his. Her fingers, locked at his back, drew him into a swaying embrace. For a moment they stood there in the dark, locked in a kiss that seemed to have no ending—and the hopeless dream of her that had tormented him in the gray rain at Chickamauga fused with a blinding reality that transcended dreams.

"Take me, Julian—please take me. . . ."

xv

Even before he opened his eyes he sensed that something was wrong. He knew instantly that this was Jane's bed and not his own; that she had fallen asleep beside him, not too long ago, with her head on his shoulder. The deep peace of his slumber had been broken when she left his side: he had sensed her departure, even as his mind struggled back to wakefulness. . . . Now that he knew she was gone, he knew just as surely that the house was astir below him, though the silence of midnight seemed unbroken.

For a moment he lay quiet in his wife's bed and held his breath, as though the suspension of the act could sharpen his hearing. Though his mind was alert, his body—relaxed, still, in the ecstasy of their reunion—was drowsy with sleep: he did not stir when he heard Jane's step in his room and saw her hurry through the door with his instrument case under one arm, his portmanteau in her free hand. Only when she placed these articles at the foot of her bed did he see her clearly.

She was wearing her riding costume, or part of it: the trousers cinched at the waist with a broad leather belt, the high boots lashed just below her knees. From the waist up she was still naked, and her hair tumbled about her shoulders in wild disorder. Half tranced, even now, he stared at her as she snatched a rough flannel shirt from a chair and hurried to the window. She stood in the frame for a moment—the shirt tossed over the sill, her hands raised to knot her hair into the familiar bandanna. A shaft of dying moonlight bathed her body, highlighting the round, firm breasts: the nipples, rosy even in that pale light, stood bravely erect in the chill of morning.

He rose from the bed with a soundless cry just as she ran from the room, diving into the shirt as she ran and plunging through the hall door with the sure-footed ease of a cat.

The house was still quiet below him as his feet struck the carpet. Fumbling for his clothes, he was dressed in a moment: thanks to his months in the field, this worn uniform was as familiar as his own palms. As he fastened the top button of his tunic, he heard the beat of hoofs outside and ran to the window.

Jane's room looked out between the ghostly white pillars of the portico, to command the driveway and the cedar tunnel that curved down to the turnpike. He leaned as far out as he dared. A dozen horses were tethered in the shadow of the house. Even as he looked, the approaching rider sounded his own warning. A black gelding burst from the driveway, and a roughly clad horseman bounced from saddle to porch in one fluent swoop. The man had vanished into the house before Julian could quite see his face; he heard the crunch of boot soles on the parquet of the entrance hall, the quick whisper of voices.

Jane spoke from the darkness as he turned. He saw that the hall door had swung wide, and guessed that she was standing in the black cave beyond.

"Come downstairs, Julian. At once."

A single candle flame outlined the stair well as he followed her: he saw that she was fully dressed now, a brace of pistols in her belt, the linen duster ready on her arm. He counted eleven heads in the candle flame as they went down. The bushwhackers were grouped in a rough half circle—all but the newcomer. The twelfth man had already returned to the driveway to rub down his mount.

Jane said, "You must listen carefully—and do what you're told. We must leave—a little sooner than we planned. And move a little faster." She was standing among the men now; he still waited on the bottom step and continued to stare down blankly into the impassive faces.

"Surely I'm coming too, Jane."

"Not now," she said quickly. "It isn't safe."

A voice rumbled in the half-dark. "Tie him up, miss. You can talk while we work."

The man stepped forward as he spoke: a broad-shouldered fellow, ambushed to the eyes in whiskers, a knotted rope swung loosely from one wrist. Julian felt the whole group close in with that motion. Every eye in the hall turned to the slipknot. Whiskers flashed a quick grin and twisted the hemp in his stubby farmer's hands.

"Tie him up," said Jane, and stepped back to make room. "I'm sorry, Julian. There's no other way."

He did not budge as the impromptu lariat snaked about his shoulders. An automatic reflex made him draw back when the rope jerked him from stair to floor; a dozen hands swooped, to anchor him where he stood, with his back to the newel post. A carbine barrel gleamed briefly in the gloom—and lowered, just as quickly, as he submitted. The rope had already taken a double turn about his waist and spiraled to include both legs. His chin went up and he stared hard at Jane, who stood alone now, watching the guerrillas work.

"Tell it your way," he said. "I'm listening."

"I'm making sure you don't follow us," she said.

"Can't you tell me why?"

"An hour ago one of our men rode in from Atlanta. Confederate cavalry is on its way here now; Crandall is riding with them. They're in force: strong enough to meet the Union group at the Chattahoochee."

She came closer, testing the rope that had lashed both his arms to the balustrade. "It seems Crandall hopes to trap us here before we can make rendezvous. If he can't, he'll trail us to the ford." She nodded to the lone rider, still grooming his horse on the driveway. "As you see, our lookout just came in to warn us. We must be gone in a matter of minutes, or they'll cut us off."

"I'm still listening," he said. "Why can't I——"

She cut in, stamping one booted foot as she spoke. "For the last time, Julian—this is my risk, not yours!"

Whiskers stepped back from the newel post, with the last knot tied. Julian strained hard at the bonds that spread-eagled him there and nodded approval. "You've made sure of that, at any rate."

Jane turned from him to snap an order. The men herded toward the portico, each with an extra bandolier on his free shoulder. The horses stirred and whinnied as the last saddlebags were loaded.

When Jane turned to him again, the hall was empty, and half her troop was in the saddle. "They'll be here soon enough," she said. "Tell me I've covered you, my dear. I've done my best."

He strained again at the hemp, and wondered if he looked half as grotesque as he felt, or half as puzzled. "You mentioned instructions, I believe."

"They're very simple. Tell the truth—up to a point. Say we were sleeping soundly upstairs when you heard horses on the drive. Say these men burst in upon us and insisted I ride away with them. Say they tied you here when you attempted to—to keep me at your side. Crandall will believe you: he has no choice."

"What about the sick bay—the stables——"

"You've been recovering from the fever; this is your first day downstairs. How could you know this was a bushwhackers' nest, if I didn't tell you?"

A harsh voice whooped from the driveway; when Jane turned, he saw that the last man was mounted. Whiskers was holding the gray hunter by the bridle: the empty saddle that waited for Jane was an invitation not to be ignored.

Her arms were around him now, her lips hard on his: he knew it was a kiss of renunciation, for all its warmth. A kiss he could not even return properly, with both arms lashed behind him.

"If there were another way," she said, "I'd take it. Won't you believe me?"

She ran out on that, into the faint moonlight. He did not see her mount after all: the other horses had begun to mill about the gray, and Whiskers swung across the portico, blocking his view. In another instant the whole troop had streaked away in line, vanishing into the night without a sound. Since there was not even a hoofbeat to betray their going, he guessed that they had quartered across the lawn, jumping fences on their way to the highroad, keeping the screen of cedars between them and Atlanta.

This, he realized, was no new thing for Jane. She had led these same wild riders down more than one midnight road, with the enemy on their heels: God willing, she would go on leading them. He could not doubt that she would escape tonight, cross the ford in the Chattahoochee, and make contact with the Yankee raiders; like all her plans, this one was too well conceived to fail.

Yes, it was her risk now—and not his own. He could only strain against the ropes that had been knotted at her orders, and wish her well—even as the bizarre excitement of her going subsided, even as the dark silence of the house settled about him like a shroud.

What if Crandall picked up their trail on the turnpike and bypassed High Cedars entirely? He tested the iron knots that Whiskers had tied with such ease, and knew that only a knife could sever them. It might be days—or weeks—before High Cedars had another visitor. He opened his mouth to shout, and choked down the bellow just in time. Already his ears had picked up a too-familiar sound—the crash of hard-riding horsemen in the driveway.

The cavalry troop rocketed from the cedar tunnel like a meteor and fanned out on the lawn with carbines at the ready. From where he stood he could see a guidon dip in the moonlight as its bearer tumbled to the grass. He wondered if they could see him too, and how good a target he would make if they failed to notice his uniform in time.

The rifles cracked overhead while he was still trying to make himself small in the candlelight. Two sharp reports that came almost as one. He saw the guidon bearer cough just once before he crumpled on the lawn; another rider spun crazily in his saddle, then sagged to the grass. The others had already taken cover with the ease of the veteran. Their returning volley seemed to mantle the portico in flame. He heard a dozen bullets sing through the hall. One of them, ripping through the chandelier, showered his hair with broken glass.

Overhead the shots repeated. He shrank aside as a bushwhacker came down the stair with the celerity of a giant crab, whisked around the newel post, and vanished through the arch that gave to the drawing room. He took the candle with him as he ran, and Julian was grateful for the sudden dark. A single rifle cracked upstairs, and he guessed that Jane had left only two decoys. By firing from different windows and moving fast, they could deceive the enemy for some time, unless the Confederates risked everything in a rush.

The attack from the lawn was steady, though the shots were scattered. No more bullets whined through the open doorway now that the two bushwhackers had shifted to opposite wings of the mansion. For some time he strained his ears to gauge the Confederate fire, but it seemed to move no closer. The answering fire from the house, so far as he could see, had produced no more casualties. If it succeeded in pinning heads down on the lawn, it would serve its purpose.

He shook his head to free himself of the worst of the glass fragments and gave another tug at his bonds. A new sound had reached his ears, and it was anything but reassuring: a kind of gnomelike crackling that seemed to begin in the area of the stables, find an echo in the west wing, and creep stealthily toward a meeting place. He guessed what it was, without daring to face the implications. He felt that the two bushwhackers had guessed too, for the tempo of their firing increased to a desperate pitch, as though they were using a series of weapons without pausing to reload. . . . A torch, whirling like a Roman candle gone beserk, plunged for an open window of the drawing room. Even before it could complete its flight, he had his first whiff of smoke from the stables.

"Come out, Yank—before we smoke you out!"

"Come and get us, Johnny!"

For two stranded marksmen, the bushwhackers were still keeping up a stiff exchange of lead, still dodging from window to window to give the illusion that a whole company stood ready to defend High Cedars. At last he saw a hardy volunteer rise from the depths of a boxwood hedge and hunch his shoulders for the run to the portico. Another rifle crack stopped him dead, with one foot on the carriage block. For an instant he seemed to freeze there and stare up at the mansion in incredulous dismay. Then he pitched forward, his face grinding deep in the gravel of the driveway.

"Come out, Yank—we'll hold our fire!"

In the quiet that followed this offer he could hear the flames behind him build to a nightmare crescendo of their own. In the drawing room the torch had already ignited the portieres: the fire, running merrily along the window frame, hardly paused before it leaped to the tendrils of ivy that ornamented the mantel. By craning his neck, Julian could see the portrait above, haloed in dancing red—before the canvas curled and crisped in the heat and hissed into combustion on its own.

A puff of smoke gushed through the double doors that gave to the dining room. He coughed and fought for breath as the smoke thickened, and knew he was bellowing for help from straining lungs, though his voice did not seem a part of him now. Outside the cavalrymen answered him with derisive yells; a tentative shot cut through the dark, and he heard a bullet spatter against the balustrade above him.

In another moment the flames would meet in the hallway, as they had already met at the back of the mansion. Once those red tongues had begun to lick the woodwork of the stair well, there would be no stopping them: the central hall would serve as a funnel, drawing the heat upward to a crescendo. Already the bushwhacker in the upstairs wing was probably cut off. The one who had been firing from the drawing room had been silent for some time now, and Julian could only infer that he had stopped a bullet at last.

"Speak up, Yank! D'you surrender?"

He bellowed again. This time he prayed his words would reach the lawn. "Cut me down, you fools! Can't you see who I am?"

The hall was black with smoke now, and he lost most of his plea in another fit of coughing. Bound as he was, there was no way to protect mouth and nose from that choking cloud, no way to flatten on the carpet, where the air was still fit to breathe. It seemed only a matter of minutes since the cavalry had circled the house; he could not believe that a place of this size could ignite so quickly, from cellar to rooftree. But there was no doubt that the whole house was blazing around him, and blanketing him in soot as it burned.

"For the last time, Yank—*will you come out?*"

Magically, the smoke seemed to clear a little at that moment. He saw a gray shadow flit between two pillars on the portico, saw a long revolver muzzle thrust out of that cover and level slowly. He was staring down the muzzle, which seemed only yards away. He was shouting one more time as his senses reeled. But he knew that a gloved hand slapped the gun down before the shot could find him. He was sure that he heard Tracy Crandall's voice giving orders as his brain spun down into darkness.

xvi

Cold water stung his cheeks. He sat up on the grass, feeling his mind rock with the effort, and then steady, as he looked up into Crandall's eyes.

The counterspy was bathed in a hideous red glare: even before he could lift himself to an elbow, Julian saw that High Cedars was belching flame from every door and window. His instrument case lay on the grass beside him, along with his portmanteau. They had carried him to a safe distance: from where he lay, the heat of the burning house reached him in waves that only accented the delicious coolness of the clean night air.

He sat up with an arm around him and looked down at his

hands. The skin was still mottled with heat, and the cuffs of both sleeves were charred; but he knew at once that he had escaped even a first-degree burn, though the margin had been slight. The counterspy took his arm away, and Julian found that he could sit up with no real effort. The wave of dizziness was passing rapidly, now that he could fill his lungs with oxygen.

Crandall was in a brand-new Home Guard uniform. He noticed the quiet for the first time, and realized they were alone on the lawn—save for the presence of a lifeless body or two.

Crandall said, easily enough, "We didn't have much time, Captain Chisholm."

"Do you mind telling me why I'm still alive?"

Crandall grinned and fanned himself with his hat. "You can thank Corporal Yates for that. He cut you down from the newel post—after deciding not to shoot you. I'll see he gets a commission for his judgment."

"What about the men who tied me there?"

"Only two were left," said the counterspy. "One is lying over there—under that sumac bush, with his coat over his face. Major Trout has taken the other along as a guide."

So Jane had left a rear guard, just as he surmised. Julian smiled inwardly as he wondered how accurate a guide the living bushwhacker would prove to be.

"We'll follow them," said Crandall. "When you've got your wind, of course." He nodded toward a cluster of tethered horses under the trees of the driveway. "You've a choice of several empty saddles, I'm afraid."

Julian got up, not too groggily, and steadied himself against a tree trunk. "Surely the others got away?"

"Not too far," said the counterspy cheerfully. "Tell me this: did you have a chance to count heads—when they surprised you?"

Julian blinked, and hoped that he could blame the reflex on the smoke that still burned his lids. Just in time he realized that the captured guerrilla had probably had wit enough to echo Jane's story. A rush of armed thugs at midnight, invading a man's bedchamber and spiriting away his wife, was excuse enough for bewilderment. . . . He continued to stare at Crandall and offered a noncommittal shrug.

"A dozen, perhaps. Yes, I think there were that many in the hall when they wakened me. Of course there could have been more outside. There was a great stir of horses in the driveway."

Crandall nodded patiently. "Take your time on this, Dr. Chisholm. I don't blame you for being shocked."

He leaned against a tree, dropping his hand into a side pocket and coming up with a flask. Julian swallowed the proffered brandy gratefully. His palate told him that it was the best French cognac. Probably Crandall had found it a valuable obbligato to his business in the past.

"I'm still trying to adjust my mind to—to what happened. Jane—my wife——"

"Your wife, Captain, is a top-drawer Union agent. Unfortunately, we were able to prove the fact a trifle too late. Does it come as a shock to you?"

"I still can't believe it."

It was a true enough statement, Julian added inwardly. Even with the evidence of his eyes, he could not picture Jane riding for her life through the Georgia barrens. He looked up as one of the pillars of High Cedars tottered into the holocaust behind it. Above the sagging rooftree the sky was inky. He prayed that it was later than it seemed: surely the minutes had telescoped crazily enough while he waited for death in that blazing hallway.

Crandall said, "I must repeat, she has been under suspicion for some time. You gathered as much when I called on you at the Atlanta Hotel."

"I refused to believe you at the time. You've yet to convince me."

"You saw her ride away with these men, didn't you?"

"She went under duress."

"It's known now that several bushwhackers posed as her caretakers here. Were none of them in the group that surprised you?"

It's coming now, thought Julian. One word out of place, and he'll think me an accomplice. He breathed deep and kept his voice steady. "Things happened too fast. I was—hardly awake when they took her from our bedroom. Of course I did my best to follow, but there were too many of them——" He paused, as though collecting his thoughts, and hoped that the pause was properly timed. "No, Mr. Crandall. It was too dark to remember faces."

"Did they carry her out bodily?"

"I'm afraid I can't answer that either. One moment I was wrestling with three of them in the hallway. The next I was tied hand and foot, as you found me—and she was gone."

"I don't question your veracity, Captain," said the counterspy.

His voice had a genuine ring; despite himself, Julian found that he could pick up hope from its timbre. "In fact, I have no wish to question you at all. It's merely a matter of routine, considering your antecedents."

"You needn't apologize, sir. I realize your position."

Crandall bowed against the crazy dance of the flames. "Still, your wife is guilty beyond a doubt. I must ask for your parole, even though I consider you blameless."

"Did you say 'parole,' Mr. Crandall?"

"Precisely, Doctor. Your word that you'll remain in this area until she's captured—and give me what aid you can. Naturally you won't be asked to testify at her trial." The counterspy bowed again. "We have enough evidence now to close our case."

"But I thought she got away." The words were out, despite himself: he knew that he had colored under Crandall's stare.

"So did I, at first," said Crandall. "As you see, the lady covered her tracks carefully. Unfortunately for her, we knew just where she was heading. Even with a head start, I don't think she'll get beyond the Chattahoochee."

"May the lady's husband ask why?"

Crandall put an arm through Julian's; they walked toward the knot of tethered horses. "As you know, Sheridan has risked more than one cavalry raid into this area. At the moment we've been warned of penetration to the northern bank of the river—less than ten miles from here. The Yankees came in after sundown and made camp in the woods, just above the north bank. Our scouts inform us that they haven't budged since. I needn't add that raiders don't behave in that manner without a reason."

"You mean they're waiting for the bushwhackers?"

"And your wife, Doctor. There's been a general withdrawal of Union agents in this county. That's why we moved in on High Cedars tonight—and why we took certain precautions, in case we arrived late."

The counterspy cupped his palms for Julian's boot and helped him up to a saddle: he stood with an elbow on the pommel, a stocky, competent figure against the blazing mansion. "Fortunately for us, there's only one road to the Chattahoochee ford; they've no choice but to take it. Major Trout, therefore, divided his forces. The vanguard rode on to the south bank of the river, to prepare an ambush——"

Julian twisted the reins in his fingers. Crandall's eyes had never wavered: they were watching him now—calmly and without pity. The collapse of High Cedars suffused his face in its pyrotechnic glare. He wondered if Crandall had placed him on the horse's back deliberately, the better to study the effect of his words.

"Won't the Yankees come to the rescue?"

"I don't think so, Doctor. They'll hear a few scattered shots in the dark when we close in, no more. Remember, our men know their business."

"Suppose they cross the ford in the meantime?"

"We're ready for that too. In fact, we'd welcome it." Crandall's eyes snapped away from Julian: if he was disappointed, he gave no sign as he swung up into another empty saddle. "Shall we observe results together?"

Julian kept face and voice impassive. "If you like."

"Of course you may return to Atlanta if you'll give me your word to stay there."

"You may need a doctor."

"True enough. I'm forgetting your instrument case."

Julian sat in his stirrups, quiet as a stone, while Crandall returned with the medical kit. There was just room for it in the saddle boot, beside the cavalryman's carbine. Crandall buckled the flap snugly before he swung into his own saddle again. Julian took in these details mechanically. He doubted if he would have the strength to ride to the river now that he understood what he might find there. Yet he knew that he must find the strength somehow. Even at this moment Jane might have need of that instrument case.

"Follow me, Doctor," said Crandall. "And try to stay in your stirrups; we haven't too much time."

The counterspy was gone as he spoke the last words, thudding down the cedar tunnel to the highroad. He knows I'll follow him, thought Julian: after tonight I don't dare hold back. He went down the driveway, too, at a gallop.

xvii

Much later he remembered the banshee overtones of that ride to the river. The endless cotton fields in the open country, where the turnpike lay straight as a ruled line to the horizon, the red clay of its roadbed bright as a wound, even by starlight. The fork that led to the Chattahoochee, churned by a hundred hoofs, beginning to shine in the misty rain that had come with morning. The echo of their passing on the corduroy that spanned a mile-long savannah, moist as a sponge in this wet autumn night. Crandall took it all at that same gallop, and he clung doggedly to Crandall's trail, blessing the boyhood training that had made this breakneck pace seem natural. Blessing the need to focus his whole mind on the soapy road, the next pothole, the next dripping arch of branches—with no time to ask what lay ahead.

It was, he thought breathlessly, not unlike a fox hunt. He and Crandall were two tardy hunters, straining to overtake the pack—and wondering if they had already closed in for the kill. Clinging to stirrups and saddle, feeling the rain pelt his cheeks, he grazed a ditch with inches to spare as the horse all but stumbled in the murk. Clearly, this was no time to think in similes. . . . And yet, when they breasted the next rise and he saw the river shining through the trees ahead, he was almost sorry that their gallop was over—that he must abandon simile and deal with realities.

Crandall reined in and answered the challenge from the dark. A wet hand appeared at each bridle, leading the two winded horses down from the shoulder of the road. The rain was a white curtain among the jack pines; Julian glimpsed a huddle of horsemen waiting in the doubtful shelter of the trees, a winking eye that turned out to be the window of a cabin. There was nothing about the group of men to suggest a successful ambuscade; the spill of light from the cabin doorway was almost friendly as it swung wide to admit them.

"Major Trout, Captain Surgeon Chisholm."

The major sat at a rough table with a map spilling over on his knees; a brace of captains, standing at attention behind him, favored the newcomers with a resentful glance. All three officers resembled wet pyramids in the lamplight, thanks to the rubber ponchos they were wearing. The dripping campaign hat that sat above the major's scowl was only an afterthought. . . . But Trout's handshake was friendly enough, despite that wet and hirsute glare. Trout's manner was completely candid as he leveled a finger at the map.

"Before you ask me, gentlemen, they got away clean."

Julian swallowed the lump in his throat and felt his knees go weak in sheer relief. He stepped back a pace, out of the lamplight, hoping that Crandall had not noticed the change in his face.

"Clean as a pack of jack rabbits," said Trout. "Don't ask me how they knew we'd be waiting. They just did. Maybe it's a blessing in disguise, Crandall. We'll know in an hour."

Watching the counterspy knit his brows, Julian half guessed the major's meaning. He ventured to look over his shoulder and saw that the forefinger was tracing a spot on the far bank of the Chattahoochee.

"Here's where the Federals pitched camp last night," said Trout. "What's more, they're still there. Sitting out the storm, if you like. Or waiting for the last bushwhacker to come through their lines." The impatient forefinger made a precise gesture. "Pickets a good mile north of the stream. My scouts had the whole line taped before I got here."

"What are you suggesting?" snapped Crandall.

"For an intelligence officer, Tracy, you're slow as molasses. I've a thousand men at this ford. Every mother's son has been chewing his navel for the past two hours. Waiting for an order to cross, re-form in open country, and charge."

Crandall said slowly, "You were ordered out of Atlanta to round up a Union agent and her group. Through no fault of yours, you've failed in that. Obviously these Yankee raiders will pull out with morning. You can do the same with honor."

"Grady snaked right up to their fires, just this side of midnight," said Trout. "He counted seven hundred head of horseflesh, including pack mules."

"How do you know they aren't camped in echelon?"

"Grady came out of the Seminole War alive," said Trout. "I trust his judgment—and his arithmetic."

"And I say you should return to Atlanta. Now, if you're sure Mrs. Anderson has already crossed the river."

Trout grinned wetly and looked up from the map long enough to wring the moisture from his beard. "I didn't say that exactly. All I admitted was she's given *me* the slip. My guess is they're holed in upriver where the woods are thickest—waiting for enough light to swim the current."

"Then it's your duty to rout them out."

"Did you ever hunt for possum in this weather, Tracy? Or bushwhackers?" The finger caressed the map, one more time, before its owner folded the parchment into a dispatch case. "Seven hundred Yanks, all in one place, are lots easier to pin down. And lots more fun, because they'll fight back. Join the party if you like: I'm through hunting spies."

Crandall shrugged. "The invitation is accepted—and the risk. I still say they'll outnumber you, but that's your responsibility."

"What about you, Doctor?"

Julian bowed his thanks. "I'm honored, Major."

"I'll detail two orderlies to help you. You can set up at the top of the bank. If they let me pick the field, we'll meet on the slope just beyond." If the major spoke vaguely, Julian guessed that his thoughts were anything but vague; his eyes were snapping as he arranged his pieces on the deadly chessboard he had chosen. "A double envelopment, and all the firing at point-blank range. The sort of charge we used to dream about at V.M.I. Maybe I'm still dreaming——"

"I'm a field surgeon, Major," said Julian. "Shouldn't we establish the field, before I set up my hospital?"

Trout looked at him shrewdly. "I know your record, Dr. Chisholm. What's your thought?"

"Only that I can't be too close to my wounded. Especially in a cavalry action. If you're putting a pincers on the Yankee camp, couldn't I ride with one of the prongs?"

"Fair enough, sir," said Trout. "Stay with me while we make the crossing. I'll give you your position on the other bank."

Crandall snorted in the background. "Don't tell me you're crossing in the dark, Major?"

"We've less than an hour to dawn, and not too much cover. I plan to be in battle order by sunrise."

"Suppose the Yanks strike camp sooner?"

"My scouts are still out," said Trout. "It's a chance we've got to take." He tossed the dispatch case to an aide and walked into the rain.

Crandall snorted once again and followed him. Julian stayed at the counterspy's heels, thankful that the bustle of war had trimmed him to proportion. Trout, he reflected, had accepted Captain Surgeon Chisholm without a single question. It was a way men had with one another, when they had smelled powder and lived down its threat.

Moving with the others into the rain, swinging into the saddle again, Julian realized that he had never been so close to battle in the making. At Vicksburg the battle—as such—had settled into the hideous anticlimax of a siege long before his arrival; at Chickamauga the main action had been muffled by the slopes of Lookout Mountain, miles away. Here he could feel the pulse of war at every throat, sense the battle look in a hundred young faces as the units streamed past the command post, offering Trout a salute blurred by darkness and the streaming sky.

Here (and his own pulse quickened at the thought) the enemy would be challenged in the open field, attacked head-on in that one leftover from the wars of chivalry—the cavalry charge. The fact that Trout planned to surprise the Yankees in their sleep was only an incidental footnote to his daring.

The movement across the ford had begun long before their arrival; only the headquarters company was waiting to clear the road as the two staff officers reined in to let them pass. They made a brave show in that graying light: even the rain was kind to their ragged shoulders, mantling them in a silver mist that hid many a discordant patch, many a strip of sacking that served in lieu of stirrup leather. A guidon lifted in the pale light, and a command was whispered: the last group of horsemen, in column of twos, vanished on the downgrade that led to the water.

"Well, gentlemen?" said Trout.

No one spoke as he followed his command. The two staff captains swung in behind him: Julian and Crandall took their own places in the file as the little knot of aides sawed on their bridles to give them precedence. The slow-moving column ahead, silent as the sodden morning, seemed to move at a snail's pace as the leaders negotiated the last steep pitch from land to river.

It was darker here, among the thick water oaks that lined the water's edge. Julian was never quite sure when his own mount slithered into the muddy current, coasted stirrup-deep in the tug of the stream, then steadied into line with the horse ahead. From where he sat the water seemed alive with Confederate cavalry as the last company fanned out cautiously to take full advantage of the ford's width; on either side of the movement a half dozen men were swimming beside their mounts to give the main body room to complete its maneuver.

He moved easily enough in that gray mass, feeling himself a part of it now. In spite of the proximity of the other riders, he had a sense of freedom, here in the open stream: the dome of the sky above him, beginning to clear as the rain lessened, winked with a few stars, though the day was growing fast behind the cloud banks to the east. Someone whispered a command in midstream, and the column halted to give its first platoon right-of-way on the far bank: there was a muted jingling of bridles, a slow, sucking rhythm of river water parting around a half thousand equine legs. Then, at a second whisper, the line snaked forward again, slowly but surely. Already the bluffs of the north bank were taking shape in the promise of dawn. . . .

The river was much deeper now: watching the arms ahead of him lift in unison to raise weapons and powder above the water line, Julian remembered to open his own saddlebag and salvage both instrument case and carbine. For a long, rather frightening moment he felt the horse lose footing on the muddy bottom and realized that he was swimming the last fifty feet in sure, deep-chested thrashing. He wondered if he should lift his own feet from the stirrups and swim, and abandoned the thought when he saw that the trooper ahead was giving his own mount a free rein and staying in the saddle. Wet manes lifted, cinches reappeared above the water line, forelegs bent and tensed one more time. He was riding out of the Chattahoochee, now, between the major's staff officers, testing the mud of the far bank and finding that the slope could be managed after all. With the last of the column he entered the road that led to higher ground.

Here, he found, the highway was no more than a gash in the bluff: the massed cavalry hardly seemed to move at all as the leaders' hoofs churned even deeper in the red gumbo that was the aftermath of the maneuver. On either side the water oaks were a dense green wall, no less forbidding now that it was light enough to make out the shapes of individual trees. Julian reflected that it was an ideal spot for an ambush, and wondered again why the Yankees had neglected to leave a picket line at the ford. Even if they were encamped a mile beyond, it seemed strange that they would not have taken this precaution. Especially now, when they were waiting to rendezvous with their agents from Atlanta.

He abandoned the question promptly as the last horseman leveled off into the open woods to the north of the bluff. Even in the half-light he could see that the trees here were free of underbrush, though the cover was perfect. The company had already deployed in tentative battle line, with the skill of veterans who knew their places without the need of commands; as far as he could see, the woods teemed with gray statues, waiting patiently for a word to sweep them into action. Men with hawk's eyes under wet hatbrims, silent as stones in the morning, alert for the slightest sound ahead.

"Captain Crowther reporting, sir."

"Left flank, ready for action."

"All present and accounted for, Major."

Julian realized that Trout was only a few yards away; he wheeled cautiously to meet the major's exultant eyes.

"We're moving out by platoons to form our right flank, Doctor. That'll be your post. If you'll be good enough to follow your orderlies——"

"And I, Major?"

Commanding officer and surgeon turned in unison. Both of them had forgotten Tracy Crandall. Though he was soaked in muddy river water to the thighs, the counterspy still had a jaunty air of dress parade about him.

"You'd better stay with my runners, Tracy. It'll be safer."

"As a Home Guard officer," said Crandall, "I resent that implication. Do you mind if I ride down the flank with Dr. Chisholm?"

"Suit yourself," Trout said just as affably. "Just keep out of the way of the charge. We'll be in battle line in ten minutes, if I know my staff. I'd hate to send you back to Atlanta with a pair of broken knees."

Someone chuckled in the wet gloom: Crandall took the slight with perfect good humor as he followed Julian and the two mounted orderlies. The group rode in silence for a time: silence, at that moment, seemed the order of the day, though it was hard to feel the presence of seven hundred sleeping enemy as the woods ahead stared back at them without a sound. Seven hundred Yankees, rolled snug in their blankets, their horses corralled, their picket line nodding somewhere ahead. . . . Once again Julian asked himself if the picture was not unduly optimistic. One of the orderlies turned in his saddle, and he remembered that his was a special task today, that battle strategy was the business of others.

"We'll check our supplies with yours in a minute, Doc. Shall I take your instrument case?"

Julian shook his head and restored the kit to his boot. The

cavalry carbine still lay across his saddlebow, and he let it stay. Obviously, a field surgeon must move into battle unarmed; still, the feel of the wet stock was good to his hands as they rode down this apparently endless file of gray.

The orderly said, easily enough, "We're proud to have you with us, Doc. Reckon I should have said that sooner, but I only just heard your name."

"Do you ride out often without a surgeon?"

"Wouldn't have come this far, sir, if we'd known about the Federals; figured we'd just do a bit of spy-catching when we left Atlanta. That's why we left the surgeon to enjoy himself at Madame Eleanor's." The orderly grinned. "Course I'm a surgeon myself, in a manner of speaking. Tied off my share of arteries from here to the Ohio."

Julian nodded, with an inward smile. The Confederate ranks were full of youths like this, who had served their apprenticeship in some doctor's office—and would come out of the war as full-fledged surgeons. He remembered the amputation he had performed behind drawn blinds in St. Augustine, and the gangling youth who had assisted. The boy on the horse ahead had the same loose-limbed frame, the same vacant stare; save for the geniality, he and Broussard's orderly might have been twins.

They were entering a copse of water oaks now: ahead, he saw, the woods thinned abruptly into open country, still muffled in mist. The two orderlies drew rein and explained their business to a lean young lieutenant in homespun, who evidently commanded this forward echelon. When the whispered parley was over, the two men rode back to open their saddlebags. Cavalry, he knew, rode light and lived by its wits: this philosophy extended to its medical arm, which was often nonexistent. But the stock of dressings in those saddlebags was adequate for a field unit.

"Do we plan on a complete envelopment?"

"That's the rumor, sir. Course the Yanks will try to fight their way out, but——"

"In that case I think we should ride behind the last wave of the charge. We can pick our spot when it's really light."

The sky had begun to open in earnest as they made their plans. The rain, he found, had stopped completely now: a brisk, high wind had rolled the clouds back from the edge of day. The last star faded as he watched, though it was not yet full daylight.

Somewhere deep in the woods a bird stirred and took flight, opening its throat wide in song as it rose to meet the morning.

From where he sat Julian could count a hundred heads. A scout rode down the lines to whisper with the lieutenant; Julian saw the man slap his thigh with satisfaction, then turn to pass on the tidings. The orderly rode up with the news in another moment.

"Still snoozing, Doc. The whole pack of 'em. Would you believe it?"

The lieutenant rose in his stirrups and lifted his sword. Julian felt his heart thud in his chest, but there was no order to charge. Instead the whole battle line seemed to knit together, even as it moved cautiously forward. He guessed that the movement was a general one, from the tip of the right flank, where he was riding, to the last platoon far to the left. A silent maneuver that placed the Confederate force as far forward as Trout dared.

It was staring daylight now, though the sun was still hidden by a dense bank of pines to the east. Not a hundred feet ahead, where the woods really ended, the Georgia countryside opened into a long stretch of meadow, thinly dotted with grazing cattle and smooth as an English park. Trees grew in scattered clumps down its length, and there was a dark swath of pines in its center, but it was a perfect spot for battle. Even a civilian in uniform, like Captain Surgeon Chisholm, could grasp that fact instantly.

"See that island of pines, Doc?" said the orderly. *"That's* their camp. Grady just went out again, on his belly, to count noses—and horseflesh."

Julian squinted at the dark oasis in that sea of green; it was difficult to estimate its size without binoculars, but he could see that there was ample space for a full-scale deployment on all sides before the woods thickened again, a good two miles to the north. The Yankees, he reflected, had chosen their cover well: at this distance it seemed incredible that seven hundred enemy cavalrymen, and their mounts, could be hidden there.

"Trout was right," he said to no one in particular. "It's a battlefield to dream about."

Crandall said, "It's too good to be true. Has it occurred to you that they might be sitting in that cover deliberately—waiting for us to come to them?"

Julian came back to the counterspy with a slight start. Crandall had been lounging in his saddle, with his eyes on the field ahead:

as usual, he had asserted his presence with a thought that echoed Julian's own forebodings. Julian handed his bridle to the orderly. "Stay where you are. I'm having a closer look."

No one spoke as he swung to the ground and walked boldly forward until he stood at the very edge of the screen of trees. Only then did he realize that he still held the carbine in his hand; he slung it over a shoulder as he knelt in the shadow of a pine and shielded his eyes from the sudden glare. The sun had pushed above the screen of trees to the east, transforming the meadow to a brilliant green carpet; the ground looked a bit spongy in places, thanks to the rain, but he knew the sun would dry it fast enough. Five hundred yards. A full gallop would bring them to that island of pines and whip their flanks around it; if it was true that the Yankees still slept, they could pen their prisoners at point-blank range.

He wondered if Jane had reached that Yankee camp during the night—and, still wondering, turned toward a sudden eruption of hoofbeats ahead and to the right. The bushwhacker troop was already bursting from the woods at the meadow's end and plunging into the open at a straining gallop. He knew them instantly, even before he recognized Jane's mount; they were riding in a tight wedge, and she was at its apex, urging the gray hunter with crop and heels.

She rode low above the hunter's neck: he guessed that she was whispering in his ear as they went into this last lap of her dash for safety. Already they were within three hundred yards of the Confederate lines. Every bushwhacker was wearing a blue uniform coat. Jane herself had discarded her linen duster and now wore an officer's tunic, complete with shoulder straps. The strategy was evident enough here: coming into view of the Yankee camp at the first flush of dawn, the troop must make its identity unmistakable.

Even at the distance he saw that the blue uniforms were dripping wet: Jane's brave new tunic, for all its dash, was soaked to the armpits. Trout, he gathered, had been right: the bushwhackers (warned by some sixth sense not to cross the Chattahoochee at the ford) had swerved into the live-oak thickets and waited out the night in hiding. When there was enough light to gauge distances, they had swum their horses across the stream, cut through the woods above the meadow, and headed for their rendezvous at this loose-reined, driving pace. Late as they were, they could not pause for caution: none of them had thought the Confederates would risk a general movement across the stream.

The picture passed through his mind in a flash as the troop swung nearer. Behind him he heard the soft slap of wood on flesh, and knew that a dozen cavalrymen had lifted carbines to cheek, to draw a tentative bead on that flying wedge of horseflesh. No one would fire without an order; but the command would come soon enough, now it was evident that the Yankees had been aroused across that strip of meadow. No one would spare Jane: from this distance it was impossible to know that a woman was leading the guerrilla band.

His own carbine was at his shoulders; he felt something snap in his brain as he fired two shots into the air, jamming the repeater on the second report and stumbling back to his horse with no conscious sense that he had moved at all.

Blank silence clamped down on their ambush. He saw the smoke drift skyward, heard the echoes of the two reports bounce back from the woods, and opened his mouth to shout another warning as the flying wedge continued to bear down upon them. For one sickening instant he thought that his warning had been misunderstood, that Jane had taken the two reports as a friendly signal from her own lines. Then the wedge changed its direction, just before the tight group of riders could be considered a really tempting target. Swerving widely in the midst of the meadow, they headed for the island of pines at another angle. In a matter of seconds, it seemed, the peril was behind them—and they were streaking for the Yankee camp in a wide arc, well outside of rifle range.

"Who fired those shots?"

He recognized the lieutenant's voice without turning, felt Crandall's stare drilling his shoulder blades as he waited for the blow to fall. Taut in the saddle, he saw his fist thrust the guilty carbine deep into the boot, as though he could conceal his betrayal with a gesture. Not that he had any conscious desire to deny the act: the gesture was purely automatic. So, for that matter, was the knot his fist made of the bridle when a long-drawn shout moved down the lines, a scant second after the lieutenant's bellow—a command that had a lilt all its own in the fresh morning air. A hundred heads lifted in unison to answer it; a hundred lithe young bodies rose in their stirrups. The rebel keen split the hush of the forest, with force enough to peel the bark from the trees.

"*Chaaaaarge!*"

Somewhere in that mad moment a banjo string twanged wildly. He had never ridden to music, but he was riding now, his own throat stretched with the rest to howl defiance at Georgia's invaders, his own fist raised at the dawn-bright sky, though it was empty of a weapon.

The horse between his knees responded too, tossing its mane as it thundered into the van. Too late he remembered that this was a cavalry charger: even with a tight rein he could hardly have sawed down that wild catapult of energy. By giving the animal his head, he had let himself be carried into the first wave of the assault.

He could never turn back now to rejoin his orderlies—to see how Crandall had reacted to his conduct just before the charge began.

The long gray arc inundated the dewy green of the meadow, trampling the fresh clover in its sweep. Somewhere the banjo still twanged madly. All around him voices picked up the tune—and he knew that he was singing it too, from bursting lungs:

"Look away! look away! look awaaaaaay!
Dixie Land."

It should have been grotesque; he should have laughed aloud at his folly; instead he felt his heart expand like a bird in flight, making him one with the swooping rhythm of the charge. To left and right the guidons pointed the way like crusaders' lances, the regimental colors taut as bright wings. Far down the line of racing horseflesh the flag of secession rode high on its standard: at the distance he could not see its tattered edges, only the crossed red bars on the gray field as it whipped in the fury of their passage.

"In Dixie Land I'll take my stand,
To lib and die in Dixie . . ."

Only then did he remember to look ahead for Jane. He was just in time to see the last buskwhacker vanish through a wall of horsemen that had grown from the meadow like magic mushrooms. An endless blue wall that seemed to thicken monstrously as fresh cavalrymen poured out of the pines.

There was no time to wonder how the enemy force had come

into being. Whether it had been packed, ant-thick, in that island of trees, or moved out, in echelon, from the forest beyond. But it was evident, even at this distance, that Major Trout of the Confederate Army had been hideously outsmarted—that the trap, adroitly baited, had teeth at every point. It was just as evident that Major Trout's force was determined to rush into that trap, pell-mell, with steel flying, with no regard for odds.

He remembered thinking how right Crandall had been about the Yankee stratagem, and turned in astonishment as the counterspy shouted at his ear. Crandall had stayed with the charge, after all. He was riding neck and neck with Julian now, a saber unlimbered and slashing the air; he was shouting at the advancing blue wall with all the force of the youngest daredevil in their ranks.

The sunlight broke blindingly on a score of blades as every point leveled at a chosen Yankee. Among the enemy the gesture was echoed with interest. A few of the veterans on both sides, sabers in teeth, were beginning to shoot from their saddles; the thin spirals of smoke curled across the lessening strip of green. . . . Already the first wounded horse had reared and screamed in their ranks.

Jane will be safe behind that blue wall, he thought. Come what may, she's out of this for a while. The horse screamed again, and he saw, without surprise, that Crandall's mount had stopped the first bullet. The animal's forelegs buckled; its head went down as it rolled to its side, sending its rider spinning to the earth a scant foot from the nearest flying hoofs.

Crandall lay where he had fallen, his body spread-eagled on the spongy earth; the charge swept over him without a pause, and Julian stayed with the leaders. There was no time to wonder if the counterspy had snapped his neck in the fall; there was no time for anything but the simple need to survive.

The two lines of cavalry met and merged; rebel keen blended with Union bellow in a cacophony that was part of the cannoning of horses' flanks, the point-blank bark of carbines and revolvers, the splinter of clubbed gunstock on bone. He was whirled into the melee, dodging a saber slash with inches to spare, feeling a bullet cut one trouser leg, and not pausing to see if it had cut flesh as well.

For the moment he was above the threat of wounds, telling

himself that he would live forever—even as the boy beside him collapsed with a blur of blood at his cheek, even as another saber cut down the trooper beyond, as casually as though the man's body were suet on a chopping block. . . . He saw two clashing horsemen, each with a point in the other's body, stare at each other in dismay before they slipped from their saddles. He saw a gutted horse stagger into the Yankee ranks as its rider lifted a blue-coated figure from his stirrups in a roundhouse swipe of steel. Then, miraculously, he was in the clear, still riding at a full gallop, still shouting a challenge without meaning.

It had happened too fast for thought. Now that the din was behind him, he could not even check his pace while he examined his surroundings. He was out of the meadow now, in the shadow of trees again; he knew, just as vaguely, that the Yankees had practically disdained him as a target when his horse found a pocket in the blue mass. For the present he could only thunder on, dodging branches with the same instinct that had saved him from that lone saber swipe.

Perhaps the Yankees had seen that he was unarmed and by-passed him for that reason. Perhaps, even in the madness of battle, they had observed that he was a surgeon out of his element and trusted him to find his way. He knew that he must turn back, when he could cut down the tempo of his mount. He must find his orderlies and set up a field unit without delay, now that a thousand men were being cut to pieces just over the rise. Or had he ridden farther, after all? Was this open square of cook wagons, tethered mules, and insolently smoking fires really the Union camp?

A cook wagon, piled high with more food than he had seen in months; a man in an apron chopping meat on a block, with the same casual competence his active comrades were exhibiting in the field—Julian had time to be sure of that. A dead weight crashed down on his shoulders, slowing his progress from a canter to a scrambling walk, spilling him from saddle to grass. He fought back by instinct as he felt the arms whip round his middle in an ursine hug, and realized that his assailant, as yet unseen, had tackled him in a flying leap as he rode past the cook wagon. But he knew, even now, that timing was against him. Feeling his nose burrow in the dirt, he jackknifed his legs and tried hard to throw the weight from his shoulders. But the man on his back was too firmly anchored. When he felt the icy prick of steel at his hairline, he could only relax in spent rage and wait for the point to thrust deeper.

"Sit up, Doc," said a pleasant voice. "Sorry, but we don't allow visitors."

Julian blew the dirt from nose and mouth as his assailant rolled away from his shoulders. They stood up together, the Yankee still a foursquare threat behind the open clasp knife. He saw now that the man was wearing a dirty uniform of the Union Quartermaster Corps—that the steel point that had just pinked his scalp was white with bacon fat.

"Lucky I saw your insignia in time," said the Yankee. "Would I be impolite if I asked what you're doing here?"

Despite the flat accent, the voice did not lack the edge of culture. A schoolmaster turned cook, Julian thought absently. . . . In another moment his mind would pin down to the fact that he had been taken prisoner by a pot-walloper, just after he had ridden through his first cavalry charge without a scratch. His brain, still reeling in the battle smoke, was beyond such ironies now.

"By this time," said the Yankee, "you're supposed to be dead. All of you. Colonel McCloud planned it that way—and the colonel's a right smart planner. How come you got this far?"

"I don't know." His voice was only a hoarse croak. As he spoke he felt a sharp pain in his thigh and saw that blood was oozing from a powder-black rent in his uniform. Suddenly his five senses awakened in unison. He breathed the good smell of bacon frying, the sour reek of the man who faced him. He saw the pine needles above the humpbacked canvas wagons and the giant at the chopping block, who leaned on his cleaver a moment to stare at him curiously. He noted the strange pattern the smoke from the cook fires made against the fresh morning sky, and knew that he preferred that pattern, infinitely, to the smudge that Mars was tracing on the meadow behind him. He could taste that broiling bacon on his tongue: realizing that he had not breakfasted, he took a tentative step toward the nearest cook fire, until the compulsion of the lardy knife point brought him back.

The Yankee said, "How come a doctor rides ahead of the army? Ain't they supposed to bring up the rear?"

"Schoolmasters," said Julian, "should mind their grammar."

He leaned on the hub of an axle and looked down at the trickle of blood on his thigh. The pain, while sharp, was not severe; it was a flesh wound only, and he could trust it to stop bleeding in time. There was worse than that awaiting him on the meadow. He would find his orderlies, set up his unit . . .

"I must go back," he murmured. "Take me to your commanding officer."

The Yankee said, "*I'm* in command of this detail, Doc. You mean you want to see the colonel?"

"What else would I mean?"

"Easy does it, now. You're a good half mile from the battle, and you're too late to help. Sit down and wait till the old man comes back for his breakfast."

"I'm a medical officer. Can't you understand that?"

"Sure I do. I wanted to be a doc once—and ended up teaching school. If you ask me, you ought to take a nice long rest—right now."

"Take me to your commanding officer!"

"Can't do it, Doc. Even if I wanted to." The man was already back in his cook wagon, chopping bacon. Julian frowned as the image blurred. Perhaps he had lost some blood after all; perhaps it was only the aftermath of the holocaust he had left behind him. He was even more furious when he felt himself obeying the quartermaster's advice, sinking slowly to the ground, with his back to the wagon wheel. . . . I won't faint this time, he told himself grimly. I'm not really hurt, I'm just tired.

Meanwhile the voice in the wagon continued, in a cheery monotone. "Don't be surprised to see Federal cavalry traveling in this style. We nabbed these wagons only yesterday—from one of your own supply depots. Course most of the food is ours, but it was easier hauling on these wood roads. Gave my mules a rest and *me* a place to sleep. . . . Our boys don't like fighting on an empty stomach any more than yours, so I aim to see they eat up strong this morning: the rest goes out in saddlebags, in the next hour . . ."

Julian knew that he had fainted after all. The voice melted into the haze that dropped on the cook wagon and the apron of grass that surrounded it. But it still droned on, as he came back.

". . . wanted to see a battle for three years now. But they left me with my mules. Wanted to capture a secesh on my own, too.

That's why I jumped you when you came in like a one-man cyclone. Course it's just my luck you couldn't fight back . . ."

The voice trailed off again. This time Julian gathered the pause was deliberate. He saw why, when two blue-coated cavalrymen rode into the clearing. Young staff officers, both of them, insolent in their newness. Both reined in sharply when they observed Julian's mount.

His eyes moved with theirs, and he saw that the horse had not stirred since the quartermaster wrenched him from the stirrups. Alert and firm-footed, the animal faced the enemy now in a kind of ferocious calm that seemed almost human. Julian remembered uneasily that this had been a cavalry charger. Not the sort of mount a doctor would choose to follow the wars.

"Easy does it," the quartermaster whispered from the wagon above him. "The one on the right is McCloud's adjutant. Just tell 'em who you are. You'll stay alive."

The cavalrymen closed in on the horse from opposite sides; Julian saw that each of them hugged a long-nosed army revolver to his side, as though they expected the animal to show fight. The adjutant leaned forward and lifted the carbine from the saddle boot.

"There's his rider, Ted."

The gun muzzles turned on Julian in unison. He sat unstirring as the young men dismounted and walked toward him with a kind of carelessness that did not hide their tension.

"Ready to surrender, Johnny?"

He found he could rise, after a fashion; despite the threat of two businesslike revolvers, he kept his hands hooked in his belt.

"I'm a doctor, gentlemen."

"He says he's a doctor, Ted. Do you recognize the insignia?"

"He's a doc, all right, Captain," said the quartermaster. "And don't you forget I captured him."

"Doctors are not subject to capture," said Julian.

The words echoed in emptiness. He stared at the two officers, wondering if they had heard. They stared back with a disbelief that was almost ludicrous. He found he was really laughing when each of them described a slow cart wheel and vanished into a thick blue mist that had, unaccountably, seeped into the clearing from all sides. . . .

"I haven't fainted," he said firmly, and felt the gritty spokes of a wagon wheel scrape against his palm as he saved himself from falling.

"I'm just a—little tired. Rode too far, after my fever——"

Someone had him by an elbow. He was walking through the blue mist, willingly enough, looking eagerly into a dozen tanned faces under the cocky visors of forage caps. Most of the faces seemed to stare at him from a great height. He understood the reason when the mist began to clear and he saw that almost everyone was on horseback. Even before the mist cleared in earnest, he realized that most of these riders were moving smoothly through the clearing, pausing only to take their breakfast in the saddle.

"He wasn't armed when you found him?"

"No, Colonel. But this is his plug, all right. And this carbine has been fired. Look at the breech——"

It was intolerable that he could hear these crisp voices so clearly and still not pick out their owners from the mass around him. The voices seemed to hang above him like a threat, though the tone was almost natural.

"Colonel McCloud, of Sheridan's cavalry," he said.

"The same, sir. Your servant."

He saluted a phantom that came slowly into focus. A squat man in a long-skirted officer's coat, unbuttoned to show a chest hairy as a gorilla's. The whiskers above that chest all but hid a pair of bright blue eyes that regarded him with easy detachment. One gloved hand held a slab of bread dripping with bacon fat. The other balanced a mug of coffee on the saddlebow.

The colonel wolfed bread and bacon before he spoke again.

"Is that your carbine, Doctor?"

"It is not, Colonel."

"Will you give your name and regiment?"

Julian gave the information, as crisply as he could. Already he guessed that the pause had been mistaken by the Yankees for indecision. "I borrowed a cavalry horse to keep up with the attack," he added. "As you see, the animal had ideas of his own."

Colonel McCloud's gloved paw all but vanished under the open coat as he scratched his fur methodically.

"Attack isn't quite the word, Doctor. Suicide is better, I think." He spoke quietly, with no overtone of humor. "As for yourself, I gather you had ideas too, as well as your horse——"

"I'm afraid I don't follow you, sir."

"Did you fire that carbine, or didn't you?"

Julian hesitated even as he remembered that hesitation was fatal. "I fired two shots. As a signal——"

"I'm afraid that makes you our prisoner."

"But I'm a medical officer of the Confederate Army——"

"Not when you ride ahead of a cavalry charge, on a first-class jumper, with a carbine in your boot."

"I've a field unit to establish. I'll be needed——"

"Not on this field," said McCloud. "Didn't I tell you suicide was the word for it?"

Again his voice took on an added impact from its conversational calm. "The cavalry don't take prisoners often, Dr. Chisholm. You should be honored."

"I tell you I'm needed here!"

"Help him up, Ted."

"But, Colonel——"

"Help him up."

The adjutant's pistol touched Julian's back gently.

He walked to his horse without turning and mounted, ignoring the adjutant's cupped palm. A trooper fell in on either side, without waiting for orders. He found that he was moving through the clearing, one of an endless column of threes. McCloud, he noted, was already buried in the map he had spread across his saddle.

Now that it was over—now that he was definitely a prisoner of war—he felt his head clear instantly. His mind was full of unspoken arguments: he turned to shout at the Yankee colonel and reminded himself in time that prisoners who shouted abuse were only wasting their breath. Besides, the shoulder of a cook wagon had already hidden McCloud from view.

The blue cavalry was clustered here, loading saddlebags as the quartermasters struck camp. When he saw her there on the high seat of the wagon, devouring her breakfast with as much gusto as any trooper, she was already part of the picture. Accepting her as such, he knew that he was indeed a prisoner—the sort of prisoner who bore his lot in silence.

Even in that staring morning light she could have passed for a slim boy. He met her eyes as his column rode past the cook wagon —met and held them, for an intolerable moment. Then, with a great effort, he pulled himself taut in the saddle and offered her a quick, ironic salute as the column swept by. Her lips moved, and he was sure that she had spoken his name.

An order passed down the line, and the Yankee column broke into a fast canter. It was too late to look back now, even if he had dared. He would never know if Jane was laughing or crying as she watched him ride away from war.

NEW YORK

THE pack ice in the river sparkled in the sun like tortured glass; the hollow-cheeked man at the barred window looked out at it without blinking, though he shivered in the blast that swept out of the west. It was part of his routine to stand thus, for a few deep-breathing moments, each morning as he wakened. Routine, he had found long ago, made most cages bearable. He wondered how soon he would identify the steep red bluffs across the water. At this instant nothing seemed more important than knowing if they were the Hudson Palisades, if this particular pen was really on the outskirts of New York. Geography was important too, when your horizon was bounded by a narrow window. . . .

Geography, your name and regiment number, the last date you had crossed off on the dog-eared calendar pinned to the wall. Captain Surgeon Chisholm, late of the 145th Georgia Volunteers, moved slowly to inspect the number he would erase tonight. January 20, 1865. It was an incredible date, but he had no choice but to believe it was accurate.

That same calendar had followed him, no matter where they had taken him. He had started it at the pen in Kentucky, when he had realized, for the first time, that his lot would be above the average, thanks to a providence he had no wish to name. It had followed him to Pittsburgh, to the grimy train shed in Sandusky—where they had marched him across the pack ice of another winter, to a fortress home on an island. . . . Johnson's Island, Lake Erie. He had crossed off almost four hundred days in those gaunt barracks before they had brought him here.

Three prisons—but one calendar served to remind him of them

all. Three windows where a man might look out at the world. At deep bluegrass shining with dew; at a Yankee lake, endless as the sea; at this ice-choked river with its escarpments and forlorn winter trees. How many mornings would he stand here and watch the weather change?

Only last night he and Devers had arrived with the provost guard; the warden had assigned them to this cell without comment, and they were too wise in the ways of prison commanders to volunteer a question. Julian stared on at the river, marking the way the land pitched steeply to meet the water, the rime of hoarfrost that still lingered on the brown winter grass, the antics of a group of small boys playing a mysterious game of their own among the ice cakes inshore. Finally he turned back to the wooden bunks, saw that Devers still slept, and went to the blackened fireplace to prod the embers.

There was enough wood in the scuttle for the day. That meant he must dip into his slender funds to buy more, if they stayed beyond tomorrow. He had nursed the last coal on Johnson's Island, fanning the dying warmth with sheets of newspapers smuggled in—for a consideration—by the guards. The Sandusky paper, he recalled, had been too dull for the price. Once there had been an old *Herald* from New York, its headlines still trumpeting the news of the Wilderness campaign, the even more heartbreaking news that Sherman was deep in Georgia now, with Atlanta in his pocket. . . . Even then he had stared dull-eyed at the tidings. After all, such things were part of the world outside, and he had tried hard to forget that world for a long time now.

Louis Rothschild had spoiled his record more than once, and he had an uneasy feeling that Louis was about to enter his orbit again. But he could hold such feelings at arm's length while he knelt beside the grate and built as opulent a fire as he dared.

Devers was yawning in his bunk when he turned for another log. His cell mate had once been a roly-poly Kentucky grain merchant who had gone with the South in the first secession, as a captain of artillery. He had ridden out the war with most of his good humor intact, until his capture at Lookout Mountain. Even now, though his clothes hung on him in folds, he gave a definite sense of vitality. Devers, in short, was a cell mate in a thousand.

"Ridden to the hunt yet, Chisholm?"

"Thanks for reminding me."

"We'd better get going. Heat sets the little devils to moving, you know."

The fire was going merrily now, lending a spurious gaiety to the drab room. Devers seated himself cross-legged before it: when he had shucked his shirt, he could have passed for a scrawny buddha in the dance of the firelight. Julian had already paralleled his move. The heat from the flames warmed their naked bodies—and raised highlights in the grooves between their ribs, where their bones stuck out like ridged washboards.

Devers scratched industriously as he held his shirt out to the warmth. "My old woman can take in washing if I'm exchanged," he remarked. "Even if there's no metal handy, my ribs will do for a while." His fingers suddenly pounced down on the seam of his shirt, and he held a tiny wriggling object to the flame. "Pretty active, aren't they—considering it's winter?"

Julian, too, speared a louse—and for a few moments they worked in industrious silence at the morning's first chore. Though they had occupied officers' quarters almost from the start, they had learned long ago that this was the only way to keep down the population that infested their clothing. No other method was possible, when there were no facilities for bathing, much less for washing their faded uniforms.

"Did I ever tell you about that hot spring on my farm at home?" asked Devers.

"Frequently," smiled Julian.

Sometimes he thought that he knew Lafayette Devers better than he knew himself. Prison routine, he reflected, is a sovereign spur to autobiography. Yet he had talked little about himself. Of late he had even ceased to wonder about his future. Perhaps he had burned out the capacity to wonder long ago; perhaps he had lost it forever when he faced a girl on a wagon seat under an arch of Georgia pines and asked himself why she had let him go when she could have saved him with a word. . . .

Devers pursued a particularly agile invader up a seam and brought him to book inside the sleeve. "First thing I'll do when I get home is jump in that spring—clothes and all. I'll cook these damn graybacks yet."

"And yourself?"

"I'll take my chance on parboiling, just to get warm again. Tell me, Chisholm, how does it feel to be clean?"

"To be honest, I've almost forgotten."

"Don't pretend you weren't deloused the last time you gave your parole. A good doctor like you wouldn't operate unless he was scrubbed and curried——"

Julian let him go on in tranquil silence. He could hardly blame the Kentuckian for wondering about his last strange absence from Johnson's Island. Yet how could he tell Devers that Dr. Louis Rothschild was waiting for him at the boat landing in Sandusky, with a clean uniform and a provost guard? That Louis had taken him South, on a special train, to help save the life of a general now industriously helping Sherman to carve out the heart of Georgia?

It had seemed only natural, then, to go with Louis. To save that corps commander's life, with no more hesitation than he had showed at the crater's lip in Vicksburg. He could never ask Devers to accept that explanation at its face value.

"Twice at Lake Erie," said Devers. "And once at that log stockade in Kentucky. Tell me this much, Doc: did you do their work for free, or did they feed you in the bargain?"

Julian felt his mouth water at the question, even before he forced down the image of the steak Louis had carved for him in that hotel parlor in Pittsburgh. The heart-warming eggnog they had shared the next morning, while he waited for his train. The rich meat pie he had devoured, with all the finesse of a wolf, in the cattle car that took him back to Sandusky. . . . Louis had insisted that these were not bribes. Rather, the food was a tangible reminder of a world he had refused to enter. A world he could still have, merely by pounding on this cell door and asking for an audience with the warden.

"Ask me why I'm here," said Devers. "I'll tell you—even if you *don't* ask. My exchange papers are in old sideburns' office now: I can see 'em as plain as though I'm going through his desk. Kentucky's still neutral: why shouldn't I mortgage some poor Yank from slow death—and then go home again? Better men than I have made a separate peace."

Julian grinned wanly. I, too, could make a separate peace, he thought: I could give my parole and take off this uniform forever. Aloud he said only, "It can't last much longer. I suppose we can sit it out right here, if need be."

"We can, and probably will," said Devers. "You won't, though, on second thought. Not if that Yankee doctor friend of yours is waiting in the warden's office."

So Devers had heard of Louis Rothschild, after all. Prisoners could have few secrets from one another, it seemed. Julian grinned in earnest. "Don't tell me you're clairvoyant?"

"Even money says we weren't transferred here for fun. I'll make a separate bet you're out ahead of me——"

They both fell silent as the footsteps sounded in the dank stone corridor outside their door. Despite himself, Julian felt a faint prickling along his scalp as the key grated in the lock and he saw that the warden himself was standing behind the guard.

"If you'll come with me, Dr. Chisholm——"

"Clairvoyant's the word," said Devers. "Whatever it means, I'm it. Don't tell me if my transfer papers have come through, Colonel —I enjoy the suspense."

The warden ignored the interruption: Julian gathered he was inured to most brands of rebel humor. "You've a visitor, Dr. Chisholm."

"Dr. Rothschild?"

"Who else would it be?" said Devers.

His laughter followed them down the hall. The sort of laughter that would never lose its bounce, no matter how stout the walls that muted it.

ii

"A year is a long time for any man to sulk," said Louis Rothschild.

"Be exact, Louis. It's a year and four months."

"Your world has fallen apart in the meantime. The war is over— Davis and his cabinet just won't admit it."

"The war won't end until Richmond falls," said Julian. "In the meantime my wife is risking her life daily, somewhere in that area."

He silenced Louis's protest with a soothing palm. "You needn't deny it, either. My guess is she's still helping to run escaped Yankees. From Libby Prison to City Point. Another guess tells me that I could find her, without too much trouble, if I were exchanged. Which is precisely why you, my best friend, continue to stand in the way of that exchange. . . . Or have we said all this before?"

He settled in his corner of the railway coach, enjoying Louis's frown. His body still tingled from the scalding bath his friend had offered him at the hotel outside the prison gate; he let his fingers caress the smooth curve of his jaw, to enjoy once again its close-shaven perfection. The sausage and flapjacks Louis had provided just before their journey were no less grateful beneath his brand-new uniform coat. He let his head rest on the red plush seat and closed his eyes on the memory of three cups of actual coffee, saturated in sugar and no less actual cream. At this moment Louis could have passed for Aladdin's djinn with only a little retouching. It was one miracle that did not stale with repetition.

"Where do you get these new uniforms, Louis? Or is that an indiscreet question? I suppose they're tailored especially for Federal spies."

The Viennese smoothed the blue sleeves of his own army greatcoat and ignored the question. "Aren't you even going to ask where you're being taken?"

"I know it's a hard job. Your jobs always are. I'm grateful for the chance to keep my hand in. Beyond that, my curiosity isn't too keen. Besides, I'm a prisoner on a temporary pass. Prisoners learn to keep their mouths shut."

"Won't you even look out the window—and ask where you are?"

"I've found the world looks much the same when a man's behind glass."

But even as he spoke Julian let his eyes stray to the sooty pane. The railroad still paralleled the river and those strange, gaunt bluffs on its western bank. On both sides of the track rolling, stone-fenced farmlands swept away to the low hills that shut in the horizon. There were square stone houses and fat red barns: the whole landscape had the tailored look of age, an unmistakable overtone of plenty. Despite their blanket of snow, he guessed that those fields would be rich and dark with spring. . . . The Yankees kept good farms: he could not doubt that they loved their neat, well-ordered acres. But he had not lied to Louis: most of their land looked oddly alike from train windows.

He leaned back and stared at the railway coach itself. Here the pattern repeated itself, without variation: the sleepy profiles of the two provost guards who watched him from a reversed seat at the end of the car; the stares of the other passengers, beginning to abate a trifle now that they had adjusted to the spectacle of a

Union and a Rebel officer seated side by side and conversing amiably. . . . The engine hooted ahead, and he turned again to the window as the tracks curved to show a vast, shining reach of river to the south, endless as a polar sea in that clear winter light.

Louis said, "We'll be in New York City in another hour. I can tell you that much, without breaking my oath." He offered Julian his sad, twisted smile. "Doesn't the prospect excite you?"

"Why do I operate this time?"

"At the moment other things are more important than the identity of your patient."

"For example?"

"You, for example," said Louis patiently. "Have you changed your mind about my—my offer of freedom?"

"Don't you know better than to ask? What's our case?"

"It's diagnosed as typhlitis. If you agree, I want you to go in for a prognosis."

"Give me the details."

"They'll keep until you're at the bedside. I was only called in yesterday, so I'm going warily."

"Then you were unwise to come for me, Louis. I might be in the mood to gamble."

Louis Rothschild favored Julian with a long, slow stare. The wisdom of centuries was in that glance—and the patience of a people who have found their strength on stony paths. . . . It's odd that he doesn't understand me better, thought Julian.

"In my opinion," said Louis at last, "and it's an opinion with authority behind it, you are the finest surgeon I have ever known."

"Thank you for the accolade. I'll try to be worthy this afternoon."

"In the past sixteen months you've performed just three major operations. How do you keep your hands from going mad?"

"By crocheting, for one thing."

"Crocheting?"

"It keeps the finger muscles limber. I'll grant you it isn't a manly occupation; somehow my cell mates never teased me. They realized I had no better choice."

"You have the escape I offered you from the start."

"I said no *other* choice, Louis."

The Viennese sighed. "When you were captured you were accused of using a cavalry carbine in action. That made you liable to imprisonment: you could be released only on parole, or in exchange. I gave you the first chance in Kentucky, the moment I heard you'd been taken."

"We've been over this too, I believe."

"It's well worth repeating, now we're rolling into New York. If you'll surrender that gray tunic, I could turn over my practice to you tomorrow. Or, if you prefer, you could go to one of our army hospitals as a contract surgeon. Make your own reputation for peacetime——"

"I'm still a Confederate officer, and I'm still hoping for active duty. *I* said that before, too. Long ago, on Southern soil. To be exact, in a house in Georgia, where you were a fugitive from Andersonville prison."

Louis smiled, unruffled. "I bow my head, Julian. And I continue to hope that you've changed your mind."

"You were rejoining your own army then. I made no effort to stop you. Why can't you return the compliment?"

"I'm an army surgeon at the moment, with a roving commission," said the Viennese. "I've nothing to do with exchanges."

"You could put in a word at the War Department. The next time you're in Washington——"

"I'm afraid your wife ranks me there, Julian."

"Even Jane can't keep me safe in a pen forever."

"Do you blame her too much for trying?"

Julian subsided gloomily. "She thinks I'd go on making trouble for her if I returned to the South. I understand that perfectly."

"Perhaps she's right."

"We made a bargain at High Cedars. We said good-by until the war's end. That morning at the Chattahoochee she could have saved me with a word. She let them take me instead. So all bargains are canceled." Julian had spoken in short, hard breaths: his voice steadied on the next words. "Of course I'll hunt her down now, the moment I have the chance. You're wise to keep me in my pen—both of you."

"Suppose you could get back, Julian. Suppose you found her. What could you do?"

"I wouldn't know. But I won't begin to live again until I can do just that."

He turned back to the window and the panorama of the river. The sky ahead was sooty now: a dozen barges moved slowly down a channel in midstream, crushing the ice with their ungainly bows. Already he could feel the presence of the metropolis beyond, though the fields were still wide open under the pale winter sky. And he felt again the indifference of this harsh and purposeful land. War and its threat had never existed here: New York would continue to grind out its own prosperity as though the South had never been.

He said only, "When do I go back?"

Louis struck the seat ahead with one fist, so hard that a cloud of dust set them both to coughing. "I've tried my best to make things easy for you. Of course, if you will refuse special quarters—and distribute the food I send in——"

"In my place, you'd do the same."

The Viennese shrugged. "At least I've spared you the worst of prison life. Conditions at Johnson's Island were reasonably good. Suppose I'd let them send you to Elmira? The death rate there is one to four."

"It was worse at Andersonville, but you came out alive."

It was Louis's turn to stare out the window. "We've hurt each other a long time, Julian. Yet we're still friends. I look forward to the day when that friendship will be complete again."

"You still insist the war will end this year?"

"By June, at the latest."

"I said that a year ago. It seemed I underestimated my countrymen."

"*I'm* your countryman now, Julian. So is everyone in this train. The War Between the States will be worth while if it teaches us that."

"Jeff Davis thinks differently," said Julian. "I still wear his uniform."

"So we're back where we started."

"Back to the operation I've left prison to perform for you. Isn't it time we discussed it?"

"High time," said Louis. "I'll begin by naming your patient. An old friend of yours called Whit Cameron."

He watched Julian for a moment of silence, as though he were enjoying the other's stare. "As you know, Mr. Cameron does considerable business on both sides of the line. He was stricken three days ago in New York. While he was the house guest of another old friend—Mrs. Victor Sprague."

Whit Cameron. Whit, prostrated by typhlitis in the home of Lucy Sprague. He tried to bring that astounding picture into focus and failed completely. Time, he found, had faded the memory of Lucy until she was less than a ghost. He brought her back with an effort. A mocking shadow in his father's garden. A fire in his veins as she gave him back his kisses in the sanctuary of the summerhouse. A naked pagan on the stair in Nassau. . . . Another man had held that phantom in his arms; another heart than his had ached to possess her. Today he could face the prospect of meeting her without a tremor.

"Mr. Cameron asked for you from the first moment," said Louis. "Fortunately I was in New York at the time. It was easy to arrange."

"Since when is a Confederate prisoner of war permitted to operate on a civilian?"

Louis waved the question aside. "Mrs. Sprague handled that detail, not I. Have you forgotten her completely?"

"I'd heard she was a rich woman, and getting richer."

"Since her husband's death she's made a third fortune in government contracts. Sprague himself couldn't have managed his mills more intelligently."

"I can believe that too."

"Unlike most contractors in this money-mad war, she gives honest weight. The government needs her now, as much as she needs the government. I won't say she has cabinet rank, but she can gratify her wishes almost as quickly. Or a guest's wish, when he falls sick in her home."

Julian came back to his profession, a trifle guiltily. "Who's with him now?"

"Noah, of course. We can operate at once, if you feel an operation is indicated." Louis just escaped smiling. "Mr. Cameron was demanding it when I left. Mr. Cameron is a very sick man, but it hasn't dampened his spirits. He insists you performed a similar operation in Nassau. Demands that he serve as a guinea pig to prove your theory——"

Julian felt a memory stir—a picture far more vivid than these forced images of Lucy. Nassau again. The morgue at Steed's pesthouse on Windward Point. His post-mortem on a cadaver, and the ruptured caecum his knife had explored so eagerly. . . . Again he came back to what Louis Rothschild was saying.

"Whit's memory is a bit at fault. I did a post-mortem in Nassau, just after the patient died——"

"Of typhlitis?"

"That was the diagnosis."

"Mr. Cameron's case is also typical." Louis's tone was clipped and precise now. "Regional pains, for the past week. Generalized, all over the abdomen. Localized now, in the right side."

"Does there seem to be general peritonitis?"

"Tenderness, yes; but I don't think that inflammation is general. There was no rigidity, except over the right side."

Julian stiffened in his seat. Whit's memory of that Nassau post-mortem was accurate, after all.

"Was there any vomiting?"

"Periodically, yes. At two-hour intervals when I left this morning."

"Would you say it was caused by a tumor around the caecum?"

Louis Rothschild's eyes widened. "I would indeed. How did you guess?"

"Would you say it centered in the region of the appendix vermiformis?"

"Precisely. It's my feeling—and I'll admit it is no more—that a localized abscess is blocking the digestive tract at that point."

"An abscess caused by inflammation of the appendix," said Julian. Despite himself, he had let his voice rise in his excitement. "Removal of that vestigial organ might remove the cause—and save a life."

To save a life. That had been his dedication once: it was good to take it up again. Especially now, when it was Whit Cameron's life that hung in the balance. Whit, he reflected, had not been born to die in bed. It was odd that he should be the bridge that led him back to Lucy. It was only natural that Whit should insist on betting his skill against the unknown malady that had struck him down.

"We'll go in on a gamble," he said. "Since our patient's a gambler, that's only proper."

"Suppose you can't reach the organ?"

"The procedure will be the same. In any case, our only hope is to open the abscess and drain. If it's localized, he'll still have a chance."

"An outside one," said Louis.

"An outside chance was always Whit's specialty. By the way, will Lucy be present when we arrive?"

"Mrs. Sprague was called to Pittsburgh. She'll be with us tomorrow."

"Are you positive she's just below cabinet rank, when it comes to wirepulling in Washington?"

Louis glanced at Julian narrowly. "What are you implying?"

"Nothing, so far. I'm just wondering if I dare ask a fee for this job."

"You may indeed," said Louis, smiling. "And you probably will."

"Be frank. Would *you* have called me in on this operation if Lucy hadn't insisted?"

"Certainly not. I know what your reward will be."

You don't know everything, thought Julian. You can hardly suspect what Lucy meant to me once. Perhaps she'll balk when I tell her why I must be exchanged. On the other hand, it may not be necessary to go into details. . . . A woman who can give those kind of orders in Washington will hardly question a Confederate officer's desire to rejoin his regiment.

"Why didn't you tell me all this sooner?"

Louis's sad smile broadened into the travesty of a grin. "I still had hopes, Julian. I still prayed you'd stay North, where you belong. I'm sure your wife is breathing the same prayer, wherever she is today."

"My wife knows where I belong—and so do you."

"We'll argue the point no more. You're practically in Richmond now."

Richmond. The word had been his talisman for more months than he cared to remember. Richmond . . . that grave queen of the South, that slightly bogus Rome, triumphant even now on her seven hills. The core of the dying Confederacy, the symbol of all lost causes, it was still his destination, and his hope. If Jane lived, he knew he would find her there. If he could face her one more time, he could ask the question on which his life depended. He had no words for that question now, but he knew it would take instant shape at their meeting.

Whit Cameron, with a daring that was quite in character, had placed his life in Julian Chisholm's hands. Julian Chisholm, staring one more time at the sooty Yankee landscape flashing past the train window knew that he would take the same risk with Lucy

Sprague. Lucy could put exchange papers in his hands tomorrow, if she chose. He would play his cards adroitly, making that choice inevitable.

"You have your wish," said Louis Rothschild. "Why don't you look happier?"

"Happiness takes practice," said Julian. "So, for that matter, does wirepulling. Besides, we've Whit to think of first."

But he could not quite conceal the strange new hope in his eyes, as he began to plan the operation with Louis, or quite ignore the all-too-familiar hammering of his heart.

iii

Outside the gaunt, sprawling terminal by the Hudson, they took the salutes of the provost guards before they stepped into the waiting carriage. The wind from the river was laced with snow; there was snow on the horses' manes, on the shoulders of the driver, on the humpbacked roofs of the slums beyond. New York, reflected Julian, offered a poor introduction to the visitor. He felt his flesh shrink as their carriage turned east on Thirtieth Street and jockeyed for place in the sullen stream of traffic; the mad blend of misery and soulless bustle had already dealt his prison-dulled nerves a savage blow.

"Is it always this dirty?"

"Not always," said Louis. "Sometimes it's dirtier. And angrier. The draft riots have still left scars." He pointed down a reeking alley that seemed to exude an almost visible miasma, despite the sketchy white mantle of snow. "A murder a day is commonplace in this corner of Hell's Kitchen: I've patched more than one broken head in that block of tenements. . . . Pull down the window, Julian: I often wonder if patching is worth while. The only remedy would be to burn down these rat warrens and start over."

"Wouldn't the city fathers object?"

"They would indeed," said Louis grimly. "Someone has said there are seven miles of tenements in Manhattan alone. All of them crowded to bursting—and all of them profitable. Perhaps it's as well you're a Southerner. This is one problem you won't be facing for a while."

The Viennese surgeon fell silent on that and stared down gloomily at the gloved hands crossed on one knee. Julian burrowed deeper in his own greatcoat and tried not to shiver as the raw west wind clawed at the carriage windows. For a time he turned his eyes from the street; then, as the carriage ground to a stop at a crossing, he glanced up irritably at the delay.

An infantry regiment was just pouring out of an armory dead ahead; from where Julian sat, the high slate-gray walls seemed to dwarf the double lines of blue, making the soldiers look more like strutting dolls than men, making their march into the snowy street more ludicrous than heroic. It was only when the column broke into route step and swung west at a kind of shambling trot that Julian noticed the faces of the men. At first he thought they were dark with cold; then he saw that these were Negro troops. They were marching to war with the same stolid calm that had marked the faces of his father's field hands when they streamed from cabins to cotton rows.

"Freedmen," said Louis. "Some even say they'll be citizens tomorrow. Don't look so startled, Julian; your Mr. Davis will be doing the same before you can offer him your services again." He came out of a brown study of his own and laughed shortly. "The world moves in spite of us, my friend."

"I wonder if it really does."

"So do I, sometimes. There is no doubt that great changes are in the wind—but they are coming too fast for me. Slow change is the only real cure for our ills." Louis subsided again. The carriage lurched in the piercing wind and plunged forward through a thickening curtain of snow.

"Does Lucy live far from here?"

"The Sprague mansion is on lower Fifth Avenue," said Louis with a touch of asperity. "Don't despair, Julian. You'll find it much more in harmony with—with what you expected."

"I expected nothing, really—so I'm not disappointed."

"What is your emotion, if any?"

"Strangeness. And a fear I can't quite define. This *is* part of America, after all. It's too enormous—and much too confident. A metropolis should be proud for a reason you can put in words. Your New York is just brash, Louis. Brash and cruel."

"Like youth itself."

"Will it grow up in time?"

"Again I wonder," said the Viennese.

The horses' hoofs rattled on cobbles as they took an upgrade swept clear of snow by the blast. Julian fell silent in turn, as he continued to stare out at the apparently endless rows of tight-packed buildings. Store and factory, saloon and church, cheap-jack lodginghouse and jerry-built dwellings seemed to elbow one another for room, like building blocks tossed down by a haphazard child. The carriage skirted an open square; he had a glimpse of tall church spires wreathed in snow and felt this city might hold glimpses of beauty after all. They crossed a narrow street hideous with the din of commerce, packed with cabs and drays—and he felt that New York was distressing as Bedlam and just as meaningless.

"Broadway," said Louis. "And don't tell me it's misnamed. We'll be at Mrs. Sprague's mansion in a few minutes now."

Julian felt his spirits lift when they turned into Fifth Avenue. At least he knew this street: for once the romantic picture he had formed coincided with reality. Muted by the snow, even the ugly granite monuments to wealth seemed to fit this wide esplanade: backed by slums though it was, and dingy with many narrow brownstone fronts, the avenue had a dignity that transcended its bourgeois smugness, a wide, almost classic beauty that was worthy of America's greatest city.

The Sprague mansion was part and parcel of that dignity: Victor Sprague might have been a scoundrel once, but his architect's eye had been true. When he stepped out under the heavy porte-cochere, Julian nodded his approval. It was a setting worthy of the woman who dominated the Sprague fortune today.

An English butler admitted them, with a dignity that matched the tall, oak-paneled foyer behind him.

"Your man is with the patient now, Dr. Rothschild." Pale, well-bred eyes regarded Julian without surprise. "Will this gentleman be staying here?"

"Naturally," said Louis.

"The bedroom next to Mr. Cameron's is ready now."

The major-domo spoke crisply to a footman who had appeared from nowhere, and Julian followed his portmanteau up a thick-carpeted stair. The whole house seemed to bask in a grateful heat, though he could not identify its source: he guessed that Lucy possessed a hot-air furnace, and smiled inwardly as he thought how well it fitted the magic of the moment. So, for that matter, did the deep comfort of his bedroom—a discreet, plum-colored chamber whose color scheme was echoed from the pile of the carpet to the tented silk valance of the bed. Even the towels in the white-tiled bath were a rich red-purple. . . . He stood on the threshold, staring at plumbing that seemed to belong to another world. Hot water gushed to his touch as he stripped to his shirt and began to scrub.

Louis Rothschild opened a connecting door as he was drying his hands; Julian glimpsed another wide, grave bedroom and a figure propped in pillows on a too-large bed.

"The patient's ready when you are, Doctor."

The two surgeons went into the sickroom together; Julian accepted Noah Heath's proffered hand, his smile of welcome.

"It's good that you could come, Dr. Chisholm. If you wish, we can operate at once. I've set up a table in Mrs. Sprague's morning room; the light is perfect there." Heath shook his head as Julian glanced toward the figure in the four-poster. "We can talk freely: he went into delirium some time ago. I administered morphia."

Julian mounted the dais of the bed and looked down at Whit. In his fine linen nightshirt, the gambler seemed to have settled into a deep, and entirely natural, slumber. Only the high flush on his cheekbones and his restless breathing betrayed him.

"Fever one hundred and three degrees," said the Negro doctor. "Pulse one hundred and ten. Vomiting at steady one-hour intervals. As you see, Dr. Rothschild, the picture's unchanged."

Julian folded back the sheet. "What's your opinion?"

"Obstruction of the colonic track seems unmistakable. I feel strongly that only an operation will clear up the picture."

Percussing lightly over the abdominal area, Julian had already nodded his agreement. The muscles under his fingers, distended by pressure within, had all the resilience of a drumhead. The mass in the right side was clearly outlined: he felt Whit stir and moan in his stupor as he defined the obstruction with his fingers.

"Does it seem larger to you, Louis?"

"Definitely."

It could be a tumor, or an abscess. In either case, surgery was clearly indicated. If suppuration had occurred in the peritoneum, nothing short of an open drain would save Whit's life. If a tumor was really choking the alimentary process, the tumor might still be excised.

He had watched Semmelweis perform such operations in Vienna, watched him close the incision immediately, with no aftermaths. The conservative surgeon might still shy away from the abdomen; that same die-hard would certainly insist on drainage, even if he dared an incision. Outlining his field one more time, Julian made up his mind.

"I feel we should go in at once. Will you have him moved?"

He felt Louis's eyes, and sensed their approval, even before Heath could summon the butler. Despite the gravity of his decision, he could hardly help smiling as he watched four stalwart footmen converge on the bed and lift Whit in the cradle of their arms. It was a moment that went with the magnificence of their surroundings, the luxurious breath of heat that mocked the snowstorm outside. The hall carpet soothed his feet as he followed the group into the morning room. Whit, he thought, would have enjoyed it all enormously.

Heath was just closing the portieres against the hiss of the storm. Julian saw at a glance that the equipment he had assembled was as complete as any hospital could offer. The four hooded gas lamps above the operating table, singing at full pressure, bathed the surface below them in a clear, if garish, light. Louis Rothschild peeled off his blue uniform coat and stepped up to check the instruments.

"Noah will give the anesthetic," he said. "You couldn't ask for better. I'll assist, if that's agreeable."

It's more than agreeable, Julian offered with a wordless smile. If the operation he was about to perform should move into territory uncharted by the scalpel, he knew that the team behind him was perfect. For a second he hesitated on the far side of the table, watching the long, dark fingers of the Negro doctor slit the cork of an ether bottle. Strange how he had felt his own hands tighten once when those dark hands had been offered to him in friendship. He was glad that he could accept their help so naturally today.

"Shall we begin, gentlemen? Time is of the essence, if an abscess is forming."

Noah Heath stuffed cloth into a paper cone and began to pour from the bottle; the room filled instantly with the strange, acrid-sweet reek of ether. The four footmen, who had lingered in the doorway in openmouthed curiosity, fled as fast as eight sturdy Irish legs would carry them; the butler, after a correct bow to each of the two surgeons, backed out as hastily as dignity would permit.

The two surgeons exchanged smiles that expanded to outright grins as Louis uncovered the operative area. The skin of Whit's midriff was profusely tattooed—a sea grotto in which a voluptuous mermaid reclined in dalliance with Davy Jones himself. The two figures quivered ecstatically as the gambler's breathing steadied under the anesthetic. . . . At the curve of the pelvic bones the artist had made what was evidently a recent addition: Union and Confederate battle flags, flaring defiance at one another across the small valley of the navel. The Stars and Bars, Julian noted, streamed across the right rectus area; the knife in his hand, outlining the planned incision, divided the flag of the rebellion in neat halves.

"Perhaps it's an omen," said Louis as he picked up a compress and stood ready to sponge the blood away.

The scalpel moved as he spoke, making a clean cut across the abdomen, well to the side and diagonally downward. The trouble it sought to uncover was localized about the caecum: Julian could be sure of that much before his first stroke. Watching Louis compress the capillary bleeding, pausing to ligate two larger veins, he moved on to the aponeurosis, the glistening white sheath that covered the muscles of the abdominal wall. The knife slit this membrane, down the entire length of the incision, and Louis grasped the edges and separated them. Below, the rich red substances of the muscles themselves bulged into the wound. The force of the swelling was already apparent here—a tension that stemmed from the disorder he would uncover in a few moments.

The steel bit through muscle tissue; there was brisk bleeding now, which was again controlled by ligatures. When the last knot was secure, Louis placed the retractor blades in the incision and widened the operative field with steady pressure. The peritoneum —that thin, fragile layer that enclosed the abdominal cavity itself —shone in the depths of the wound. Julian let out a sigh of relief when the gas jets above him picked out those highlights. General peritonitis might still lurk beneath that tensile membrane; there might be a localized abscess where it would impede his progress most. From this angle there was no evidence of infection beneath: only the tensile strength of an incipient inflammation that had stretched the peritoneum to the bursting point.

"Whatever it is, it's local."

He kept his voice steady with an effort as he eased the scalpel into the wound and nicked the membrane. He heard Louis suck in his breath and felt his heart jump a beat as the dark red coil of the small intestine appeared just under the knife. But there was no rush of fluid to indicate an abscess, no telltale reek of death in the making. True, the intestinal wall was taut with the aftermath of interrupted digestion, but there was no evidence of perforation here. The trouble—and he dared to hope that his guess was accurate—was still near at hand, even though he had not yet reached it.

Letting his fingers think for him, he found that part of his brain was reviewing his anatomy. Obviously this area was a blind jungle for the surgeon; one false stroke of the knife could bring disaster. The blood vessels that served the leg, he recalled, were a safe distance away. Directly under his hand he could feel the great, blind-alley pouch of the large intestine, the caecum. Surely the inflammation centered here: he had gambled on the hope that its focus was the appendix vermiformis. True to its name, that dependent organ might be as difficult to pin down as an angleworm in seaweed. Yet each exploration of his fingers convinced him that the infection—if it had reached that stage—was localized around the tip of the caecum. Until he could be sure of that much, he could not chance a possible hemorrhage that would flood the cavity in a blind dissection.

And yet how could any fingers, however trained, recognize the shape of an inflamed organ that the eyes themselves had had no chance to study properly? In that Nassau autopsy the appendix had been ruptured almost beyond recognition. At the dissection table in Vienna he had sectioned dozens of this organ, in a healthy state—there, again, experience could hardly serve as a guide. On the other hand, he could not continue this fumble indefinitely: Whit Cameron was a hard man, but Whit's alimentary tract was only mortal.

His fingers paused and went back, to mark a change in the texture of the wall he was exploring. This was no mere intestinal loop, though it compared in size with the tissue above and below it. He traced the dimensions carefully, letting his fingers move back for a second check. No doubt about it, this was an extension of the caecum, not a continuation—an unwieldy, sausagelike extension that was a good six inches in length and all but adhered to the intestinal wall about which it had twisted like a fat, choking root.

Gently yet firmly, moving with the utmost care, he began to break up the adhesion, starting at the distended tip of this new discovery and working slowly down to its even more swollen base. Then, one by one, he separated the loops from the barrel of the intestine they had all but closed in their embrace. Across the table he heard Louis gasp as the released organ popped into the operative field at last. From this angle it looked more like a sausage than ever: a bloated, badly stuffed sausage, its skin iridescent with the decay that throbbed beneath it like an all but visible pulse.

"The appendix vermiformis," he said quietly. "Swollen to the point of incipient rupture. It seems we were wise to go in immediately, gentlemen."

The silence in the room was absolute, broken only by the rasp of Whit's steady breathing as Noah continued the ether. Louis's hands were just as steady as they spread the retractor to its fullest width. The operative field was a small, compact square now—thanks to the persuasion of those flat steel blades. The Viennese spoke hoarsely as Julian took up a fresh scalpel and bent once again to his work.

"So it was the appendix, after all."

"There's no doubt of it now."

"You're the first surgeon to remove that organ as a cure for typhlitis. You're making medical history."

"I haven't removed it yet."

Julian selected a strong ligature from the table with his free hand as the steel blade outlined the fanlike mesentery attaching the appendix to the wall of the caecum. He had dissected out this organ in more than one cadaver; the present structure, like the appendix itself, was so inflamed that he could recognize it only by its relative position. A false move could ruin their chances, even now: the mesentery was channeled with blood vessels that would hemorrhage instantly if the ligature was incorrectly placed. Once again he must move by instinct: he had never seen this operation, never even heard of a surgeon daring enough to attempt an appendectomy.

"Appendectomy. Is that the word for it, Louis?"

"It's your idea," said the Viennese. "You've the right to name it." "We must ligate the mesentery, then cut away. It should be feasible, if we can control the bleeders."

A slender forceps, administered cautiously, separated the inflamed fan of the mesentery in gentle installments. Now he could outline the wall of the caecum distinctly, see where it became one with the appendage he had delivered with such care. The ligature snaked in smoothly, and out again; he drew the ends taut and said a short prayer before he completed the knot, snug against the intestinal wall. As he had expected, the horsehair thread cut through the inflamed tissue in several spots—but his luck held. The blood vessels beneath it were tough-fibered, after all: though the tissue throbbed under the knot, the knot held firm, with no hint of hemorrhage. He set a second knot, and a third. The scalpel followed swiftly, cutting close to the appendix itself, freeing it completely from the mesentery which conveyed its blood supply.

Again Louis Rothschild let out his breath in a sigh of pure relief. "Now for your appendectomy—is that what we're calling it?"

"With your permission."

He tested the next ligature with the greatest care. This was the climax of the operation: pioneering though he was, he could sense that fact instantly. The horsehair sang like a taut fiddlestring between his fingers; he looped it about the appendix, easing it along the bloated surface until it encircled the organ at its very base. Automatically, his fingers tested the broad, pouchlike surface of the caecum itself. Quite as he had expected, there was hardly a trace of inflammation here: the entire disorder had been limited to the appendix itself.

He forced his fingers to be fluent and unhurried as they arranged the horsehair knot and tightened it. It cut through tissue, all but losing itself in the distended mass, but it held firm. He placed his supplementary knots at the same careful tempo, then took up a clean scalpel from the instrument table. One swift stroke, and the operation was over. The clean bite of steel was pure as poetry—anticlimactic, too, as the distended six-inch curve of sausage came away in his hand.

He laid it on the instrument table and stared at it curiously, knowing that the other two doctors had bent forward as well. Then he tossed it into the waiting basin, bisecting it in mid-air, and smiling, despite himself, as the whole green-skinned thing burst in that release of pressure, inundating the basin with a flood of bright yellow pus.

"How's the time, Dr. Heath?"

"Operating time, thirty-two minutes," said the Negro in a shaking voice. "Pulse still one hundred ten, respiration steady."

"Next time we'll move faster," said Julian. "It helps to know where things are—and why."

They came back to their job in unison, still working as a team—a team that did not forget to be methodical despite the note of triumph that hung over the table. Louis Rothschild's voice was almost normal as he eased the pressure on the retractors.

"Any sutures?"

Julian nodded. "We can close now."

"So we can." Louis stared down into the wound as though he could not quite believe his eyes. "The focus of infection is gone. You've left only clean tissue."

Both doctors watched in a kind of fascinated silence while Julian threaded his suture needle. Semmelweis had closed more than one abdominal incision with the same operative picture behind him. Julian himself had assisted at one such operation in Budapest, when the great Hungarian surgeon had excised a tumor as big as a man's two fists—and closed the wound within an hour. Here, as Louis said, the seat of Whit's infection was swimming in the basin on a side table; nothing but scalded steel had touched the amputation point. It was unnecessary to leave the incision open; barring an accident, Whit Cameron's recovery seemed assured.

"You may discontinue the anesthetic, Dr. Heath."

He worked swiftly after Louis had whisked away the retractor blades: this was routine, and a joy. But he permitted himself to smile only when he had stepped back from the table at last. The red line of the incision was neatly joined by purse-string stitches that would have put most housewives to shame. Again he noticed how neatly the scalpel had divided the Confederate flag that still fluttered feebly in the area between hipbone and umbilicus. In another month a white streak of scar tissue would split that flag in half, absorbing one blood-red bar. . . . He met Noah Heath's eyes across the table and saw that the Negro doctor was smiling too.

"You saved his life, Dr. Chisholm. But you ruined his tattooing."

Julian walked to the window in an effort to hide his elation. The snow was still thick as flying swansdown above Fifth Avenue; the few pedestrians he could make out seemed bent double by the blast. He had a sudden urge to feel that wild wind on his face, to match his mood against the driving storm.

"Suppose I went for a walk, Louis? Would the heavens fall?"

"Not if you come back promptly." Louis Rothschild, working busily with Heath, seemed to understand Julian's urge instantly. "You're under my jurisdiction now."

"It's only that I want to breathe." The verb was inadequate, yet he felt that it summed up his desire.

"My greatcoat's in the hall," said Louis quietly. "It will be simpler if you wear it. New York is shockproof, but it might startle people to see a Confederate officer strolling alone in a snowstorm."

In the hall, soothed by the empty silence, Julian cracked his heels just once, in a solemn buck and wing. Then, grinning sheepishly at his own exuberance, he went down the stair on tiptoe. Louis's blue overcoat hung in a cloakroom just off the foyer: he found that it concealed his uniform perfectly.

The English major-domo loomed beside the entrance door as he emerged, muted as ever, his composure unshaken by the spectacle of a rebel officer in a Yankee greatcoat.

"You're leaving, sir?"

"Only for a short walk."

The Englishman glanced at the snow-blurred afternoon with perfect composure. "I trust you'll return for dinner, sir. Mrs. Sprague will be expecting you."

"I thought Mrs. Sprague was in Pittsburgh."

"She's returning early. I just had a telegram. Are you sure I can't call a cab?"

"Thank you, no," murmured Julian. "This walk is strictly anonymous."

It's a bit foolhardy, too, he added to himself as he felt the first claw of the wind. Yet he leaned against the snowy blast gladly for the first block, letting it whirl the last of his staleness away. It was good to be free again—to remind himself that he had only to lift a finger to make that freedom actual.

Perhaps he had allowed his mind to leap ahead too fast, after all. Lucy might refuse point-blank to help him when she learned why he was so anxious to be exchanged. Jane—and this was even more likely—might be working far from Richmond. Jane might even be dead. . . . He had cursed that specter in more than one sleepless prison midnight: it faced him again, without pity, as he let his thoughts stream free in the icy wind.

There had been no word from her in months. He had sensed that much on the train this morning: Louis would have assured him on that score, if Louis had had recent news. Her work was no less important as the iron ring tightened about the Confederacy; he could hardly deny that it grew more desperate. Somehow he must rescue her from that senseless risk before the end. Somehow he must tell her, once and for all, that the score was evened.

"I love you, Jane. I can't let you die."

He found that he had spoken the words aloud into the teeth of the New York storm, and turned quickly, before he lost his sense of direction in the murk: too much freedom had apparently gone to his head. Now he was walking south again, with the worst of the wind behind him. Lucy's gray-brown mansion already loomed ahead: the lighted windows looked down on him with friendly eyes. He would never have guessed that a part of Lucy's world could seem friendly—even welcoming. That he would hurry toward her porte-cochere to ask a favor. The major-domo had said she would return this afternoon. He was behaving like a fool—walking in a snowstorm, when it was Lucy who held his future in her hand.

A whip cracked in the dimness; he stepped back in time to let the carriage swing into the porte-cochere ahead of him. He knew that it was hers even before he glimpsed her profile at the frost-rimed window. He could have met her face to face merely by hurrying forward to open the door ahead of her coachman. Instead he hesitated on the Fifth Avenue pavement, letting the snow build its own ambush between them.

Lucy was bundled to the eyes in a gray squirrel coat and muff as she hurried from carriage step to door; but she paused for an instant in the entrance to give an order to her coachman, and Julian saw her face clearly. *She hasn't changed*, he thought swiftly. *If her blonde beauty is intact, so is her assurance. So, for that matter, is her lure.* . . . She could not see him in the murk, and he thanked his luck for that; yet her pale siren compulsion seemed to hang in the air long after the heavy door had sighed shut behind her.

Memory rushed into that void, to beat him with its soft fury's wings. How reluctant those same memories had been only a few hours ago! Already he could feel her kisses on his lips, with all their teasing invitation. The little broken laugh she had offered him in the summerhouse before her first surrender. The proud thrust of her breasts, lifted like twin victories from the filmy trap of her gown as she took the last step forward to mold her body into his.

That whole body had been born to vibrate to the high, wild note of passion; from too-full mouth to fluent thighs, she was Lilith reincarnated. A supremely casual Lilith, who could step over the body of a dead husband and go on to other loves. Who could renew an old love now, if she chose.

His starved body trembled, and it was not from the cold; he continued to stand there, ankle-deep in snow, the fresh flakes powdering the blue of his masquerade—and that same starved body began to yearn for her. The yearning of man for woman, as uncomplex as hunger. In that flash he knew that it would be quite easy to possess her in this house whose walls defied the world with such casualness. His hunger, he added, was legitimate enough, after fourteen months in prison. If he should satisfy it tonight, would he be disloyal to Jane?

The wind stung his mind back to normal. He thrust his hands deep in the pockets of Louis Rothschild's greatcoat and marched twice around the block while he waited for his calm to return.

This, he reminded himself, was the home of Mrs. Victor Sprague, a lady whose name wrought its own magic in Washington. He would go to her presently and ask her to speed his exchange. The fact that he and Mrs. Sprague had been intimate once was beside the point; in fact, the poets insisted that a man must fall in love with a woman—and fall out again—before he could achieve the status of friendship. . . . The corollary (that he was trudging in a snowstorm now, and remembering each detail of that passion with thundering heartbeats) was only natural—and not too important, when he measured his need against his wary pride.

He turned the corner into the avenue for the second time and saw that a row of windows was glowing in the upper story of the house. Lucy, he judged, was now in her own quarters. The hall door opened under his hand without sound: he walked in without ringing. The warm air seemed faintly scented with her presence, but he dismissed that fancy as he went up the stairs to his room. Feeling its comfort close around him, he did not pause to wonder if he had traded one Yankee prison for another.

iv

Noah Heath sat at Whit's bedside with a book open on his knee; Whit himself, still under the ether, rested tranquilly with his head propped on pillows. There was no sign of Louis as Julian paused at the half-open door, and he did not disturb the tableau. There would be time enough to spell Heath at the bedside when he had made his peace with Lucy.

In his own room, he closed the connecting door softly and resumed his pacing: Lucy's thick carpet, he reflected, would do as well as the snowy pavement outside. . . . When the knock came, he was as ready as he would ever be. Holding the prepared words before him like a shield, he flung the hall door wide—and found himself staring into the impassive eyes of the major-domo.

"I thought I heard you return, sir. Mrs. Sprague sends her compliments—and hopes you're free to see her now."

"I'm at Mrs. Sprague's disposal."

He wondered just how true that statement was as he followed the butler down the upstairs hall.

"Mrs. Sprague's office is on this level, Doctor. She'll see you there." Major-domo was opening double mahogany doors with a flourish as he spoke; he stood aside, with all the punctilio of a Cerberus at the sanctum entrance, as Lucy's voice came out to meet them.

The apartments, as Julian had surmised, were in a spacious corner of the mansion's second floor. Lucy had furnished them in her own taste, from the pale paneling to the spindly rosewood desk at which she sat. The room was part study and part boudoir: one whole side was mirrored, to echo the French water colors on the other walls, the handsome buhl cabinet spilling over with potpourri, the jewel-like hearth of white marble in which a coke fire danced brightly. Above the mantel (Julian noted the detail even in the shock of that first encounter) a portrait of Victor Sprague stared down coldly at the room. Oddly enough, the immaculate, frock-coated figure seemed to belong here, to find its obbligato in the black bombazine that Lucy was wearing so regally, the well-remembered rivière of diamonds that sparkled at her breast.

Sprague, thought Julian, would have rejoiced to find his wife seated at this desk, dictating a letter to a young man in snuff-brown tweeds, who was evidently a private secretary. A letter addressed on equals terms to a Mr. Vanderbilt, dealing with the sale of railroad holdings west of Chicago. Sprague, who had always been the first to applaud true ruthlessness, would have admitted that his empire had found a worthy successor after all. . . .

Lucy's voice continued in an even, confident monotone. She did not look up at once from the closely printed brochure in her hand. It was only when she raised her head that Julian noticed she was wearing horn-rimmed spectacles. The glasses were the crowning touch in a picture that should have been bizarre—and wasn't. Lucy Sprague had been born to hold power in her two hands, to reap the harvest as she saw fit. It seemed only natural that she should be talking back to a Vanderbilt—and moving at ease through freight-rate statistics.

"Come in please, Julian. This is my last letter."

The mouse in tweeds closed his notebook as she spoke and bowed out like a well-bred shadow. Major-domo had already crossed the room, to bring a decanter and glasses to the desk. Julian found that he could enter almost as easily, to bow over Lucy's hand.

"It's been a long time, Mrs. Sprague."

"Too long, my dear," said Lucy, not quite so casually, and with a twinkle he remembered too well. "Will you join me in a brandy—as a concession to the weather?"

"With pleasure, Lucy," he said, taking her tone, to a point. Talking against the butler's presence, he could pause to wonder what was coming next as he accepted a thin-stemmed glass.

"To your victory over death, Dr. Chisholm."

"And yours over Vanderbilt," he offered, seating himself in the chair the secretary had vacated and doing his best to meet her appraisal boldly. She was still wearing those heavy-rimmed glasses. He knew her too well not to suspect she had left them on with a purpose.

"That victory isn't complete yet," she said, and tossed her papers aside.

"It will be—if I know you at all."

The butler went out, closing the double doors behind him. Lucy offered him her hand again.

"I'll accept that compliment, Julian. May I add that it's good to see you—if I mean it?"

"Have you ever said anything you didn't mean?"

Lucy Sprague laughed softly. He rediscovered the fact that it could be both mocking and provocative. "Frankness is the one virtue my enemies admit. Are you my enemy—or my friend?"

He rose with the glass in his hand and glanced at himself in the huge wall mirror, obscurely glad that the brand-new uniform was a perfect fit. "Does this answer your question?"

"Don't be a fool," said Lucy. "I knew you'd be wearing that uniform, five years before it existed. Naturally you're the sort who'd wear it to the end." She sipped her brandy, then tossed it off. "I've friends in both camps, Julian—as you must know by now. I hoped to include you too."

"Even after what I saw in Nassau?" he asked boldly.

"I've lived that down nicely. So could you—if you'd put your mind to it."

"You said we'd meet again, as I remember."

"Did you think it would be like this?"

He shrugged a silent admission. "I'm still trying to take you in, Lucy."

She removed the horn-rimmed spectacles with a little flourish and poured herself another brandy: he guessed that she had saved both gestures deliberately. "Does it shock you too much—to see what three years have done to me?"

Three busy years, he thought, and more millions than you dreamed existed. Even now it was hard to realize that Lucy's money was more than a toy to her—that she could be as grimly efficient with those millions as Victor Sprague. This bland room, with its feminine overtones, was a business office nonetheless: wiser men than he must have discovered that fact too late.

Aloud he said only, "It's always a shock to find that someone's life has worked out exactly as you thought it would. How long ago did you plan to sit in a house like this and give the orders? Since you married my brother Mark—or before?"

Lucy took the questions with her good humor unshaken. "It's my turn to be shocked, Julian. I didn't think you understood me so well."

He smiled. "Of course, if you'd rather not answer——"

"I'll answer by the book," said Lucy. "Since I was old enough to think—and you'd be surprised to learn how young that can be, with a woman—I wanted to be my own master——"

"Mistress," he corrected gravely.

"Never mind the grammar; you know what I mean."

He found that they were smiling together: was it possible for a man to be friends with Lucy, after all? Involuntarily, he glanced at the portrait of Lucy's late, and unlamented, husband. The man's stare seemed to belong to the centuries now. . . . He told himself that Lucy had not really been responsible for Sprague's death in Nassau, and all but swallowed his own sophistry. Lucy, he added wryly, had merely assumed the Sprague mantle, as a matter of course.

"Isn't it a bit lonely on the mountaintop?" he asked.

"So far," said Lucy, "I've been too busy to notice."

"Busy, and loving it?"

"Busy, and loving it," she echoed. "Perhaps I should have been a man, Julian—I sometimes wonder about that. And yet I've always enjoyed being a woman too."

"I believe you," he said gravely.

"Being a woman, I'm allowed to be unpredictable on occasion." She picked up a stamped paper from her desk and offered it to him. "This came from Washington today, at my request. I'm sure you can use it."

Julian stared at the document blankly. It was a printed form from the Union War Department, filled in neatly in ink. The notations instructed the provost marshal of the New York area to arrange for the transport of one Captain Surgeon Chisholm, Confederate States Army, from that area to City Point, Virginia, where arrangements would go forward to effect his exchange. He had seen similar documents in the hands of more fortunate brother officers, when the provost guards had called for them at Johnson's Island. Each word of the transfer order had been engraved on his brain for months. Now that his own name was written here, he could not quite take it in.

"Aren't you going to thank me, Julian?"

"Why did you do this for me?" he asked harshly. He had planned to campaign for this helping hand, with every trick in his repertoire. Now that it was offered unasked, he could control neither his voice nor his amazement.

"Isn't it what you wanted?"

"How could you know?"

"You're forgetting that Whit Cameron is also a friend of mine. Three days ago, when he told me that you were a prisoner, he added the request that I might help you to"—she lowered her eyes romantically and poured again from the decanter—"shall we say, to rejoin your regiment?"

"And you consented that easily?"

"Why not? Surely you deserve some reward for that operation, Julian. Dr. Rothschild has only just finished singing your praises."

He watched her narrowly as she sipped her new drink. It was incredible that the path to Richmond could open before him so smoothly; worse than incredible that Lucy should have no inkling of his real reason for going there. He breathed deep, and plunged.

"You've heard that my wife is a Union agent?"

"I met your wife in Washington six months ago," said Lucy calmly. "At a levee in honor of Mr. Stanton, our Secretary of War. May I say once again that I approve your choice?"

"Can you tell me if Jane is in Richmond now?"

Her eyes dropped for the first time; he watched her hands stack the reports on her desk top. "After all, Julian, the government has a few secrets from me."

"Then I must tell you that it's her wish that we—separate until the war's over."

"Do you concur in that wish?"

He waited until Lucy had lifted her eyes to his again, then answered steadily. "I love her too much to lose her. If I can find her, I mean to take her out of this war, once and for all."

"Suppose you can't find her, Julian? Suppose the very fact you're searching puts her in new danger?"

"I've thought of that too," he said. "It's a risk I'll have to take."

"Suppose she's dead?"

He stared down blankly at his exchange papers. So Lucy knew more than she was telling; so, for that matter, did Whit and Louis Rothschild. Suddenly the whole picture came clear in his mind. Jane was dead—or, at least, they believed her to be dead. So there was no reason for keeping him penned in the North. Lucy could give him his freedom—and a ticket to Virginia; Louis could stand aside and let him go, with understanding, if not with approval. . . . If Jane was out of the picture, Captain Surgeon Chisholm could serve his stubborn gods to the end.

"I won't admit she's dead," he said at last. "Show me proof, if you like: I still won't admit it."

"Even if I tell you there's been no word of her since fall?"

He got up slowly, folding the provost marshal's order between his fingers. "You know me better than that, Lucy. I won't give her up."

She was on her feet too; for the first time he noted the tired half-moons under her eyes, saw that her hands were trembling a little as she stacked her papers one more time.

"How do you find it, Julian? Being in love, I mean?"

"We were in love once," he said, "don't you remember?"

"That wasn't love. I know you thought differently at the time. You were younger then, my dear."

"And you, Lucy?"

She smiled, and despite the bleak despair that enveloped him, he found that he was smiling faintly too.

"I was never that young, Julian. Still, it was pleasant while it lasted."

"Pleasant is hardly the word I would have chosen."

"You were always gallant," she murmured. "Don't spoil your record."

"Not for the world," he said, and kissed her hand again. Her fingers were hot in his: she clung to his hand for an instant, then released it.

"Come back if you change your mind."

"I won't."

"Don't be too sure of that," she said. "Your worst fears may be justified when you reach Richmond."

"I tell you, she isn't dead!"

"Nothing is lonelier than that sort of obstinacy," she said. "Not even this mountaintop. I'll—share it with you when you like, Julian. That goes without saying."

So his guess had been right, after all. He could possess Lucy Sprague when he liked, on his own terms. Possession would naturally include the Sprague millions, an assured position in the heart of this Yankee world. He could team with Louis, build the sort of hospital he had dreamed about. . . . The nebulous picture faded in the compulsion of the moment. Lucy took a step toward him, and he saw her again as a woman any man would desire, a woman whose sweetness would open to him at a word. And he knew that he had never wanted a woman more than now—when a cold voice, deep in his mind, assured him that he had lost Jane forever.

"Is that offer good, as of now?" His voice was hoarse; he steadied it with an effort.

"As of now," said Lucy. "Need you ask?"

"I must decline with thanks," he said just as steadily. "You see, I've still a war to finish—and a wife to find."

"Good luck with the search, Julian."

"Do you mean that?"

"No, my dear," she murmured. "I want you too much."

He turned on his heel and left the room: in another second she would have been in his arms.

On the stair he paused to steady his pounding heart and looked at the transfer paper one more time. It was a real thing now—real as freedom, that abstract word he had clung to for so long.

RICHMOND

SPRING foamed green at the windows of General Clayton Randolph's office, and the general bloomed almost visibly with the season. The fact that a city was all but starving just outside was another of those nightmares that could not presume to enter here; the fact that the general's nephew had insisted on occupying the armchair facing the desk (like another unwanted ghost) was hardly more important. He's trying hard to be magnanimous about it, thought Julian; he's trying still harder to assure himself that he's done all he can for me. After all, if a man's own kin persists in finishing the war like a dim-witted fool, the interview should be ended, as painlessly as possible.

"Does it seem good to be back, Julian?"

"I'm afraid it seems like a bad dream, Uncle. Unfortunately, I know I won't really waken until Grant's on Shockoe Hill."

"That butcher will take Richmond dearly, sir. We'll defend it to the last man." Uncle Clayton swallowed the balance of the cliché, a bit too hastily for comfort. "My only regret is that duty calls me elsewhere."

"Must you really go to Nassau?"

"An order's an order, my boy. Now that I've been transferred to ordnance, I realize how important it is to keep our sea lanes open——"

He's talking like an out-of-date editorial, thought Julian. One of those blood-and-thunder scareheads that have turned yellow long ago in the files of the *Examiner*. Yet the *Examiner* continued to print the same bombast, when all Richmond knew that Grant would rumble north from Petersburg any day now. That Sherman, crossing yet another flooded river in the Carolinas, already strained to throw the last iron loop around this beleaguered capital. Even the *Examiner* had been forced to admit that last menace. He had read the news only this morning, at the hospital. As usual, the editor had buried it among his advertisements; the banner head described Lee's heroic repulse of another cavalry raid that threatened, for a time, to reach the upper James.

"I thought our sea lanes were closed, now that Wilmington is invested."

"Have you forgotten that Captain Semmes is now in Virginia?"

Julian blinked, despite his good resolves. The skipper of the *Alabama*, that legendary privateer, had come back from the seven seas to command the Confederate squadron on the lower James. A last-ditch fight to keep the Federal gunboats from pushing even farther up the river. . . . And yet General Clayton Randolph had uttered Semmes's name with all the old reverence. Precisely as a bankrupt might ring his last gold piece on the counter, to convince a remorseless shopkeeper that there were a hundred others in his purse.

"Do you suppose Captain Semmes will drive the Yankees into the sea?"

"I've every hope of it; so, I might add, has our Navy Department. Unfortunately, my business is too urgent. I shall be forced to slip out of a tidal estuary in Carolina, like a thief in the night."

"Might I ask your mission?"

"A large shipment of gold went to the British before Wilmington harbor was closed. I shall make sure it's well spent in London."

"What if the war ends before you reach London?"

"I've more confidence in General Lee than that, sir."

Julian smiled blandly and waited for Uncle Clayton to come to the point. As a hard-working surgeon, he could begrudge the wasted time; yet Uncle Clayton, as always, was both amusing and terrifying. Like all classic types, his oratory was audienceproof. Like all bores, his antics sometimes aroused one's laughter—until one paused to realize the strength of bores.

"It is still evident," said his uncle, "that General Lee cannot hold his present line forever. I offer you that thought in confidence, Julian—and suggest you weigh it carefully. What will you do if Richmond falls?"

"Give my parole, I suppose, and go back to Chisholm Hundred. If I can still find the house for weeds."

"The city may be under siege. You lived through the siege of Vicksburg. You might not be so lucky here."

"Lucky or not, I'll still be needed."

"The sentiment does you credit, my boy." Uncle Clayton made a dramatic pause. "As it happens, you may be needed elsewhere. I could use a medical aide, to check my inventories in Nassau."

"Forgive me, Uncle—but are you suggesting we cut and run together, just because the Yankees are closing in?"

It was gratifying to watch the general turn a slow brick red as his rhetoric backfired from other lips than his own. "Young man, if you dare to imply that I'm a coward——"

To hell with implications, thought Julian. I'm stating a bald fact about you—and the other fat rats who are scrambling for Europe by the boatload. What really puzzles me is why you lingered so long.

Aloud he said carefully, "I need no proofs of your courage, Uncle. I only think it unlikely you'll return to America in the future, with a price on your head. No man would be so foolhardy."

Clayton Randolph settled at his desk again as his flush subsided. "Everyone above a colonel will have a price on his head. That's common knowledge."

"In that case, you'll do well to stay in London. I must take my chances here. I've a living to make, when the fighting's over."

"And a wife to find, I gather."

"If she's living."

Uncle Clayton seemed disappointed by his nephew's calm. "Naturally I've heard all about that unhappy business in Atlanta. I'm sure you acted in good faith—to help a lady in difficulties. That was always your family's way."

"A gentleman could not do less, Uncle." Julian tried not to smile as he echoed Clayton Randolph's tremolo.

"You still hope for a reunion, when the war's over?"

"It's my only hope, at the moment."

"There's no finer name in the South than yours, my boy. You gave it to a spy, in good faith. There's time enough now to repent of the error."

"But she wasn't a spy!" Julian found that he had all but shouted the words. "She risked her life for one purpose: to help starving men on their way—to a place where they could eat again."

"Prisoners of the South were fed the same rations as our troops."

"You were on the commission that visited Andersonville, Uncle. You know the death rate there. And the death rate at Libby Prison, which you can all but smell from this window."

Clayton Randolph dismissed the invitation with a soothing gesture. "Have it your way, Julian. Your wife was still an enemy of our cause. It's my honest opinion that she is dead."

"And I say she lives." In his heart he whispered a plea to Jane. Asking her forgiveness for even discussing her with this avuncular windbag. For speaking of her in the past tense—as though he shared Clayton Randolph's conviction.

"Very well, my boy. The question is really academic. How long since you've heard from her?"

"I've had no word since my imprisonment."

"And no proof?"

Only a crazy hope that won't die, thought Julian. Aloud he said, "Libby was mined a week ago. Twenty men broke for freedom. As many more have swum the James from Belle Isle in the past fortnight. Someone is helping those men to the Union lines. I'll tell you to your face that I hope it's my wife. You're too loyal to the family name to let such sentiments get beyond this room." It was madness to talk thus, he knew, but he was past caring. It was too great a luxury to give his hopes free rein.

"I'm an old man, Julian," said Clayton Randolph. "If the times would permit, I might add that my spirit is broken. My boy was all I had: when I heard of his death, life lost its meaning. At least I hoped I could be proud of you."

"You'll never be ashamed of me. I give you my word."

The general sighed deeply. "Is it true that George died of tetanus in a hospital wagon?"

"Too true, I'm afraid."

"George wanted to die in a charge. He said so a hundred times. He wanted to go down killing Yankees with his last breath."

You're speaking for the textbooks now, thought Julian. Posterity will yawn soon enough—why should I pretend to listen? But he forced hushed respect into his voice as he answered.

"George was a gallant officer. After all, he gave his life for the Confederacy."

"As I'd give mine, if I had the strength." Clayton Randolph considered a peroration, abandoned the idea, and got up briskly from his desk. "You won't change your mind about that trip to Nassau?"

"I'm afraid not. May I wish you a pleasant journey?"

The general's gray felt sombrero was jaunty with newness: it made a brave flourish as he set it at a slight angle on his grizzled curls. Clearly, his mind was at rest, now that he had done his duty by his own.

"Since you insist, Julian——may I leave these papers in your hands?" His gloves flicked a pile of manuscript on the desk, a stack of glossy photographs. "My memoirs—and a pictorial record of my various commands. Unfortunately, I can't risk taking such valuable records abroad. They might fall into the hands of the enemy."

Once more Julian suppressed a smile by a tremendous effort. "Are you making me your literary executor, Uncle?"

"Let's not put it so solemnly. On the other hand, there's no doubt that such a record will have value when peace comes. I'm trusting you to see that it finds a publisher."

The general stripped off one glove and offered his hand. The liver spots were as abundant as ever above the well-fed wrists; the handshake was pulpy but firm. Julian returned it heartily. Now that Clayton Randolph was walking out of his life, he could see him clearly. A puffy old man whose life was over. A harmless peacock whose tailfeathers would take on an added luster in the next London season. . . .

"I'm late now for an appointment with Mr. Davis. Wish me luck, Julian—and I'll return the compliment."

"Even in my search for Jane?"

Clayton Randolph paused in the doorway to throw his nephew a pitying smile. "You'll live down that heartache in time, young man."

Alone in the office, Julian took the throne chair without compunction and riffled the pages of the manuscript. He made no attempt to read: his sense of humor had already been strained to the breaking point.

Instead he stared for a long time at the top photograph under his hands. It was, he recalled instantly, the one General Randolph had posed for so proudly when they had first met in this same city, over two years ago. The alert hawk's eyes still glared out at posterity beneath iron-gray brows: the brigadier's stars glowed dully

on the stiff tabs of the gold-encrusted collar. The photograph had
painted out the crow's-feet admirably; the liver spots did not show
on the two hands knotted firmly on the hero's sword.

A half century from now—or sooner, with luck—a generation of
schoolboys would study that picture and wonder what enemies this
man had stared down so proudly. There was no avoiding the
dignity that glowed from within like a sacred altar flame. The
photographer had simply ignored the brass and made the most of
the contours. If that picture found its way between the covers of a
history book, General Clayton Randolph—the defender of Richmond from afar—would establish his fame with no contenders.

Julian watched his hands obey a sudden impulse that could not
be gainsaid. For another moment he sat quietly in his uncle's
throne chair staring at his uncle's photograph, all but obscured now
in the debris of a catchall wastebasket beside the desk. His hands
moved mechanically, shredding the other pictures into the receptacle, wadding the manuscript and thrusting it after them. Just
in time he remembered that paper had been salvaged for years in
Richmond and touched a match to the destruction he had caused.

The paper burned quickly in the wind-swept room; the smoke
eddied at the window sill, losing itself in the clean spring day.

"Now you belong with the ages," said Captain Surgeon Chisholm to no one in particular.

He walked out of the office without remorse. On the street he
found that his breathing was normal again. Somehow he had never
breathed properly in his uncle's presence: the air had always
seemed heavy with the mummy smell of death.

ii

The office stood on the slope of Shockoe Hill. Obeying another,
more tranquil impulse, he followed an alley of fresh-leaved lindens
until he emerged on the square before the Capitol. The city and
the James were at his feet, heavy with the smoke of the ironworks
along its banks. Behind him the handsome statehouse of Virginia
threw its classic silhouette against a flawless spring sky. The flag
of secession made a brave show in the breeze. On a pediment near
by, the state flag whipped just as bravely against the blue. Watching that gallant duel, Julian reminded himself that the oligarchy
responsible for the war was a sovereign confederation, not a union.

390

Virginia had accepted the Confederate president and his cabinet: the Old Dominion could hardly do less. Richmond had, just as consistently, snubbed the President's wife from the start. The two flags merely confirmed that fatal dualism.

Richmond, reflected Julian, was not the South in microcosm; yet the faults and the heroism of the Confederacy were packed in its crowded heart today. Balls were still given for the Home Guard officers in more than one mansion; even now champagne corks popped behind the profiteers' doors at the Spotswood Hotel. He had refused more than one such invitation to eat his fill in the midst of this hungry city. True, those same rich bombproofs had been stoned on occasion, when they ventured abroad in their finery: he could count them by the dozen today, here in the crowded square, or bustling into the Capitol itself. Perhaps Richmond would never know the end had come until Shockoe Hill was all homespun and tight-lipped misery. . . .

He stood aside without bowing to a plump, swarthy individual with a black lazy-man's beard that contrasted oddly with his sleek frock coat and almost oriental manner. Judah Benjamin, the inscrutable Jew, the Secretary of State for the Confederacy. The man—it was whispered—who had already insured his own future in a secret deal with Washington. Julian watched without surprise as the Secretary mounted the steps of the statehouse and vanished in the chill gloom of the rotunda. Political bigwigs, like simon-pure heroes, were plentiful on Richmond's streets these days. He had seen Mr. Davis more than once, pacing behind his frown, his tragedian's locks lank on his collar. It seemed only yesterday that his heart had thudded as he came to attention, and saluted General Lee himself in the lobby of the Spotswood House.

He wondered where the general had bivouacked last night—and whether the news he had telegraphed the President was good or bad. Benjamin's thin smile could have meant almost anything: Mr. Davis's Secretary was always smiling at a joke peculiarly his own.

And yet the spring was heady as wine in Richmond's streets today, after the bitterest winter in Richmond's memory. There were still whispers of miracles afoot, of a juncture of Lee and Johnston's forces to take Grant on the flank and smash through to Washington. . . . Certainly the town looked serene as time in the sunlight.

He faced the river again, watching a side-wheeler nose into a landing. He had come in on just such a side-wheeler six weeks ago —direct from Aiken's Landing, the place of exchange downstream. The riverbank had been thick with black ice that morning as he stood among the sick and wounded on the crowded deck—still childishly pleased that the War Department had seen fit to swap a Yankee brigadier to get him back. It seemed incredible that the Yankees were swarming only a few miles downstream today, awaiting the signal to fling themselves against the city's defense arc. . . . The sunlight picked out a golden spark on the musket barrel of a picket on Belle Isle. The whole island was white with prisoners' tents: even at the distance he could see a group of Yankees, stripped to the waist in the sunlight and pounding their shirts clean on the stones of the riverbank.

A dozen prisoners were said to swim the James each night, to filter through the city and rejoin their lines. Had his wild guess been true, after all? Did Jane still have a hand in those bids for freedom?

He crushed the hope before it could take shape and bring her image back. Walking down the steep pitch to the river, he remembered that he had been away from work too long.

Like more than one convalescent ward in Richmond, his hospital had been set up in a tobacco barn on the river's edge, almost in the shadow of the busy bridge that crossed the stream to the suburb of Manchester, on the southern bank. Thanks to his status as a returning veteran, he had been able to extract several barrels of chloride of lime from a harassed commissary. After the place had been scrubbed from floor to rafters, he had permitted his staff to settle again into the routine of nursing the endless stream of dysentery and fever cases brought to their door by barge and hospital train. While the ominous stalemate at Petersburg had lasted, he had found his daily schedule one long anticlimax: there had been little to interest a surgeon in these rows of emaciated bodies, little to vary the dull despair that brooded above the wards as he watched their occupants die and realized he could do little to ease the agony of their dying.

Even now, it was said, certain warehouses just across the river were bursting with food—held by speculators in the hope of a last-minute victory, and rotting in the storage bins. The government's own warehouses were packed too—or so ran the rumors: there simply was not enough rolling stock in the freight yards to take this sorely needed food to the armies in the field. . . . Julian knew only that the hospital ration was barely enough to sustain a normal life. The fevered boys in his cots, perishing for nourishing soups and jellies, retched at the ill-balanced diet of bacon and corn pone, but it was all he had to offer them. He had donated his own portion this noon and dined on yams with his orderlies.

His office was a lean-to shack that had once served the warehouse. He sank down wearily in the lone armchair and glanced through the memoranda on his desk. Dr. Tanner would call again this afternoon: he smiled faintly as his eye fell on the name. It seemed only natural that Tanner should go through the war without a scratch, that he should be operating in Richmond now.

The fracture case had died this morning, precisely as he had expected; he had used all his skill to set the broken elbow joint, knowing in advance that the gunner would never come out of shock. He had seen too many such cases since Vicksburg—when once-healthy young bodies, debilitated by dysentery and the hopeless army diet, simply failed to respond to treatment.

He signed the death certificate and added it to the neat stack at his elbow. Now that he had made his desk tidy again, a letter caught his eye, stuck in a corner of the blotter. He felt his breath catch in his throat as he saw the censor's seal across the flap and recognized Macalastair's copper-plate hand in the address.

It was, of course, ridiculous to be upset by his overseer's letter, to hold it gingerly in his hands and admit that he was afraid to open it. He had been expecting that letter for a long time now—long before the last batch of bad news had been relayed from the Cape Fear.

The manager of Chisholm Hundred came straight to the point, with true Scotch forthrightness:

. . . writing from my forced detention in Wilmington, I have made up my mind *not* to spare your feelings. So I tell you, at the beginning, that the plantation is a casualty of war—looted—raped of its riches—the slaves fled to the four corners of the compass—the quarters and work buildings leveled to the ground—the house gutted to its walls . . .

Macalastair's pen had stuttered on the last word before it went resolutely on. That January the Yankees had cut their way up the river, engaging what Confederate cavalry they could coax into the open, living on the land while their main force continued a slow squeeze on Wilmington itself. The overseer drew a detailed picture of that inexorable military advance: though the advancing blue column did not repeat the excesses of Sherman's bummers in their march from Savannah northward, the occupation had been distressingly thorough.

Chisholm Hundred might have escaped the worst if a certain Colonel Fraser, commander of a Home Guard cavalry unit, had not decided that the landing had strategic importance. The Confederates, said Macalastair, had dug in along the river in the hope of blunting the Yankee column moving with insolent deliberation on the river road; the Confederates had planted a battery of howitzers on the hill where the former Mrs. Mark Chisholm had once built a summerhouse. Dr. Chisholm would recall that the ridge commanded a wide sweep of valley below: from that elevation even a few howitzers could do considerable damage. . . .

Dr. Chisholm remembered perfectly. He saw it all clearly again, as he sat in this pine-and-tar-paper office, staring down at the neat, closely written sheet. The way the gulls walked under the live oaks; the curve of the path just above his mother's rose garden, where it was cool even in August; the blue-green cup of the valley, melting into heat haze along the river's rim. The grave beauty of the house itself—the serene permanence of its lines, its patrician calm as it faced the broad acres below. Yes, he had kept it all inviolate in his mind. Somehow he had managed to believe that it would last forever.

. . . I make no attempt to tell you what happened when the two hostile forces met. There was sharp firing for more than an hour. It seemed to come from all corners of the estate: I learned later that the howitzers on the ridge had used their last round when the Union forces outflanked them and cut the gunners down. All that time I was in the cellar, working to hide the plate and the plantation records. Black Lolly (you will remember he had been our headman since '48) stayed to help: most of the other hands had taken to their heels long before. I regret to add that he was but ill repaid for his loyalty—for he stopped a bullet when they fired the house and we were forced to run for our lives.

Black Lolly. He remembered when the Negro had taken the ritualistic glass of whisky from Harrison Chisholm's own hand; he remembered the proud lift of the slave's shoulders as he accepted the duties of headman. Had it really been almost sixteen years since he had looked down on that ceremony from the shadow of his father's portico? He tried to picture the headman's death and found no image in his mind. Black Lolly was only a name—a ripple of shoulder muscles—a rich bellow to drive the field hands to their tasks. There was no face to go with these details.

As for the burning of Chisholm Hundred, Macalastair refused to express an opinion: an outlander who took his pay in gold could not afford to be partisan in the matter. Some said that a shell from the howitzer had fallen short and exploded in an open cellar door; others insisted that the Yankees had fired incendiaries into the rooftree, to smoke out the snipers clustered behind the chimney-pots. Be that as it may, the house had been burning at a dozen points when Macalastair ran into the open with his hands above his head.

He was fairly certain that Lolly had stopped a stray bullet. They were still fighting among the boxwoods when he crossed the lawn. He had watched the Yankees smash the fanlight above the main door to clear the stair well for their fire; he had heard sabers clash in the formal drawing room, just before the smoke obscured his view. The house had burned for a half hour by his own watch before the rooftree collapsed under the last sniper. . . .

Julian found that his eyes had refused to read on. Prepared as he was, the shock was far greater than he had believed. In a moment, he knew, this flaming image would be all too real: Macalastair's careful recital of facts had merely numbed his mind. Though he had never been a part of it, Chisholm Hundred was still his only synonym for home, the only haven he had known. He could not picture it now, a skeleton against the sky.

The warehouse beside the steamboat wharf, said Macalastair, was filled to the rafters with the cotton they had baled three years ago. He had begged for that cotton with the Union commander, and watched the warehouse go up in flames even as he begged. Secesh die-hards had holed in there for a final stand, the Yankees said. . . . Their commander, Julian gathered, was a good sort, on the whole. At least he had vetoed the suggestion of an aide that Macalastair be shot in the general roundup. The overseer had spent the night penned in a slave cabin—the only building on the estate with four solid walls. In the morning he had been sent down-river with the wounded, arriving in Wilmington a day after the city's capitulation under the guns of Fort Fisher.

Julian looked back dully at the date of the letter and saw that it was weeks old. Macalastair explained that too, logically enough. He had been too shaken, at first, to make an adequate report; in any event, the Yankees had imprisoned him for a while, until they had assured themselves that he had been an unwilling spectator to the battle that had raged across the estate. At present he had the freedom of the city, which was still under martial law; he had even bought himself a cot at a hotel that was livable enough, save for the fact that part of the roof was gone. Most of his time, this past month, had been devoted to an intensive search for the insurance records of Chisholm Hundred. . . .

Despite himself, Julian all but laughed aloud at this commendable zeal. Macalastair had always shown a deep respect for documents. Surely he must know that whatever insurance Harrison Chisholm had carried on the estate was valueless now—that there is no insurance against war. His eyes went back mechanically to the letter:

. . . Perhaps I should add that I have little hope of recovering anything by legal means. But it helps to pass the time here, while I wait for news from Richmond. Perhaps it has fallen as these lines are written: perhaps we will meet again before this letter can reach you. It has been a hard letter to write: I can almost hope that your eyes will never see the words.

All is not lost, Dr. Chisholm: believe me when I assure you that we can build again on the ashes. I know that thought is cold comfort now; but I hope that I may continue to serve you, if and when I can. . . .

There was more, in the same gruffly sympathetic vein; there was no inkling of how the letter had found its way through the Union lines. Discretion had prevented Macalastair from naming his messenger; Julian did not doubt that he had paid out of his own Scotch purse for the service, and paid high.

He knew that he should be grateful to his father's overseer, but his body seemed drained of all feeling as he crumpled the letter in one fist and walked to the window. The cobbled street was empty, save for a ragged soldier who dozed in the shade of the boarded warehouse across the way. He stared at the man for a moment—wondering if he was on furlough or if he was waiting for a train to return him to the trenches before Petersburg, some sixty miles to the south. . . . Petersburg. He had passed through that battered city more than once, on his way to Wilmington and Chisholm Hundred. Perhaps he should take the train, along with that tattered casual of war. If he applied for an assignment in the field, there would still be time to die before the war ended.

He had never thought of death in quite this friendly light. Staring at the exhausted soldier as though the man embodied that same dark essence, he saw his next move clearly. On the edge of battle it was absurdly easy to make oneself a living target. A man had every right to choose his own exit from a collapsing world. . . . Even Jane had said that he would not be happy among the ashes of the world he had known.

This, he told himself firmly, was more than self-pity. The pattern of his ruin had been repeated a thousand times in this ravaged land; a thousand other aristocrats, real or imagined, would sit down to die in the ashes of their past—or rise up to carve themselves a new future. The strong, as always, would survive: eventually they would build a better South, enriched by the old traditions yet freed from the old taboos. . . . But the strong had their own reason for being. Now that Jane was gone, he was existing on borrowed time. Living without savor, and—he faced the fact squarely now—without hope.

No, there was little reason to deceive himself from this point on: in his secret heart he had abandoned hope of finding her long ago. His return to the Confederacy, his work in this Richmond hospital, were only the last stand of a stubborn nature that would not admit defeat, even when defeat stood eye to eye with him and administered the deathblow. Jane was dead, and life without Jane was meaningless. A Yankee sharpshooter could finish that syllogism nicely.

He turned with a strangled cry as someone knocked on the office door—and fought for composure as Dick, his orderly, stepped across the threshold. Dick had rejoined him some time ago, thanks to Tanner's helping hand. The pale ex-pharmacist had done a great deal to make these weeks in Richmond bearable. Waiting for the orderly to speak, he wondered if Dick would mourn his loss. . . .

"The insuttusception case is waiting, sir."

"Insuttusception?" He stared at Dick blankly, as though the word were new to him.

"You said you'd be operating at three, Dr. Chisholm. Dr. Tanner is waiting to assist you."

Corporal Petty. He remembered instantly now. The boy was from his own corner of Carolina, the son of a swamper on a tributary of the Cape Fear. Corporal Petty was a likable youth—like so many others, he was too young to give up. Even now, when his preliminary examination had convinced him that insuttusception —the telescoping of the small intestine into the large—had occurred as an aftermath to the dysentery that had brought him to the hospital. . . . In Vienna it had been established that the condition could be relieved; he had consulted with Tanner only this morning and agreed to take the risk.

His mind began to tick again, and he stood quietly for a moment, rejoicing in that steady rhythm. They must open the abdomen and retract: space was needed for a technique that was dependent on manual dexterity. In Vienna he had watched a surgeon professor manipulate the small bowel, so adroitly that the telescoped area had disengaged itself in a matter of minutes, like a stocking turned in on itself. . . .

"Put him under, Dick. I'll be along at once."

When the door closed he stood for a while in the cluttered office, waiting for his heartbeat to steady. Come what may, he thought, the worst is over. Jane may be dead; I must still find a way to go on. . . . He corrected the thought gravely: already the way was open wide before him. His wife might be lost forever and his world burned to the ground. With a scalpel in his hand, he would always have a reason for being.

iii

An hour later—alone in that same office, knowing now that a certain Corporal Petty had a better than even chance to live—he felt that he could afford a symbolic gesture. The cigar came first, of course—the fabulous cigar that Tanner had handed him as they left the operating room. He had not smoked a cigar in weeks: Tanner himself admitted that this roll of genuine Havana had cost him two hundred Confederate dollars when he had purchased it sub rosa. . . . Julian squared the end carefully before he struck the lucifer. Only when the cigar was drawing did he touch that same flame to Macalastair's letter, still lying in a crumpled ball on the window sill.

He watched the letter burn with deep satisfaction. The salvage committee would never approve, of course. Still less would it have approved his wholesale destruction in Clayton Randolph's office.

398

But he was burning a link with his past, and he knew the gesture was valuable.

The cobbled street outside still drowsed in the late afternoon sunlight. It was only when he bent to blow the ashes from the window sill that he thought to glance at the door of the warehouse across the way. The ragged soldier (his synonym for death only an hour ago) had vanished. But he was in time to see Tracy Crandall whisk back into the shadows and out of sight.

It was only a glimpse, but he could not doubt that it was Crandall—or that Crandall was watching the hospital entrance. In that same flash he guessed that the apparently innocent soldier had been there with a reason, too. Soldiers asleep in doorways were a commonplace in crowded Richmond. If he knew Crandall at all, the counterspy had relied on that fact when he placed his substitute lookout. . . .

Julian found himself in the armchair again as his eyes still clung to the sunlit window frame. The empty street, that had seemed dreary beyond belief a moment ago, was alive with interest now. If Crandall thought him worth watching, there could be but one meaning behind the vigil. Jane was alive, despite his craven doubts; Jane was still an active menace to the Confederacy. Last, and most important, Jane was in Richmond or near by—and Crandall fully expected Captain Surgeon Chisholm to lead the way to her hiding place.

He was still weighing that miracle when he heard the ring of boots on the cobbles and saw Whit Cameron cross the window frame. The gambler, in immaculate broadcloth and beaver, was something of a miracle in his own right. The tilt of his hat had lost none of its old jauntiness; the twirl of the rattan between his long, pale hands had a tempo that only Whit could give a walking stick. . . . The shadowed doorway of the warehouse looked as empty as ever as Whit paused to scratch a match on his boot sole. Julian wondered if Crandall had drawn in his breath on the same high note of tension. If Grant himself had swaggered across his own line of vision at that moment, he could hardly have been more startled.

In the hall outside he heard Whit's voice boom in greeting; he heard the click of an orderly's heels and grinned at the man's instinctive reaction: with that cane and that swagger, the gambler could have passed for a general in disguise.

"Mr. Cameron for Captain Chisholm. He's expecting me."

God knows *that's* true enough, thought Julian. Now you're here, I'm not really surprised. From the moment I took out your appendix in New York, I've been expecting you when I needed you most.

"It's quite all right, Dick," he said. "Mr. Cameron is an old friend."

"To put things mildly," said Whit. He lounged in the doorway for a moment, until Julian remembered his own manners and held out his hand.

Julian's voice, when he found it again, was full of that same manufactured politeness. "Did you have a pleasant journey?"

"Expensive but uneventful," said Whit. "It's still nice to be back—and find Richmond the same as ever."

They turned in unison as Dick snapped his heels in a correct salute. "You might show a little more surprise, Julian."

"I gave up being surprised a long time ago. Especially by you."

It was good to laugh aloud again. Good to wave his friend to a chair, settle behind his desk, and feel his tension melt away. That, too, was part of Whit Cameron's genius. Despite the implications of this visit—despite the fact that a counterspy of the Confederate Army was watching this office window—he had not felt more at ease in weeks.

Whit put down his hat and stick on the desk top and hooked one gleaming boot in an angle of the window sill. "You're looking tired, my friend."

"So would you if you'd operated all last night." That would do for now, thought Julian. He could not bring himself to speak of the ruin at Chisholm Hundred.

"Isn't it about time you let someone else do your operating?"

"Never mind me, Whit. You never looked better."

"Thanks to you. What was that item you removed from my innards in New York?"

"The processus vermiformis—sometimes called the appendix. Do you miss it?"

"Very pleasantly, so far. Aren't you going to ask me how I got here?"

"I'm waiting for you to tell me, your own way."

The gambler smiled. "The same old Julian, I see. Always patient with my natural talent for self-dramatization."

"The same old Whit, you mean."

"Be that as it may, I'm still an honest government contractor for the Confederacy. Would you care to see my papers?"

"Don't tell me you were buying shoes for Lee's army in New York?"

"Believe it or not, I was doing just that. Somehow, I don't think the shipment will arrive in time."

"So you came South to apologize?"

"I came to Richmond to see how you're faring, Julian. It cost me just five hundred Yankee dollars to buy my way through your lines." Whit studied his boot top carefully. "You might say you're glad I came."

Julian swallowed hard. The gambler had made this slightly fabulous statement with his usual air; there was no doubting his sincerity. He *has* come back to check on me, thought Julian; but that isn't all. This visit to Richmond in her eleventh hour ties up with Jane, as surely as Tracy Crandall's presence in the shadow of that warehouse door across the way.

"Must I turn handsprings to show you how glad I am?"

"A simple declaration will do," said Whit.

"I'll do better than that. I'll warn you that we're being spied on now."

"I know—by Tracy Crandall. He and I tangled horns more than once in Atlanta. Don't give him a second thought, Julian. Of course he knows where my sympathies lie, but he can't prove a word of it."

"I'd keep my voice down, just the same. At the moment he's standing across the street, watching us."

Whit glanced carelessly at the sagging bulk of the tobacco warehouse. "We came into town on the same train. Naturally he'd guess that I was coming here."

"He can arrest you now, if he likes."

"True enough. But he won't dare. Leave Crandall to me, Julian. I've made up my mind just how to handle him."

Julian let his own eyes stray to the window and turned away as casually as he could. They were both in plain view as they talked; it would never do to let Crandall know that they suspected his presence.

"I thought he was dead in a cavalry charge," he said. "It seems his neck is tougher than I suspected."

Whit shrugged again. "Nemesis is hard to kill, sometimes. Just remember this particular Nemesis can't hurt us, unless we give him a chance."

"He's after Jane, not us!"

"Precisely. Have you any intention of bringing them together?"

Julian leaned sharply across the desk. He wondered if Whit had framed their meeting in the window deliberately; certainly it was impossible for him to show emotion with Tracy Crandall's eyes upon him.

"Where is she?"

"A great many people in Washington were asking me that question, day before yesterday."

"*Where is she, damn you?*"

"Keep your voice down, my friend; and if you must curse me, smile while you curse."

"You know she's alive, Whit. You know where to find her."

"In Washington she's officially listed as dead."

"Washington knows better. So does Crandall."

"And so do I. Is that what you're implying?"

"I'm stating a fact. You're here with messages for Jane, and you needn't deny it. Tell me that much is true, at least. I won't ask for more."

Whit took up the flexible rattan and tapped his boot sole with the point. "I'll tell you this much—if she were alive, I'd have a message of great interest to her."

"Does it bear repeating?"

"Only in a whisper. Tomorrow is the second of April, 1865."

"So it is. Our calendar is the same as yours."

"There's where we differ, Julian. Your calendar says it will be a peaceful Sunday here. Mine says that Richmond will be evacuated by nightfall."

Julian stared at the gambler for a moment of openmouthed silence. "Who told you this?"

"Friends in both camps," said Whit calmly. "Fact one: General Lee is now hopelessly outnumbered. Fact two: he is being decisively defeated at this moment, if odds mean anything in your dictionary."

"They haven't in the past."

"They will tonight," said Whit just as calmly. "My information is that Lee will work out of this defense arc and establish a line to the south. Which can only mean that President Davis must move his seat of government. Sunday is an unlucky moving day, but it will serve. . . . With Richmond fallen, the war must end in a week. I bet a thousand dollars in Washington that Lee will surrender before the tenth of April. I'll bet you another thousand now. Gold against shinplasters."

"And that's the message you bring to Jane?"

"Don't confuse your tenses. That's the message I *would* bring if she were still alive."

Julian felt the blood hammer in his temples. "She's in Richmond. You know where to find her."

"Where else would she be if she were still running prisoners?"

"Have it your way, Whit. You're bringing her this news. Telling her to stop her work—that Grant will do the liberating in Virginia from now on. The war has ended for her as of today."

Whit smiled sadly at his boot top. "It would be providential— if I could find her and tell her that."

"Tell her, by all means. I give you my word I'll stand aside——" He swallowed the rest as Tanner burst into the office without the formality of a knock and pulled up on the threshold as he met Whit's level stare.

"Your pardon, Chisholm. I didn't realize you were busy."

Whit was already on his feet, with his most formal bow. "Come in, sir, by all means. A civilian's business can always wait. Shall we meet at the Spotswood bar, Julian—around six?"

"Stay where you are, Whit." Julian faced Tanner with the best poker face he could assume. "Mr. Cameron's an old friend. You can speak freely."

"Did you know we were to evacuate this hospital tonight?"

Julian ignored Whit with a great effort and forced surprise into his tone. "When did you have the news?"

"It just came down the hill. By courier." Tanner laid a printed form on the desk top. "This came by the same messenger. Do you blame me for being puzzled?"

Julian stared at the paper. It was a two-week furlough, made out in his name and stamped with the next day's date.

"Signed by the commanding general himself," said Tanner. "Countersigned by my own esteemed uncle, the Secretary of War. How do you explain it?"

Julian dared to glance at Whit now, but the gambler had withdrawn delicately to the window and was staring out at the sun-drenched cobbles.

"Believe me, I'm quite as puzzled as you."

Tanner tossed up his hands. "Of course I can sympathize. A man who's just learned that his estates are in ruins deserves a breathing spell. But why should it come now—on top of this order to evacuate?"

"Ask that it be revoked, if you like."

"I wouldn't hear of it. The leave doesn't begin until tomorrow morning; you can see me through the worst of the moving."

Julian found that he was almost calm now. If he could keep his eyes away from that precious document on the desk—and ignore Whit's expressive back—he might even part friends with Tanner.

"Does the evacuation order sound like bad news to you?"

"If you ask me, I think it's merely a precautionary measure. We're to move our cases by train to Danville. That's only a short haul. Naturally we must wait for darkness to begin the transfer; it would never do to alarm the civilians." Tanner glanced quickly at Whit and forced a laugh. "Your pardon, Mr. Cameron. We can trust you not to repeat this news in Richmond?"

Whit bowed, without turning from the window. "My lips are sealed, sir."

Julian spoke quickly. "I'll find Dick now and check supplies."

"I've already given Dick his orders." Tanner's voice had eased off a little, though he still looked puzzled. "It's fortunate that nearly half our cases are walking wounded. We should be out of here by midnight, if they give me enough litter bearers."

"I'll come too, if I'm needed."

"You'll do nothing of the kind," said Tanner decisively. "You've earned this furlough, Chisholm." He glanced at Whit, hesitated, then spoke his mind regardless. "Perhaps it'll outlast our war. For your sake, I hope so. It'll give you a good start to the Cape Fear——" He walked out of the office on that note—quickly, as though he feared to say more.

Whit was still at the window; his voice seemed far-off and resigned. "Strange, isn't it, how quickly the War Department can move when it's on its last legs?"

Julian snatched up the paper and studied it carefully. "This looks authentic."

"It is authentic."

"You arranged it, nonetheless."

"Naturally. I might add that it cost me a pretty penny."

"Why?"

"Why not? This isn't the first leave I've bought for a friend."

"You want me out of Richmond—is that it?"

"Precisely, Julian."

"Why not let me go with the hospital unit to Danville?"

Whit smiled. "I'll admit I was a trifle taken aback when *that* order came through. Unfortunately, even a man in my position can't foresee everything."

"Now that I'm free, what's to keep me from following you?"

"Only your word, my friend. Don't forget you just promised to stand aside—and let me spirit Jane out of Richmond in my own way."

"So you finally admit she's in Richmond."

"To the best of my knowledge."

"You haven't seen her yet?"

Whit shrugged. "Aren't you forgetting our friend across the street?"

"But you know where she is staying?"

"Of course. And I'll tell you more. Even without Crandall to dog my steps, I'd have come here first. You're a greater problem to me than Jane. Authentic heroes always are, at this point in a war."

"Never mind me, Whit. Tell me where she is hiding."

The gambler spread his thin hands expressively. "I was afraid of this."

"I've got to know she's safe. Suppose Crandall heads you off? I can still go to her——"

Whit slapped the desk top. "You, my friend, are quitting town tonight, as you promised."

"And leaving Jane here?"

"With luck, I'll have her out of Richmond ahead of you."

"Tell me where you're taking her, at least."

"Never in this world," said Whit. "I may still lose my bet on General Lee."

Julian capitulated on that, none too gracefully. "I suppose I should thank you for that furlough, but I won't. Tell me what my orders are. I'll try to obey."

The gambler sat on a corner of the desk and flexed the rattan between his palms. "Get out of Richmond. If the trains are running in Carolina, try to reach Wilmington. The country's wide open. You're a noncombatant. Chances are you can reach Chisholm Hundred without being stopped——"

"Tanner just told you what happened to Chisholm Hundred."

"The land's still yours," said Whit. "You've a right to look at your land and decide on its future."

Their eyes met and held on that. Julian's mind swung back to a night at High Cedars, under the chandelier of the formal dining room. The night he had offered Chisholm Hundred to Jane, to do with as she liked. Remembering that offer, he knew that it answered all his questions now. Jane would find her way to Wilmington, and the estate on the river; Jane would be waiting there for him. . . . The fact that they could not share that journey was not too important. He could trust Whit Cameron to serve as guide.

"Perhaps I should thank you after all," he said at last.

The gambler took this tacit apology with his good humor intact. "Chisholm Hundred, then," he said. "When and if you can reach it. It's as good a rendezvous as any." He got up on that, folding the rattan cane under one arm and setting his tall beaver over one eyebrow.

"You're going to her now?"

"With your permission."

"What about Crandall?"

"I promised to eliminate Crandall," said Whit. "Stay where you are and watch me perform."

"You'll find him rather hard to eliminate."

"Watch," said Whit. "You're positive he's still inside that doorway? There's no way he can dodge me?"

Julian nodded mutely. He had begun to sense Whit's plan, and knew he was powerless to stop it.

"Come when you're called, and come fast," said the gambler.

He went out quickly, slapping the rattan against the doorjamb. Julian sat inert in the window frame, hearing the click of Whit's heels in the street outside, watching his friend come into view again as he crossed the cobbles at an angle. In the shadow of the warehouse he paused to select a cigar from his case—and took a careless step into the doorway, to scratch the match on the boarded surface. . . . The rattan stick lashed downward; he heard Crandall bellow with pain, saw him catapulted into the sunlight with Whit's hand knotted in his collar. The rattan whipped down again in a merciless arc; there was blood on the counterspy's face when Whit released him at last.

"How dare you take this liberty!"

"That's my question, not yours," said Whit. "How dare you follow me from the station—eavesdrop on my visit with an old friend? How dare you take offense at a punishment you deserve?"

Even before that clash of voices, the street seemed to fill magically with uniforms. A swarthy young infantry captain, who had been visiting in the wards, stood bristling at Crandall's side. There was Tanner, looking vastly competent as he hurried up to thrust his bulk between the antagonists. There was a whole quartet of privates on crutches, hobbling down from the hospital entrance to watch two gentlemen settle their quarrel by time-honored means.

"What's the trouble here?"

Julian watched Crandall's fist double, then fall to his side; even from where he sat he could see the great veins throbbing at the base of the counterspy's jaw. But Crandall was a gentleman in uniform—as such, he had just one way to revenge the blow.

"As the injured party, Mr. Cameron——"

Whit's voice cut in, with studied contempt. "Dr. Chisholm will act for me, I'm sure."

But Julian had vaulted from window sill to street without waiting to be called. Honor had put its own ritualistic glaze over the faces as he walked toward the group. Crandall stepped back a pace; his eyes sought the swarthy young captain, who—like Julian—had come forward without being summoned.

"Captain Crittenden, sir. Your servant."

Pistols at twenty paces. The dry meadow under the bluff, on the Manchester side of the James. Even if the meeting was put off until six, there would be light enough. He had assisted at too many such affairs to fumble his details—or his lines.

"Your servant, Captain Crittenden."

No one stirred in the taut group as the two seconds-to-be walked up the street together; no one smiled but Whit, as he tossed the broken rattan into the gutter.

"It's served its purpose," he said to the silence.

In his heart Julian murmured a fervent Amen. Whit had taken longer chances in his time, and won. Crandall was the injured party, and Crandall was the challenger: if Crandall's death was in the cards, he was powerless to ask for another deal. It would be strange indeed if that broken walking stick could smash the last barrier that lay between Jane and safety.

iv

Crittenden closed his pocket inkpot with a flourish. "I think this statement of particulars is in order, Captain Chisholm. Will you verify it?"

"Your own verification is sufficient, sir."

Crandall's handsome young second knitted his brows over the sheet of paper on his knee. "Colonel Whitford Cameron of the Raleigh Home Guards—is that correct?"

Julian kept his face impassive. Whit's colonelcy was news to him; he could not doubt that Whit had the papers to prove it. He touched the wallet in his pocket, which the gambler had passed over to him on their way to the field. "Colonel Cameron," he murmured. "Temporarily on leave from his command." He watched Crittenden narrowly, glad that punctilio was served so easily. Crandall was in uniform, after all: it was always simpler for one officer to shoot another.

"Shall we place them now?"

"The light will hold, I think."

Julian walked to the riverbank for another needless glance at the sky. April still bathed the James in a silver glow. The dry meadow on which they had just marked their ground seemed to glow silver too: even the rough escarpment above them was softened by the approaching twilight. Across the stream Richmond sat proudly on her hills, ignoring the antlike bustle of these visiting firebrands. . . . There was no sound beside the murmur of the river, the soft clump of a horse's hoofs as the animal sought what grass he could reach from the shafts of the buggy. Tanner had insisted on that buggy, in case one of the parties was wounded; Julian's instrument case was already open on the seat where Dick sat contentedly, honing a scalpel. Placed well out of the line of fire, it could be brought to the field in a moment.

The two principals in the quarrel stood on the field of honor with folded arms. Crandall's eyes were on the ground, his face impassive. Whit, whose demeanor had been faultless now that the dare was taken, stood a little apart from the others, apparently lost in reverie. Julian had seen that expression before, when the gambler had sat behind a straight flush in poker and waited for the betting to start. . . . This is his moment, thought Julian; come what may, he'll play it to the hilt and love it. He pulled his mind back to realities as Tanner walked around the buggy with a flat satinwood case under his arm.

"Let's get it over, Chisholm. We've work to do in Richmond."

Like the others, Tanner's calm was genuine enough. The duel was a common thing in all their lives, especially during these years inflamed by war. Few of them had ever paused to question its essential rightness as a short cut across an argument. Whit had accused Crandall of spying without justification; Crandall had insisted on disputing the charge on this field of honor. No one had asked if Whit deserved to be spied upon: even Crandall's mind had been trapped by the iron compulsion of a code. Tanner's flourish in opening the satinwood box merely set the seal to their ritual.

The two seconds withdrew to inspect the dueling pistols; Tanner, as the senior surgeon on the field, had already folded the cartel into his wallet. The postscript to the challenge would be added when the affair was over.

Crittenden sighted down a burnished barrel and offered the pistol for Julian's approval. "Smoothbore, Captain. Hair-triggered. A nine-inch barrel. A beautiful weapon—and a dangerous one. Will your man stand at thirty feet?"

"Thirty feet will do."

"As you see, I've paced the field. Will you check my measurements?"

"They'll do also, Captain," said Julian. "I think we should place them now. Will you toss?"

Crittenden took a coin from his pocket: Julian noted, without smiling, that it was a Federal two-bit piece. He wondered idly if it was a trophy of war—or a hedge against the future.

"Heads!"

"Heads it is, Captain Chisholm. You may choose the position; I'll give the word."

Whit stepped forward at his signal, and they paced down the field together to the spot Crittenden had marked with his sword. The gambler toed the mark with all the nonchalance of a dancing master heading a cotillion. Julian dropped his voice to a quick, savage whisper.

"For the last time, tell me where I'll find her."

"For the last time, that's my job."

Julian tried another approach, knowing in advance that it would leave Whit unruffled. "You aren't immortal, you know. What happens if Crandall knocks you down?"

"I'm betting the other way," said Whit. "Suppose I gave you Jane's Richmond address now—and lost. You'd have to kill our friend across the meadow before you dared visit her. I won't let you have his death on your conscience."

"I'd find some way of dodging him!"

"He's too stubborn a leech. Leave him to me, please." The gambler fitted the stock of the pistol into his right palm; the muzzle outlined the breast pocket of Julian's tunic. "You've my wallet safe? And my money belt?"

"Dick's holding that in the carriage."

"They're yours if I fall, my boy. Step back where you belong. Your opposite number is getting impatient."

Julian played his last card. "Tell me where to find my wife, or I'll stop the duel."

"How can you now?"

"By telling them who you really are."

Whit profiled to the field and sighted down his gun barrel. "No one knows who I really am, Julian. Or where my loyalties really belong. Myself, least of all." He considered that thought a moment as he rocked easily on his toes, an alert steel spring of a man who could face eternity with his tensile strength intact. "However, I can see you're desperate enough to ruin everything. Promise you won't fight Crandall?"

"I promise."

"You'll find Jane's address in the wallet," said Whit. "It's written across the top of her orders, in red ink. Read the street number backwards: it was my only precaution when I took it down in Washington."

Once again the pistol touched Julian's heart lightly. "And don't dare open that wallet until this is over. Stand where I can watch you. If your hand touches that pocket, I'll shoot you instead of Crandall."

Julian nodded and stepped out of the line of fire. Crittenden was repeating his instructions in a deep baritone. That, too, was part of the ritual: a singsong that most Southern gentlemen—and

410

many Southern rascals—had memorized since their teens. Julian glanced at Crandall. The counterspy had already profiled to the field and toed his mark as calmly as Whit. He breathed easily, the pistol lax in one fist. Julian knew that he would suck in his midriff with the last command, in case Whit should aim low. His gray bulk made a much better target against that fresh green background. By contrast, Whit's black broadcloth made him look knife-thin as he waited for the word. At this distance he still seemed wrapped in his tranquil dream; but Julian knew that his eyes would never leave Crandall now. Probably they had already drilled a neat hole in the counterspy's tunic, where the last button opened incautiously to show a triangle of shirt front beneath.

"Gentlemen, prepare to receive the word."

The two duelists tightened within themselves, as though invisible levers had snapped their shoulders taut. The pistol arms snapped downward like flails that needed only a touch to fan into action, though the long barrels, pointed rigidly downward, all but grazed the earth.

"Are you ready?"

The next pause seemed hours long, though Julian—timing it by the throb of Crandall's jugular—knew that pauses were needless now, as needless as the twin nods of affirmation from both ends of the field.

"Fire!"

The double bark of the pistols bounced from the bluff above them; the twin plumes of smoke, fanning the afternoon air, vanished instantly in the breeze. Watching Crandall rather than his own man, as punctilio demanded, Julian saw that Whit had chosen another target after all. The great vein at the base of the counterspy's jaw had burst like a small red volcano, drenching the tunic beneath it—though the crash of the report had blunted the deadly chunk of the bullet as it smashed the spinal column and roved upward into the brain. Crandall was dead on his feet: Julian had seen that same wound too often to doubt his verdict. Captain Crittenden could sprint across the meadow if he liked: a field surgeon knew that his man would go down like a poled ox long before the second could reach his side.

Then he heard Dick slap the reins in the buggy, the screech of the wheels on grass—and turned to Whit for the first time. Even before he could kneel beside him, he knew that there was no need

411

for the orderly to bring his instrument case. Graceful even in death the gambler had spread-eagled on the grass; the red stain that welled across his tightly buttoned broadcloth was the only jarring note.

"Straight through the heart," said Dick. "Instantaneous. They aren't all so lucky, are they, Doc?"

But Julian's hand had already darted to his own breast pocket. He would hate himself afterward for this, though the movement was purely instinctive. After all, he could not breathe until he had assured himself that there was an address inside Whit's wallet. A Richmond street number, scrawled backward, in red ink.

He looked down at his friend to ask a silent pardon. The gambler's eyes were wide open in a grotesque stare. The gambler's lips still curved faintly, as though he were smiling at a joke all his own.

v

Tanner's eyes were on him as he emptied the contents of Whit's wallet on the desk top, but Julian's hands were steady enough. The senior surgeon could not see Jane's orders: he had stolen a moment, on their return from the hospital, to hide them in his shirt, where the parchment still seemed to betray itself by a faint crackle. There had been no time to check further: he was trusting to luck, now, as he exposed his friend's effects in the office lamplight.

As he had hoped, the wallet's contents were quite normal. A neatly folded wad of Confederate bills enclosed a dozen gold pieces. An address book contained only the names and office numbers of commissary bigwigs in Richmond. In a leather frame, a strange but very pretty girl laughed out at them impudently. . . . He studied the inscription across the bottom:

Toute à toi. Odette.

"His wife, perhaps?" hazarded Tanner.

"I think not. Mr. Cameron wasn't a marrying man."

The senior surgeon frowned. "He was well known here in Richmond—and well liked, according to young Crittenden. . . . You signed the final statement of particulars?"

"It's on its way to headquarters now."

"Then we can consider the affair closed. Poor young man, he

should have thought twice before challenging Tracy Crandall. The fellow was a bit of a parvenu, but he's given his proofs a dozen times. Never failed to drop his man."

Julian just escaped smiling. "Nor had Whit."

Tanner put his hand on Julian's shoulder. "May I say I'm sorry, without giving offense? Our friends can't always win, even when they're in the right."

"You think the attack was justified?"

"Entirely. As I say, Crandall was an incurable busybody—and a boor in the bargain. It's too bad he was also a dead shot at twenty paces."

So that was Tanner's verdict on the affair; if it was Richmond's judgment as well, reflected Julian, he could take heart. So far he had not dared ask himself what his next move would be.

Fortunately, the business of transferring their cases to the hospital train had kept him much too busy to think. Tanner or one of the orderlies had been at his side every moment since they had returned from the dueling ground with their ghastly burden. . . . He shook off his inertia, now that he could relax into his first breathing spell. Tanner had already settled on the desk top to hug a booted knee, and Julian tried to keep the resentment out of his stare. The senior surgeon had been more than understanding, yet it seemed now as though he would never leave.

"Perhaps I should make sure about the funeral?"

"Dick is handling that for you," said Tanner. "Burial's at Hollywood Cemetery, tomorrow forenoon." He arranged the gold pieces from the wallet in a neat stack. "There's enough here to buy Mr. Cameron a soldier's grave and a suitable headstone."

Julian choked a protest. After all, it would have amused Whit mightily to learn that he was to rest with military honors—and a colonel's bays: it was an epitaph he could hardly have improved, even with his talent for improvisation. . . . Once again he asked himself why Whit's death should refuse to register on his brain. It still seemed a grotesque joke that they would both be chuckling over tomorrow.

Tanner's voice brought him back. "It's hard to say good-by at a time like this. Shall we just shake hands and hope for an early reunion?"

"That's much the best way, isn't it, sir?"

"Can we give you a lift to Main Street?"

"Thank you, no. I'll close my desk and walk; I'd like to get used to this furlough gradually."

"I'm sorry again that it didn't come at a happier time."

He could not believe that Tanner had really gone, even when he heard the last hospital cart rattle down the cobbles. Standing at the window, he was in time to see it round the corner on its way to the yards and the waiting train. Behind him the big whitewashed barn that had housed their wards echoed with emptiness in the dark. He was alone in that emptiness at long last; alone with Jane's address burning in its hiding place. . . . Free to go to her when he wished, free to bring her the news that her work was ended. Yet he was almost afraid to move.

Why, when Whit Cameron had given his life to remove the last obstacle, should he fear to stir? Why should he be positive that eyes were still watching him, from that warehouse across the way?

He shook off the too-tangible nightmare and sat down at his desk again. Spinning his chair so that he sat with his back to the window, he fumbled cautiously in his shirt and drew out the square sheet of parchment that Whit had guarded so well. Now that there was time to read it, he felt the print blur in his eagerness.

Like the paper he had uncovered at St. Marys long ago, this one was merely a printed form, stamped with the great seal of Union and signed with the squiggle of Lincoln's Secretary of War. An order instructing one Harriet May to terminate her local services on receipt, to consider herself on inactive duty thereafter. There was no formal address: apparently it was understood that the order would be delivered by hand. Whit's memorandum of the street number in Richmond had been jotted down on the margin: the red ink clashed with the neat spider scrawl on the ruled lines.

Harriet May, 427 Stanhope Street, Richmond, Virginia. He knew the street well enough—a narrow, second-class residential thoroughfare that snaked its way downhill from Main to the river. He had followed it a dozen times, as a short cut from hotel to hospital; he even remembered that number 427 stood less than a half mile from the hospital door, though he could not describe the house itself.

Harriet May. He wondered how she had chosen such a nondescript title when she ceased to be Mrs. Kirby Anderson of Atlanta. Or why she had dared to make her new residence in the heart of the Confederate capital. He could not doubt now that it was Jane who had helped the last break from Libby to a successful conclusion—that 427 Stanhope Street was the headquarters for another underground railroad. Perhaps she had felt that the time for elaborate façades was past, that only speed and daring counted now.

If such was the case—and how could he think otherwise, knowing Jane so well?—he was worse than cowardly to linger here, afraid that he would be followed if he paused at her door.

A step sounded in the cave of the warehouse. He thrust the Union order into his shirt front again and whirled to the door. But it was only Dick, his orderly—asleep on his feet from weariness.

"Thought you'd gone, Doc. Just came through to douse the glim."

"I'm going now, Dick."

"Shall I stop for you at the hotel in the morning?"

Julian reeled a little as he got up from the chair: his mind, whirling in its tight vortex of indecision, had forgotten how tired his body could still be after a day like this.

"You needn't, Dick. Perhaps you've forgotten I'm on furlough—as of now."

He verified that statement with his watch. Two antemeridian, April 2, 1865. Whit had said that this day would go down in history as the date that Richmond fell.

"Maybe *you've* forgotten the funeral, Captain." Dick's voice was faintly reproachful.

"My friend Mr. Cameron was a strange man," said Julian. "He expected to die with his clothes on; he insisted that he be buried without mourners."

"You mean we can both sleep late?"

"As late as you like." For an instant he played with the temptation to pass on Whit's warning to the orderly, though he was sure that Dick would never believe it. Since winter the air had been filled with rumors of capitulation; one more would hardly ruffle the soporific calm that brooded over Virginia tonight.

"Have you thought what you'd do if Richmond fell suddenly, Dick?"

He had expected the question to startle the ex-pharmacist, but the boy only grinned and nodded as briskly as his drowsiness would allow. "I'd head for home, Doc. Make me a separate peace. What about yourself?"

"I wish I knew," confessed Julian. "Right now I'd like to sleep a week. I think I'll start in on that part now. Don't come near the hotel tomorrow: I'll shoot you on sight."

The orderly blew out the lamp as Julian locked the main door of the hospital. They left together by the emergency entrance; it seemed odd that the admitting orderly's desk should be empty now, the candle in its hurricane lamp vanished with the record book. Only the villainous reek of boar's-head tobacco lingered. Julian could picture that same orderly now, still champing on his corncob, still laboring through his endless paper work as the hospital train rocked south to Danville.

"I sleep on the river side," said Dick. "Good night, Doc."

He stood in the blue moonlight, watching the boy vanish in the shadows along the James; then, obeying a sudden impulse, he walked up to the warehouse across the way and thrust a lighted lucifer into the cave of the entrance. Black-boarded emptiness leaped out of the darkness: not even the ghost of Tracy Crandall was there to molest him now. Yet he was sure that his departure had not gone unnoticed. He cursed the stupidity of that insistence as he walked toward the center of town, choosing the long way to Main Street by instinct, shunning the short cut that passed 427 Stanhope.

At the first crossing he pulled up just in time to avoid the soldier who sprawled across the sidewalk in sleep, with his head propped on his haversack. The bundle of gray rags was inert, though the snore that ruffled the matted whiskers was real enough. Even in the wash of moonlight he could not see the man's face clearly as he stepped over the spread-eagled legs and continued on his way. Memory stirred only as he turned into the steep pitch that led to the lights of Main Street. It was too late, then, to check the accuracy of the picture that leaped at him like a tangible banshee. . . . This afternoon he had told himself that dozing soldiers were a commonplace in Richmond, at any hour: he had not even tried to remember the gray bundle that had slumped in the warehouse door. Tired as he was, it had never occurred to him that Crandall's deputy and this other gray bundle might be one and the same.

He was sure of it when he paused at the next crossing and heard the pad of feet behind him. He tested his conviction at the corner of Main Street, pausing to light a cheroot with his back to the route he had just traversed, hearing the soft shuffle of footsteps hesitate too. When he swung down the pavement again, he risked a quick glance. The street seemed empty in the moonlight, but he was positive that gray rags had melted into the shadows with his turning.

Perhaps it was only a footpad, after all—or a deserter eager to ask his help in rejoining his command. Doctors were approached with stranger requests in times like these. He could wait, just this side of the Main Street lights, and give the man a chance to come up; he could emulate Whit, and collar him. But if this were really Crandall's deputy—and only his desperately tired mind refused to grant that certainty now—he guessed that he had seen the last of him tonight. Only by leading him to Jane's door could he bring the fellow into the open.

He walked on, with that thought riveting the back of his brain; the soft pad of footsteps picked up the rhythm of his own. Hesitation, he knew, was fatal; nor could he wander aimlessly about these empty streets. There were still lights on Main, a few drunken whoops from the nearest bar. He turned through the swinging lattice and drank three bourbons without tasting them at all—taking care to stand at the plate-glass window, in full view of the street, while he drank. . . . There was no stir of gray in the shadows outside, no sign that the presence of a tired young surgeon in this bar was marked on the calendar of the Confederate counterespionage service.

The fourth bourbon tapped its own warning between his eyes, though he could still focus clearly enough as he glanced out casually at the street. Somehow he must shake off that incubus outside. He could not let his brain insist that there was no incubus, now that it had begun to loosen its tension in alcohol. Perhaps he could outrun the threat, if he could not outwalk it. He stepped boldly to the sidewalk again, ready to put the hope to the test.

This time the soldier was dozing—or pretending to doze—under the tin awning of the hardware store across the way. A streak of lamplight outlined his figure clearly: Julian saw that he had chosen the vantage point with care, for it commanded both doors of the bar, while allowing the watcher himself to remain invisible to anyone standing inside. Only his quick exit had revealed the soldier's hiding place: the fellow faded from view instantly as Julian started across Main Street, and the sidewalk under the tin awning seemed empty of life when he stepped up from the curb.

It was small comfort to know that his menace was flesh and blood, and not a phantom of his own devising. Yet he felt his spirits rise as he swung up Main Street—walking as fast as a Southern officer could on a night in April, without being accused of running. His heels rang a brave rhythm on the plank sidewalk —loud enough, now, to cover the whisper of his pursuer's feet in the shadows that lay deep along the store fronts.

At the next crossing he paused one more time, grateful that he had a reason. The moonlit peace was disturbed by a strange sound for Richmond—"Yankee Doodle," sung from bursting lungs, the happy-go-lucky cadence bouncing in crazy echoes from the shuttered business houses on both sides of Main. The singer, Julian perceived, was idling down the street in a decrepit buggy, with a horse to match; as he drew nearer, it was evident that he was as drunk as he was happy. An infantry lieutenant, wearing the insignia of Ewell's corps with proper pride, and flaunting his dizzy bliss to the world. Even the song he was caroling fitted the picture, now that Julian could make out the words:

> "But Doodle knows as well as I
> That when his zeal has freed 'em
> He'd see a million darkies die
> Before he'd help to feed 'em!"

"Am I right, Captain?"

The buggy wheels screeched as the boy slammed on his brake; the horse started to rear in the traces, then thought better of the effort. Julian put a foot on the hub and steadied the lieutenant in time to save him from pitching into the street.

"Which way's the Spotswood?"

"I live there—shall we drive up together?"

"Surest thing y'know, Cap'n."

He was in the buggy before the boy could speak, with the reins twined in one fist. The horse gave a start as he felt the whip tease his back, then broke into a splayfooted trot that threatened, for a moment, to rock the wheels from their axles. The lieutenant whooped with joy and surrendered the situation to Julian.

"Watch that plug. I promised to deliver him in one piece."

"Easy does it," said Julian. "You want another drink, don't you?"

"How'd you guess?"

The lieutenant lolled on the worn upholstery and raised his voice again in song. Julian found that he could join with no effort at all. In spirit he was still striding down the pavement a block behind, and fighting the desire to break into a run.

As the carriage rocked on, he looked back and saw his pursuer —a forlorn silhouette in the moonlight—standing in the empty street with arms akimbo. . . . Tracy Crandall, he thought gleefully, would have anticipated this and kept a horse of his own in reserve. I must keep rolling, before that gray ghost has the same idea.

At the Spotswood he shouted for the night porter and prayed that the bar had defied the law again and stayed open for the benefit of Saturday-night furloughs, like the boy at his side. The porter's seal-brown face opened in a grin as he felt hard money slap his palm.

"Get him a drink, if he insists, then put him to bed. I'll see to the buggy."

The lieutenant protested mildly, with the hotel porter's arm already linked in his. "Why not join me, Cap'n? Orderly's about somewhere; *he'll* put the plug to bed."

"Thank you, no. I've an errand to run anyhow." Instinct told him to move quickly, and keep moving, before this amazing piece of luck slipped through his hands.

The wheels protested as he swung the horse's head in a wide arc and headed up Main. A detour first: the porter must have no chance to report his direction later. . . . But he could not resist the temptation to force the animal into another trot once he had dropped the hotel entrance behind. He had waited a long time for this moment; he would have been less than human had he not rushed headlong to meet and explore it.

The back alleys he had chosen seemed interminable, and he threaded them at the nag's best speed, risking a collision with more than one rainspout and sagging wall. Stanhope Street at last —and a dour anticlimax as the horse took the steep pitch with spavined legs flying. Julian soon found that he must mend his pace or jettison the buggy on the curb; he had forgotten that a man on foot could move more nimbly than a buggy on a hillside.

Twice he reined in to consult house numbers by the uncertain light of the corner lamps. The whole street seemed boarded to the eaves or snoring behind its padlocked doors. . . . He remembered the portico of High Cedars and how proudly it had soared against this same moon. The operator of an underground railroad could not always work from a country estate.

He had swung wide, to enter Stanhope Street almost from the top: 427 was nearer the river than he remembered, and the houses seemed more down-at-heel with each screech of his unoiled axles. He wondered if that screech would waken her from sleep—if some inner sense would warn her that he was coming.

The carriage step at the next corner had a number carved on its face; even before he deciphered it by the wan light of the street lamp, he knew that this was her block. Between the lights the street was bathed in the blue dusk of moonlight sifted through the leaves of a few stunted lindens. A bleak, empty-faced street, lifeless as that cold, pale radiance pouring from the sky. . . . Only at 425 was there a stir of life. He heard the ribald thud of the piano and saw the lamplight through drawn blinds. A half dozen horses were hobbled at the stoop; most of them were patiently dozing as they waited for their riders to emerge.

He could not believe that Jane would establish herself next to a bordello, however discreet the exterior; but there was no mistaking this blind-eyed house or the profession it housed so casually. He gave the horse its head and jumped down to the carriage block at 427 with his heart thudding in his throat. The music followed him across the rank lawn; he heard a cork pop behind the drawn blinds and the rumble of male laughter—but it was too late to stop for details or prying eyes. Especially now, when 427—a gaunt misanthrope of a house in its half acre of weedy, unfenced garden —looked untenanted and content in its desolation.

Perhaps the dark had deceived him. He paused on the grass-choked walk to make sure that the glimmer at an upstairs window was only the reflection of the moon on glass, and not the winking flame of a candle inside. Then he was on the porch, with no memory of a headlong dash up the steps. Dust choked him as he stamped on the rotting floor boards; the door under his hands was solid as an extension of the wall, its lock nailed down from the outside; the windows along the veranda had been nailed down, too, and boarded from within. So, he discovered, had the folding cellar doors, when he tested them with a reckless boot heel; so had the kitchen door, when he groped his way through the weeds to put his weight against it.

He risked a lucifer to verify the address on the carriage block—427 Stanhope. He could not doubt that Whit had copied it correctly in Washington. Yet this house had surely been empty for months, and boarded solidly to keep out unwanted scalawags. He could see the picture clearly: the solid family, with just enough money to decamp to the mountains at Grant's inexorable approach, with just enough brains to make their home thiefproof against an eventual return. . . . The cellars of 427 Stanhope had never harbored men with prison sweat upon them. Those boarded stables had never sounded to the stamping of a mounted bushwhacker guard. He could be sure of that much, without forcing a lock.

Whit, and the War Department in Washington, had been in error after all. If Jane had planned to use this house, she had been stopped short long before she could cross the threshold.

Behind him, in the cozy half-darkness next door, the piano began to thump again; even the hobbled horses at the stoop stirred unhappily as a man's basso profundo all but rattled the blinds. He caught up to his own horse just as the animal had started to meander downhill on business of his own. With one hand anchored on the bit, he paused long enough to heave a stone against the harlots' shutters—then stepped into the buggy again. The crazy rhythm of the song did not even slacken as he drove away, though an angry shout followed him down the pitch of Stanhope Street. . . .

At the hotel entrance again, he tossed the reins to the groom and wakened the man promptly by ringing a coin on the pavement.

"Stable this bag of bones. He's brought me bad luck tonight."

In the entrance to the bar he paused to shake himself together. As he had hoped, the tall, ornate room was still wide open and roaring with trade. His lieutenant was at a corner table, even drunker than before—but Julian elbowed his way to the bar before the youth could shout a greeting.

"Bourbon. You can bring the bottle."

He had not sought this kind of oblivion in years. Not since the days when Lucy Sprague was a hunger gnawing at his heart. But the frustration that had begun to creep over him was too great to be borne. Later, perhaps, he could adjust his mind to his loss. Later still he would try to convince himself that he had been mildly insane tonight. Only a hopeless romantic, overwrought by a friend's death, could hope to find a wife again so easily. Only a die-hard lover would go on believing that Jane was still alive.

Proof to the contrary had offered its mute negative to that optimism, among the weeds on Stanhope Street.

He tried to face that proof squarely, to accept it at last. For tonight, at least, it was easier to pour another drink—and raise it in a solemn toast to the officer standing at his elbow. The man's face had already begun to merge with the others in the crowded room as they clinked glasses. Whisky slopped over the bar as he poured again, but the fresh glass reached his lips without mishap. He heard a voice propose another toast, and recognized it vaguely as his own.

"To war, sir!"

"To our Cause!"

"No, Major. Just to war—the normal state of man."

He waited for the room to still under the blasphemy, but the babble went on regardless. The bar at the Spotswood House had seen years of war and shouting officers; the bar could afford to smile back at this drunken young doctor. Perhaps it was a tacit admission that the young doctor was right. Packed to the doors with officers, jingling with silver spurs, shining with gold-crusted collars, it seemed a living proof that war could last forever.

He drank once more to that conviction—and again to the memory of Whit Cameron, who had bet wrong for once. He tried to drink to the memory of a wife he would never see again, and threw the glass aside to cradle the bottle in his arms. He had felt alone before, in larger crowds than this; but this was a new loneliness. Even in wartime a man seldom lost his best friend and the woman he loved in a single day.

When he weaved up the stairway to his room he noted, with no surprise, that his gray ghost was waiting at the end of the hall —and feigning sleep again in the curve of the stair well. For a moment he almost yielded to the temptation to waken him from that spurious doze. Then he remembered that it was hardly an hour to dawn. Even a ghost had the right to a little rest. Even a ghost (he all but laughed aloud at his consideration) would resent the assurance that he was wasting his time.

vi

Church bells pealed through his stupor in great billowing waves. He shivered and groped for sleep again, and knew vaguely that the sun was blazing at his windows now, that the heavy rep curtains were swelling in the breeze, as though they moved with the cadence of the bells. It was quiet after the bells, though the curtains still whipped across his bed, breaking his semi-slumber. Then—with no sense of transition—he heard scattered pistol shots from the street outside. The shouts of riders, mingled with the sound of wagon wheels turning at top speed. The thud of an explosion that seemed to come from far away.

Wide awake (and realizing that he had been half waking for the past hour), he sat up in bed and groped for his watch on the side table. The table was bare, and so was the topsy-turvy room. Even his carpet slippers were missing when he dropped his feet to the floor and felt his bare legs cringe in the whip of the breeze at the wide-open window.

He remembered distinctly that he had opened those windows wide last night, just before he had shucked his uniform to the floor and sprawled his way into the bed. There was no uniform now; even the strip of carpet had gone. So had his other clothing in the open armoire. So had his instrument case, his portmanteau, and the military cloak he had worn since Vicksburg. . . . He staggered toward the dresser, tripping over the empty drawers that had spilled pell-mell to the floor. His silver-backed brushes had vanished, along with his toilet set. The pier glass in the wall above had been cracked deliberately. Across it the same vandal's hand had scrawled an obscenity in lampblack, no less pungent because of its brevity.

Julian stared at his broken image, while his naked body shivered in the blast from the window. No, he wasn't quite naked: a leather belt surrounded his chest like a *ceinture*. The handles of two dueling pistols were thrust between the leather and his skin, along with a folded sheet of parchment. . . . As his mind groped back to complete sanity, he saw that this was Whit Cameron's money belt, which he had worn since the duel.

He remembered thrusting the two pistols into it just before he stripped off his shirt last night. The folded parchment, it seemed, had been another afterthought—one of those solemn precautions that inebriates and children practice so carefully, long after the need is past. Yet he was glad that the thieves had not taken Jane's final orders from Washington. It was good to hold that bit of parchment in his hand, to stare down at her neatly written *nom de guerre*, as he sank on the bed again and struggled to collect his thoughts.

From where he sat he could look into the empty hall, which seemed ominously quiet for this late hour. He shivered again in the draft as he pushed the door shut with one foot and reached for a blanket. The vandals had left him one, after all, though they had stripped his bed of pillows and counterpane while he slept the sleep of the just—and the drunkard. Apparently the blanket had been twisted about his body as he snored his way through that last pint of bourbon; finding his wallet and watch on the side table, they had not risked wakening him.

So much for the pattern of thoroughgoing robbery. His assets at the moment were an untouched skin, two thousand dollars in gold, a pair of discharged smoothbores, and an official order from an enemy that might even now be marching in force on Main Street. He crossed to the window and saw that that fear was premature, though every carriage and gig in Richmond choked the roadway. Judging by the way the sunlight slanted, it was already late afternoon; if he read these desperate faces right, they were not the first in the sluggish cavalcade that wound downhill to the river bridges.

He stood in the ambush of his window curtain, mesmerized by the sight. This was no cross section of the Confederate capital, despite the hodgepodge of vehicles. The rich, as always, were fleeing with their jewels sewed in their women's bodices; the poor would stay behind, to taste the Yankees' mercy at first hand.

He counted new beavers and smartly frilled bonnets by the dozen—their owners hunched under buggy hoods and the sunshades of phaetons and surreys, a shamed aristocracy decamping before the first smell of powder. There were uniforms in the rout, though most of them were worn by members of the Home Guard: government clerks who had been forced to man the breastworks since winter, graybeards who flaunted their Mexican War medals even at this moment of shame. . . . Every eye had the same glaze, the same inward stare. Terrified by their own scareheads, shocked by the inevitable choice that they had put off too long, they were running for their lives—bombproof and his wife, government potentate and reluctant guardsman alike.

He felt no urge to join the scramble for the bridges and the sanctuary of the south bank of the James. There was something grotesque about that elbowing hurry, something repelling. A fragile racing sulky danced through the procession like a gadfly, only to splinter a wheel against a cruising dray. Julian watched the dandy at the reins leap for his life as the dray rolled on, watched him cut harness and canter down the sidewalk on his trotter's back, for all the world like a circus ringmaster out of his proper element.

No one laughed at the sight; no one so much as raised his eyes from his own obsession. Julian drew back from the window frame: he had seen enough of exodus.

His own exodus still required attention; a second glance at the mirror reminded him that he could not leave the room as he was. The blanket, he found, made a toga of sorts. He kicked open his door and strode into the hall.

At first glance the hall seemed as gutted as the bedroom had been—the carpet slashed, the floor boards trampled by a score of muddy boots. Doors gaped wide on either side: he saw that most of the bedrooms had been ransacked quite as thoroughly as his own. The clean-picked desolation shocked his mind awake more effectively than the actual glimpse of Richmond in full retreat. If the town had started to empty long ago, so had the Spotswood House: the fact that the vandals had dared to be so thorough was proof enough of that.

He heard a quick, ratlike scurry in a room to the left and pivoted with a pistol in his hand—just as a brace of Negro chambermaids burst into the hall with their arms full of plunder, squealed at the sight of the gun, and plunged for the shelter of the stair well. They were still squealing as they vanished; he lowered the dueling pistol and all but smiled at his own melodrama. The wenches, he reflected, had waited a long time to rob their betters. There was rough justice in the fact that the carpets of Richmond's best hotel would grace the puncheon floors of shanty town tonight.

One door at the end of the hall was closed and locked. He rattled the knob automatically. Inured to shock though he was, he found himself staring when he met General Clayton Randolph's eyes in the cautiously opened crack.

Uncle Clayton stood motionless as the door swung wide—an aged jack rabbit frozen in the act of flight. He wore the dark traveling clothes of a civilian, and his manner was as modest as his cravat. To Julian he seemed as ludicrous as the gutted rooms that flanked his own neat suite. . . . He took a tentative step forward and laid a hand on his uncle's broadcloth arm—if only to assure himself that this apparition was flesh and blood. He had known that General Randolph reserved a suite at the Spotswood at all times. It was simply incredible that he should be stranded in Richmond now.

"What's the meaning of this?" Even now the general's voice had lost none of its forensic boom.

"I might ask you that same question, Uncle."

"Come in, my boy. Come in quickly. No gentleman should walk through a public hall naked."

His uncle's suite was in wild disorder, but Julian saw at once that the disorder had been created by its occupant: trapped though he was, General Randolph had been shrewd enough to double-lock his door last night. Two small carpetbags stood packed and waiting. A uniform coat sprawled over a sofa; enough linen for ten men spilled unwanted from a mahogany highboy; in a clothespress several pairs of riding boots winked reproachfully at their owner from between the skirts of a full-dress brigadier's overcoat. For all the havoc, Julian noted that Uncle Clayton's civilian garb was a perfect fit—save for the slight bulge at both armpits which advertised a well-stuffed money belt.

"In another moment you'd have missed me," said the general. He frowned abstractedly at Julian, as though his nephew were a stranger. "I'm to join the Cabinet now as a military aide."

"Don't tell me Mr. Davis is still in town?"

"Mr. Davis was warned at church that Richmond must be evacuated today. General Lee has abandoned his lines at Petersburg and is moving to the west." Uncle Clayton spoke with a kind of controlled bitterness, as though he were lecturing a child who could not be expected to understand. "Naturally the rumor has spread like swamp fire since noon. Look out the window for the result."

"But you, Uncle! I thought you were dispatched to Nassau."

"I *was* dispatched to Nassau, as of yesterday. Unfortunately, I was ordered to a Cabinet meeting for instructions, and the session was late. I missed my transport—a hospital train to Danville." Uncle Clayton took up an ornate beaver and tested it before his cheval glass. Julian saw that he was all but pouting with regret as he discarded it for a less conspicuous slouch hat.

"Surely you can still get through."

"Naturally," snapped the general. "As it happens, my mission to Nassau is canceled. Tomorrow the government moves to Carolina. Who can say where it'll move next?"

"And you must stay with it to the end?"

"Such are my orders."

The pout deepened as Uncle Clayton drew his hatbrim over one eyebrow. In that rig, thought Julian, he looks like a gentleman masquerading as a cattle thief. No wonder he's sulking in his broadcloth. It'll make a poor ending to his memoirs.

"Don't let me detain you, Uncle," he murmured. The sympathy in his tone was real enough: he was almost sorry for Clayton Randolph now.

"I've still a moment. They're holding the presidential train in Manchester. The archives train went out hours ago." Even in his discontent the general could not avoid strutting a little. "You may believe this or not, Julian, but our Cabinet is still discussing ways and means to stop the enemy. Mr. Davis sent two additional telegrams before he'd take Lee's order as final."

"I can understand your impatience. Might I ask why you're out of uniform?"

"You may indeed. I feel that my life is too valuable to risk. Later, perhaps, I shall don the Confederate gray again."

Much later, thought Julian. When the shooting's well behind us, and the first reunion of the Old Guard is legal. You'll be even heavier in the midriff then, but your tailor will see to it that your tunic fits perfectly, that the stars at your collar are still burnished.

Aloud he said only, "As you see, my room was robbed last night —rather thoroughly. Could you spare enough clothes to make me decent?"

"Help yourself, my boy. The place will be rifled soon enough."

Julian tossed off his impromptu toga and upended a drawer packed with linen. Ignoring Uncle Clayton's scandalized eyes, he selected a pair of underdrawers, a uniform shirt with his cousin George's monogram.

"Do you have any of George's coats left, Uncle? They'll fit me better than yours." George would have grinned at this moment, he thought. Particularly at the snort of disapproval the old goat feels duty bound to give me now.

"There's a duster of mine in the clothespress that'll do nicely, Julian."

"Sorry, Uncle. You can make your separate peace when you like. I'm still on furlough."

Watching Clayton Randolph in the cheval glass, he saw that his eyes had widened in simple incredulity as his nephew stepped into a pair of George's fawn dress trousers.

"That's a cavalry uniform, Julian."

"Does it matter now?"

"Surely you can wear civilian clothes today with honor."

"George's uniform suits my purpose better."

He did not elaborate on that flat statement as he tried on a brand-new campaign hat. A slash in the band, and it fitted well enough. George's frogged dress coat was another matter. He had outweighed his cousin by a good twenty pounds; the seams cracked as he tried to force his shoulders into a semblance of a fit.

"Am I too young to pass for a general, Uncle?"

He kept Clayton Randolph's face in view as he profiled before the mirror in the gold-starred coat. Surprisingly enough, it was both snug and comfortable, save for a slight fulness at the midriff. He found time to wonder if his uncle had dared to lace himself in stays before he strutted at a levee. . . .

"Take off my coat, Julian!"

He came back to Clayton Randolph's sputter with a good-humored smile. Thinking of his uncle's peacock-bright past, it was hard to believe that this dingy old gentleman and the foppish brigadier were one and the same.

"After all, I must have a uniform——"

"Take off my coat! I forbid you to wear it!"

"I think you forget yourself, sir."

Clayton Randolph could merely sputter now: words were lost in that choking anger. "I tell you, I forbid——"

Julian stepped back from the glass. "Look at yourself, Uncle. You've given up the right to forbid anything."

The words shocked General Randolph into an icy calm. Here, at least, was an insult he could understand. "Go on, sir."

"Yesterday you were prepared to run out on your government in its last hours. Today you'll drop off the President's train at the first division point. What can it matter if I wear the uniform you're deserting?"

Clayton Randolph bore down on him with a hand upraised, and pulled up short when Julian pressed the barrel of one dueling pistol hard against his chest.

"So you'd commit murder, too?"

"Why not? Posterity would thank me, if it knew the truth."

He sensed that his point was made before Clayton Randolph dropped his eyes. "You'd better hurry to the depot, Uncle. Even a special train won't wait forever."

With a carpetbag in each fist, General Randolph was something less than imposing. But he paused for an exit line just the same.

"Julian Chisholm, you're no longer my nephew."

"May I count on that?"

The door slammed, and Julian sat down weakly before the clothespress. He found that he was laughing, though he was in no mood for laughter as he fumbled through the uniforms for a pair of riding boots.

He found George's pistols later, in a corner of the wardrobe chest. There was even a bullet mold and percussion caps. He tested the lead pellets in his own smoothbores and found that they fitted well enough, with a bit of greased leather folded ahead of the charge to make them snug in the barrel. . . . The solemn business of providing himself with weapons preoccupied him for a time: with the two pistols thrust in his belt, he did not mind the lack of a sword. Swords, after all, were anachronisms when an army is on its last retreat.

For a long moment he stood before the cheval glass to plan his next move. The mirror gave back the very image of a black-browed brigadier, complete from spurs to scowl. He drew on George Randolph's riding gloves, and forced himself to smile a little as he asked his dead cousin's pardon once again. The initials of the Confederate Army were a bit tarnished on the webbed belt that girded his waist; he burnished them absently with a gloved thumb, and hoped that George would smile down from Valhalla on the gesture.

Then he clicked his heels smartly to his own image and walked out of Clayton Randolph's suite, leaving the door wide for the looters. Even now he guessed that his gray ghost would be waiting for him, somewhere in the gathering dusk. With Richmond falling about their ears, it was high time they struck a truce—or shot out their quarrel, once and for all.

vii

At the curb of Main Street he saw at once that there would be few, if any, street lamps lighted in Richmond tonight. Not that it mattered, with fires already dancing on more than one hillside. He felt the pavement rock with another explosion as he started to force his way across the street. This one seemed much nearer: windows glowed blood-red for an instant, as a pulse of flame leaped and died against the wild evening sky.

The solid mass of carriages that choked the roadway moved doggedly on, though heads ducked in unison under the threat of the blast. That one was an ammunition dump, thought Julian. Or a gunboat in the James blown up by its own crew. He remembered that General Ewell had given orders long ago regarding the cotton and tobacco warehouses along the riverbanks. Perhaps the military was beginning to fire them now, as it pulled out in earnest. There was nothing like one fire to start another—whether a spark leaped in the wind or in an arsonist's brain.

Crossing Main Street, he found, was a major risk to life and limb while the traffic was really moving. He jumped back to the curb in time to avoid the threat of flying wheels, and dodged downhill with the stream until it slowed and blocked itself again. Then, ignoring the shouts of its occupants, he clambered over the roof of a bursting stagecoach, risked a flying leap to a farm wagon piled mountain-high with household goods, and, from that tottering perch, dropped to the axle of a second wagon and stepped down to the far sidewalk.

The turn to Stanhope Street was only a short block ahead. He must hurry, before Richmond's fast-merging fires destroyed his purpose in advance.

It was hard to resist the temptation to pause and make sure he was being followed; on that jostling sidewalk it was harder still to keep on one's feet and still risk a backward glance. Twice he swung wide to avoid fist fights that threatened to become general at any moment; once he doubled his own fists to force his way through a milling mob that had just burst the doors of a government commissary depot.

Here the air was full of a whitish haze as a score of men disputed the possession of as many flour sacks. There was a stench

430

of brine in the air from overturned hogsheads, a more pervasive reek of whisky which seemed to rise from the pavement itself. He saw why when he slipped in a rich brown flood and heard the ax crunch into a keg on the stoop above. Negroes and whites fought for position under the spurting bung. At the curb others knelt to drink from the flooded gutter. He stepped over a drunken Negro who had passed into oblivion with both arms embracing a side of bacon, his face clown-white from the battle of the flour sacks. He elbowed a soldier who had slashed off his insignia and was rocking on his heels like a shoddy bacchante, with a girl on each arm.

"Way for the general, folks! He's got important business!"

He ignored the whoops of laughter that followed him, the salt fish that missed his ear by inches and mushroomed against the store front ahead. Uncle Clayton's stars had made a path for him, after all; the jeers were real, too, but they had none of the undertones of riot. . . . More important, he was sure that he was followed now. He had sensed it even before that drunken shout had drawn a circle about his progress.

It was much quieter when he turned into Stanhope Street: this time he rejoiced in the strategy that had caused Jane to seek a hideaway in this mean quarter, where there was little to tempt the prowler. The pad of footsteps in the gloom behind him was all he had hoped for. Tonight he would meet his gray ghost face to face—at a meeting place of his own choice. To be precise, on the stoop of 427 Stanhope. He would prove beyond a doubt that the prize they both sought was gone forever, and insist he be followed no more. If his Nemesis refused to accept the evidence, he would prove that ghosts can stop bullets too.

With that much settled in his mind, he walked on almost tranquilly. A brisk but easy pace, to keep Nemesis alert without tiring him: the stride of a man who knew where he was going, a man who had no fear of pursuit. Here was the carriage block with 400 carved on its street side; here, in the center of that same city block, was the outline of the bordello, prim as ever against the light of burning Richmond.

Another explosion shook the air. He knew that it came from the river's edge, and flattened instinctively as a haze of sparks skyrocketed in the dark. Even at the distance he could hear the hiss of fire stabbing wood along the bank, the hungrier gasp of the river itself as it swallowed the aftermath of the burst. The rumble died, but the red glow continued to build against the sky. Stanhope Street dropped back into darkness with its sturdy silhouette untouched.

The ghost waited politely as Julian got to his feet. Only there were two ghosts, not one, when he looked a second time. A third shadow, patient as the others, blocked the street ahead. Even had he planned otherwise, he had no choice but to turn up the weed-choked path that led to 427.

He moved warily, with both wrists cocked; at that distance he could drop two of the trio, if he could get the pistols out in time —and if the carbine at the third ghost's armpit missed fire. . . . Then he was on the rotten floor boards of the porch, with both hands in the air and the muzzle of a second carbine hard against his lumbar muscles. Ghost number four, it seemed, had been waiting here for him since the beginning.

He forced a grin—and kept his hands discreetly high—as ghost number five stepped from the shadow of a pillar. He knew the whiskers instantly, and the scar that zigzagged up one cheekbone. Amos was anything but wraithlike as he chuckled in the dusty gloom. Amos, in a Confederate corporal's uniform, seemed to fit the moment perfectly. So, for that matter, did the trio on the lawn, as they moved up to the porch and ranged themselves beside their leader.

Amos came up easily and lifted the pistols from Julian's belt. "Seems we got each other wrong, Doc," he said pleasantly enough. "Let's don't go on makin' mistakes."

"Was it *you* in the warehouse door?"

"Course. Crandall could keep an eye on you. Why not us?"

Julian felt a great light burst behind his eyes. He steadied himself on a rotting porch pillar, feeling the intent stares and returning them with interest. "So this is your hide-out, after all?"

"You knew better than that last night," said Amos. "We wondered when you'd come back to make sure you were wrong. Fact is, Doc, 427 was bought as a blind—just in case. Too bad you didn't drop in next door and ask if all the girls were busy."

Julian vaulted the rail on that and went across the lawn on the run, with five gray-uniformed bushwhackers on his heels. A sixth bushwhacker, also in gray, barred his path as he stormed up the porch of 425 and raised his hand to the ornate brass knocker. Amos strolled up without reproving the guard and held Julian a moment more with his voice.

"Funny thing about 425, Doc. It *was* a sporting house until we bought it last fall. Business was wonderful, but the madame was nervous. Figured her young ladies needed a change of air with the Yankees coming. We left it just so when we took over. Lots of beds, when our friends from Libby and Belle Isle needed to rest up awhile. Lots of would-be customers too, of course—but it was easy to turn 'em away. All we did was hobble a string of our horses on the lawn and say the girls were busy."

Amos kept a wary eye on Julian as he came a step closer. The carbine in the guard's hand was still level. "Course it meant keeping a piano going and popping a wine cork now and then. Timmy here has a boy soprano to go with the music. Outside you'd swear it was a gal with a skinful of French champagne. Miss Jane claimed that Timmy carried things too far sometimes—but I figure he saved our lives."

"Is my wife here?"

"In the downstairs parlor, Doc. Sorry it isn't the best place for a lady to greet her husband, but this is war."

Bushwhacker and surgeon stared at each other for a silent moment; when the surgeon staggered a little under the bushwhacker's news, four pairs of hands steadied him instantly.

"I've news, too," said Julian. "Whit Cameron——"

"We know about Whit."

"Did you know he brought orders?"

Amos stared down at the folded paper that Julian slapped into his palm. The other heads bent over it, in unison with his own, as the door opened and slammed again.

She was waiting on an ottoman in the midst of the dim wilderness of Turkey carpet. A silk tent arched above her in lieu of ceiling. All about her there was a dusty sheen of mirrored walls: as Amos had said, their final hiding place had been a bordello in the grand manner. Now the mirrors echoed Jane endlessly, as she sat in her modest bonnet and the pelisse she had worn that day in Glasgow. Her hands were demure in her lap, and her eyes were downcast. Like the guardians on her lawn, she seemed to be waiting here for him—alertly patient, and certain that he must come to her at last. Here, in this bizarre silken cave, was the alembic that would help him to banish his private ghosts; here, at long last, were hands to open the dark garden that had prisoned him.

A great cry of thanksgiving welled in his throat, but he made himself pause in the doorway. He stood for a moment, taking her in as deliberately as he dared. Storing the memory deep, lest she vanish in that mirage of mirrors when he looked again.

Jane spoke, without raising her eyes. "You promised to wait. Until it was really over."

"It's over for you now, darling."

"You promised to let me decide that."

"Would you forgive me, if I had?"

"Not now," she said, and raised her face to him at last. He was already on his knees beside the ottoman, and his arms were about her. Only when their lips met could he be certain that she was real.

viii

Across the James, the burning city made a patina of red against the night. On the southern bank—where a bluff rose sheer above a meadow at the river's edge—a little cavalcade had just reined in. Six dragoons in Confederate gray, a man in a brigadier's uniform, a slim girl in a bonnet and pelisse, who rode her sidesaddle with an easy grace. An observer would have guessed that each rider was praying. Perhaps the group was paying a silent tribute in its own way. . . . There was no mistaking its eagerness, when it cantered briskly down the slope of the hillside to the turnpike that ribboned southward in the moonlight.

At the first turning the man in the general's uniform reined in, drawing the others about him with a glance. The girl in the sidesaddle was already close; as he spoke, she gentled her own mount and edged even closer.

"It's fifty miles to the Carolina line. We can make it by dawn, if you're willing to ride hard."

"We're all hard riders," said the girl.

He smiled at her in the moonlight. "I should have remembered that, of course. Are you sure—all of you—that it's wise to ride together?"

"Don't forget you promised to sell us Chisholm Hundred," she said. "I've one witness to that bargain beside me now. There'll be others waiting, when we reach the Cape Fear."

"It's still a bargain, then?"

"It always was," said the girl.

Julian Chisholm stripped off his cavalry gauntlet to seal that bargain one more time. After he had taken his wife's hand, it seemed only natural to repeat the ritual with each man in their escort. Natural, too, that they should ride together in a close group, and sing as they rode. A lilting rhythm that would never ring hackneyed in Southern ears:

> "In Dixie Land I'll take my stand,
> To lib and die in Dixie!"

Each of them, reflected Julian, had done just that, in his own stubborn way, for a whole war's span. Now that their war was ending, it seemed a good augury that they could sing that song together, without missing its meaning or its challenge.